VI KEELAND

The Boss Project
Edited by: Jessica Royer Ocken
Proofreading by: Elaine York, Julia Griffis
Cover Model: Daniel Harris
Photographer: Wander Aguiar
Cover designer: Sommer Stein, Perfect Pear Creative
Formatting by: Elaine York, Allusion Publishing
www.allusionpublishing.com

The Boss Project

CHAPTER 1

Evie

"I, uh, was eating cherries." I looked down at my stained blouse and offered an apologetic smile. "When I'm nervous, I snack, and I passed a fruit stand that had Bing cherries. They're my weakness. Though I realize now it wasn't a good idea fifteen minutes before my interview."

The woman's forehead wrinkles deepened. To be fair, my shirt was speckled with more than one or two cherry stains. If there was any shot of saving this interview, I had to jump in and try to make her laugh with the truth.

"I dropped one cherry," I continued. "It bounced and left red dots in three places before I could catch it. I tried to get the stain out in the ladies' room. But this is silk, and it wouldn't come out. So then I had the bright idea to make it look like a pattern. I had a few cherries left, so I bit them open and tried to replicate the marks." I shook my head. "It didn't work out too well, obviously, but my choices at that point were to go shopping for a clean shirt and be late for our interview, or try to pull it off as fashion. I thought it wouldn't be that noticeable..." I sighed quietly. "Guess I was wrong."

The woman cleared her throat. "Yes, well... Why don't we get started with the interview, shall we?"

I forced a smile and folded my hands on my lap, even though it seemed like I already didn't get the job. "That would be great."

Twenty minutes later, I was back out on the street. At least she didn't waste too much of my time. I could grab some more delicious cherries and still have time to stop at a store for a new shirt before my last interview of the week. That put a spring in my step.

After I stopped back by the fruit stand, I jumped on the subway. I'd grab a new shirt somewhere between the train station and my appointment.

But two stops into my trip, we screeched to an abrupt halt and didn't move for the better part of an hour. The guy sitting across from me kept staring in my direction. At one point, I dug into my purse for something to fan myself with, because the train was really starting to get hot. He looked down at his phone and back up at me two or three times. I tried to ignore it, but suspected I knew exactly what was coming.

A few moments later, he leaned forward in his seat. "Excuse me. But you're that bride, aren't you?" He turned his phone to show me a video that I wished did not exist. "The one that blew up her wedding?"

This wasn't the first time I'd been recognized, though it had been at least a month or two since the last encounter, so I'd hoped the insanity had finally passed. Guess it hadn't. People sitting to the left and the right of us on the train were now paying attention, so I did what I had to in order to escape being bombarded with questions once I admitted the truth: I lied straight through my teeth.

"Nope. Not me. But people have told me I could be her twin." I shrugged. "They say everyone has a doppelgänger somewhere. I guess she's mine." After a pause, I added, "Wish it was me, though. She's a badass, isn't she?"

The guy glanced down at his phone again and then back up. He didn't look like he believed a word I'd said, but at least he let it go. "Oh. Yeah, sure. Sorry to bother you."

Another hour later, the train finally started moving again. No one had even bothered to make an announcement about the holdup. By the time I got off, I only had about twenty minutes before my next interview, and I still had on my cherry-stained shirt. And...I'd dropped a couple more as I binged while sitting on the hot train. So I rushed up the subway stairs, hoping I could find something presentable to wear on the way to my appointment.

A few buildings down from my interview, I finally found a store with both men's and women's clothing in the window. A saleswoman with a heavy Italian accent offered to help as soon as I walked into Paloma Boutique.

"Hi. Would you have a cream silk blouse? Or white? Or..." I shook my head and looked down. "Basically anything I can put on with this skirt?"

The woman eyed my top. I gave her credit for not reacting. Instead, she nodded, and I followed her to a rack where she pulled out three different silk blouses. Any of them would do. Relieved, I asked where the fitting room was, and she started to walk me toward the back of the store. But when someone called out from the register, she pointed to a door and barked something at me in a mix of Italian and English. I thought it might be *"I'll check on you in a moment,"* but whatever. It didn't seem too important.

Inside the dressing room, I looked at myself in the mirror. My lips glowed bright red. The pound of cherries I'd eaten on the train must've stained them. *"Shit,"* I mumbled and rubbed at my mouth. But it wasn't coming off before my interview. Thankfully my teeth had been spared. Those damn cherries had turned out to be a disaster. Though I didn't have time to deal with anything else, so I shook my head, pulled off my ruined top, and took one of the blouses from the hanger. Before I slipped it on, it occurred to me that perhaps I should clean up a bit. The hot subway car had left me feeling not too fresh. So I grabbed my purse and fished out an old wet wipe from a wing place I'd gone to a few weeks ago. Thankfully, it was still moist. A lemony scent wafted through the air as I raised my right arm to wipe, and I wondered if that smell would transfer to my skin. Curious, I bent my head and sniffed. Which was exactly the position I was in when the fitting room door whipped open.

"What the...?" The man on the other side immediately went to close it. But he paused halfway with his brows knitted. "What are you doing?"

Of course, because my day couldn't get any shittier, the guy had to be gorgeous. His stunning green eyes caught me off guard, but I quickly regained my wits when I realized I was still holding up my arm and he'd just watched me *sniff my armpit.*

Flustered, I folded both hands over my lacy bra. "Does it matter? Get out!" Reaching forward, I yanked the door shut, brushing it against the intruder as it closed. "Go find the men's room!" I yelled.

From the bottom of the door, I could see the man's shiny shoes. They weren't moving.

"For your information," his gravelly voice rumbled, "...this *is* the men's room. But I'll let you wash your pits in peace."

When the shiny shoes finally disappeared, I blew out two cheeks full of air. This day just needed to end. But I still had one more interview left, which I was going to be late to if I didn't hurry my ass up. I didn't even bother to wash under my other arm before trying on the first shirt. Thankfully, it fit, so I changed back into my own lovely blouse and rushed to the cashier while still tucking it in. I expected to see the guy who'd busted into the fitting room waiting around, but thankfully he was nowhere in sight.

As I waited for the salesperson to ring me up, I looked back at the fitting room and noticed that the door I'd thought the woman had pointed to was actually right next to another door, and that one had the *Ladies* sign above it. The one I'd been in was clearly marked *Men*.

Crap. *Perfect.*

The shirt cost me a hundred-and-forty dollars—about a hundred-and-twenty bucks more than the one it replaced, which I'd picked up at Marshalls. Since that was almost enough to deplete my sad checking account these days, I needed to land this last job—the interview for which I only had a few minutes left to get to. So I rushed to the building a few doors down, did a Superman-speed change in the ladies' room in the lobby, ran my fingers through my hair, and applied an extra layer of lipstick over my already too-red lips to even out the cherry stains.

The elevator ride up to the thirty-fifth floor was about as speedy as the train ride downtown had been. The car stopped at almost every floor to let people on and off, so I took out my phone and scanned my emails to avoid stressing about being a minute or two late. Unfortunately, that turned out to be even more draining, since I'd received two new email rejection letters from jobs I'd submitted my resumé to—including one from the place I'd interviewed earlier today. *Great.* I felt completely defeated, especially since I was now walking in to interview for a job I knew I wasn't qualified for, even if Kitty had put in a good word for me.

The elevator dinged at my floor, and I took a deep breath to compose myself before stepping off. But I barely had one foot over the threshold when whatever morsel of the calm I'd managed to find flew out the window. Tall, double-glass doors with big, fancy gold letters announcing *Crawford Investments* intimidated the hell out of me. Inside, the reception area was even worse, with sky-high ceilings, stark white walls featuring boldly colored art, and a giant crystal chandelier. The woman behind the desk looked more like a supermodel than a receptionist, too.

She smiled through glossy lips. "May I help you?"

"Yes, I have a five o'clock appointment with Merrick Crawford."

"Your name, please?"

"Evie Vaughn."

"I'll let him know you're here. Please, have a seat."

"Thank you."

As I walked over to the plush white couches, the woman called after me. "Ms. Vaughn?"

I turned. "Yes?"

"You have..." She motioned over her shoulder to her back. "...a tag hanging off your shirt."

I reached around, patting until I found it, and tugged it off. "Thank you. I got something on the shirt I put on this morning, so I had to buy a new one before I got here."

She smiled. "Thank God it's Friday."

"Most definitely."

A few minutes later, the receptionist walked me back into the inner sanctum of offices. When we reached the proverbial corner office, there were two men inside embattled in some sort of a screaming match. They didn't even seem to notice us. The entire office was glass, though, so I could see them standing toe to toe as they yelled. The shorter of the two was balding and talked animatedly with his hands. Every time he flailed his arms, he flashed giant sweat rings in his armpits. The taller of the two was definitely the boss, based on his stance. He stood with his feet spread wide and arms folded across a broad chest. I couldn't see his whole face, but from the side, it looked like some of the confidence he oozed probably came from being extremely attractive.

"If you don't like it..." the boss finally growled, "... don't let the door hit you on the ass on the way out."

"I have socks older than this kid! What kind of experience could he possibly have?"

"Age isn't a number I give two shits about. It's the other number that calls the shots around here—*profit*. His are double digits, and yours are in the toilet for the third quarter in a row. Until things improve, your trades all need to be approved by Lark."

"Lark..." He shook his head. "Even the name pisses me off."

"Well, go be pissed off somewhere else."

Short Guy grumbled something I couldn't make out and turned to leave. He wiped sweat from his ruddy face as he marched toward the door and swung it open, brushing past us as if we weren't even here. Inside, the boss walked toward his desk. Apparently, we were invisible.

The receptionist looked at me sympathetically before knocking.

"What!"

She cracked open the door and peeked her head inside. "Your five o'clock interview is here. You told me to bring her back."

"Great." He frowned and shook his head. "Bring her in."

Apparently, Kitty's grandson didn't inherit her kind demeanor.

The receptionist extended her hand with a hesitant smile. "Sorry," she whispered. "But good luck."

I took a few steps inside the palatial office. When the glass door clanked closed behind me, and the guy still hadn't looked up or greeted me, I got the urge to turn and run back out. But while I stood debating doing exactly that, Mr. Grumpy lost his patience.

He kept his back to me as he put something on his bookshelf. "Are you going to take a seat, or do I need to get a tin can and string to interview you?"

I narrowed my eyes. *What a jerk.* I wasn't sure if it was the day I'd had, or just this guy's attitude that made me lose my cool, but suddenly I didn't care if I got the job. Whatever happened, *happened.* The nice thing about the point when you stop giving a crap about whether you win or lose is that it takes all the pressure off playing the game. "Perhaps I was allowing you a minute in the hopes it would improve your mood," I said.

The guy turned around. The first thing that caught my attention was his smirk. But when my eyes lifted to meet his, and I got my first good look at that startling green, I nearly fell over.

No.

Seriously?

Just no.

It can't be.

Kitty's grandson is the guy from the fitting room?

I wanted to crawl into a hole somewhere.

But while I was quietly dying of humiliation, the man who fifteen minutes ago had walked in on me sniffing my armpit was forging ahead.

Merrick held out his hand to the chair in front of his desk. "Time is money. Have a seat."

Does he not remember me? Is that even possible?

8

After watching the exchange he'd just had with his employee, I didn't think he seemed like the kind of man to not speak his mind.

Maybe he didn't get a good look at my face... I had yanked the door shut pretty quick. And I'd been standing there in a bra, and now I was fully clothed.

Or maybe... Could I have been wrong and he wasn't the guy from the store? I didn't think so. While I might be forgettable to him, this man had a face I couldn't forget—chiseled jawline, prominent cheekbones, flawless, tanned skin, full lips, and thick, dark eyelashes that rimmed nearly translucent green eyes. Those were currently staring at me like I was the last person he wanted in his office.

He put his hands on his hips. "I don't have all day. Let's get this over with."

Wow. *What a peach.* He sounded as excited as I felt about the prospect of working for him. Nevertheless, I'd put in quite a lot of effort to be here, so I might as well finish my shitty week with one more rejection and play along.

I walked to his desk and extended my hand. "Evie Vaughn."

"Merrick Crawford." We locked eyes while we shook, and I still didn't see any sign that he recognized me, not from the fitting room or as a friend of his grandmother's.

Whatever. Kitty got me in the door, but the rest was up to me.

My resumé sat in the center of his massive glass desk. He lifted it and leaned back into his chair.

"What's Boxcar Realty?"

"Oh, it's a nonprofit company I started a few years back. It's more of a side project, but I spent a good portion of the last six months working on it full time while I was between therapist jobs. I didn't want to leave it off and show a gap in my employment."

"So you left your last therapist position six months ago and haven't had outside employment since then?"

I nodded. "That's right."

"And Boxcar is involved in real estate of some sort?"

"It's a rental-property company. I own a few nontraditional spaces that I rent out through Airbnb."

Merrick's brows pulled together. "Nontraditional?"

"It's sort of a long story, but I inherited some property down south that's great for hiking and escaping the city. It wasn't developed at all, and I didn't want to spoil the land by building homes, so I built a glamping site and two treehouses that I rent."

"A...*glamping* site?"

"It's camping, but done with a little more glamour. It means—"

Merrick interrupted. "I've heard the term *glamping*, Ms. Vaughn. I'm just struggling to figure out how it relates to being a therapist."

Ugh. Not off to a good start. I sat up a little taller. "Well, it doesn't directly—unless you consider that most of the people I rent to are looking for an escape from their stressful jobs. It's sort of my passion project. All of the proceeds go to charity. After I left my last position, I took some much-needed time off to focus on growing it a bit." I leaned forward and pointed to my resumé. "If you look at the job before that, you'll see my experience as a therapist."

Merrick studied me a moment before looking down at my resumé again. "You were employed at Halpern Pharmaceuticals. Tell me about what you did there."

"I monitored and treated patients involved in clinical trials for antidepressant and anxiety drugs."

"So every patient was treated with drugs?"

"Well, no. Some people receive placebos during a clinical trial."

"Were these people who worked in a high-stress environment?"

"Some. They were people from all walks of life. But they all suffered from depression and anxiety."

Merrick rubbed his lip with his thumb. "I would assume these were people seeking drugs because traditional therapy didn't work."

I nodded. "That's right. All participants had to have had at least one year of therapy in order to qualify for the trial. The studies Halpern did focused on whether the drugs helped a person who had not responded to counseling."

"And did the drugs prove effective?"

"The ones I worked on did, yes."

Merrick sat back in his chair. "So the only experience you have is working with people who don't respond to counseling and needed drugs to get an improvement. Do I have that right?"

I frowned. *God, he's a jerk.* "Unfortunately, not everyone responds to counseling. Many of the people I treated saw improvements. However, because of the double-blind nature of drug trials, I couldn't tell you how many patients took placebos and improved solely from my therapy. I'm sure some did."

He tossed my resumé on his desk. "I run a brokerage firm. I wonder if I could stop reporting the rate of return my company earns its clients? It must've been nice to not worry about anyone gauging the success of your efforts."

I felt my cheeks heat. "Are you insinuating that I didn't do my job because no one could tell if it was my counseling or the drugs making people better?"

His eyes gleamed. "I didn't say that."

"Not in so many words, but you implied it. I counsel all patients the same, to the best of my ability, whether

11

anyone is watching or not. Tell me, Mr. Crawford, if your clients didn't, in fact, see their rate of return, would you perform your job differently? Perhaps slack off?"

A ghost of a smile lurked at his lips, as if he was enjoying being a dick. After a few heartbeats of staring at me, he cleared his throat.

"We're really looking for someone with experience treating people in a high-stress work environment, *before* they resort to drugs."

It hit me that it didn't matter what I'd said since I walked in the door. And that I wasn't in the mood for any more ridicule, especially since it was clear from his attitude that I wasn't going to get the job.

So I stood and held out my hand. "Thank you for your time, Mr. Crawford. Good luck with your search."

Merrick arched a brow. "Is the interview over?"

I shrugged. "I don't see any reason to continue. You've made it clear that you don't think my experience is what you're looking for. And you've said time is money, so I'm sure I've already wasted what...a grand or two?"

That smirk he'd had earlier came back out to play. His eyes roamed my face before he stood and clasped my hand. "At least twenty thousand. I'm very good at my job."

I tried to withdraw my hand, but Merrick clasped his fingers tighter. He pulled unexpectedly, leaning me over his desk. Then he leaned in, too. For a second, I thought the guy was going to try to kiss me. But before my heart could start beating again, he veered to the left and his face went to my neck, where he inhaled deeply. After, he simply let go of my hand like nothing had happened.

I blinked a few times as I righted myself to stand. "What...what was that?"

Merrick shrugged. "I figured since you weren't going to be my employee, it wouldn't be harassment if I took a quick sniff."

"A quick sniff?"

He slipped his hands into his trouser pockets. "I've been curious since the dressing room."

My eyes bulged. "Oh my God. I knew it was you! Why didn't you say anything sooner?"

"Seemed more fun not to. I wanted to see how you'd handle yourself. You looked like you were considering bolting when you first walked in. But you recovered pretty nicely."

I squinted. "No wonder you need help with your employees' stress level. Do you often play with people for your own entertainment?"

"Do you often hide in fitting rooms and sniff your pits?"

I frowned, and my squint narrowed further. Merrick seemed amused.

"I'll have you know, I was cleaning up because I got stuck on the..." I shook my head and growled. "You know what? It doesn't matter." I took a deep breath and reminded myself that I was a professional and sometimes it was better to take the high road. I straightened my skirt and stood tall. "Thank you for your time, Mr. Crawford. Hopefully, we won't cross paths again."

CHAPTER 2

Evie

"I take it the interviews today didn't go too well?"

I poured the last drops from the now-empty bottle of wine and held it up to my sister. "Gee, whatever could have given you that idea?"

Greer grabbed another bottle from the wine rack and sat down at the kitchen table across from me with the corkscrew. "Why couldn't we be born rich, instead of just smart and beautiful?"

I chuckled. "Because we're not assholes. I swear, every person I've ever met who was the full package—money, brains, and beauty—was also a giant asshole." I sipped my wine. "Like the guy I interviewed with this afternoon—drop-dead gorgeous. His eyes were really light and his lashes so thick and dark that it was hard not to stare. He owns one of the most successful hedge funds on Wall Street—but a total arrogant jerk."

Greer pulled the cork from the wine with a loud *pop*, and Buddy, her dog, came running. It was the only sound he got up for. People could ring the doorbell or knock, and he wouldn't get out of his bed. But open a bottle of wine, and he was suddenly Pavlovian. She held the cork out for him to lick, and he went to town.

I shook my head, watching. "Your dog is strange."

She scratched the top of his head as he slurped the cork. "He only likes red. Have you noticed the dirty look I get when he comes running only to realize it's white and he got up for nothing?"

I laughed and poured Greer a full glass of merlot.

"Let's get back to the hot, rich, arrogant guy you met today," she said. "He sounds awful. Any chance he wants to make a donation for your sister?"

Greer and her husband were currently picking a sperm donor after five years of trying to get pregnant. At thirty-nine, she was almost ten years older than me and starting to feel the squeeze of Mother Nature. They'd done four rounds of IVF with Ben's sperm, because his little guys had motility issues. But they still had no luck. Recently they'd given up and decided to go the donor route.

"Pretty sure you have a better shot at getting his sperm than I do of getting his job."

"What happened? Not the right experience fit again?"

I sighed and nodded. "Honestly, it's my own fault. I never should've taken the job with Christian's family's pharmaceutical company. It's a very specific industry, and people are pretty distrusting of drug trials these days, so it casts a weird light to have been involved with them. Plus, it was dumb to intertwine my entire life with a man."

My sister patted my hand. "Keep your chin up. Next week is your interview at Kitty's grandson's company, right? Maybe that'll work out."

"Uh, the arrogant jerk I just told you about? *He* is Kitty's grandson."

Our grandmother and Kitty Harrington had been best friends for nearly thirty years. They'd lived next door to each other down in Georgia until my Nanna died four years ago. When I'd decided to do my PhD at Emory in Atlanta, I'd moved in with Nanna and gotten to know Kitty pretty well. When Nanna died after a short battle with cancer during my last year of school, Kitty and I helped each other through it, and we'd been close ever since. It didn't matter that there were nearly fifty years between us. I considered her a good friend. Even after I moved back to New York for my internship, we never lost touch. I went down to visit her at least once a year, and we talked on the phone almost every Sunday.

Greer's eyes widened. "Oh, wow. I thought that interview was next week. I can't believe Kitty's grandson would be such a jerk to you, knowing how close the two of you are."

I sipped my wine and shook my head. "You know, Kitty never came up. He wasn't the kind of guy to waste time with small talk. But I realized after I left the office, it's possible he didn't know who I was. You'd think he'd at least mention it, right?"

"Why didn't you mention it?"

I shrugged. "It was a crazy day. I actually ran into him at a store a few doors down before the interview, and we had...a little incident. The whole thing threw me off, and then he gave me a hard time, questioning whether I was qualified. I get that I might not be *the best* candidate, but why did he invite me to the interview if he didn't think I had the basic qualifications?"

"I'm really surprised. Kitty's such a sweet lady."

"She is. But she's also got a mischievous side. I could never tell when she was kidding because of her smirk." I shook my head. "I realized they have that in common—an unreadable smirk."

"Are you going to tell her he was a jerk to you?"

I wrinkled my nose. "I don't want her to feel bad. Plus, she always lights up when she speaks about him."

"Well..." My sister squeezed my hand. "Everything happens for a reason. I bet there's something bigger and better waiting for you. And even if it takes a while to find it, you don't have to go anywhere. You can stay with us as long as you want."

I knew she meant it, and I had enjoyed spending time with my sister and her husband since I'd moved in, but I was looking forward to getting settled into my own place.

"Thank you."

Later that night, as I lay in bed unable to fall asleep, I tossed and turned, like I'd done most nights since my life had been turned upside down. In one day, I'd lost a fiancé, a best friend, a job, and my apartment. On top of it all, my wedding speech—where I'd called Christian and Mia out for their affair—had gone viral. As did the video I showed of them having sex in the bridal suite the night before my wedding. Last count, the "crazy bride's best friend and groom porn video" had more than a billion views—that's B for *billion*, not M for *million*. Mainstream news had even picked up the story, and it had taken more than a month for the interest on the Internet to die a slow and painful death. Then, just when I thought it was okay to breathe again, Christian and his family had filed a lawsuit against me for fraud and misappropriation of funds, claiming I'd had them pay for an elaborate wedding to get even for something I knew about all along. As if being served with that ridiculousness hadn't been bad enough, when the news got wind of it, the craziness started up again. Paparazzi had even parked outside my sister's apartment building for a few days. What is this world coming to when you can't even blow up your own wedding without *a billion* people getting involved?

Since I couldn't sleep, I grabbed my phone from the nightstand and started to scroll. Finding nothing to catch my attention, I made the mistake of opening my email. Two more rejections had arrived since I'd checked this afternoon. Sighing, I went to log back off. But then I noticed an email I'd missed. It had come in two hours ago, and the domain name definitely caught my attention.

Joan_Davis@CrawfordInvestments.com

It was probably another rejection, yet I opened it anyway.

Dear Ms. Vaughn,

Thank you for taking the time to talk to us about the stress therapist position. Mr. Crawford has selected the candidates to advance for additional consideration, and we'd like to invite you for a second interview at our office.

Kindly let me know your availability next week.

Sincerely yours,
Joan Davis
Director of Human Resources

I blinked a few times, sure I must've misread the email. But nope, a second read confirmed I was indeed being invited back. Must've been that great first impression I'd made sniffing my armpit.

CHAPTER 3

Merrick

"**M**r. Crawford?" My assistant, Andrea, poked her head into my office while I was eating lunch with Will. "Sorry to interrupt, but HR asked me to find out if you might have time to talk with one of the candidates for the in-house therapist position?"

I shook my head. "I don't need to talk to the applicants. I already gave my input to Joan. HR is holding second-round interviews and will let me know what they think when they're done."

"Apparently one of the candidates asked if she could have a minute with you after her appointment with HR. But her meeting is starting now, and I know you don't like anything on your schedule during trading hours."

"Which candidate?"

"Evie Vaughn."

I leaned back in my chair with a chuckle. "Sure. Why not?"

She nodded. "I'll let her know."

Will lifted his chin after Andrea shut the door. "What was that little grin about?"

"One of the candidates for the stress therapist job is *interesting*, to say the least."

"In what way?"

"Her first-interview appointment wasn't until five one day last week, so when the market closed, I ran downstairs to Paloma to pick up a suit I'd bought and had tailored. After I left the store, I thought I'd forgotten my cell phone in the fitting room, so I went back to check. When I opened the door, I walked in on a woman."

"I hate those places that have one fitting room for both men and women."

"Actually, this place has separate ones. The woman was just in the men's room. But that's not the best part. When I walked in, she was half undressed...and smelling her armpit."

Will's brows shot up. "Come again?"

"You heard me right. Anyway, a few minutes later, my five o'clock appointment walks in, and it's her. The woman from the fitting room."

"The pit sniffer? Get the hell out of here. What did you do?"

"Nothing. I played it off like I didn't recognize her, though she definitely recognized me. I could see her squirming."

"Shit like this only happens to you, my friend. So what went down? How did the interview go?"

"She was the least-qualified candidate. I don't even know how her resumé made it into the group that got called for interviews."

"Yet she's back here today for a second interview?"

"She is, indeed."

Will shook his head. "What am I missing?"

"When I got home that night, I started thinking about how the board is shoving this position down my throat.

They mandated that I hire someone, not that the person be competent."

Will smiled. "Genius."

I shook my head. "It wasn't enough that I offered to pay for counseling for anyone who wants to go. They had to push me into getting a full-time person onsite and requiring every employee to attend during their workday at least once a month. I need my people to be focused and ruthless while they're here—not getting in touch with their emotions."

"I hear you."

As we finished lunch, Andrea returned and knocked. Evie Vaughn stood right behind her. Her wavy blond hair was up today, and she wore a simple black skirt and jacket with a red blouse underneath, giving her the sexy-librarian look every male fantasizes about at least once in his life. I tried to ignore the stir seeing her caused in me and forced my gaze down.

Andrea peeked her head in the door. "Do you need more time?"

I looked at Will. "We need to discuss anything else?"

He shook his head. "Not that I can think of. I'll get the Endicott buy order placed as soon as it hits forty a share."

"Good." I turned my attention to Andrea. "Please show Ms. Vaughn in."

Will left, tossing me a smirk over his shoulder as he passed Evie.

When the door shut, she took a few steps forward, then hesitated. "Thank you for seeing me."

I nodded and gestured to the guest chairs on the other side of my desk. "Have a seat."

"Your assistant mentioned you don't usually take appointments while the market is open."

"I don't." Leaning back, I tented my fingers. "What can I do for you, Ms. Vaughn?"

"It's Evie, please. And...well, I was hoping you could clear something up for me."

"What would that be?"

"Why am I here? For a second interview, I mean. You made it pretty clear during the first one that you didn't think I had the right experience for the position, and I didn't exactly make a winning first impression in that fitting room. So...why am I here again?"

I folded my arms across my chest and deliberated how to answer. The politically correct and professional response would've been to say I'd reconsidered based on how she'd handled herself during the interview. But I'd never been accused of being politically correct or professional.

"Are you sure you want the real answer? Sometimes it's better not to know and just accept the outcome."

She folded her arms across her chest, mimicking my posture. "Maybe, but I'd like to know anyway."

I liked her spunk. It was a challenge to keep myself from smiling. "You were invited back because you are the least qualified of all of the people we interviewed."

Her face fell, and I felt a tinge of guilt, even though she'd said she wanted the truth.

"Why would you do that?"

"Because hiring an in-house stress coach wasn't my idea. My board of directors is forcing my hand."

"Is it a problem because it wasn't your idea?"

"I employ a hundred-and-twenty-five people whose jobs are to give me ideas." I shook my head. "No, I don't have an authority issue, Ms. Vaughn."

She pursed her lips. "Doctor—it's *Doctor* Vaughn. I prefer to be called Evie, but if you insist on using formal etiquette, you might as well use my proper title. I hold a PhD in clinical psychology."

I couldn't hold back the smile that time. I nodded. "Fine. No, I don't have authority issues, *Doctor* Vaughn."

"So you're against the position, in general, and you wanted to hire the worst person to prove a point?"

I nodded once. "You could say that."

"Are you against therapy?"

"I believe some people can benefit from therapy."

"Some people? But not your employees? Do you believe your employees don't have any stress in the workplace?"

"This is Wall Street, Ms.—*Doctor* Vaughn. If it weren't a stressful job, my average trader wouldn't earn seven figures. I just prefer my people to be focused while they're here in the office."

"Did you ever consider that you might be looking at things backward? Taking an hour out of the day to speak to someone isn't what's interrupting a stressed-out person's focus. They're already not focused because of their stress level. Therapy could help center someone so they can concentrate better."

"Noted that there's more than one way to look at things." I studied her for a moment. "Is there anything else you wanted to ask? Or have we reached the point in the discussion where you tell me you hope we never see each other again?"

She smiled shyly. "I'm sorry about that. It wasn't an appropriate thing to say."

I shrugged. "It's fine. Believe it or not, I've been accused of being inappropriate a time or two myself."

She laughed as she stood. "Gee, I never would have guessed that from the man who sniffed me during my interview." Evie held out her hand. "Thank you for your time. And your honesty."

I nodded and shook.

"One more thing. I hope you don't mind if I push my luck by making a suggestion."

I arched a brow. "I can't wait to hear it..."

She smiled. "If you have to hire someone, why not hire the best person you can? Your employees deserve it, and you never know, the outcome might surprise you."

That night, my head of HR, Joan Davis, waved as she passed my office. It looked like she was on her way out for the night. I opened my door and called after her. "Hey, Joan?"

She stopped and turned back. "Yes?"

"Can I ask you a question?"

"Sure. What's up?"

"Why did we pick Dr. Vaughn to interview?"

Her forehead creased. "You emailed and asked me to have her come in."

"No, I don't mean for round two. I mean the first time. The other candidates all had more experience, so I was curious as to what made you pick her for the initial interview."

The line between her brows deepened. "I was referring to the initial interview. You instructed me to include her when we started the hiring process."

"*I* instructed you? I'd never met her before the other day when she came in."

"But you told me your grandmother might refer someone for the position, and when her resumé came in, to include her in the first interview round."

"I didn't think that resumé ever came in. The woman my grandmother knows is..." I closed my eyes. "Shit. Evie is short for Everly, isn't it?"

Joan nodded. "I assumed you knew all this. She wrote that she was referred by Kitty Harrington in her cover letter, which was included with the resumé I gave you."

I hadn't bothered to read the cover letters. They were usually bullshit, just a place to drop annoying buzzwords. "I must've missed that."

"Oh. Well, I apologize. I should have pointed it out before you started the interviews."

I shook my head. "It's fine. My fault. Have a good night, Joan."

Later that evening, I decided to give my grandmother a call. It was almost nine by the time I got home, but she was a night owl. Besides, I was overdue, which I was certain she'd remind me of. So I poured two fingers of whiskey and picked up my cell.

"Well, well, well..." she said when she answered. "I was beginning to think I was going to have to get on a plane and open a can of whoop ass on you."

I smiled. That didn't take long. "Sorry, Grams. It's been too long. Work's been really busy."

"Ah, that's horseshit and you know it."

I chuckled. "How are you?"

"Probably about the same as you, only better."

I really missed this woman. "I'm sure you are. What's new? You still dating that guy, Charles?"

"Oh honey, it really has been a while. Charles got the boot at least two months ago. I've moved on to Marvin."

"What happened with Charles?"

"He ate dinner at four o'clock, wore house slippers out of the house as shoes, and didn't like to travel. I'm seventy-eight years old. I don't have time for that boring stuff. Did I tell you we're related to Ava Gardner?"

"Ava Gardner was an actress, right?"

"A damn good one, too. She always had these big, full lips. It's probably where you got that pouty mouth of yours."

My forehead wrinkled. Grams was already halfway down the road, and I was still stuck at the intersection. "How does Ava Gardner relate to Charles?"

"She doesn't. Ava is one of my new finds on Ancestry."

"Oh..." I'd almost forgotten about my grandmother's hobby. Over the last two years, she'd charted over six-thousand connections on Ancestry. Every week, she Zoomed with whatever new distant relatives were willing to talk to her. Some she even met in person. The woman had never sat still a day in her life. Hell, she'd only retired five years ago from the domestic violence shelter she'd founded, and she still went back to volunteer once a week.

"So how are we related to Ava?" I asked.

"My father's great grandfather—so that would be my great-great grandfather—was first cousins with her great grandmother."

"That branch is pretty far up the tree for my lips to come from her."

"We have strong genes. Lord knows your stubbornness runs at least five generations back."

I was pretty sure the woman on the phone had enough of that for five more lineage lines.

"What've you been up to lately, besides not calling to see if I'm dead?" she asked. "Still blowing through models instead of looking for the mother of my great grandchildren? I'm not getting any younger, you know. It would be nice if you could get started sooner, rather than later."

"I'm busy running my business, Grams."

"Bullshit. Life gave you some lemons. Stop sucking on 'em and make some lemonade. Then go find a girl with vodka."

I smiled, but it was definitely time to change the subject. And speaking of lemons... "Listen, I wanted to ask you about Evie Vaughn."

"Ah, Everly. I never could get used to calling her Evie."

"Apparently she goes by Evie."

"I figured she might be the real reason for your call. Everly told me the two of you met last week."

Shit. "What did she say?"

"The usual. That you were just as debonair as I'd said and very polite and professional."

Polite, huh? My grandmother did *not* pull any punches. She would have reamed into me if she knew I'd treated Evie the way I did. I was grateful *Dr.* Vaughn had kept the truth about our meeting private.

"She's a looker, isn't she?"

"Evie's a beautiful woman, yes."

"Nice rack, too," she said.

That I definitely knew from the fitting room. But I wasn't having a conversation about any woman's tits with my grandmother. "I wouldn't know. I was interviewing her, not ogling her."

"Good. I love you. You're my favorite grandson. But the last thing my Everly needs is a workaholic with commitment issues. Just give her a job, not a ride on the Merrick Express."

"First of all, I'm your *only* grandson, so I better be your favorite. And second of all, I don't have commitment issues."

"Uh-huh. So are you giving my girl the job or what? She's had a rough year with her breakup and that dumb video and all."

"Dumb video?"

"Do you listen to anything I say? I told you about it. It was probably six months ago now. The week after my gallbladder surgery, to be exact. That's why I couldn't come up for the wedding."

Now that she said it, I did remember she was supposed to come up for a wedding, but she'd had a gallbladder attack, and instead I'd gone down there for her surgery. "I remember the wedding... So they broke up? Evie called it off?"

"Not quite. The night before the big day, Everly found out her fiancé was shtupping her maid of honor. Rather than break it off, she married him, and then at the reception she showed a video of the two of them doing the horizontal mambo before walking out. Somehow the whole world saw the video because of the damn Internet. She annulled the marriage the week after."

Holy shit. I vaguely remembered my grandmother telling me that story, and I even remembered seeing a partial clip of the video on the news. But I hadn't put two and two together. "I didn't connect the dots to realize it was the woman I interviewed."

"Yep. Though I hope you don't hold that against her. It took a lot of guts to do what she did."

"Of course not," I told her.

My grandmother and I talked for another ten minutes. After we hung up, I grabbed my laptop and typed into the Google search bar: *Everly Vaughn wedding disaster.*

I hadn't paid close attention to the video when it was popping up all over the place earlier this year, but the very first video that showed up when I hit enter was definitely

Evie. And the damn thing had a shit ton of plays. The still was her face as she spoke into a microphone wearing a wedding dress. I hit play and watched the entire thing once through with my mouth hanging open. I couldn't believe this was the same woman I'd halfheartedly interviewed, the same woman from the fitting room. When the video ended, I hit the button to play it a second time. But when the bride came on the screen, I hit pause and took a good look at her.

Evie—*Doctor* Everly Vaughn—looked gorgeous in a fitted, strapless, white-lace gown. Her hair was styled the way women wore it back in the forties, with soft blond waves framing her pretty face. The sexy librarian glasses she'd worn both times I'd met her were gone, making her big, blue eyes look even bigger. Damn... She really was a knockout.

I rattled the ice in my almost-empty glass with my eyes glued to the screen. The first time I'd watched the video, I'd concentrated on the groom—trying to see if he'd had any clue what was about to go down. He definitely hadn't, and it made watching the asshole get what was coming to him that much more enjoyable. But this time I focused on the bride. And as beautiful as she looked, I could now see the hurt in her eyes. It reminded me of this afternoon, when I'd been truthful about why she'd been invited to a second interview—except the hurt was magnified times a thousand.

I pressed play and watched as Evie took the microphone and asked for everyone's attention. Zooming in, I noticed her hands shaking. A few months ago, when it hit the news, I'd chalked the video up to a crazy bride. But now, I saw things differently. Sucking back the last of the amber liquid in my glass, I gave her credit for standing up for herself. My grandmother was right. It took balls to do what she did, putting her emotions on display in front of a room full of people and calling out two people she loved. When the video got to the part where her fiancé and best friend started to go at it, I shut my laptop and stared out the window at Manhattan.

Evie Vaughn. The woman went through with marrying a guy just to blow up the wedding at the reception. It didn't seem like she had a grip on managing her own stress too well. Not to mention, she also seemed like a real handful—bold, smart, the type of woman who called people out when she saw fit, whether that was her own wedding or in an interview with a prospective employer. She was sexy as shit, especially when she showed no fear. Yep, Dr. Vaughn was *exactly* the type of employee I *didn't* need, even in a position I didn't want. My company was filled with enough strong-willed people.

And yet I couldn't seem to get her out of my head the last few days.

Which was dumb.

Just dumb.

I knew what I needed to do to nip this shit in the bud. So I called up the email HR had sent after they interviewed the final candidates and reread it before answering.

Mr. Crawford,

I met with the two candidates you selected to come in for a second interview. Both interviewed well, were able to share different stress-management techniques they might employ, and had clearly done their homework on the industry. However, Dr. Wexler has more one-on-one anxiety and stress counseling experience

*than Dr. Vaughn. Therefore, it is my recommen-
dation that we extend an offer to Dr. Wexler.*

*Please let me know if you would like to discuss
things further, or alternately, if you would prefer that we reopen the search to locate new potential candidates.*

*Sincerely,
Joan Davis*

I sat for another twenty minutes, staring blankly at
the screen. The list of reasons not to hire Evie Vaughn was
endless. Even human resources recommended another
candidate. Yet...

I was a man who often went with instinct over logic. It
had mostly served me well. And for some reason, I couldn't
shake the feeling that rejecting Evie Vaughn would be a
mistake—and not just because my grandmother wouldn't
be happy. Though I couldn't honestly say my leaning toward the less-qualified candidate was for entirely professional reasons. Something about the woman had gotten
under my skin. Which is precisely the reason I should heed
the advice of my HR director. Yet instead of writing back to
HR, I clicked back to YouTube and hit play again. *Twice.*

Eventually, I shook my head. *This is just stupid.* Why
the hell was I wasting time ruminating over who got hired
for a position I didn't even want in my company?

So I hit reply and started typing.

Joan,

Please extend an offer to Dr...

CHAPTER 4

Evie

"**H**oly shit," I laughed and sipped my coffee. "Seriously?"

"What?"

I looked up from my laptop at Greer. "I just opened an email from that investment firm I interviewed at a couple of days ago, the one Kitty's grandson owns. You know, the guy who basically told me I was incompetent."

"The hot one whose sperm I want?"

I nodded. "That's him."

"What did the email say? Does he need me to drop off a sterile collection jar?"

"No, this is even crazier. They offered me the job."

"Oh, wow! That's great!"

I nibbled on my fingernail. "Is it? Do I really want to work somewhere that the big boss doesn't believe the job needs to exist, or that I'm able to fill it properly?"

"That depends. What does it pay? And can you negotiate for extra vacation time and a side order of sperm?"

I turned back to my laptop. I'd only made it through the first few lines that said I'd been selected for the job. There was an attached employment contract. Scanning the nine-page document, I was surprised to find the salary was more than my last job—definitely not commensurate with the experience Merrick Crawford felt I had. And the vacation time was very generous, too, not to mention the potential for a hefty bonus.

"*Ugh*. It pays really well, has four weeks of vacation to start, and profit sharing after one year."

"And you're saying *ugh* because you'd rather have shitty pay, no time off, and zero cut of the profits?"

I shook my head. "It wouldn't be so painful to turn down a shitty-paying position."

"Why would you turn it down?"

"The owner only wants to hire me because he found me the least-competent candidate. He admitted that. He said his board is forcing him to create this position."

"So? Who cares what he thinks? Do *you* think you could do the job?"

I considered it for a moment. "I'm sure there are more qualified people who know the industry and would be able to jump in and have no learning curve. But I'm good at my job, and I think I'd be fine after I understood more about what causes the stress at work. I mean, aside from the boss, who clearly has a unique management style."

"What's the problem then?"

"Did you miss the part where the owner thinks I'm incompetent?"

She shrugged. "Prove him wrong. What happened when Mom told you you'd never be able to play on the volleyball team because you were too short?"

"I made the team and became captain the next year."

"And when everyone suggested you apply to some 'safety schools' for your PhD, instead of just your top three choices, because all of them had a less-than-ten-percent acceptance rate?"

I smiled. "I got into all three."

"Do I need to go on? Because I'm still bitter over me staying behind after I told you you'd never get backstage to meet Justin Timberlake when you were sixteen." Greer shook her head. "You want to know what I think the real problem is?"

"I'm not sure. Do I?"

"The boss. You think he's a bigger challenge than the job itself, and maybe he is. But so what? Look at him like a project you need to tackle, separate from the position. *The Boss Project.* It sort of has a nice ring to it, doesn't it?"

I nibbled on my bottom lip. "I don't know. This guy made me nervous for some reason. I felt like he was trying to read my mind or something."

Greer scoffed. "Trust me. You wouldn't have been offered a job if he could see what was going on in there. I sort of imagine it like Cirque du Soleil, only the performers are a little drunk and also doing mind-bending, complex math problems while folding themselves into pretzels."

I laughed. "I don't know. Maybe I'll think about it more later." I finished my coffee and got up to rinse my mug in the sink. "Right now, I need to get dressed and go meet with my lawyer about the lawsuit. But don't worry, I'll be at the store to cover you by five, like I promised."

"Thanks. Our appointment isn't until six, so you can even come closer to five thirty. But when did you hire someone to represent you? You didn't mention that."

"I didn't yet. But I think I finally found the perfect man for the job."

"Where did you get him?"

"It's someone I've known for years."

My sister's nose scrunched up. She knew all of my friends. "Who?"

"Simon."

Her eyes flared. "You're kidding?"

"Nope."

"I'm kind of surprised he agreed to take the case. He's a nice guy and all, but he always treated Mia like she was some sort of queen."

"Well, he doesn't know he's taking it yet."

Greer laughed. "Oh, Lord. This should be interesting. I'll grab an extra bottle of wine for when you get home tonight."

"Thanks, sis."

She shook her head. "I still can't believe Christian is suing you. The guy has giant balls."

"I know. Such a shame his penis wasn't a matching set."

"Evie? What are you doing here?" Simon asked.

I looked at the receptionist, who had just walked me back for my eleven-AM meeting. She looked confused.

"Evie is what they call me for short," I explained.

Her nose wrinkled. "For Jill?"

Simon waved to the receptionist. "It's fine. Evie, or Jill, come on in."

He came around from behind his desk and kissed me on the cheek. "So you're my eleven o'clock? What's with the fake name?"

"I'm actually surprised you didn't crack the code. You must be slipping, Simon."

"Code? What do you mean?"

"The name I gave."

Simon walked back around his desk and looked at the printed-out calendar on top. "I thought the last name was unusual. Tedbride."

"Say it with the first name."

He looked down again. "Jill Tedbride."

"Now put them together."

"*Jilted bride*. Cute. Guess I'm a little slow on the sixth-grade gags. I might've gotten Ben Dover or Mike Hawk. But what did you make an appointment for?"

"I have some legal trouble I was hoping you could help me with."

"Oh, I'm sorry to hear it. What's going—*oh*, wait..." He shook his head. "No. Definitely not. If you're here about what I think you're here about, I can't help you."

"*Please*, Simon. I know you were mad that I didn't give you the heads up before my speech at the wedding, but I thought we were past that."

Simon ran his hand through his hair. "I'm not mad at you for not telling me. It's just... I'm trying to put what happened behind me."

"So am I. That's why I need you to help me with this ridiculous lawsuit."

"I can refer you to someone."

"Come on, Simon. Isn't there a little part of you that wants to stick it to Christian?"

He took a deep breath. "There's a big part of me that would like to pummel him. But I promised Mia I'd work on letting it go."

My head reared back. "Mia? Why would you promise her anything?"

Simon looked back and forth between my eyes. "You don't know we're back together, do you? Mia and I are trying to work it out."

My face twisted. "What? Why would you do that?"

He took off his glasses and tossed them on his desk before rubbing his eyes. "It's complicated, Evie."

My face grew hot. "No, it's not. When your girlfriend is caught screwing her best friend's fiancé, it's pretty simple. You throw her shit out on the lawn and change the locks. How could you take her back?"

Simon sighed and pinched the bridge of his nose. "I love her. She made a mistake."

"She didn't make *a* mistake. She made it dozens of times. It wasn't like they had too much to drink one night, wound up in bed, and regretted it the next morning. They carried on an affair for months—with her supposed best friend's fiancé. We went out to dinner as a foursome all the time, Simon! Her hand was probably on his dick under the table while the two of us sat there like fools."

"I know you're upset, but... Mia feels terrible about what she did to you."

"They slept together in the honeymoon suite the night before the wedding. My dress hung five feet away from where he had her bent over. She was staring at her *best friend's wedding dress* while Christian stuck it in her ass, Simon! *Her ass!* She's told me she didn't let you do that to her!"

He looked over my shoulder. "Please. Keep your voice down. I work here."

"I'm sorry." I shook my head. "I shouldn't have come. I just... I thought we were friends, and I needed legal help, and... I don't know. I guess I thought we could exact revenge together somehow."

Simon frowned. "We are friends, Evie."

"No, we're not. You can't be friends with someone who's on the other side of the enemy line. I have no hard feelings toward you, but let's be realistic. We're never going to hang out again. Maybe you'll write Happy Birthday on my Facebook wall, and I'll post an LOL on the occasional Instagram picture, but that's the extent of it."

Simon's mouth set to a grim line. There wasn't anything he could say, because he knew I was right. And really, I felt sorry for him. Mia had screwed over him and her best friend. That wasn't a mistake; it was a character flaw. And she would do it again to the poor bastard.

I stood and held out my hand. "Goodbye, Simon. Good luck."

He stood. "Do you want me to at least refer you to someone?"

"No." I smiled sadly. "That's okay. Thanks anyway."

I walked out of Simon's office feeling like a layer of new flesh had been ripped off a gaping wound. I'd known coming here to talk about what had happened wouldn't be easy. But I hadn't been expecting this. Six months had gone by, and it seemed I was the only person left behind. Christian had posted a photo while out on a date the other night, and Mia... She'd gotten her boyfriend and her old life back. Meanwhile, I was unemployed, homeless, a laughingstock to a billion people, and about to be sued for everything I'd earn over the next ten years—*if* I could actually find a job.

"That sucks. I'm sorry." Greer frowned. I'd arrived at her specialty wine shop a little earlier than she'd needed me to so I could fill her in about Simon and Mia. I hadn't been able to shake the conversation I'd had with him, and I'd wound up going out to Brooklyn to take a long walk on a beach where I often collected sea glass before coming to the shop.

"I expected he might turn me down. Simon was never big on drama—that was Mia's forte. But I never anticipated he'd turn me down because he and Mia were back together."

My sister shook her head as she finished unpacking a box of wine, lining the bottles up on a shelf. "I can't believe someone as smart as Simon would be stupid enough to take her back."

"I know. I tried to put myself in his shoes. He and Mia were only boyfriend and girlfriend, not engaged like Christian and me. But I honestly don't think I would feel any differently if Christian and I hadn't been engaged when I caught him. Cheating sort of has levels. If you have a drunken one-night stand, that's a three on the cheat-o-meter. If you have an ongoing relationship with someone else, that's like a six and a half. If it's with your significant other's friend or family, it rockets the offense up to a ten. Maybe, *maybe*, I could forgive a three. But anything higher, it's no longer a mistake. It's absolutely a choice. The whole thing just makes me so crazy..." I lifted my chin to the locked glass cabinets behind my sister. "I might bust open your fancy reserve cabinet and drink a few bottles."

She pointed to the shelf behind me. "You can get just as drunk on the cheap stuff, sister."

I walked behind the counter. "Don't worry. I like to match my alcohol with how I'm feeling, so the cheap and crappy stuff it is." Pulling open a drawer, I tossed my purse inside. "Now go—get out of here. I don't want you to be late for your appointment to pick out my future niece or nephew's genetic benefactor. Actually, hang on a second..." I reached into my pocket and pulled out a piece of bright red sea glass. Leaning over the counter, I held it out to my sister. "Take this with you."

Greer kissed me on the cheek as she took it. "You and your lucky sea glass. I'll see you at home later. If it's slow, lock up at seven thirty. You don't have to wait until eight." She grabbed two bottles of wine from a display. "We're going to need these to continue our conversation about what an idiot Simon is when I get in. Ben has to go back to work after we're done, so it will be just us girls."

"I feel like he's never home lately."

"His company needs twenty-four-hour IT support since they're global. Both the night-shift guys quit the same week, so he's basically been working nonstop. It's a good thing we're getting help with our fertility because we're never in the same room long enough to conceive."

I smiled halfheartedly. "Love you. Good luck."

"Thanks. Love you, too."

For the next hour and a half, I helped a few customers, washed the front windows, and stalked my phone for unhealthy fast food within a three-block radius. When seven thirty rolled around and no one had called or come in for forty-five minutes, I decided to do as my sister said and close early. I needed to feed my soul to make myself feel better—literally, not figuratively. So I turned off the neon OPEN sign, locked the door, and walked one block over to Gray's Papaya for the best hot dogs in the city. It had been a long time since I'd had one. Lord knows I'd been watching everything I ate earlier this year so I could look my best in my wedding dress. And I hadn't had anything but coffee all day today, since I'd lost my appetite after my appointment this morning. I actually salivated as I watched the cashier add chili and cheese to my order. When she was done, I was so anxious to dig in that I grabbed the bag and started to walk away.

"*Excuse me.* That'll be nine sixty-two, please."

I turned around and shook my head. "Oh my God, I'm so sorry. I got so excited, I forgot to pay." I pulled out my credit card, as I'd used the last of my cash earlier today to buy coffee from a street vendor.

"Here you go."

The woman swiped and then frowned. "The card was declined."

"That can't be. I have plenty of credit available." I motioned to the credit card machine. "Can you try it again?"

She did, and the same thing happened.

"Shoot. Alright. I'm not sure what the problem is." I pulled another card from my wallet. "Use this one."

The cashier swiped and then sighed. "This one's not working either."

"What do you mean it's not working?"

She pointed to the screen. "It just says declined."

"But that's impossible. Your machine must be broken." I looked around and noticed the woman next to me paying. Her card seemed to go through without a hitch. I pointed. "Can you try that register?"

The teenage cashier barely stopped herself from rolling her eyes. "Sure."

But the same thing happened at the other register. And now a line was forming since I was preventing *two* rows of people from paying.

"Ummm... I'm sorry. I'm not sure what's going on. Can you hold my order aside, and I'll call my credit card company? There must be some sort of mix up."

Since the store was loud, I stepped out front. After way too many prompts and pushing zero angrily five times, I finally got a human on the phone.

"Hi. My credit card was just declined, but it shouldn't have been. I have plenty of available credit."

"Account number?"

After I read the number to her and went through a few verification questions, the woman put me on hold for a moment. When she came back, I was hungry and frustrated.

"Hi, Ms. Vaughn?"

"Yes."

"It seems your card has been closed."

"What do you mean it's been closed? I didn't close it."

"It's a joint account. The joint account holder closed it."

"What joint account..." *Oh my God.* I felt my face turn redder than the delicious hot dog I should've been eating. *Christian.* I'd forgotten that we'd applied for this card together. They'd offered it to us when we opened our joint bank account, even though I'd been the only one to ever use it.

I shut my eyes. *The joint bank account that I now used as my personal account.* I guess that explained why my ATM card wasn't working either. I was seriously going to kill that man.

I took a deep breath. "Can I reopen it under my own name?"

"Of course. I can take the application over the phone for you, if you'd like. And if everything gets approved, we can have your new cards shipped to you in three to five business days."

No Gray's Papaya. So no point to this call right now.

"I'll call back tomorrow and do that."

"Okay. Is there anything else I can help you with this evening?"

"Can you buy me a hot dog?"

"Excuse me?"

I shook my head. "Never mind." I just wanted to go home and crawl in a ball. Except I didn't *have* a home. I lived at my sister's.

So with shoulders slumped and my stomach growling, I started toward her place. But that route took me back past the wine shop again, and as I approached the store, I realized I could at least borrow ten dollars to get something to eat from her register and leave her a note. So that's what I did. I unlocked the door, rang in a one-cent sale so the drawer would open, and took out a ten, replacing it with a note in case I forgot by the time I got home.

When I shut the drawer, I tossed the ten in my purse and headed out. But not before grabbing another bottle of wine from the display Greer had looted earlier.

CHAPTER 5

Evie

On Sunday, despite thinking about it for most of the last forty-eight hours, I still hadn't decided whether or not to take the job with Kitty's grandson's company. My sister thought I was insane to turn down the only offer I'd had after searching for a while, but the idea of taking a job where I wasn't really wanted didn't sit right with me. I'd asked the woman from human resources if I could get back to her in a few days, and we'd agreed I'd let her know by Monday morning. I'd figured at some point a moment of clarity would hit me, but now I'd begun to think having any type of clarity in my life would never happen again. Oddly, the person I often talked to when I had doubts was the grandmother of the man who was giving me doubt about accepting the job.

But this was also the day I usually spoke to her, and I felt like that might not be a coincidence. So I picked up the phone and dialed my unlikely friend.

"Hey, Kitty."

"Hello, sweetheart. How's the world treating you this week?"

Like that poor ninety-eight-year-old man who died the day after winning the lottery in Alanis Morissette's song. "Pretty good. How about you?"

"I can't complain. At my age, you can either see your aches and pains as a burden or see them as a reminder that you're still alive with plenty left to do. I choose the latter."

Ten seconds into our call, I already felt better than I had in days. Kitty had such a simple way of looking at things, and I needed the reminder. Things could always be worse. "Talk to any new relatives this week?" I asked.

"I did indeed—a bit of a crazy story actually. A woman who came up as a second cousin got the DNA testing kit for Christmas from her daughter. Her results came back saying her uncle was only a half uncle. She did some digging, and it turned out her grandmother had an affair and got pregnant. She'd passed the kid off as her husband's her whole life. The grandmother was long gone, but the grandfather was still kicking. They did a little investigating and discovered the grandmother had had an affair with a guy who lived in the same town. When the grandfather found out, he went to his wife's grave to talk to her about it, only to realize his wife was buried right next to the guy she'd had the affair with. The grandmother had bought the plots and never said a word. Talk about taking a secret to your grave."

"Oh wow. The dirt you get from genealogy is better than watching a soap opera."

"And to think, I used to say those shows were too outlandish. Turns out, most people do have a dirty little secret that could turn their world upside down."

Don't I know it. "There's no such thing as a secret these days with the Internet."

Kitty laughed and then told me all about a trip she was planning to take with the new guy she was seeing. They were going to try ziplining for the first time. It dawned on me how much more exciting this seventy-eight-year-old woman's life was than mine.

"Are you sure I'm the one who's twenty-nine?" I asked.

"Age is just a number, my dear. What are you doing for excitement lately?"

"Well, I did cross against the light the other day."

Kitty tsked. "Child, you need to rejoin the world. I know that moron ex of yours threw you for a loop, but there's a big world out there just waiting to make you smile. Take what today has to offer. Don't dwell on what yesterday has taken away."

I sighed. "I know. You're right. It's just... I'm not sure how to start fresh again. It's like I'm weighed down with so much resentment, I'm struggling to keep my head above water."

"Well, that's a problem. But there's a simple solution."

"There is?"

"Mmm-hmmm. You need to make a decision to be happy and let it guide your future. Then make a left instead of a right, zig instead of zag. Sometimes that's the only way to find a new path."

"How do I do that?"

"You do the opposite of what you would normally do. I don't mean you say yes to a date with a guy who just got out of prison for murder. Or you dive into a pool without water. Because those are just dumb. But if a handsome, sixty-eight-year-old man asks you to go ziplining? Go for it. Your life course has been changed, and you're never going to find out where you should go next by sitting home. Believe it can happen, and it will. Take some chances."

The idea sounded good, though I felt more stuck in place than stuck deliberating over turning one way or the other. But Kitty was trying to help, so I didn't want her to feel bad. "Thanks, Kitty. You're right. I'll give it a try."

"That's my girl. Now, what's new on the job front? Did you get the job with my grandson?"

"I did, actually. Though I haven't accepted it yet. I'm not sure I'm the right person for the position."

"Do you have any other prospects?"

I frowned. "No, I don't."

"Welp. You do what you want, but I think maybe your first opportunity to zag instead of zig is staring you in the face."

She had a point... But I still wasn't sure.

After we hung up, I sat in the living room for a little while. Greer and her husband were out to dinner with some friends, so the apartment was quiet. I pondered what Kitty had said—not so much her suggestion about zigging and zagging, but about what I might tell a patient who was struggling with change. I would tell them to focus on the opportunities, not the loss. And isn't that what the job at Kitty's grandson's firm was? An opportunity? One I believed I could excel at. So why was I struggling to make this decision so much? It all came down to one thing...or one man, that is: Merrick Crawford. He was a challenge. Could I rise to conquer The Boss Project?

I chewed on my lip as I opened my laptop. I had to give Joan Davis an answer one way or another, and staring at the screen wasn't going to help bring about the clarity I was searching for. Yet I spent another twenty minutes doing it anyway. Then I opened my email, took a deep breath, and decided to zag instead of zig.

CHAPTER 6

Evie

A week later, I arrived at my new office with a belly full of first-day jitters.

Was the building this tall when I came for my interviews?

I stood at the front entrance, staring up at the skyscraper, feeling as tiny as an ant. It was still dark, but as the old saying goes, *New York never sleeps*, so the block was almost as lit up as it would be midday. People in suits were already rushing all around me, even though it was a little before six AM.

I'd wanted to be early, but now that I was here, maybe this was a smidge *too* early. I debated going back to the coffee shop where I'd stopped for my caffeine fix on the way from the train. Perhaps I could sit at the table and watch some TikToks to pass the time until seven, but then a man jogged past me. I didn't give it much thought until he stopped a few paces later and backed up.

"Evie?"

I blinked. "Merrick?"

He plucked an earbud from one ear and looked me up and down. "Are you coming to work this early?"

"Ummm... Yeah, I thought it would be good to get an early start."

My new boss looked at his watch. "It's five fifty."

"I guess I was a little overeager."

He smiled. Damn, he really was good looking. I'd always had a weakness for a man who wore a suit well, but today he was dressed in running gear—black shorts and a body-hugging, long-sleeved Under Armour shirt. His forehead was damp with sweat, and his thick neck glistened in the overhead lights.

"The office doesn't open until seven."

"Oh. I'll just go get some coffee or something."

Merrick eyed the large cup in my hand. "Why don't I show you where your office is, and you can get situated."

"Oh, no. That's okay. I don't want to interrupt your run."

"It was my last lap, anyway." He tilted his head toward the door. "Come on."

In the lobby, Merrick stopped at the security desk.

"Hey, Joe. This is Evie Vaughn. *Dr.* Everly Vaughn." He turned to me and winked. "I'm sure HR will be sending down the paperwork to get her building cards later today. Just figured I'd introduce you and tell you not to forget the *Doctor* part before her name."

"No problem, boss."

Merrick extended his hand for me to walk first toward the elevator. I waited until we were out of earshot to say anything.

"You know, I'm not a jerk about being called doctor. I could care less about the title. You were just being difficult that day and brought out a side of me."

The elevator doors slid open, and Merrick held them and grinned. "What side would that be? Your bitchy side?"

I squinted. "Did you just call me a bitch on my first day of work? I think I've already figured out the root of your stressed-employee problems here at the office. This job is going to be easier than I thought."

Merrick smirked. "I never claimed I wasn't part of the problem. Your job is to get people to learn how to deal with it."

"Or...you could act more professional."

Merrick pressed a button on the elevator panel. "What fun would that be?" He paused. "By the way, your office is on a different floor than the one you interviewed on. Not sure if Joan told you that."

"Oh yes, she mentioned it. The traders are all on one floor and everyone else is a floor down?"

He nodded. "We don't all fit on one, but it's better split this way, anyway. The traders yell across the bullpen all day long. It can get pretty loud, and the language isn't great when a stock they've invested in heavily tanks."

"I bet." The doors slid closed, and I felt Merrick's presence, even though he was standing an appropriate distance away in the elevator car. "So...do you come to the office early to run every day?"

"I live in the building. The top few floors are residential."

"Oh, wow. Guess that cuts down on commute time. It also explains where all your papers and photos are."

"Papers and photos?"

"Your desk is so clean. I was in your office twice, and both times I saw no sticky notes, notepads, files, or paperwork. And your credenza didn't have any personal items like framed photos or signed baseballs or whatever."

"I like things organized. My files are in drawers, and my sticky notes are electronic."

I snorted. "You're not going to love my office then."

Merrick raised a brow but said nothing. The elevator dinged at the thirty-fourth floor, and he led me down a series of hallways. It didn't dawn on me that every one of the offices was a glass fishbowl until we came to the one he said was mine. It was glass, too, but the glass was different, frosted so you couldn't see inside.

He unlocked the door and opened it for me. The lights turned themselves on as we entered.

I sniffed a few times. "Do you smell that?"

He pointed to the glass. "It's the glue from the film we installed to make the privacy glass. It was just done over the weekend. HR thought it was necessary to shield people who are having appointments with you from prying eyes."

I nodded. "Thank you. Privacy is important. Without it, patients will be apprehensive about opening up."

Merrick thumbed toward the door. "The coffee room is a few doors down, and restrooms a few after that. I believe your desk has been filled with basic supplies. You have a laptop there, and I can see the HR manuals are behind you on the shelf. Joan will give you the full tour when she gets in. I'm going to go upstairs and take a shower, but if you need anything, you know where my office is."

"Okay, great. Thank you. I'm anxious to get started. Will you have some time to talk later today? I'd like to learn about the company's culture."

"I'm sure HR can fill you in on that."

"Actually, I'd prefer to hear it from you. Things like values and priorities are usually set at the top level and trickle down. But I'd also like to talk about the expectation of communication between management and me, as I learn things from employees."

Merrick frowned and looked at his watch. "Fine. I'll come by when I'm done upstairs."

"Thank you."

As he walked out, I stole a glance at Mr. Grumpy from behind. His running shorts stretched across the muscles of his rear end as his long strides ate up the distance to the door. Good Lord, even the man's ass was toned—the kind of toned that reminded me I needed to get my own butt back to the gym. Only I didn't have one any longer. The apartment I'd shared with Christian had a gym in the building—another thing I'd lost in wedding Armageddon.

I'd been lost in that thought, my eyes still glued to the boss's derrière, when he turned back around. The slight smirk at the corner of his lips told me I'd been caught.

"You might want to leave your door open to air out the smell. Wouldn't want you high off glue fumes your very first day."

I nodded and willed my face not to show embarrassment. "I'll do that."

After he left, I took a deep breath and looked around my new home away from home. This office was bigger than the one I'd had at Christian's family's company, and I also had a decent view of the city from the windows on the back wall. All in all, it felt like I'd made a good decision. So maybe there was something to Kitty's advice to manifest my own happiness...

My nose was deep in the employee manual when I heard footsteps approaching. I looked up to find Merrick's appearance very different than it had been just a little while ago. His hair was slicked back, still wet from the shower, and those little ends I knew would curl up when they dried brushed against the collar of his navy blue suit jacket. His face, which had been peppered with scruff earlier, was now shaved clean, making the chiseled line of his jaw even more pronounced.

God, he was too damn handsome.

Until he spoke, that is...

"You know the glue smell in here might work for you. No one will be able to tell if your deodorant stops working again."

I gave him a look. "Cute."

"That's what all the ladies call me. But you should probably watch it. Sexual harassment causes stress in the workplace, you know."

I shook my head. "Like I said, trouble usually starts at the top and trickles down."

Merrick nodded toward the door. "How about you psychoanalyze me in my office so I can get settled in?"

I grabbed one of the notebooks from the drawer and stood. "Whatever works for you."

Inside his office, he turned on all of his electronics and leaned back in his chair as they whirred to life. "I wasn't so sure you were going to take the job."

"I debated it for a while."

"What was the deciding factor?"

"It was something Kitty said, actually."

"Ah...my grandmother. The woman can be very persuasive."

"She can." I tilted my head. "Is that why you hired me? Because of my relationship with Kitty?"

Merrick shook his head. "To be honest, when you came in for your interviews, I didn't know who you were, other than someone who'd applied for the job. I found out after the fact."

"So you hired me because I was the least-competent person?"

He stared at me for a moment, then sat up and folded his hands on his desk. "I hired you because my gut said to. I rely a lot on instinct."

I let that sink in a moment before nodding. "Okay. Well, thank you."

"Any other questions about why you were hired, or shall we get started?"

I flipped open my notepad and clicked my pen. "I'm ready. Can we start with you telling me a bit about why your board decided an in-house therapist was necessary? I asked you that during our first interview, but you didn't elaborate. It would be helpful to know the specifics."

Merrick sighed. "We were sued civilly."

"For?"

"Emotional distress. I believe the legal term was *negligent infliction of emotional distress*."

I jotted down some notes. "Has the case concluded, or is this an active lawsuit?"

"Lawsuits."

I lifted a brow. "How many?"

"Four. We won two, settled one because it was less expensive than going to trial, and the last one is still in the early stages. Though that case is bullshit. The guy is just lazy, but he was friends with the guy we settled with and thinks he can also capitalize on our generosity."

"Anything else I should know about?"

"I guess I should also mention that there was a small fistfight here in the office recently, too. The board mentioned that as one of the determining factors in the mandate to hire someone."

"Small? So two employees?"

Merrick's lip twitched. "Eight. But it started as two. The others just joined in, taking sides."

"Do you know what the fight was over?"

"Bonuses, who had the higher profit rate, whether a trade was a good investment or not." He shook his head. "It's always something, and it always stems from competitiveness. The people on the floor all make a good living. Most of them could retire by thirty, if they wanted to. Money isn't what drives them; it's being the best."

"And what makes someone the best? I don't mean how do you determine who did the best—obviously that's a numerical test. But what qualities does it take to become the best broker?"

Merrick nodded. "That's a good question. Being intelligent is a given. Most of the traders on the floor went to Ivy League schools and graduated at the top of their class. What sets the best apart? I'd say nerves of steel. You have to be able to tune out the noise around you and stay the course some days, and other days you have to take a risk that could lose you everything. You ever hear the saying, 'You use the same boiling water to harden an egg that you do to soften a potato'?" He tapped his fingers to his chest. "It's about what's inside, not the circumstances you're in."

I smiled. "I know you weren't in favor of adding this position, but that quote actually supports bringing someone on board to help people deal with stress, since everyone processes things differently."

"Or I could just fire the soft potatoes and keep the hardened eggs."

I chuckled. "Speaking of which, how is your retention rate with employees?"

"The financial-service industry has one of the highest attrition rates. Ours tends to run a little higher than average."

"What's a little higher?"

"Ten to fifteen percent. It's not a coincidence that our profits also run in tandem with that higher-than-average turnover rate. We've been the highest-performing firm three years in a row because I only employ the best."

"So I take it that means you fire a lot of people?"

Merrick shrugged. "They tend to quit when they can't keep up."

I wrote some more notes and then nodded. "Okay. And how many hours would you say your employees work, on average?"

"Most are in by seven and clear out by seven or eight, unless something is going on."

"Is that every day?"

"Weekdays, when the market is open."

"Do they work weekends?"

"Usually. But not like weekdays. The analysts tend to work more than the traders on the weekends when it's quiet. The traders might work half a day on Saturday and then take off until the following evening. They usually start back Sunday night when the international markets begin opening."

"So twelve to thirteen hours a day, five days a week, and then five to six hours on weekends each day? Does that sound right?"

I did the math as he thought about it and nodded.

"So seventy to eighty hours a week would be the norm?"

He shrugged. "I guess."

"And what about you?"

"What about me?"

"How many hours do you work?"

"I'm always the first one in and usually one of the last to leave."

"Can I ask you a personal question?"

"That depends on what it is."

"Are you married?"

"No."

"Were you ever?"

Merrick shook his head. "Engaged once. Not any-more."

"Don't you find it difficult to maintain a relationship while working that many hours?"

"The divorce rate in this country is fifty-one percent. I think most people find maintaining a relationship difficult, and the majority of them work nine-to-fives. But to answer your question, no. It's not impossible to have a relationship. Both parties just need to have the right expectations about how much time they'll have available." He leaned in. "Here's the thing about this job—it's all about expectations. You need to learn how to set them and meet them. The job is not easy. The time commitment is not for everyone. But it's a choice. And if you can't hack it? Leave. But don't sue me on the way out because you couldn't put in the work."

I tapped the pen in my hand against the top of the notebook I'd closed ten minutes ago. "So you think the only people who need a little help with their stress are the people who can't hack the job?"

"I think that's the case the majority of the time, yes."

I smiled. "I think we've found the root of the prob-lem."

"And I assume you're still inferring it's me? After what—has it been an hour you've been here yet?"

"You set the tone in this office. It must be difficult to live up to your standards, if not impossible. That's bound to trickle down to the employees at every level."

"So I should lower my standards to make this a more pleasant place to work?" He locked eyes with me. "I don't bend. People need to reach."

"Have you ever seen a therapist?"

Merrick sat back in his chair. "You won't be counseling me, Ms. Vaughn."

"*Doctor* Vaughn. And I thought all of the employees were mandated to have monthly sessions."

"I'm not an employee. I'm an owner. And if you read through the board minutes, you'll see that I made sure their mandate for therapy was very specific in not including me." He reached up to the two monitors on his desk and turned them on before checking his watch. "If you don't have any other questions, I need to start my day."

I nodded and stood. "Thank you for your time." But as I reached the door, Merrick spoke again.

"Evie?"

I turned back. "Finally, he calls me Evie and not Ms. Vaughn..."

The corner of his lip twitched. "I just wanted to say that while I may be strong willed, I can admit when I'm wrong... And I am. I shouldn't have hired you."

My face fell.

"My goal was to hire someone incompetent to prove a point. But I can already tell you're not."

"I think there was a compliment buried in there somewhere, wasn't there?"

Merrick looked like he tried not to smile, but failed as he shook his head and turned to face his monitors. "Try not to soften my troops too much on your first day."

CHAPTER 7

Merrick

It was almost eight by the time I shut down for the day. On my way out, I took the stairs down one flight to the other floor we occupied to drop off a package in the mailroom. The hallway lights on both floors ran on motion sensors, so most of the corridors were dark by now, with the majority of the staff gone. But as I turned left, I noticed light streaming into an otherwise dark hall to my right. It looked like it might be Evie's office, so I diverted to pass by.

She was talking on her cell, but smiled and held up one finger when I stopped.

"Dave, huh? What's the story behind that?" she said into the phone. Evie's smile widened as she listened. Her eyes twinkled. "Oh my God." She covered her mouth in laughter. "That's hysterical. And you're right, it's good information to keep tucked in my back pocket." After another minute, she said, "I have to run. My boss just came into my office. But thank you for checking on me." She laughed again before saying goodbye and tossing her cell on the desk.

"That sounded interesting," I said.

Her smile widened. "Oh, it was interesting, alright. That was Kitty."

It took me a few seconds to backtrack through the conversation, but I realized what they must've been talking about. *Dave.* I closed my eyes and hung my head. "*Fuuuck.*"

Evie laughed. "I've never heard of anyone being terrified of Dave Thomas. What did the guy do, other than being the founder of Wendy's?"

"I'm going to kill my damn grandmother."

She smiled. "Seriously. Why were you afraid of him when you were little?"

"I have no damn idea. I just saw him on a commercial once, and he looked scary to me, I guess. I was only like three years old. My sister made it worse. She used to threaten that she was going to call him if I didn't do whatever she said. Why did Kitty have to share that shit with you?"

"She called to ask how my first day went. She said she knows you well enough to know I might need some pointers on how to keep you in line."

"Pointers? With an S? As in Dave wasn't the only thing she shared?"

"The rest weren't bad."

"Let's hear them anyway."

"She told me if I want to get my way with you, to bake anything with peanut butter in it—cookies, pie, brownies..."

"If you can bake a peanut butter pie like Kitty, you might work out here after all." My phone vibrated in my pocket, so I slipped it out to see if it was important. I shook my head and turned it to show her Kitty's name flashing on the screen. "I only heard the tail end of your conversation. Am I about to get my ass kicked for something you told her?"

"Nope. I told her you'd been nothing but sweet to me." She winked. "Basically, I lied."

I pretended to scowl and swiped to answer without moving from the doorway. "Hello, grandmother dearest."

"What did you have for dinner?"

"Dinner? Nothing. I haven't eaten yet."

"Good. Neither did my Everly. She's still in the office, so take her to grab a bite. And be nice. You've been giving her a hard time, and I know it. I can tell even though she covers for your sorry ass."

I looked up and locked eyes with Evie. "How can you tell she's lying about me being nice?"

"She oversold it—called you delightful. We both know that's a load of crap. Now, are you going to do this for me or not?"

"Don't you have some fourteenth cousin to bug?"

"Yes, and he might be going in my will if you use that tone with me much longer. Oh, and while you're at dinner, give Everly the name of a bulldog lawyer. She needs one."

"Goodbye, Grams."

"Later, masturbater."

The phone went dead, and I pulled it away from my ear and shook my head at it. "Aren't people supposed to mellow in their old age?"

"Not Kitty, and she'd kick your ass if she heard you refer to her as old."

I smiled and stuffed my phone back in my pocket. "How did your first day go?"

"It went well. I think I got a lot accomplished. I went around and met everyone, started reading employee files, and made my first few appointments."

"Good." I nodded and thumbed behind me. "I should get going. Don't stay too long."

"I won't. I was just cleaning up to head out."

"See you tomorrow." I turned, but Evie's voice stopped me after my first step.

"Also, I'll make sure to tell Kitty you didn't take me to get that bite to eat."

I squinted. "You heard that?"

Evie shrugged. "Kitty talks loud on the phone."

"Are you blackmailing me for a meal?"

She opened a drawer, pulled out her purse, and shut her laptop. "I'm starving and broke. Plus, I have questions about the hierarchy here at the company and the structure of compensation. I'd like to understand where all the different pressures come from."

"What if I say it's not appropriate for us to have dinner?"

She rolled her eyes. "You've seen me in my bra, and you told me you hired me because I was the least-competent person. Plus, this is a business meal, not for pleasure. You're not my type."

I felt oddly offended. "Why not?"

"Because you have a penis. At least I assume you do. And I haven't forgiven your kind for all the wrongs they've caused."

I couldn't help but crack a smile. "Good. You're not my type either."

She batted her eyelashes. "Not into hot girls who are batshit crazy?"

I grinned. "Definitely not."

"Perfect. Then let's go." She flashed a gloating smile and walked toward the door. I stepped aside for her to exit first, but she stopped in front of me. "If you want to go to Wendy's, I'll treat."

"Keep walking, wiseass."

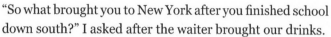

"So what brought you to New York after you finished school down south?" I asked after the waiter brought our drinks.

Evie shrugged. "My ex-fiancé—well, sort of. Christian and I met when we were both students at Emory. I applied for my doctoral internship year in New York because he was planning on moving back to work for his family's company, which has its corporate offices in Midtown. My sister also lives up here, so it worked out well at the time."

"Is she still here?"

Evie nodded. "She and her husband are up in Morningside Heights. But we actually lived in New York for a few years when we were kids. My mom moved us around a lot. I lived in eleven different states before I was thirteen."

"Wow. Did she move for work or something?"

She shook her head. "No, usually we moved when my mom left my dad, which happened every few months."

My brows pulled together. "They didn't get along?"

"Oh, sorry. I assumed you knew since Kitty and my grandmother were so close. Kitty was the one who finally got my mom to leave my dad for good. Almost thirty years ago, my mother stayed at Kitty's women's shelter for the first time. My father was abusive. My grandmother didn't know what was going on back then. Mom kept it from everyone until Kitty encouraged her to speak to family. After she did, my grandmother came down to the shelter to get my mom, and she and Kitty hit it off. They became friends, and a year or two later, the house next door to Kitty went on the market. My grandmother had been looking for a one-story house, so she bought it. The two of them were inseparable after that."

Shit. Evie's mom was someone from the DV shelter my grandmother had run for most of her life? "I knew your grandmother was Kitty's neighbor and close friend, but she never mentioned anything about your mom being..."

Evie smiled sadly. "Abused. It's okay to say it. That's one of the things Kitty taught me when I lived next door to her during school. It's not something I'm ashamed of. Kitty made me realize that the more people talk about domestic violence openly, the less victims will feel like it's something they need to hide. Anyway, there was a period of about nine months, when I was ten, where we lived with my grandmother. She had been trying to get my mom to leave my dad for years, but it was Kitty who got through to her before we finally left for good. That summer was one of the best years I had growing up, so when I got accepted into a few PhD programs, I decided to go to Emory so I could stay with my grandmother. In my third year, she was diagnosed with an aggressive metastatic cancer and passed away only a few months later. Your grandmother and I were always friendly, but we became close after that."

I nodded. "She's talked about you a lot over the years. Though of course, she calls you Everly, so I didn't put two and two together when I was interviewing Evie."

She sipped her wine with a grin. "Maybe you would have been a little nicer during my interview if you'd known."

"Or maybe if we hadn't met when you were sniffing your armpit in the men's room..." I fought past a smile.

"I never did get a chance to explain that. I had dropped a cherry on my shirt and stained it, then got stuck on a hot subway for two hours and had to rush to buy a new blouse. While I was getting changed, I realized I should freshen up a bit, but all I had was a wet wipe. When you barged in, I was trying to see if the lemon smell had transferred onto my skin."

"Number one, you didn't lock the door. And number two, you were in the men's fitting room."

She waved her hand at me. "Technicalities, technicalities. You still used me to amuse yourself. Letting me sit there and squirm, wondering whether you recognized me or not."

"It wasn't one of my finer moments. I guess we'd both had a bad day. In my defense, I'd gone to a board meeting the night before and went another round trying to talk them out of forcing my hand to fill this position, only to have them inform me we'd been served with another lawsuit just that morning. Any shot I had of swaying things my way obviously went out the window."

"How about we make a deal? You won't mention what you saw in the dressing room again, and I won't bring up Dave Thomas?" She held out her hand. "It'll be like having a fresh start."

I smiled and reached across the table, liking the feel of her tiny hand in mine a little too much. "You got a deal."

Evie pushed a lock of hair behind her ear, and it opened up a clear view of her slender neck. My fucked-up brain immediately imagined licking along her smooth skin. I had to force my eyes to look anywhere else and cleared my throat. "By the way, my grandmother told me to give you the name of a bulldog lawyer. Do you really need one?"

She sighed. "I do, actually."

"What kind of lawyer?"

"To represent me in a civil suit. My ex is suing me."

"Is he trying to get your engagement ring back?"

"No, I gave that back. Actually, I threw it at him. But I did something he claims harmed his reputation."

"You mean the video you showed at your wedding?"

Evie frowned. "You saw it?"

I wasn't about to admit I'd watched it several times recently. So I shrugged. "I saw bits and pieces of it."

She took a deep breath and exhaled. "Okay, well, that kind of makes it easier anyway. Less to explain at least. My ex, Christian, and his family are suing me for fraud and defamation. He's claiming I knew about the affair he was having for longer than I did, and that I purposefully racked up unnecessary bills for the wedding with fraudulent intent. He's also claiming that I harmed his reputation when the video went viral."

"How long did you know about the affair?"

"Twelve hours maybe? I found out on the evening of our wedding. We'd checked into the hotel where our reception was being held. When we got engaged, Christian's father had given him the money clip his mother had given to him the day they were married. It was engraved with a sweet note and their wedding date. I'd secretly taken it from his drawer and had our wedding date and a note engraved underneath his parents' names and message. I'd thought it would make a nice family heirloom. You know, maybe something that could continue being passed down through generations with dates added. Anyway, I wanted to video his reaction when I gave it to him, so I'd set up a camera in the honeymoon suite and told Christian to meet me there. But while I was waiting for him, my sister called to tell me a cabbie had just jumped the curb and run over her husband's foot. I wound up going to the hospital to be with her for a few hours and forgot all about the camera that was recording. When I got back later that evening, I gave Christian the money clip, and afterward we said goodbye for the night since we were sleeping in separate rooms—the groom's not supposed to see the bride before the wedding and all." Evie rolled her eyes. "As if my luck could have gotten any worse. In any case, I'd forgotten all about the camera until after he left. I figured it had probably stopped recording hours ago, but I checked anyway and got the surprise of my life: Christian having sex with my best friend and maid of honor, Mia."

"Jesus Christ." I shook my head. "And you had no clue anything was going on between them until that point?"

"Nope. Well, I didn't at the time, but in hindsight there were some clues I'd missed. Like, Mia's name popped up on his cell phone once, and the message said something about them meeting. But when I asked Christian about it, he told me to stop being nosy because I was going to ruin the surprise of my bridal shower. And then another time I found Mia's phone stuck in the cushions of our couch, and she hadn't been over in a few weeks. She said she must've lost it when she was there last time and had been looking all over for it. But I thought it was strange that she'd never mentioned she couldn't find it, if it went missing right after being at my house. We're all so attached to our phones, and a new one is like a thousand dollars." She sighed and frowned. "But never in a million years would I have thought the two of them would do what they did to me. Even after I found the video, I didn't want to believe it right away. I thought it was a joke at first."

"Guy's got some balls suing you after what he did. Even if you did know about it and didn't call things off to run up the bill, he damn well deserves it. And how can he sue you for defamation? The defense to a lawsuit like that is the truth."

She smiled halfheartedly. "I think he's trying to get even with me for embarrassing him publicly. His family has a staff of in-house attorneys, so there isn't any cost for him. But I'm sure it will wind up costing me a fortune I don't have. The ironic thing is, I didn't even want a big, expensive wedding. Christian and his family did. They had more business associates on the guest list than I did friends and family."

"I'm sorry. That sucks. But I do have a good attorney to recommend, and he owes me a favor or two. I'll call him tomorrow and see what he can do."

"Thank you. I'd appreciate that."

I nodded. "Not a problem."

The waitress came with our dinners. I'd ordered the salmon while Evie had chosen the chicken piccata. She licked her lips, looking over at my plate. "Yours looks good. Are you sharing?"

I shook my head with a chuckle. "Sure. Anything else you'd like?"

Evie reached over and grabbed my plate. She smiled while cutting off a piece of my salmon and replacing it with a piece of her chicken. "Actually there is."

"Why am I not surprised..."

"Oh, pipe down. I just want to ask you some questions about the office."

I took my plate back. "What would you like to know?"

For the next half hour, she peppered me with questions about trading, mostly how things ran and what my staff were and weren't authorized to do. She seemed to have a pretty good grasp on a lot of industry terminology.

"You don't have any experience in a brokerage house," I said. "Yet you seem to understand a lot about how things work."

"I read a bunch of books when I was offered the job."

I nodded. "Anything else you'd like to know?"

"Actually..." She drummed her fingers on the table. "When I was reading up on your company, I found an old article from the year you opened. It said you had a partner. But I read your last few prospectuses, and the name disappeared from the stockholder section a couple of years back. Amelia...Evans, I think it was?"

I looked away. "That's right."

"What happened with her?"

I looked around for the waitress. Catching her eye, I raised my hand to call her over before returning my attention to Evie. "I don't think that's relevant to the job you were hired to do." When the waitress walked over, I requested the check.

She slipped a leather padfolio from her apron pocket and set it on the table. "I'll take it whenever you're ready."

"I'm ready now." I pulled out my wallet and tucked a credit card into the slot before handing it back.

"Okay. I'll be back in a minute."

Evie waited until the waitress disappeared, but didn't miss a beat picking up right where she'd left off. "I'm asking because oftentimes a change in management can have a major effect on employees."

"If anything, Amelia's departure relieved the firm of stress, not added to it. She ran the IPO division—bringing companies public for the first time. There's a lot of pressure involved with that type of deal. We no longer take on that type of work."

"Oh...okay. How long ago did she leave the company?"

"Three years."

"Did any staff go with her when she left?"

I shook my head. "No."

"Was the split amicable? Did she start her own firm?"

The waitress returned with the credit card receipt, so I scribbled my name. When I looked up, Evie was still waiting for an answer. So I gave her one.

"There was no split. Amelia Evans died."

CHAPTER 8

Merrick

NINE YEARS AGO

"**W**ho's filling in for Decker tonight?" I ripped open the cardboard Budweiser case and bent to fill the mini fridge—the one we kept in the living room next to the card table because we were all too lazy to get up and walk the ten steps to the kitchen.

"Someone from my stats class," Travis said. "Her name is Amelia. She's going to let me cheat off her for Tuesday's midterm if she can play."

My head swung up. "She? You invited a girl to play cards with us?"

Travis shrugged. "I gotta pass this damn test. Besides, it's not like we ever made a rule that girls couldn't play."

Maybe we hadn't. But the four of us had been playing cards once a week since freshman year. For three-and-a-half years it had been a guys' night. Whenever one of us couldn't make it, we got someone to fill in. Up until today, that had always been a guy. One of our regular foursome was doing a semester abroad this term, so we'd been taking turns recruiting his replacement each week. "I guess

we never needed a rule because we all had a silent understanding."

Our friend Will Silver walked in. He set a bottle of
Jack in the middle of the card table.

"Hey, Will," I said. "How come you never invited a girl
to play cards with us?"

"I don't know." He shrugged. "It's a guys' night."

I looked to Trav. "See?"

He waved me off. "Stop bitching. She probably sucks
at cards, and you'll be taking home some easy money. You
should be thanking me."

Will pointed to the beer I was transferring to the
fridge. "Toss me one."

"They're warm. Cold ones are in the kitchen."

"Have you been paying attention the last three years?
I don't give a shit if it's cold. Just pass me one."

I tossed him a warm beer.

Will peeled back the top of the can with a loud *tssSSS
kr-POP*. "Does she at least have nice tits?"

"Yes. She has great tits," an unexpected voice said
from behind us. "Tell me, how's your dick?"

All three of our heads swung toward the woman, and
the room grew quiet. I lifted my beer to my lips and noticed
she hadn't been lying—her tits were pretty great. Though,
unlike Will, I was smart enough to keep my thoughts to
myself.

The woman lifted a brow. "Well?"

She was waiting for an actual answer about Will's
dick. I tilted my beer toward his junk. "I've seen it. His
dick's pretty sad."

"Fuck off," Will said. "I'm a grower, not a show-er."

The woman looked at me. She wasn't smiling, but I
could see it lurking at the corner of her lips and in the spar-
kle in her eyes. She tilted her head. "And how's your dick?"

I shrugged. "Spectacular. You want to see it?"

Her smile peeked through. "Maybe later. I'll take all your money first."

I might've been willing to hand my wallet to this girl right now, if that was all it was going to take. She had fire red hair, pale skin, and a few freckles on her perky little nose. Not to mention, the green tank top she had on made it impossible to not stare.

"Sounds like a plan to me," I said. "Except I'm pretty sure I'll be the one taking the money tonight."

Her smile widened. "Would you like to wager on that?"

"You want to bet you're going to be the big winner tonight even though we haven't dealt the first hand of cards?"

"Yep."

"Shouldn't you at least wait to see how the people you're up against play?"

"Nope. If we wait that long, you won't make the bet..."

"Because you're that good?"

She rolled her eyes. "Do we have a bet or not?"

"Sure. Why not? How much we betting?"

"A hundred bucks?"

My buddies whistled. We only played with fifty bucks each, sometimes less if someone was broke. But I worked and had plenty of money. Besides, I could only count a handful of nights when I'd lost big. More times than not, I was the winner. I was good at cards, because cards were essentially numbers. And I was even better at numbers. Though I didn't want her money.

I rubbed my bottom lip with my thumb. "I'll give you the hundred if you win. But if I win, I want a kiss."

Amelia's eyes sparkled. "Deal. Let's play."

Two hours later, I sat back in my chair and dragged a hand through my hair. Travis and Will had tossed their cards on the table and gone out back to smoke a joint. "How the hell did you learn to play like that?" I asked.

We'd played Texas Hold 'Em, Five-Card Draw, Crazy Eights, and even Sevens Take All, and Amelia had won almost every single hand.

She leaned forward to rake the last of the pot to her side of the table. "My father loved to play. He taught me how to count cards when I was four, and I'm good at reading people."

"You count cards? That's cheating."

"No, it's not. It's using your brain to get an advantage. Cheating is when you hide a few aces under the table and give yourself a winning hand. Or when you help yourself to a view of another player's cards."

"But you didn't mention that you could count cards before we started."

She shrugged. "I told you I was good at cards and was going to take your money. You didn't believe me." Amelia held out her hand, palm up. "By the way, I'll take my hundred dollars now."

I shook my head as I dug into my pocket. "I should at least get the kiss I bet since you already fucked me."

"You didn't earn it."

I counted five twenties and held them out. But when she tried to take them, I didn't let go. Her eyes lifted from the bills to mine.

"Let me earn it a different way," I said. "Go out with me?"

She plucked the bills from my hand and tucked them into her front jeans pocket. "No thanks."

"Why not?"

"That would be too easy for you." She picked up her purse and pulled the strap over her head so it laid diagonally across her body. "But I'll give you a consolation prize."

"What's that?"

"You can watch me walk out." She turned and strutted toward the door, yelling back over her shoulder. "My ass is even better than my tits."

She wasn't wrong. But I was still confused as shit about what had gone down this evening. "Wait. What do I have to do to get you to go out with me?"

She stopped with her hand on the door but never looked back. "Now if I told you that, *anything* you did would be considered easy, wouldn't it? Goodnight, Merrick."

CHAPTER 9

Evie

"Andrea!"

The bellow came from behind Merrick's closed door. I'd just come upstairs to talk to his assistant about scheduling an appointment, but Andrea wasn't at her desk. I looked around, and she was nowhere in sight. So I walked to his office and waved so he could see me before popping my head in.

Two people were arguing loudly through his desk speakerphone. But Merrick waved me inside and pushed a button, which I assumed was mute.

"Sorry, I see you're on a call," I said. "I heard you yell for Andrea, so I figured I'd let you know she's not at her desk. I just came up to speak to her myself."

"Shit."

"What's the matter?"

"This call I'm on was in my calendar for this afternoon, not eight in the morning. I think she might've flip-flopped two clients when she input the appointments."

"Oh. Well, do you need something?"

"I need Andrea to run upstairs to my apartment and grab a file that has the reports for this call."

"I can do that."

He hesitated. "You sure she's not around?"

I looked back over my shoulder. "I don't see her anywhere. But I can check the break room for you, and if I don't find her, I can grab your file."

"You don't mind?"

"Not at all. I'm happy to help."

Merrick nodded. "If you don't find her, the file should be on the living room table. Some of the contents are probably outside the folder, so just grab whatever you see." He pulled out a set of keys. "Top floor, apartment two."

"Okay. Be right back."

I quickly checked both the break room and the ladies' room, but there was no sign of his assistant. So I headed to the elevator and pushed the button for the highest floor on the panel.

When I arrived, I realized apartment two was really *penthouse* two. I stood with my jaw hanging open as I let myself inside. Merrick's place was ginormous, with an open floorplan that swept from the gourmet kitchen to the living room and dining room, separated only by a few steps down. I made my way to where he'd said his file was, drooling over the stainless-and-marble kitchen as I passed. Then I completely forgot why I was up here once I got a load of the view from the living room. Floor-to-ceiling windows lined one wall, looking out onto the river and bridge, while the adjoining wall showcased a skyline of tall buildings. I bet it looked incredible all lit up at night.

I could've gazed all day, but the boss needed his file—and I needed thirty seconds to nose around the rest of the apartment. At the far end of the living room, there was a long hall, which I assumed led to the bedrooms. So I scooped up the file I'd come to collect and the papers scattered around it, and went to check out the rest of the place.

The first room was an office, with gorgeous built-in bookshelves and one of those ladders attached at the top that could be rolled from one end to the other. *God, I always wanted a ladder with my bookshelves.*

The next room was a bathroom, and there was a bedroom across from that. At the end of the hall was a set of double doors. I might've gasped when I creaked them open and got a look at the master. The man had *a terrace* off his bedroom, with enough room to have a small party. And the bed? It had to be a California King—or bigger? Was there anything bigger? The four dark-wood, carved posts were so masculine and definitely matched the bossman downstairs.

Speaking of which...I needed to get the hell out of here. I would've loved a little more time to poke around, maybe check out the closet and master bath, but I wasn't about to push my luck. As I pulled the bedroom door closed, a flash of color caught my eye on the nightstand on the far side of the bed.

Goldfish?

I don't know why, but it struck me as odd that two plain jane, orange goldfish were sitting in a small bowl on a nightstand. Now, if there had been a five-hundred-gallon tank filled with exotic saltwater fish? That wouldn't have seemed strange. But two simple fish that probably cost a dollar? While I stood there trying to make a piece fit into a puzzle, my phone rang. The number was familiar, although I couldn't place it until I swiped to answer and heard the voice.

"Where are you?"

Crap. Merrick. "I'm...waiting for the elevator."

"That thing is slow as shit. Take the stairs, please. I need the damn file."

"Okay. I'll be right there."

I swiped my phone off and rushed out of his apartment, double-checking that the door locked behind me while looking around for the stairwell. But as I headed toward it, the elevator dinged, so I backed up and rushed in as soon as the doors slid open—and almost collided with a woman coming off.

"Oh my God, I'm so sorry."

The woman had to be over six-feet tall with the statuesque heels she had on. And five of those feet were legs.

She looked me up and down. "Why are you on this floor?"

"I, umm..." I pointed over my shoulder to penthouse two. "I had to pick up a file for Merrick."

She tilted her head and squinted. "And you are?"

"I work at Crawford Investments."

"Oh." The woman gave me a last once-over and seemed to lose interest. She stepped around me. "I should've guessed that."

What the hell did that mean? I was pretty sure it was an insult, but when the elevator doors started to slide closed, I realized I didn't have time to worry about it. So I jumped inside, glancing over my shoulder toward where Miss Daddy Long Legs was heading. Apparently, she lived in penthouse one—or at least she had the key.

Andrea was back at her desk when I returned, so I explained what had happened, and she quickly took the file to the boss.

The rest of the day was pretty unremarkable. I didn't see Merrick again until his voice made me jump at seven that evening. I'd been reading and hadn't heard him approach my open office door.

"Did you get here at the ass crack of dawn again this morning?"

I smiled. "Maybe a little later."

He had a leather strap diagonally across his chest, with a stuffed briefcase hanging behind him. He looked at his watch. "Why don't you go home? You don't have to work twelve hours a day."

"Thanks. I was just going to pack up." I lifted my chin, motioning toward his bag. "Looks like you plan on working a lot more than twelve hours with that bag."

He nodded. "I have a lot of shit to catch up on. Unfortunately, I have a dinner meeting first."

Merrick's phone rang. He pulled it out of his pocket, looked at the screen, and swiped to answer with a groan. "I'm on my way."

The other person said something I couldn't make out. It made Merrick roll his eyes. "I'll avoid it. Thank you. See you in a bit."

He swiped his phone off, shaking his head. "Don't become one of those annoying New Yorkers who has to tell everyone what route to take to get somewhere."

"I don't think that will be a problem. I barely know my right from my left."

Merrick smiled. I thought it might be the first real, unguarded one I'd been treated to. I pointed to his face. "You should do that more often."

"What?"

"Smile. It makes you seem like less of an ogre."

"So I'm an ogre?"

"Well, I think you have to be a minimum of nine-feet tall to be an ogre. So maybe a mini ogre."

Tiny wrinkles creased around his eyes as he smiled again, even as he tried to hide it. "By the way," he said. "That reminds me—I never thanked you for not dropping a dime on me to Grams."

"What do you mean?"

"She told me you said I was polite and professional in our first interview. In hindsight, perhaps I was a little curt."

"A little?"

Merrick smiled some more. His phone buzzed in his hand, and he glanced down before shaking his head. "Now I'm supposed to avoid 144th at Convent Avenue for some reason."

I nodded. "Oh, that's two blocks from where I'm staying. They actually have the entire block shut down. They're filming something. I tried to get a peek at it when I passed this morning."

"You live uptown?"

"My sister does. I'm staying with her until I can find something."

He nodded toward the hall. "Come on. I'll drop you on the way."

"Oh no, it's fine. I can take the subway."

"I'm going right near you. I have a car waiting outside."

"You sure?"

He nodded. "It's not a problem at all."

We rode the elevator down together and got into the waiting Town Car, where I gave the driver my sister's address. As we pulled away from the curb, this time my phone rang.

"Would you excuse me for a minute? It's my sister."

"Do whatever you need to." Merrick sat a few feet away, scrolling through his phone while I answered.

"Hey," Greer said. "I just wanted to tell you I walked Mrs. Aster's dog for you. I was taking Buddy out anyway. Plus, you've been getting home so late. Just figured I'd tell you in case you planned to stop in her apartment on your way up."

"Oh, thanks so much. You didn't have to do that. Why are you home so early?"

"I have that part-timer who closes on Tuesdays and Thursdays now, remember? So I can walk her dog Thursday, too, if you need it."

"Thanks, but Mrs. Aster will be back tomorrow. She's away at her sister's."

"You and your crazy barter deals. What does she give you in return, anyway?"

"Homemade cat treats."

"Cat treats? But you don't even have a cat."

"Yes, but I trade them to a guy who does website development. He's making one for me, for my rentals. If I rent direct, I can save the Airbnb fees."

Greer sighed. "Why can't you figure out how to trade for some primo sperm for me?"

Through my peripheral vision, I noticed Merrick glance over. His brows pulled together as he looked back down at his phone.

"Are you still at the office?" she asked.

"Actually, I'm on my way home."

"Okay, be careful on the subway."

"I'm in a car. My boss was heading uptown, so he offered to drop me off."

"Oooh... Is this hot boss?"

This time my eyes flashed to Merrick. If he'd heard, he didn't react. "I gotta run. Thank you for doing that for me. I'll see you in a little bit."

"Get me some sperm from hot boss!"

Now Merrick's eyes definitely widened. *Did she have to yell that?* I closed my eyes. "Goodbye, Greer." I *felt* the man next to me staring. I sighed. "You heard that, didn't you?"

"Do you want me to pretend I didn't?"

I nodded. "That would be great. Thank you."

The corner of Merrick's lip twitched, but he went back to staring at his phone. After a few minutes of awkward silence, I gave in.

"My sister and her husband have had some fertility issues. They're in the process of looking for a donor. It's been a running joke since I interviewed that she wants your sperm."

"Why?"

"She wants someone with good genes—you know, smart, good looking, successful."

"Did she and I ever meet?"

I shook my head. "No."

"Did she see a picture of me somewhere?"

"Not that I'm aware of."

Merrick's mouth slid to a cocky grin. "So she got her information about my appearance from..."

Shit. I rolled my eyes. "You don't have to be obnoxious about it. You're good looking. Big deal. So are a lot of men."

Merrick chuckled. "And the cat treat-website development barter?"

"Man, you heard everything, huh?"

He smiled. "Perhaps you should turn the volume down on your phone."

"Or...you can just mind your own beeswax and pretend you didn't overhear."

"Why would I do that when you were engrossed in such a riveting conversation? Your sister is bartering for sperm?"

I laughed. "No, the bartering part of the conversation didn't have anything to do with the sperm part—not really, anyway. I'm taking care of my sister's neighbor's dog. That neighbor makes organic cat treats that have CBD in them, so she pays me in those. I don't have a cat, but the guy who's building the website for my rental properties has one with bad anxiety, so it works out all around."

Merrick shook his head. "Just curious. What could I get for sperm in the racket you have going?"

"Sadly, I probably can't do much better than organic cat treats right now. I'm still establishing my network here in New York. I stopped doing it for a few years because Christian, my ex, hated when I bartered."

"Why did he hate it?"

I shrugged. "I think it embarrassed him. He didn't like people thinking I couldn't afford things. But I had fun organizing all the barters and getting stuff for free. I sort of find it exhilarating. In hindsight, I should have bartered his ass for a backbone and done what makes me happy."

Merrick's eyes swept over my face, and he smiled. "Tell me what else you've bartered."

"Everything." I shrugged. "Anything. I've babysat for frequent flyer miles, got my oil changed in exchange for tutoring a mechanic's daughter in math. Once I even traded baking forty dozen cookies to get my friend's nursery painted with a Pete the Cat mural."

"What's Pete the Cat?"

"A cartoon."

"Who needed forty dozen cookies?"

"A couple getting married who wanted to give everyone a small box with fresh-baked Italian flag cookies as a parting gift."

"You make those things?"

I nodded. "I bake a lot. My grandmother owned a bakery when I was a little girl."

"Milly did? I didn't know that."

"Yep. She sold it a year or two after my grandfather died. She said it wasn't the same without him. But she still baked a lot, and it was something we did together every time I visited. I don't remember ever walking into her house without it smelling like a fresh batch of cookies or a cake. I'm more of a mood baker than a regular baker, though. I don't usually bake if things are just rolling along in my life. But if I'm happy or sad, I get a certain energy and need to keep myself busy, so I wind up in the kitchen. I also tend to snack when I'm nervous, so I suppose the baking and snacking go hand in hand. And..." I laughed. "I have no idea why I'm telling you all this."

Merrick smiled. "I'm not even sure how this conversation started anymore."

"Ah..." I raised a finger. "My sister wants your sperm."

Merrick's phone buzzed. "We might've needed this call as an interruption. God knows where this discussion would go next."

He swiped to answer and brought the phone to his ear. "What's up, Bree?"

Unlike the way he'd listened to my entire conversation, I couldn't make out more than a word or two of his. Though the voice on the other end was definitely a woman. After a minute, he shook his head.

"Sorry. I won't be around next week. I have a business trip."

He listened again. This time, he looked over at me before he spoke. "That's nice of you to offer, but I'm not home now either."

Quiet.

84

"Probably not. I'll be pretty late. But thank you anyway."

He swiped his phone off and went silent. I just couldn't
help myself.

"You know, your phone is so low, I could only hear
one side of the conversation."

"That's because I turned it down after you were able
to hear my entire conversation with Kitty the other day."

I shifted in my seat to face him. "So you're not going
to tell me who you just blew off?"

"How do you know I blew someone off if you didn't
hear the person on the other end?"

"A woman knows when she hears a blow off, whether
it's for her or someone else. It's one of our innate talents."

Merrick's lip twitched. "Bree is my neighbor."

"Is she super tall?"

"Yes, why?"

"I think I met her when I went upstairs to get your file
earlier today. I'm pretty sure she insulted me, but I can't
be sure."

Merrick smiled. "I don't even know what she said, but
I'm sure it was insulting. Bree's not a big fan of women."

"The entire gender?"

He shook his head. "She's a model, and apparently it's
very competitive."

"She's a model—one who is very pretty with great
legs. So why would you blow her off?"

"I don't shit where I eat, Dr. Vaughn." His eyes
dropped to my lips for a fraction of a second. If I'd blinked,
I would have missed it. He caught my gaze again. "Getting
involved with a neighbor is almost as stupid as getting involved with a coworker."

An odd disappointment hit me. "Oh... Yeah, that
makes sense."

When we turned the corner to my block, my sister was coming out the front door of her building with Buddy on a leash. I leaned forward to let the driver know which building it was, and we pulled up right next to where Greer and her dog were standing. I had a sneaking suspicion she was out here on purpose, waiting for me to pull up so she could take a look at the man sitting next to me since she'd told me she just took out her dog with the neighbor's.

"Thank you very much for the ride home."

Merrick nodded. "Of course."

I grabbed the door handle, but Merrick stopped me. "Hang on. Don't open that side. This is a busy road, and no one pays attention. I'll let you out on this side."

"Umm... You might want me to risk it." I pointed to my sister, who was smiling like a loon. "That's my sister, Greer, who wants your sperm. I'm not sure you want to get out."

Merrick chuckled. "This should be interesting." He climbed out of the car and offered his hand to me.

Greer's eyes sparkled as she watched the scene. I had no choice but to make the introduction. "Uh, Merrick, this is my sister, Greer. Greer, meet my boss, Merrick Crawford."

The two of them shook, and Greer looked Merrick up and down. "You're tall."

He smiled politely.

"What, about six two?"

"Exactly. Very good guess."

She nodded. "It's nice to meet you. I've met your grandmother. She's a hoot."

"That she is, indeed."

I could see the wheels spinning in my sister's head. "How old is she now? She and our grandmother were born the same year. So that must make her close to eighty?"

"Seventy-eight. But if she were seventy-nine and three-hundred-and-sixty-four days, I wouldn't call her *close to eighty* to her face."

Greer smiled. "Longevity in the family. You must have good genes. Any family history of severe illness?"

Oh my God. I shoved my sister toward the apartment building and waved behind me to Merrick. "We definitely need to run. Thanks again for the ride, boss."

He chuckled.

Inside the lobby, I shook my head. "I cannot believe you just did that."

"What?"

"Questioning him like he was a serious sperm-donor candidate. He's *my boss*, Greer."

"Sorry. I got carried away. He's even better than you described, though. *Those eyelashes.* I pay eighty dollars a month, and mine aren't nearly as full and dark. If I can't have his sperm, you definitely should take some."

"That's not happening."

"Really? Are you ignoring the way he looks at you?"

Lines creased between my brows. "What are you talking about?"

"I was around the man one minute, and I know he's hot for you."

"You're crazy."

I turned and looked back through the front door. Merrick was still standing outside the car watching me.

But that didn't mean anything...right?

CHAPTER 10

Evie

The following Monday, I had my first one-on-one counseling appointment at the office. I was excited and nervous, and both were showing—to me anyway. I'd been up since three AM making cookies, and was now arriving at the office before it even opened.

I'd decided to bring some of the goodies with me to keep out on a pretty tray next to the patient couch. Joan in HR had warned me that some of the traders had been vocal about not wanting to be forced to meet with a therapist, so I thought it might soften the blow if they could nibble on some cookies.

On my walk from the subway to the office, my hands were full with three containers of cookies, a gallon of milk, some disposable cups and paper goods, a half-dozen files I'd read at home last night, and my unnecessarily large purse. At the door to the building, I was attempting to juggle it all into one hand when an arm reached around me and opened the door.

"Thank you so..." I turned to finish the sentence and realized it was the boss. "Oh, you again."

He offered his signature half smile-half smirk. "You sound so thrilled..."

Merrick wore black running gear again, except today his outfit had a short-sleeve shirt. He reached up to pluck one earbud from his ear, and the muscles of his brawny biceps bulged, catching my attention. *Well, maybe a little thrilled.* Luckily, he seemed oblivious to my ogle.

"What the hell is in all the bags?" He reached over and scooped everything from my right side into his arms.

"Thank you. I made some cookies, but then I realized I can't serve cookies without milk. And I haven't checked out the supplies in the break room yet, so I picked up some paper goods and cups and stuff, too."

"You baked?"

I nodded.

"Uh-oh. Was it me?"

"What are you talking about?"

"You said you bake when you're angry."

I laughed. "No, I said I bake when I get into a frenzied mood. This was excited baking."

Merrick peeked in the bag. "Looks like a shit ton of cookies in here."

"And I left more than half at home." I smiled. "I'm *really* nervous."

We arrived at the elevator bank, and Merrick pushed the button. "What are you nervous about?"

"Oh, I don't know... Starting therapy with a bunch of super-intelligent Ivy League millionaires who don't think they need therapy."

"You want me to let you in on a little secret for keeping them in their place?"

"Duh—is that even really a question? *Yes.*"

The elevator doors slid open, and Merrick held out his hand for me to enter first. It was just the two of us in the car, yet Merrick lowered his voice. "Okay, this is the secret. When you feel like they're challenging you or questioning your authority, stand like Superman."

"How exactly does Superman stand?"

"Stand tall and plant your hands on your hips with your feet apart. Maybe puff out your chest a little."

"I think that might work better for you since you're six two and actually are a little intimidating."

Merrick tapped his pointer to his temple. "It's nothing to do with size. It's what's in here. Trust me. You can pull it off."

I wasn't sure he was right. But I appreciated him trying. At least I thought I did... Unless... "Wait, you're not telling me that to sabotage me and asserting a power pose is going to make them go ballistic, are you?"

Merrick grinned. "No, I'm not."

I sighed. "Okay. Well, then thanks for the advice."

He nodded. "You're welcome."

When we arrived at my floor, I turned to Merrick. "Here, give me those bags. You're probably going upstairs to your apartment, right?"

He used his free hand to hold the elevator door open and lifted his chin, motioning for me to walk out first. "It's fine. I'm going to grab a file from one of the analysts down here anyway."

He followed me into my office and set the bags down on the coffee table in the patient treatment area. Then he picked up a shard of glass I'd forgotten when I left Friday night. He looked around the room. "Did something break?"

"No, I brought that with me."

He flipped it around in his fingers. "Is it sea glass?"

I nodded.

"It's an unusual color."

"Turquoise is the second rarest color for sea glass. Orange is the first."

Merrick lifted a brow. "Sea glass expert?"

"A little. I collect it." I walked over and took the piece from his hand. "I shouldn't give you any more ammunition to think I'm a quack, but that's one of my lucky pieces. I meant to put it in my desk drawer the other night for safekeeping before I left."

He smirked. "Lucky sea glass, huh?"

I wagged a finger at him. "Be nice."

"Who are your first patients today?"

"Ummm... Let me check the order." I went to my desk and got my calendar out of the drawer. "I started with the most senior people, so I have Will Silver at nine, Lark Renquist at eleven, and then this afternoon I have Colette Archwood and Marcus Lindey."

"Will is a cocky bastard, but he has good reason to be. He's talented. Lark was promoted last year. He's young, and the older guys don't like to report to him because they don't feel like he's paid his dues. It doesn't help that he looks even younger than his age, and won't grow a five o'clock shadow even after a marathon forty-eight hours in the office. Colette hates my guts. And Marcus is currently interviewing with our biggest competitor and doesn't think I know."

"Oh, wow. I appreciate the insight. But why does Colette hate you?"

"It's a long story." Merrick nodded toward the bags he'd set down. "Did I earn a cookie?"

I smiled. "Help yourself. There's chocolate chip and peanut butter chunk."

He reached into the bag and slipped a cookie out of each of the top two containers. Biting off half a peanut butter one with a single chomp, he waved it at me. "Peanut butter is my weakness."

I might've remembered that when I was figuring out what to bake. But I kept that to myself.

He popped the rest in his mouth and spoke with it full. "You probably shouldn't have told me you make these when you're excited or angry. These cookies are the shit, and I'm really good at pissing employees off."

I laughed. "You can also just ask."

Merrick nodded and reached for the bag a second time. He swiped a few more peanut butter cookies and winked before heading out. When he reached the door, I called after him.

"Hey, Superman."

He looked back.

"You think a Wonder Woman stance would work, too?"

His eyes did a quick sweep over me before a dirty grin spread across his face. "Had a huge crush on Wonder Woman when I was a kid. Whoever designed her outfit was a damn genius."

"Should I lie down?" Will pointed to the couch.

"If you'd like, but you don't have to."

He jumped into the air and flounced down on the couch. He stretched his long legs out and propped his head up on a pillow with his hands tucked behind it. "Ah... This is kind of nice. I don't know why everyone is moaning and groaning about having to come here. It's better than kindergarten. You get milk and cookies, and then it's nap time."

I smiled. "Well, nap position anyway. The idea isn't really for you to go to sleep."

"No worries. I couldn't fall asleep during the day if someone had a gun to my head." Will motioned to his head and twirled his finger around. "Once this on switch gets flipped, it's on until it runs out of power, around two AM usually."

"Two AM? I saw you here at seven the other morning."

"I don't require a lot of sleep."

"Were either of your parents that way?"

Will nodded. "My mom. She could sleep four or five hours a night and be good to go. My dad always said she was just afraid she'd miss a conversation."

"It's actually genetic for some people," I said. "A few years ago, they found a gene mutation that can get passed through families. It's called the ADRB1 gene. It causes a shortened sleep cycle."

"No shit? I always knew I was a mutant."

I chuckled.

Will sprang upright and put his feet on the floor. "It feels weird to talk to you without looking at you. Why is it always that way in the movies?"

"Freud believed having patients not make eye contact made them feel freer, that people were more relaxed and likely to say whatever came to their mind when they weren't focused on being watched and were in the supine position."

"Is that true?"

"For some people. It's whatever makes you feel more comfortable."

Will nodded. "So how does this work? Where do we start?"

"I like to start slow, get to know each other a little bit."

"Okay. Shoot. What do you want to know?"

I picked up the steno pad and pen I had set on the table next to me and flipped to the first open page. "Have you ever been to therapy before?"

"Does marriage counseling count?"

I nodded. "It does. Are you still actively in therapy?"

"Nope." He held up his hand to show me a ringless finger. "Happily divorced."

"How long ago were you divorced?"

"It was finalized about eighteen months ago."

"And how long did you go to therapy?"

"Six sessions."

"Oh. Did you not feel like it was working?"

"No, that's how long it took for my ex to admit she was sleeping with the neighbor."

"I'm sorry. Are you comfortable talking about your marriage?"

Will shrugged. "It's not my favorite topic, but sure."

"Do you mind if I ask if you were having marital problems before she had an affair?"

"I didn't think so. But apparently we were. I work a lot. Brooke complained about it, but she also liked the lifestyle that came with the type of job I have. I suggested she take up a hobby. So she did: banging the neighbor."

I smiled sadly. "How many hours a week do you work?"

"I'm usually in the office from seven-to-seven weekdays. Saturdays I work a half day from home."

"When you go home in the evening, what do you do?"

"Now that I'm single? I play racquetball twice a week. Other than that, I usually order in or pick something up, and read the *Journal* while I eat. Watch a little TV maybe, answer some emails, do research while I have a drink. I also leave my socks on the floor, the toilet seat up, and snore without getting yelled at."

"So you work about sixty hours a week in the office, plus another five or six on Saturday. And then you also spend your evenings reading business-related news, doing research, and answering emails, which probably adds another few hours each day. Would it be unreasonable to say you work eighty hours a week?"

Will shrugged. "I love my job. It's not like I'm miserable doing it."

"What about the people who report to you? Do they work as much?"

"Some. The good ones anyway."

"Is it impossible to be good at your job if you only work say, fifty hours a week?"

"I didn't say that. But this is a career that requires a lot of knowledge—knowledge of the market, trends, individual industries and corporations. And that knowledge changes by the moment."

"Can you farm out any of the knowledge acquisition and just have someone give you the summary version?"

Will smiled. "That's what an analyst does. It would be impossible for one person to dig deep into everything. But even just sifting through all of the different sector analysts' summaries is a job."

"How long have you been at Crawford Investments?"

"Since day one. Merrick and I have been friends since freshman year of college. We went to Princeton together."

"I didn't know that."

He nodded. "We both worked over at Sterling Capital right out of college. After three years, he was a VP, and I was still an analyst. People don't make VP in three years anywhere. But Merrick was smarter and worked harder than the guys who owned the place, so they moved him up fast in an attempt to keep him. When he said he was leaving, they offered him a piece of the business. He wasn't even twenty-five yet."

"But he didn't take it?"

Will shook his head. "Nope. Would have been easier on him if he did. But the owners didn't like Amelia. She worked at Sterling, too. So the two of them went out on their own."

"Why didn't they like Amelia?"

"Back then, Merrick said it was because Sterling was a good-old-boys club and women weren't given the same opportunities. If we talked about it today, he might have a different opinion. Amelia was brilliant but reckless. This is a job you have to have balls for—excuse my French—but there's such a thing as too big of balls."

Interesting. "Merrick and I spoke a little about Amelia," I said. "He seemed to think her departure from Crawford Investments didn't have an effect on the staff. Would you agree?"

"Merrick spoke to you about Amelia? As in, he said her name?"

My brows drew together. "Yes."

"Wow. You must be a good shrink. The man hasn't uttered her name in three years, that I'm aware of."

"Really? Well, we didn't get into details, only the fact that she was a partner and that she'd passed away. Often a change in leadership can cause stress among the employees." I suspected there might've been more between Merrick and Amelia than just a business partnership, but it wasn't my place to ask. "I take it the split wasn't a friendly one, if he doesn't speak of her?"

Will nodded. "It didn't affect the office nearly as much as it did my friend. They were engaged."

"What happened?" Inappropriate as it was, I couldn't stop that question from popping out. After I asked, Will's face changed. A wrinkle formed between his brows and his mouth dipped down.

"It's not my place to talk about. Let's just say she annihilated my best friend."

That didn't sound good. Of course, it also made me more curious, but I didn't want to push my professional boundaries any further on his first visit. So I rounded our conversation back to his job. Will seemed open to discussing anything about his work, which was good. And his cooperation went a long way in settling my nerves. I was glad he was my first client of the day.

When the alarm I'd set to signal the end of our session dinged, Will slapped his hands to his thighs. "So? Did I win a prize?"

"You sure did. Your first session is over. You've won your freedom for another month."

"Nice. Wasn't so bad."

Considering we'd spent the hour mostly discussing the elements of his job and not really any emotions or feelings, I was glad he didn't think it was too painful. I had a learning curve and needed to take my time with these people to earn their trust and respect. But it felt safe to push my luck a little with Will, since he was so easygoing and friendly.

"Can I ask you one more question, Will?"

"Sure."

"If you had a do-over in your marriage, would you work less and try to be present at home more?"

He looked me in the eyes and smiled sadly. "Yeah, I probably would."

I couldn't believe it was already seven o'clock. Between seeing my first patients, a meeting with HR to go over the corporate org chart, and writing my session summaries, the day had flown by. I flicked off my laptop and took out my phone to text my sister to see if she wanted anything on my way home.

Before she could respond, Merrick appeared at my door. His evening visits were becoming common, but since he worked on another floor, I had to wonder if he stopped down just to see me. He had his usual worn leather brief-case flung over his shoulder, and the bag was bulging again.

"So? You survived meeting with your first employees today." He looked me up and down. "I don't see any bumps or bruises."

I pulled my purse from a drawer and plopped it down on my desk. "I think I made it out unscathed."

"How'd it go?"

"Pretty well, actually. Only one person canceled, or rather, she rescheduled."

"She? I take it that means Colette?"

I nodded. "She had to leave early because her son was sick at school."

"But the others didn't give you a hard time?"

"No, they were really friendly. We talked a lot."

"So I can go tell my board we're cured? We won't be getting hit with any more lawsuits?"

I laughed. "Not quite. But speaking of lawsuits, I called the attorney you recommended, and I'm meeting with him tomorrow night."

"Good. Hope it works out. Barnett is a good guy, but he's also a bulldog of a lawyer."

"Any chance you have a real-estate-agent referral, too?"

Merrick nodded. "I do. Nick Zimmerman. He'll probably disagree with you when you tell him where you want to live, but he's a great agent. I can send an email making an introduction, if you want?"

"That would be great. Thanks a lot. And as long as you're so amenable, could we also meet tomorrow morning for a few minutes?"

"Can't. I'm flying out first thing."

"Oh. How long are you gone?"

"Five days. Is it important?"

"No, not really. I'm just trying to get a handle on the culture, and I can't discuss my thoughts or opinions with staff or employees. I have to remain neutral and encourage them to talk. Joan from HR has been great, but she doesn't have experience living in the action like you do."

Merrick looked at his watch. "You want to do it now?"

I held up my hands. "No. I'm supposed to be helping people reduce stress. I don't want to get in the way of what little free time you have."

"It's fine." He nodded toward the hallway. "Let me run upstairs and drop off my bag and get changed. Did you eat yet?"

"No, I didn't."

"Pub food okay?"

I nodded. "Sounds perfect."

"There's a good place a few buildings over. You can grill me again while we eat."

"That would be great. Thank you." I smiled. "Look at us making nice all on our own. I didn't even have to threaten to tell your grandmother."

Merrick shook his head. "I'll meet you by the elevator in about ten minutes, wiseass."

"Okay."

Fifteen minutes later, we were already seated at a table. The waitress came by with menus and asked if we wanted to order a drink. I could've really gone for a glass of wine, but Merrick opted for water, so I followed his lead.

"So have my managers confirmed I'm the ogre you think I am?"

I shook my head. "No. Obviously anything said in session is privileged, so I can't share specifics. But I will say that all of your people respect you very much."

"Ah... So they think you're a mole and are telling you what I want to hear."

I laughed. "I don't think that's it."

Merrick leaned back, resting his arms casually across the top of the booth. "People are talking to you, though? Not giving you a hard time?"

"The ones today did. I mean, therapy tends to start slow, so I don't push or delve into personal things right away. We just get to know each other a bit."

"Will liked you."

"Oh?"

"We eat lunch together a few times a week. He mentioned you were easy to talk to."

"That's good to hear. I liked him a lot. He has a quick wit and dry sense of humor."

"You can say that again. Will likes to bet on random things. Last year he came in on New Year's Day when no one else was here. He collected all the personal photos from every employee's desk, scanned them into Photoshop, and superimposed his own face on every kid, spouse, and dog. He egged me into betting who would notice last."

"Oh my God," I cracked up. "Who was it?"

Merrick shrugged. "I'll let you know when we finally have a winner. Two people still haven't noticed. It's been almost seven months."

"That's hysterical."

The waitress stopped by and asked if we were ready to order, but we hadn't even looked at the menu yet. Merrick told her to come back in a few minutes.

"Do you have a favorite thing here?" I asked, looking down at the menu.

"I usually get the pub burger or the turkey club."

"Mmm... Both sound good." I set my menu on the table. "Want to order one of each and share?"

Merrick smiled. "Sure." He drank some of his water. "So how do you like the job so far?"

"It's definitely better than I thought it was going to be."

"You thought it was going to be bad?"

"I thought it might be hell. The guy hiring me told me he was only offering me the job because I was incompetent, some of his staff recently got into a brawl, and they don't want to see a therapist. Not exactly a rosy picture."

Merrick tilted his head. "Yet you took the job."

"I thought I might be able to make a difference."

"It must be nice to have a job where you get that satisfaction."

"Are you saying you don't find your job satisfying?"

"It's a different kind of satisfaction. I love the adrenaline of my job. I love to discover a needle-in-the-haystack small company that's going to do big things, get in on the ground floor, and watch them take off. Having financial independence is definitely satisfying, but making more money for a bunch of already rich people doesn't leave you feeling like you've made a difference in someone's life."

"What made you go into your line of work?"

"If I'm being honest, I went into it for the money, and I love the rush of the game. What about you? What made you become a therapist?"

"I went to one when I was little, and he helped me a lot. After my mom finally left my dad for good, she put me into therapy."

"I'm sorry. I didn't mean to pry."

"It's okay. I'm not ashamed of it—not anymore anyway. I was when I was little because I thought people only went to doctors when something was wrong with them. But as I got older, I realized getting help doesn't make you weak, it makes you strong. That's actually part of the mindset that needs to change about counseling. There's a stigma about people who need treatment for their mental health, and that stops a lot of people from seeking help. We don't look at people differently because they go to the dentist or cardiologist, but we do if they see a psychiatrist or therapist—as if only certain parts of the body should be treated."

"True. But I also wouldn't have asked you to talk about your cardiologist appointment. I was apologizing for getting too personal, not because you went to a psychiatrist."

"Oh." I smiled. "Maybe I jumped up on my soap box unnecessarily there."

The waitress came back and took our order. When she left, our conversation flowed back to the office, and I had Merrick explain the authority of each of the floor traders and all of the different levels of approval that were in place. I also had him walk me through who had the ability to hire and fire who, and what recent promotions had been made. I was trying to collect all the different stress triggers, so eventually I could help determine how to manage them.

"Anything else you want to know?"

"Actually, I do have another question. It's more personal than the organizational structure, though."

"Okay..."

"How many weeks of vacation did you take last year?"

"I'm not sure. Why?"

"One of the things I asked the first few people I met with today was where they went on vacation last year. I wanted to make friendly conversation and get people talking openly. I was surprised to learn that none of them went anywhere, except a weekend trip or two. Your team is highly compensated, and people who make seven figures or more tend to spend money on lavish vacations and summer homes."

Merrick nodded. "In order to really take a vacation, you need to disconnect from the office. That means you have to trust someone else to manage your portfolio while you're gone, which isn't easy to do. Or you have to work while on vacation, and that doesn't go over well when you're supposed to be on a family trip."

"But then they never get a break from stress, and we know chronic stress causes memory impairment. If you don't disconnect, you become less productive at work over time. I took the liberty of asking Joan in HR for a list of vacation days taken over the last year versus how many days they were entitled to. What would you guess is the average percent of allocated days off people are taking?"

Merrick shrugged. "I don't know. Fifty...maybe sixty percent?"

"Nineteen."

"Shit. I didn't know it was that bad."

"The average person gets five weeks of vacation and takes less than one."

"What am I supposed to do? I can't force them to take a trip."

"No, you can't. But you can force them to take their time off. You can institute a policy that all employees must utilize the majority of their time off. You could even cut their access to the company's systems during that time."

"I don't know about cutting access. I think most of them would go ape shit if I did that. But maybe making vacation time mandatory could work."

"I think that would be a great place to start. Though, like with most things, you should set the example. You can't expect your staff to think it's okay to disconnect for a week or two at a time if the boss isn't doing it."

Merrick nodded. "Point taken."

"Can I ask you something else personal?"

He shook his head. "No, I'd rather you didn't."

"Oh...okay."

"I'm just screwing with you. I wanted to see how you'd react."

I narrowed my eyes. "Sort of like when you pretended not to know I was the woman from the fitting room for your own amusement?"

He smiled. "What's your question?"

"Are you dating anyone?"

"Are you asking because you're interested in filling that role if I say no?"

I felt heat in my cheeks. "Oh no... I wasn't trying to insinuate..."

"Relax, I'm teasing. "You're actually turning pink, Dr. Vaughn."

I hated that my face always gave me away. Touching my warm cheek, I shook my head. "Well, it's a little embarrassing if your boss thinks you're hitting on him your second week on the job." Merrick looked completely amused. "You really enjoy watching me squirm, don't you?"

He seemed to take a moment to think about it before he answered. "Oddly, I do."

"Is this a thing you do with all your employees?"

Merrick shook his head slowly. "Just you."

"Why?"

He shrugged. "I have no damn idea. But to answer your question, not seriously, no."

"Oh my God, I don't even remember the question now."

He grinned. "You asked if I was dating anyone."

"That's right." I shook my head. "My question was related to the lack of vacation time being taken. You had said it was difficult to disconnect. But I feel like it shouldn't be when you have someone who really captures your interest. I think we all need something that can distract us from our work."

Merrick's eyes flickered to my lips, causing a flutter low in my belly. He lifted his water to his mouth. "I'll keep that in mind."

Luckily our food arrived just then. I swapped out half my sandwich for half of his and quickly picked up the burger, feeling the need to *distract* myself from the way my boss made me feel. "You know, if you decide to take some time off, I know a great glamping Airbnb."

He winked. "I think I'm more of a treehouse kind of guy."

"Seriously, though, I know you're exempt from the mandatory therapy, but we can all use some time off to decompress. How do you destress if you don't even take time off?"

"There are plenty of ways to work the stress out that don't require weeks off. Though I'm not sure HR would want me to tell you my personal favorites."

"Ah. I guess I forget about those methods since it's been so long."

A little while later, we walked out of the restaurant together. I had to go left to the subway, but Merrick would be going right, back to the building where he both lived and worked.

"Thank you again for taking the time to answer all my questions—and for dinner," I told him.

"No problem."

"Well, have a safe trip." I nodded toward my train. "I go that way."

"No, you don't." Merrick lifted his chin. "You go that way."

I wrinkled my nose but followed his line of sight. The dark Town Car he'd dropped me off in the other night was waiting at the curb. The driver stepped out and opened the back door.

"It's after eight. My employees take a car service home if they work this late."

"That's very generous of you, but I'm fine on the subway."

"I'm sure you are. Take the car anyway."

I squinted. "Back to being bossy, I see."

"Back to being a pain in my ass, I see." He tried to keep his face stern, but he couldn't hide the amusement in his eyes. "Goodnight, Ms. Vaughn."

"*Doctor* Vaughn."

His lip twitched, but he said nothing more. So I walked to the car. Before I climbed in, I looked back to say goodbye and caught Merrick's eyes glued to my ass. I expected a sheepish look, or feigned embarrassment, at least—like I'd felt when I'd gotten caught checking him out the other day.

But there was not a morsel of either to be found.

CHAPTER 11

Merrick

"She's smoking hot," Will said, though I hadn't really heard him. My mind was somewhere else, as it often had been the last couple of weeks.

"What?"

He lifted his chin toward the hallway where Evie stood a few feet from my door, talking to Joan from HR. "The doc. She's hot. I usually go for the ones who have it all on display. You know my type—dyed blondes, a mountain of cleavage, lots of makeup, the ones who know they have it and aren't afraid to flaunt it. But the doc? She's got that sexy-librarian thing going. I'd make her leave those thick glasses and pumps on when I ripped her clothes off."

"Don't be a dick. She works here, for Christ's sake."

"Seriously? You were just staring at her. I lose you mid-conversation every time she walks by. You know what it reminds me of? When my little brother was two or three, we got a dog—a husky with two different-color eyes. Thing was beautiful. But anyway, Jared was potty training at the time, and he was obsessed with the dog. Whenever he'd stand at the toilet, I'd hear *tinkle tinkle tinkle*. Then the dog would pass by, and the sound of the urine hitting the water would stop until the dog cleared the doorway. Then it would start up again—*tinkle tinkle tinkle*. Every damn time. He'd piss all over the floor because he was so distracted."

Will picked up one of his French fries and waved it at the hall. "She's your husky. Guess I should be glad we can't see her from the men's room, or I'd have piss on my shoes from standing next to you at the urinal."

My face wrinkled. "What the fuck is wrong with you?"

"All I did was say what you were thinking."

"You don't know what you're talking about."

"Oh yeah? So you wouldn't mind if I asked Evie out?"

The muscle in my jaw spasmed. "I wouldn't mind. But we do have a corporate policy against it."

Will grinned. "Oh yeah? Hang on a second." Joan and Evie had finished their conversation and started to walk away. Will cupped both sides of his mouth and yelled. "Hey, Joan!"

The head of HR looked into my office, and Will waved her inside.

She cracked the door open. "Do you need something?"

Will nodded. "Can you refresh my memory, please? What's our policy on interoffice dating?"

"It's against the rules to date a subordinate."

"And why do we have that rule again?"

"To avoid putting an employee in an uncomfortable place. Someone might feel obligated to say yes for fear of consequences if they don't. And on the flip side, when an employee dates their boss, how does it look when that employee is promoted?"

"So it's not a companywide rule then, right? If someone works in a different department, two employees can get together?"

Joan shrugged. "I don't see why not. John Upton's wife, Allison, used to work in accounting. He's a trader, and she did accounts payable, so there wasn't any conflict of interest. A lot of couples meet at work, actually."

Will leaned back in his chair, locking his hands together behind his head in a smug posture. "Thank you, Joan."

"Sure. Anything else?"

He shook his head. "Nope. You've been very helpful."

Will's gloating smile widened as she closed the door. "So, as I was saying... You don't mind if I ask her out? We have that charity fundraiser this Friday night, and I haven't asked anyone yet."

"Whatever," I grumbled. "Just stop talking and finish eating. I have shit to do."

The following Friday afternoon, I'd forgotten all about Will trying to rattle me. I'd convinced myself he was screwing around about asking Evie out—that is, until she knocked on my office door.

"Hey. Do you have a minute?" she asked.

"Sure. Market just closed."

She smiled. "I know. I was waiting."

"What's up?"

"So I met with a bunch more employees this week. And two things that seem to be a common theme are a lack of trust and inaccessibility to senior management."

"What do you mean?"

"Some of the employees don't feel like their supervisor trusts them. For example, they'll make a trade, and then a few minutes later their manager will walk over and question their decision. It leaves them feeling like their judgment isn't respected."

"It's the manager's job to watch transactions and raise potential issues."

"But when you question someone about something they've already done, it automatically begins the conversation with a negative tone."

"So what do you propose? There's no point in managers if they aren't watching over things."

"Could they flip the table and do that while setting a positive tone? Perhaps managers and employees could meet at the start of the day to talk about things they're considering. Then when the manager sees a questionable transaction come through, they'll already understand why it's happening, and they won't have to second-guess the employee's decision. The end result is the same, but instead of feeling monitored in the background, the employee might feel heard in the forefront."

"Let me guess. The complaints all happen to surround one manager: Lark Renquist? I told you the old timers don't like reporting to a guy young enough to be their son. They wouldn't have a problem being second-guessed by one of the managers who's been around longer."

"I'm not here to point fingers, nor would I want to reveal specifics that violate people's trust. But I've heard it enough times to think it's something that might be causing unnecessary stress."

"Fine. I'll talk to the managers. Is that it?"

"I also get the sense that people don't feel senior management is accessible."

"Are you talking about me?"

"You and your senior team."

"I'm here every day, and so is my team. My door is glass, for shit's sake. People can see if I'm busy and stop in if I'm not."

"Maybe *accessible* isn't the right word."

"What is?"

"*Approachable*?" She nodded. "I think that's a better way to put it. You might be here in your office, but I don't get the sense that people feel comfortable approaching you and others."

"And that's my fault? I'm not a mind reader to know when someone would like to talk to me so I go over and start a conversation."

"I actually don't think it's your fault. I think you're just naturally intimidating."

I shook my head. "That sounds like a *them* problem, not a me one."

She chuckled. "Would you consider doing monthly town-hall-type meetings? Maybe go out to the bullpen area where most of the staff sits and hold a team discussion? Perhaps give them some updates and take questions? A team-building workshop of some sort held offsite might be a good idea, too."

"You mean where one person falls back, and the other person is supposed to catch them?"

"Something like that."

"You think that's going to stop people from suing me after they can't hack it here and brawling because the tension runs high?"

Evie shrugged. "Humor me. I can work with Joan to set it all up."

I sighed. "Anything else? Should I go find some babies to kiss or save some kittens stuck up a tree?"

Evie stood. "Thanks, boss."

"Yeah, yeah, yeah."

She walked to my door. "I'll see you later?"

I'd been planning on leaving when she walked in, so I stood. "Actually, I'm getting out of here on time tonight. I need to get ready for a charity event."

"Oh, that's what I meant. I'm leaving to get ready now, too. If I don't hurry, Will will be at my house before I am."

I froze. *That motherfucker*. He'd asked her out after all.

I was in the middle of a conversation with Erin Foster, the woman who ran the Home Start program we were raising money for tonight, when Evie and Will walked in. The event had started more than an hour ago, with no sign of either one of them, so I'd started to think Will had put her up to saying she was coming to screw with me—not that it made any sense, but neither did the way I felt whenever I thought of the two of them together.

Evie and Will stood together at the bar, waiting for a drink. I watched from a distance as Will scanned the room. When he found me, a diabolical smirk raised the corners of his lips, and his hand moved to Evie's back. She had on a red dress with a low-cut back, so his fingers touched bare skin. I stared with so much intensity, anyone watching might think I was trying to do some sort of Jedi mind trick on him.

"Merrick?" Erin said. She turned to look over her shoulder, in the direction I was staring. "Is everything okay?"

I blinked a few times and shook my head. "Yeah, sorry. I was just... I apologize. What were you saying?"

"I was telling you about our new initiative. We've been having a lot of success asking our corporate sponsors and partners to add a giving page to their website. We provide all the copy, graphics, and HTML, so it's a pretty simple add for your webmaster. It shows your clients that your company is socially conscious, and it gives us a chance to tell potential donors who we are and what we do. We've had one financial management partner add a giving page, and also put a little button on the home page where their clients signed in. It made for one of our highest capital-contribution months, even though we never reached out directly to anyone. Do you think that's something Crawford Investments might be able to do for us?"

I nodded. "Sure. I'll talk to my IT person and let you know how we can set it up."

Erin silently clapped her hands. "Thank you!"

My eyes wandered back to the bar. Will and Evie were now talking to a banker I'd met a few times. She was facing me, though looking at Tom or Tim or Tucker—whatever the hell his name was. I couldn't tear my eyes away long enough to figure it out. The front of her dress had a V neck that hugged her curves. She was definitely showing more skin than she did around the office, yet she still looked classy and elegant. When she leaned forward to shake the hand of someone who walked over, a hint of her thigh popped out of the high slit in her dress. *Fuck.* She had great legs.

I thought I'd been discreet, but when I peeled my eyes away from Evie and returned my attention to Erin, she was grinning. "She's beautiful. What's her name?"

I attempted to play dumb, raising my drink to my lips. "Who?"

"The woman in the red dress you haven't been able to take your eyes off."

I looked around as if I had to figure out who she was referring to. I may have oversold it. "I'm not sure what you're talking about."

She smiled. "Mmm-hmm." She pointed to Will and Evie. "Well, I guess you're about to figure it out, seeing as she's heading this way."

Sure enough, Will and Evie were halfway across the room, walking straight toward us. Will still had that shit-eating grin stuck on his face.

"What's up, boss?" He bounced heel to toe.

I offered a curt nod to each of them. "Will. Evie."

"I don't think we've met." Erin extended a hand to Evie. "I'm Erin Foster. I run Home Start."

Evie shook her hand. "It's very nice to meet you. Will was just telling me all about your program on the way here. My mom was a victim of DV, and we relied on a lot of temporary housing over the years. Helping survivors find something permanent like you do, where they can plant roots, is so important."

"Absolutely. Making people safe for the short term is understandably the priority of most DV nonprofits. But we focus on what comes after that. Abuse survivors who own their own homes are ninety-three percent more likely not to go back. So, our goal is to make it easier for women to buy homes by providing down-payment assistance and low-interest loans from partner banks."

"That's amazing. I'm not sure what I could do to help, but I'm available."

"Are you a broker?"

Evie shook her head. "No, actually. I'm a therapist."

"Oh my gosh. I need to introduce you to Genie. She runs a group that helps people make the transition to living alone in their new homes. I'm absolutely positive she needs you."

Evie smiled. "Okay."

Erin glanced at Will then me. "I hope you don't mind if I steal her for a few minutes."

We both shrugged, but it was Will who spoke. "Steal away."

Erin looped her arm with Evie's, and the two of them continued chatting as she guided her away. Will and I watched as they walked over to a group of women sitting at a table.

Will leaned toward me. "*Tinkle tinkle tinkle.*"

I looked at him like he had two heads. "What the fuck?"

"Just like my brother and his piss with the dog." Will sipped his drink with a gloating smile.

I rolled my eyes.

"Not that I can blame you," he said. "My date looks insanely hot tonight, doesn't she?"

"Don't be a dick."

"Why am I a dick?"

I ignored him. "Why are you so late?"

His shit-eating grin spread so wide, it looked like his annoying face might crack. "Evie needed a little help getting into her dress."

I scowled at him. Luckily, the emcee came over the speakers and asked everyone to please find their seat. We'd bought a twelve-seat table at the event, so I had no choice but to sit with Will. Four other people from Crawford Investments and their dates or spouses were already seated, so I made the rounds and said hello to everyone before sitting down. The spot between Will and me was empty when Evie walked over a few minutes later. I stood and pulled out her chair since her date was too busy flirting with a woman at the next table to even notice she'd returned.

"Thank you," Evie said as I tucked her in.

The emcee took the stage, and for the next half hour, we listened to speeches about all of the things Home Start had been able to accomplish over the last year. Well, most of us listened. Will was too busy typing into his phone. I was reasonably certain, based on the glances being exchanged, that he was texting with the woman at the table next to us. Luckily, his date didn't seem to notice. When the speeches finally concluded, they opened up the dance floor and said dinner would be served shortly.

Will wasted no time pulling back from the table and standing. "I'm going to dance."

My jaw flexed, assuming he meant with the woman he'd brought tonight. But instead, he walked over to the table next to us and took the hand of the woman he'd been flirting with.

I frowned, but Evie at least pretended to be a good sport. She smiled as we watched Will make a spectacle of himself, twirling the woman around on the floor. When a second song started and Will pulled his partner close, it felt awkward, so I tried to distract Evie.

"I should have warned you about Erin. If you so much as look in her direction, the next thing you know she has you opening your wallet or working for her."

"Oh, no. I'm happy to volunteer. Home Smart is an incredible organization. I really need something like that in my life." Evie smiled. "Thank you for inviting me."

I thought it was strange that she thanked me since I hadn't been the one to invite her. But she probably assumed the company paid for all of the seats, which it had. "My grandmother is the one who told me about the program," I said. "Some of the people she's worked with got housing through Home Start."

"Ah. I should've known Kitty was involved somehow." She smiled. "I'm sorry I made us late. Will feels horrible about ripping my dress."

"He...ripped your dress?"

"Oh, I thought you knew. He said he was going to text you to let you know we were going to be late. I was all dressed and ready, but I needed to use the bathroom before we left. My zipper was stuck, so I asked Will to see if he could get it. He did, but he tore the zipper right from the seam. I only had this dress with me at my sister's, since the majority of my clothes are still in a storage unit. So I had to wait for her to come home and sew it for me. I don't have a clue how to sew, especially not the fabric of a dress. Then when she finally got me fixed up, and we were about to leave, one of my contacts popped out." She shook her head. "So it worked out well that you asked Will to pick me up. Otherwise, I would've made you late, too."

"*I* asked Will to pick you up?"

Hearing the question within my question, Evie paused to study me. Her brows drew together. "He said you had to come early, so we'd meet you here."

I was missing something. First she'd said I invited her, and now she thought I'd arranged to have Will pick her up. Something was off, but I'd been hanging out with Will for too long to not know that the best way to handle it was to go along with things.

So I nodded. "Right. Some of the sponsors come early to work the door, greeting people with the staff of Home Start."

When the second song ended, Evie excused herself to go to the ladies' room. Will walked back over to the table a minute later. He sat in Evie's chair next to me, rather than his own, and leaned down to speak quietly next to my ear. "I'm going to duck out early."

"What the hell are you talking about?"

He motioned over his shoulder to the woman he'd been dancing with. She was already standing with her purse in her hand. "Carly suggested we go in the other room, so we don't have to talk over the music. I suggested we go to my apartment instead. She's in, so I'm out."

"What about your date?"

"What date?"

"You came with Evie, didn't you?"

Will smiled. "Bros before hoes for life, man. Do you really think I would date the woman you're hot for?"

"What the hell are you talking about? She just told me you picked her up, and I saw you walk in together."

"I told Evie *you* invited her." He shrugged. "That all the executives attended, and you asked me to share a car and introduce her around since you had to come early."

"Why would you do that?"

"Because you're a damn idiot and weren't going to ask her yourself."

"Did you ever think that's because I didn't *want* to ask her?"

"Not for a second. You like her, and we both know it. You just think it's a bad idea because she works for your company."

"Maybe that's because it *is* a bad idea."

"Some of the best times in life start off as bad ideas, my friend."

Will slapped his knee before standing. "Speak of the devil." He held out a hand to Evie, whom I hadn't seen coming. "I'm going to ditch this place. Merrick will give you a ride home."

"Oh, okay. Though it's fine. I can call an Uber later."

Will smirked in my direction. "I'm sure the boss will insist. You two have fun."

Evie looked confused by the sudden turn of events, yet not bothered by Will's departure in the least. She laughed. "You, too, Will. And thanks for breaking my dress."

He winked at her before taking off. "Anytime, gorgeous."

CHAPTER 12

Evie

I didn't even realize I'd been staring until a slow, sexy smile spread across Merrick's face.

He was halfway across the room, talking to two men. In my defense, he was almost directly in my line of sight, so how could I not look at him? It had nothing to do with how good he looked in his black tuxedo, or the way he slipped one hand into his trouser pocket, his thumb staying casually hooked on the outside. And it definitely had nothing to do with how broad his shoulders looked in the suit, or the way his shirt tapered down to a narrow waist. Nope. He was just standing right where I happened to be looking. At least he had been, anyway, because now he was walking right toward me.

He put a hand on the back of Will's empty chair. "You haven't danced all evening."

"I didn't see you out there either."

He held out a hand. "Fix both of those right now?"

I hesitated but then realized I was being ridiculous. Colleagues had been dancing together all night. This was a work function, not a date. So I put my hand in his and smiled. "Sure."

Merrick led me to the dance floor and pulled me close. Suddenly I realized he was the first man I'd danced with since the night of my wedding fiasco. I'd had to dance with Christian at the reception when we'd been announced—ten minutes before all hell broke loose.

Merrick must've noticed my face. He loosened his grip and pulled back. "We don't have to dance."

"No, no." I shook my head. "I want to dance. My head was just somewhere else."

He looked into my eyes. "You sure?"

I nodded. "Positive."

I didn't get the feeling he believed me, but he nodded, nonetheless, and we went back to dancing. After a minute of awkward silence, I sighed.

"The last time I danced was at my wedding." I smiled sadly. "I love to dance. It just brought back a memory. That's all."

A look of understanding came across Merrick's face, and he nodded. He opened his mouth to say something but then shut it and looked away.

"What?" I asked.

"Nothing."

I assumed he was going to make a comment about my wedding, so I prodded. "No, you were going to say something and stopped yourself. I want to know what it was."

Merrick frowned. "I was going to say you look beautiful tonight."

Definitely not what I'd expected. "So why did you stop yourself?"

"I didn't want to be inappropriate."

"Need I again remind you that you told me you only wanted to hire me because I wasn't qualified?"

"You're never going to let me forget that, are you?"

"I doubt it." I smiled. "But thank you for the compliment. You don't look so bad yourself."

Merrick's eyes twinkled "Is that why I caught you staring at me a few times?"

"Oh my God." I laughed. "Full of yourself much? You were standing right in front of me."

"Uh-huh."

"And to think I was going to compliment you on your cologne, too. But you'd probably think I want to marry you."

Merrick twirled me around the dance floor. "Nah. It means you want to make out with me, not marriage just yet."

We both laughed.

His teasing was exactly what I needed to forget all about the last time I danced. "By the way, thank you for introducing me to Nick, your real estate agent. I'm going to check out some apartments with him soon. He's hysterical, and you were right. I told him the areas I thought I might want to live, and he ruled out all but two."

Merrick nodded. "He's not shy about sharing his opinions, but he also won't waste your time showing you crap you don't want. Though he may also try to strong-arm you away from things *he* thinks aren't important, so you have to stand your ground. He was adamant that I shouldn't live in the building I work in, but it works for me."

I nodded. "Yeah, I pushed back about a pet-friendly building. I'd told him I wanted an apartment that allowed pets because I'd like to get a dog someday, and he sent me back an article titled 'Ninety-nine Reasons You Shouldn't Own a Pet in New York City'. I told him it was a deal breaker."

Merrick smiled. "I told him I already had a pet when I was looking for my place. He sent me a list of no-kill shelters that took pets for people who had to move to buildings that didn't allow them."

"Fish count as a pet?" The minute the words left my mouth, I realized I'd just stuck my foot in it. Merrick tilted his head and looked down at me.

I shut my eyes. "Could we...just pretend I didn't ask that?"

"Not a chance."

At least there was amusement in his voice and not anger. I opened one eye to see if his face matched his tone, and he arched a brow. The smirk he wore now was a lot more readable than usual—this one said he was a cat who'd just caught a mouse and was about to toy with it before deciding whether to let it go or bite its head off.

I shook my head and sighed. "I can't even come up with an excuse I'd believe, and I have a feeling I'm a lot more gullible than you. So I'm just going to admit I snooped in your apartment and take my lumps."

Merrick's smirk grew to a full-blown grin. "You went in my bedroom."

I felt my face heat. "I'm sorry. I didn't actually go in—I swear. I just... I don't know. The whole thing lasted thirty seconds or less. Your apartment is gorgeous, and I couldn't help myself."

Merrick wasn't letting me off the hotseat. He just kept looking at me, not saying a word, which caused me to ramble to fill the dead air. "What size bed is that anyway? It has to be bigger than a king. I was thinking California King, but it seems even bigger. You could have a party on that thing." I closed my eyes again. "Please tell me I did not just insinuate that my boss has multiple people in his bed at once."

"I believe you did."

I shook my head. "I'm going to shut up for the rest of this song. Speaking of which, when the hell is it going to end so I can go crawl in a hole somewhere?"

Merrick smiled and pulled me closer. "It's fine. As long as you didn't look in the nightstand."

My nose wrinkled. "What's in the nightstand?"

He laughed, and I play-smacked his chest. "You're just screwing with me, aren't you?"

"Yes, but you really want to check out that nightstand now, don't you?"

I grinned. "I totally do. Though I'll tell you what... I will never again bring up that you only hired me because I was the least-competent person, if you can forget the conversation we've had these last few minutes."

"Don't we already have a deal where I can't bring up the incident in the dressing room and you can't bring up a certain Wendy's founder?"

"We do. This is a second deal."

Merrick pulled me close again. "Whatever makes you happy."

A few seconds later, the song ended and the emcee announced it was time for dessert. Even though I'd just embarrassed myself and wanted to hide, I also felt a pang of disappointment when Merrick let me go.

Back at the table, we both got pulled into conversations with different people, and a little while later, when others started to say their goodbyes, Merrick leaned over to me.

"I'm ready to get out of here when you are," he said.

"Oh, it's okay. I'm all the way uptown, and you're all the way downtown. I can call an Uber."

"It's not a problem. I'll drop you."

I decided not to argue.

Outside, Merrick's usual black Town Car pulled up. He waved off the driver who had started to get out and opened the back door for me himself. I'd arrived in a stretch limo with Will, yet the big boss was in a regular-size sedan.

"Your employee's car on the way here was flashier," I teased, scooting over to make room for Merrick.

He pulled the door closed after getting in. "Is that a surprise, based on what you know about Will?"

"I guess not."

"I think the cars most people choose match their personality. Will is definitely a stretch limo. Probably one with a sunroof and hot tub, too."

I laughed. "Well, he does like attention, and he has a big personality." A funny thought hit me. "Oh my God, your grandmother's car—Kitty drives that souped-up red Dodge Charger convertible. I've always thought it was an odd car for an older woman, but now that I think about it, you're right. It matches her personality to a T."

"When she bought it, it didn't come standard as a convertible. She had a body shop make it into one just for her. Before that, she drove a Ford Mustang. Always had a car with some muscle, and in a bright color." Merrick shrugged. "Suits her."

"Oh crap." I covered my mouth with a laugh. "The car I had before I sold it to move to New York was a Prius."

Merrick smiled. "Economical and practical. Fits the woman who barters things, I'd say. Wouldn't you?"

"I guess... But a Prius is so ugly and unsexy."

Merrick's eyes flickered to my legs before lifting to linger on my mouth for a heartbeat too long. He swallowed. "It suits the personality. Not the appearance."

I felt my skin blush and was thankful for the darkness. "Do you own a car, other than this Town Car you always seem to be driven in?"

"I do."

"What kind?" I shook my head. "No, wait—let me guess."

"This should be interesting..."

I tapped my finger to my lips. "Hmmm... Let's see... I feel like it would be something expensive, but not flashy like a Ferrari or a Lamborghini. That's more Will's style."

"First big bonus he earned, he bought a cherry red Ferrari."

I laughed. "Of course he did. But that's not you. I suppose a car like this would suit you—a simple Mercedes or a BMW or something in a luxury class. But I don't feel like that's it for some reason. Am I wrong?"

He shook his head. "You're warm..."

I smiled. "I prefer to be called hot, but I'll take it. Anyway, I think your car wouldn't be just for driving around town. You use this Town Car for that. So whatever you drive probably has some meaning." I paused. "Oh, I know! It's a classic car."

"Keep going..."

I rubbed my hands together. "I don't know that much about cars, so I'm not sure I can tell you the make and model. But I can see you in one of those cars in old movies, the ones people take out for a Sunday drive in California. You know, the woman wears big sunglasses and a pretty scarf around her neck and looks like a celebrity. Maybe it's a convertible. Probably a dark color with a saddle brown leather interior."

Merrick shifted to one side and dug his cell from his pocket. He punched some keys and turned the phone to me. "Something like this?"

I pointed to his cell. "Exactly like that. What kind of a car is that?"

"A 1957 Jaguar convertible."

"Okay. That's what kind of car I can see you in."

He shook his head. "That's an actual picture of my car. I keep it in a garage not too far from the office."

My eyes widened. "*No way.*"

He went to his photo app and swiped through a bunch of pictures before turning his cell to me again. The picture was black and white, but it looked like the same type of car. Two men stood proudly in front of it with their arms folded.

"That's my grandfather and his buddy."

I took the phone from his hand. "Is that Kitty's Redmond?"

"It is. I guess she's mentioned him?"

"Only in every other sentence."

"My grandfather bought the car for my grandmother as a wedding gift. It was used and a little beat up, but she loved it. He passed away pretty young, and she didn't have a garage. Back then they used actual steel in cars, so it got rusted over the years. A guy knocked on her door one day thirty years ago and offered her more than it was worth, so she sold it. Coincidentally, that was where she got the money she put down on the first women's shelter she opened. She claims a few weeks earlier, she'd decided that was what she wanted to do with the next chapter of her life, so she wrote about her plans in a journal—even though she had no idea how she could afford it." Merrick shook his head. "The woman is as no-bullshit as they come, but she believes she 'manifested' that guy knocking on her door to make it happen."

I smiled. "I've heard the *manifest your destiny* speech a time or two from Kitty myself."

Merrick chuckled. "I'm sure you have. Anyway, I only knew about the car because of the picture I just showed you and my grandmother talking about it. I never actually saw it."

He stared at the photo a moment. "Ten years ago, when I got my first big bonus payout, I went to a car swap. I wasn't really looking for anything, but I figured I'd see if something caught my eye. There was a 1957 Jaguar convertible on display, and the thing was sparkling. It looked brand new. I tried to buy it, but it was already sold. The seller was a nice guy, though, and we got to talking. He mentioned he had a friend who had the same car, though it wasn't in nearly as good of shape, so I'd need to have it restored myself. A couple of weeks later, I went to go see it." He shook his head. "The thing didn't need a little work; it was a disaster. I was about to say I wasn't interested when the guy mentioned he'd gotten it from a woman in Atlanta almost two decades ago."

My eyes widened. "*No!*"

Merrick nodded. "Turned out to be the same exact car. It was just too big of a coincidence to walk away from, so I bought it. Fixing it up probably cost more than buying a completely restored one, but I love that damn car. I tried to give it to my grandmother as a gift for her seventy-fifth birthday a few years back, but she insisted my grandfather would rather have me keep it. Then she told me her DV house could use some new siding if I wanted to be a big spender."

I laughed. That sounded like Kitty. "Wow. That's a really cool story. I'd say that car was definitely meant to be yours."

He nodded. "What made you decide that car matched my personality?"

"I don't know. I guess it's kind of a rich guy's snobby car, but it's understated and quiet at the same time."

"Snobby, huh?"

I smiled. "How do you think I feel? I'm a damn Prius."

We both laughed, and a few minutes later, we pulled up to my sister's building.

Merrick told the driver to wait and walked me inside to the elevator bank.

I pushed the button. "Thank you again for inviting me," I said. "I haven't gotten dressed up and gone out in a long time."

He looked down at his feet in an oddly shy gesture. "Well, you clean up good, so you should."

"Thank you. I'd say the same to you, but honestly, you look good all the time."

Merrick's brows shot up.

I rolled my eyes. "Don't let it go to your head. You know you're handsome."

"You pretty much just say whatever is on your mind, don't you?"

I shrugged and pulled out my keys. "I guess so. As long as I'm not going to hurt someone. Don't you?"

Merrick's eyes flickered to my lips before returning to meet my gaze again, causing my stomach to do a little dip. *Oh my.*

"I guess I filter some things to make sure they're appropriate," he said.

I tilted my head coyly. "That's a shame. Sometimes the inappropriate things are the most interesting."

On that note, the elevator doors slid open. I stepped inside and turned to face Merrick.

I tried to hide how flustered I felt. "I'll see you Monday?"

"Actually, you won't. I'm traveling all week again."

"Oh."

Merrick winked. "I'm disappointed I won't see you, too."

VI KEELAND

"I didn't say I was disappointed."

"Didn't have to. Your face did."

I rolled my eyes as if he was crazy. Thankfully, the doors started to slide closed a few seconds later. I wiggled my fingers. "'Night, boss. Sweet dreams."

"Oh, they will be, Dr. Vaughn."

The next morning, I baked up a storm. My sister padded out from the bedroom, squinting at the sun streaming in through the kitchen window like it was her archenemy.

"Why do you always open the blinds so much?"

"Umm... To let in some sunshine? You should've been a vampire. It's almost ten o'clock."

Greer walked over and pulled the blinds closed before leaning across the other side of the kitchen counter. She reached for the plate of unfrosted cupcakes that were cooling, but I swatted her away. "Those are for Mr. Duncan."

"Who the hell is Mr. Duncan, and is he letting you crash at his place rent free?"

"Fine. Have one. But that's it. Mr. Duncan lives in 4B. He's got that cute little four-year-old daughter who always wears a backward baseball cap and braids."

My sister's face scrunched up. "Do I live in the same building as you?"

I laughed. "Don't you know anyone?"

"This is New York. We don't make friends with our neighbors. We put our AirPods in and avoid eye contact at all costs when we pass other humans in the hallway."

"Well, not me. I met him on the elevator a few times. He's a single dad. He owns the cell phone repair shop a few doors down. Anyway, tomorrow is his daughter's birthday. She wants to bring cupcakes to nursery school. He said he was a horrible baker, so I traded him two dozen for a screen repair."

"You broke your phone, too?"

"No, I use a case, so that doesn't happen. *Unlike you.* The repair is for you, silly. He said it will take about ten minutes. Just pop in and tell him you're my sister."

"Oh, awesome. Thank you." She sighed and slouched. "I wish I had your energy. I started a new batch of hormones to get ready for the next round of IVF, and they're sucking the life out of me."

I frowned. "Sorry."

Greer waved me off. "Not your fault. Hey—what do you call men with a low sperm count?"

"I don't know, what?"

"In*cum* Inequality."

I laughed. "I hope you didn't share that with your sweet husband."

She shoved the rest of the cupcake in her mouth. "Of course I did. And since we're on the subject of sperm, how was your date last night? That Will was hot, too. Is every guy gorgeous where you work?"

"I told you, it wasn't a date."

"He picked you up and broke your zipper. What do I call it, a hookup?"

I shook my head. "It wasn't like that at all. The zipper was stuck, and I asked him to try to wiggle it down, but it tore away from the dress. We just went to a work function together. I'm new, so the boss asked him to ride with me so he could introduce me around when we arrived. He disappeared an hour after we got there with some woman who'd been making googly eyes at him since the minute we walked in. Plus, he's not my type."

"Oh..." She nodded. "So he's faithful and not a douche?"

"Let's not remind me about Christian. I actually haven't given him much thought lately."

"Well, that's good. Maybe it's time you move on, then. You know, put yourself out there."

My mind instantly went to Merrick last night. I'd found his eyes focused on my lips more than once. "Let me ask you something. When a guy's eyes linger on your lips, does it always mean he's thinking about kissing you?"

"Definitely not."

I frowned. "Oh."

"Did you have lipstick on?"

"Yeah."

"Might some have been on your teeth?"

"No, I don't think so. I looked in the mirror after I applied it."

She pointed to her teeth. "Did you eat spinach?"

I shook my head.

"Is he deaf?"

I chuckled. "No."

Greer shrugged. "Then yeah, he was thinking about using your lips for dick pillows."

I laughed. "And here I thought maybe it meant he wanted to kiss me."

"Nah. Women think about kissing. Men think about blowjobs."

I sighed.

Greer walked to the refrigerator and pulled out the orange juice. "Who was fantasizing about your mouth?"

"I don't know if he was fantasizing about anything, but I caught Merrick's eyes lingering a few times."

"As in your jerk, hot boss, Merrick? The one I met for two minutes and noticed looking at you in that sort of way that's more than a look?"

I nodded.

"Oh boy. I know I teased you about how hot he is, but do you think it's a good idea to go there?"

I shook my head. "Definitely not. He's my boss. Been there, done that, burned the T-shirt. But I am undeniably attracted to him. He's softened a lot since we first met. I don't know what it is—aside from the obvious, he's very handsome—but I'm drawn to him. He's kind of hard and stern on the outside, but then every once in a while, you get a glimpse of a soft inside. Being around him kind of awakens something in me. It's made me realize just how dead my relationship with Christian was, long before he buried us."

"What's bossman's deal? Does he have a girlfriend?"

"Not that I'm aware of—he's said he isn't dating anyone seriously. Though he's pretty private about his personal life. I know he was engaged to a woman he started his firm with. She apparently died, but Will once mentioned that she'd annihilated him—whatever that means. I'm not sure what happened there."

"Well, I want you to get back out there and enjoy yourself. You deserve to be happy. But maybe you should tread lightly with that one. The only thing more wrought with issues than dating your boss is dating a guy who's carrying a ghost around with him."

CHAPTER 13

Merrick

NINE YEARS AGO

"**H**ey, wait up!" I jogged to catch up to Amelia. I'd been looking for her all over campus for a week.

Her stride never broke as I fell in step. "You?" she said. "Are you back to invite me for another card game or just to watch my ass as I walk?"

I shrugged. "Both?"

She snickered. "Now why would you want to play cards with me when you know I'll kick your ass and take all your money again?"

"Will you go out with me instead?"

She shook her head.

"Welp, then cards it is for now."

"For now, huh?" She rolled her eyes, but there was an unmistakable twinkle in them. "When's the game?"

"Tonight. Seven o'clock."

"Where?"

"My apartment."

She stopped short. "If I show up at your apartment and you're the only one there and there isn't really a card

133

game..." She shook her head. "I carry a Taser in my purse. I'll have it ready."

"There'll be a card game."

"Fine." She started walking again. "Where do you live?"

I rattled off my address. When I was done, she again stopped, this time holding up her hand. "This is where my next class is. You stay here and enjoy the view."

My forehead wrinkled. But I quickly figured out what she meant as I watched her ass sway from side to side climbing the stairs to the Lincoln Building. I waited until she disappeared inside to take out my cell and text my buddies:

Emergency card game tonight. Who's in?

"I can't believe you're making me do this." I peeled two twenties and a ten off the wad of cash I'd taken out of my pocket and slapped them into Travis's hand.

He shrugged. "I don't have the money to lose again so soon. If you need me to play cards so badly, it's your dime." He shook his head. "I can't believe this girl's got you handing out cash."

"She won't go out with me. The only way to see her was to invite her to play cards again."

"Did you ever think the reason she won't go out with you is because she emasculated you playing cards? Maybe doing it a second time is just going to turn her off more."

"Then I guess I'll have to kick her ass and show her who's boss."

Amelia's voice came from behind me. "Umm...whose ass are you going to kick?"

I looked at the door, now closed behind her. I hadn't heard a knock.

She smiled. "It was open, so I let myself in. I figured if I needed to Tase you, I was better off with the element of surprise." Amelia looked at Travis and the card table. "I'm glad there's an actual poker game."

Travis shook his thumb toward me. "I'm playing with his money. I didn't have the cash to ante, so he gave it to me just so I'd come. He's pretty desperate to hang out with you."

Amelia looked to me with a smug smile. I shut my eyes. "Thanks, buddy. I appreciate you sharing."

Travis laughed. "No problem. You want a beer, Amelia?"

"Sure. That would be great. Thanks."

A few minutes later, there was a knock at the door before Will let himself in. He was always the last to show up for anything. He grabbed a beer, and we all settled in around my kitchen table. Travis tossed the cash I'd given him across the table to exchange for chips, and Will reached into his pocket. But Amelia stopped him before he could pass cash my way.

She pointed to me. "Your game is on Merrick tonight, Will."

"Uh, no it's not," I said.

"Why not? You paid your other friend to play."

Will looked back and forth between Amelia and me. "Is she serious?"

"Travis didn't have any cash," I said.

"Playing cards is the only way he could get me to hang out with him." Amelia shrugged. "If we don't have four people we can't play, and I'm leaving."

Will stuffed his cash back into his pocket. "Thank you for letting me know." He lifted his chin to me. "I'll take whatever you kicked in for Trav. Or I guess we don't have a game, and Amelia here will be on her merry way."

I narrowed my eyes at Amelia, who looked damn proud of herself. But I knew Will. He'd probably made two grand day-trading between classes today, yet he wasn't about to put out cash now that he knew I was stuck. Groaning, I pulled out fifty dollars more and tossed it into the pile.

"Thanks, guys. I can't wait for one of you to need a wingman."

A few hours later, I hadn't lost all my money. I'd lost all mine *plus* the cash I'd kicked in for Travis and Will. Once again, Amelia had kicked our asses.

I leaned back in my seat, still shaking my head. I was a damn good card player. It was rare that I took a beating. But Amelia had won at least seventy percent of the hands. "I don't get it. You said you count cards, but I looked it up. You can't count cards in poker the way you can in blackjack. You'd have to memorize the likelihood of winning with all the different combinations of hands and then compare that to what you see face up on the table from every other player."

She shrugged. "That's right."

"And you've done that?"

"It's not hard. I'm good at numbers."

"I'm good at numbers, too. I'm going to open my own brokerage firm in a few years. Maybe I'll hire you."

She smiled. "Maybe I'll hire *you*."

The other guys laughed and got up. After a quick round of *laters*, it was just Amelia and me. She slipped her winnings into her purse, and it looked like she was about to leave, too.

"Stay for a little while?" I asked.

"Why?"

"Because I want to hang out with you."

"Why?"

"Is *why* your favorite word?"

She stood. "I'm not a very trusting person."

I grinned. "Why?"

She tried to contain her smile, but failed.

I reached out and took her hand. "Because you're obviously smart. You like to play cards. You can dish it out to my buddies as good as they give it to you. And...you're hot."

Amelia looked into my eyes. She searched the same way she did when she was trying to figure out if one of the guys was bluffing his hand. "Do you have a girlfriend?"

"Wouldn't be asking you out if I did."

"So that's a no?"

"It's definitely a no."

She folded her arms over her chest. "I have trust issues. If I get it into my head that you're lying to me, I'll probably search your phone when you're not paying attention. I fact-check people—if you say you were somewhere, you darn well better have been there, because I'll find out if you weren't. I pick fights when I'm feeling down. I assume the worst of most people. My father's in prison, and I don't even know what state my mother lives in anymore." She held my gaze. "Still want to go out with me?"

I nodded. "Yep."

She shook her head, pulled her purse up to her shoulder, and headed for the door. I figured I'd flunked whatever test she was trying to scare me away with. But halfway to the doorway, she stopped without turning back. "I like foreign movies with subtitles. Friday at seven. I'll meet you here, but outside."

I blinked a few times, confused at the sudden turn of events, but I wasn't about to give her a chance to change her mind. "Can't wait. I'll see you at seven."

CHAPTER 14

Evie

The following Friday afternoon, I was in a session with one of the traders when the receptionist knocked on my door.

"I'm very sorry to interrupt, but you have a call. The gentleman said it was urgent, but your phone is showing as do not disturb."

I held my hand out toward Derek, my patient. "I turn it off when I'm meeting with someone. Do you know who it is?"

"Marvin Wendall. He asked for Merrick first, but when I said he was out of the country, he asked to speak to you."

My forehead wrinkled. I would think Will was the "next of kin" for any business matters. But okay... "Thanks, Regina." I looked over at Derek. "I'm sorry. Would you excuse me? I'll just be a minute."

He nodded. "No problem. Take your time."

At my desk, I picked up the phone. "This is Evie Vaughn."

"Hiya there, Evie. This is Marvin. I'm a friend of Kitty Harrington."

"Oh. Hi, Marvin. Is everything okay?"

"Not really, honey. That's why I'm calling. I'm a little worried about Kitty. I tried to reach her grandson, but they tell me he's out of the country. She talks about you a lot and had mentioned you're a doctor and that you work there now, so I figured I'd talk to you since I couldn't reach Merrick."

"Merrick's on a business trip to China. I think he flies back in the next day or two. But tell me what's going on?"

"Welp, Kitty broke one of her ankles and twisted the other."

"Oh, that's terrible. How did that happen?"

"It's a long story. But we were roller skating and—"

"Roller skating?"

"We're old, missy. Not dead. Anyway, some little turd knocked her over, and she twisted one ankle. I helped her up, but when she tried to put weight on it, she fell again and someone rolled right over the other ankle. I heard the crack on that one."

I winced. "Oh gosh."

"But that's not the worst of it."

"It's not?"

"Nope. We went to the ER, and they took some X-rays and did some bloodwork, mostly just routine stuff. But she came back anemic. Turns out she's also been having some lady problems and hasn't gotten checked—a lot of bleeding, apparently. So they had a specialist come see her about it, and that one told her she needed some surgery. They wanted her to stay in the hospital, but you know Kitty. Nothing keeps that woman down. I'm afraid she checked herself out. Now she's in a wheelchair with two bum ankles and some woman problems, and she won't talk to me about those. I didn't know what else to do. She's going to kick my ass when she finds out I took her phone and called you, but right now she can't run to catch me, so I have some time to worry about that."

I blew out a big breath. "No, you definitely did the right thing, Marvin. I'm glad you did. I'll talk to her."

"Woman's one of the most fascinating people I've met in my life. But she's also pigheaded."

I smiled. "I see you've gotten to know Kitty pretty well."

"I'm sorry to dump this on you. But I would never forgive myself if anything happened to her and I hadn't done all I could."

"Of course. I'm with a patient right now, but I'll give Kitty a call in about a half hour."

"Thank you, dear."

After I concluded my session with Derek, I settled in at my desk to call Kitty. But while I was collecting my thoughts on the best way to approach her, I realized that if I did get her to go back to the hospital, she would need someone to look out for her and be there to help make decisions. And if I didn't get her to go back, no one would be checking her vitals to see if her anemia got worse—not to mention, she had two injured ankles, so she wasn't getting around too well to begin with.

So rather than call, I decided this should be taken care of in person. I figured I should run it by Merrick to see what he wanted to do, but when I Googled the time in China, I realized two in the afternoon on Friday here meant it was three in the morning there. I wasn't sure when he was flying home, so I called his assistant.

"Hey, Andrea. Could you tell me when Merrick is flying back from China? I need to talk to him about something important."

"Of course. Let me pull up his itinerary." I heard the clickity-clack of her keyboard before she spoke again. "He's on a nine-AM flight out tomorrow morning, China time. But between the twenty hours of flights and time change, he gets into JFK on Saturday about four in the afternoon."

Shoot. Even if he hopped on a different flight, with twenty hours of travel, he wouldn't get to Atlanta until late Saturday night, at best. This didn't seem like something that should wait. So I decided I'd just go. Besides, Kitty might find it easier to talk to another woman about her issues than her grandson. And my grandmother would want me to take care of Kitty. So I made the choice to get on a plane and delay telling Merrick until he landed. There was no point in having him worry for twenty hours of flying when there was nothing he could do until he got here anyway. If I flew down tonight, I'd know more by then, too.

"Do you want me to contact his hotel or anything for you?" Andrea asked.

"No." I shook my head. "I'll talk to him when he gets back. But thank you."

"No problem. I'll email you his itinerary, in case you need it after I'm gone for the day."

"Thank you. Have a good weekend, Andrea."

"You, too, Evie."

After I hung up, I searched for flights. There was one at 6 PM that would get me in at 8:30. As long as I didn't check a bag, that would have me to Kitty's by 9:30. The later flights arrived too late to knock on Kitty's door. I didn't want to disturb her rest. I could also wait until tomorrow, but I would feel better going now. So I booked the flight and let Joan in HR know I needed to leave a little early. It felt like the right thing to do—though I hoped Merrick didn't disagree.

By Saturday evening, I was starting to worry that I hadn't heard from Merrick yet. I'd flown down to Kitty's yesterday and spent the night at her house. She was stable and doing well. This afternoon, I'd sent Merrick a long email, telling him everything that had happened over the last day and a half. I'd waited to send it until two hours before his flight was scheduled to arrive, but when he hadn't responded more than two hours after I confirmed his flight had landed, I tried calling. My call went straight to voicemail. Another hour later, I tried again and texted. Still no response.

At 9 PM, I checked my phone one last time before checking in on Kitty. She'd taken the pain pills the ER doc had prescribed, and they'd knocked her out. So I grabbed a towel and took a hot shower, hoping it would help me relax enough to fall asleep. But just as I got out, I heard what sounded like glass breaking in the kitchen. I assumed Kitty had woken up and tried to get something to drink, but when I passed by her room, she was still sound asleep.

Oh shit. Was it a broken window and not a glass? Could it be a burglar? Or maybe Marvin had a key and had let himself in to check on Kitty... Though he'd been over earlier for dinner and obviously knew I was here. I wasn't sure, but I also wasn't about to find out empty-handed, so I looked around for something to use to defend myself. The closest thing to a weapon I could find was the toilet bowl cleaner, a plastic stick with a brush on the end. It would have to do, because someone was most definitely in the kitchen—I could hear rustling now, even through the closed door.

My heart pounded as I approached. If it did turn out to be Marvin, I hoped I didn't give the old guy a heart attack. I wanted to use the element of surprise to my advantage, so I wasn't about to announce myself. Instead, I took a deep breath and whipped the door open. But it stopped abruptly when it whacked into something.

Everything after that seemed to occur in fast forward.

A person was down on the floor, bent on all fours.

I lunged forward with the toilet bowl brush high in the air and brought it down with a loud *smack* across the back of the intruder's head.

He yelled.

I lost my balance, tripped over the man, and went flying through the air.

It wasn't until I landed on my ass that I realized what I'd done.

Oh my God. Shit!

"Merrick! I'm so sorry!"

He rubbed his head. "What the hell? What did you hit me with?"

I held up the toilet bowl brush, the head of which was now missing. "This. It's..." I pointed to the bristled top on the floor nearby. "I guess I broke it on you. It's all I could find. I thought you were a burglar. I'm so sorry. Are you okay?"

He shook his head. "I'm fine."

"Why were you on the floor?"

"I broke a glass and was cleaning it up. I didn't turn on the lights because I heard the shower running and didn't want to scare you. That worked out great, huh?"

He climbed to his feet and leaned toward me, offering a hand to help me get up. "Are you okay?"

"Yeah, I think so." But once I got to my feet, I felt something pinching my butt. I twisted to look over my shoulder then patted around my ass. Hitting a spot on my left butt cheek, I felt the pain again.

Merrick's brows drew together as he watched me. "What's the matter?"

"I think I might've landed on a piece of glass."

"You've got to be kidding me."

I patted my butt again, and this time I felt a little wetness. There was a tinge of blood on my fingertips. "Shit... I'm bleeding."

"Let me see."

"It's my ass!"

"Well, how are you going to see what's going on?"

"I don't know. A mirror, I guess?"

Merrick looked down at my bare feet and sighed. "Don't move. There are probably still slivers all over. I hadn't finished cleaning up."

"Well, could you fi—" Before I could complete my sentence, he lifted me into the air and didn't set me back down on my feet until we were in the living room.

I smoothed my shirt, which had ridden up. "A little notice you were going to do that would've been nice."

"I didn't feel like wasting time arguing about it." He lifted his chin. "Go fix your ass."

Twenty minutes later, there was a quiet knock at the bathroom door.

I sighed and creaked open the door enough to stick my head out.

"You okay in there?" Merrick asked.

I frowned. "No. I can't get it. I feel it, but it's not sticking out enough for me to pull it with my tweezers. I think it's in pretty deep."

"Let me take a look."

I shook my head. "I'm just going to leave it."

Merrick put his hands on his hips. "You'd rather leave a piece of glass in your ass than have me see a little skin?

Pretend you're wearing a bathing suit. Then strangers see half your ass."

"I'd rather strangers see my whole ass than you see part of it."

Merrick thumbed over his shoulder. "There's an overpass a few miles away with a bunch of people living in tents. You want me to go get one of them to examine your cheek?"

I narrowed my eyes. "It's not funny. This is all your fault, you know."

"Would it make you feel better if I showed you my ass first?"

I tapped my finger to my lip. "Maybe?"

He chuckled. "Just let me in."

"Fine." I sighed and opened the door.

Merrick came into the bathroom and pointed to the shower curtain, which was no longer hanging and now on the floor of the tub, along with the rod. "What's going on there?"

"Oh. In order to see my ass, I had to stand on the toilet. I lost my balance at one point, so I grabbed the shower curtain to steady myself, and it all came down."

The corner of Merrick's lip twitched. "Sounds like you have things under control."

I squinted. "Just shut up and look at my ass."

"Yes, ma'am."

Merrick sat down on the ledge of the tub while I turned around. I'd been dressed for bed when I heard the noise, so I had on a pair of flimsy pajama shorts. I lifted the back to expose my left cheek.

"Do you see anything?"

"I see a lot of red, which I'm guessing is from you trying to get it out. I'm going to touch the area, okay? See if I feel anything."

I nodded. "Yeah, go ahead."

Warm fingers gently ran across my skin. *Oh God.* My traitorous body liked it. Thankfully I was not facing him, so at least he couldn't see the heat creep up on my face.

"Anything?" I asked with a shaky voice.

"Not yet. I need to push a little harder, okay?"

Push a little harder. Jesus Christ. He needed to stop talking like that, too. I blew out a puff of air. "Just do whatever you need to do."

He rubbed his fingers over my ass again, this time pressing down as he went.

"Ow!"

"Yeah. I feel it right there. It's definitely fully beneath the skin. I'm going to need to squeeze it like a buried splinter to tease it out."

I took a deep breath and nodded. "Fine. Go ahead."

His fingers moved around the area for a few seconds before he stopped. "Can you...lie over my knee?"

"I'm not lying over your knee!"

"I need leverage, and it's hard to squeeze with you in the upright position."

I huffed. "Maybe we should go get that person under the bridge after all."

Merrick laughed. "Come on. I'll do it as fast as I can."

"Fine." I shook my head. "I can't believe I'm doing this."

For the next five minutes, I laid, with my bare ass cheek hanging out, over my boss's knee. And I hated the thoughts running wild through my head.

I kind of like it here.

I wonder what he'd do if I told him I wanted him to spank me?

He has such big hands. I bet the print he'd leave on my skin would be huge.

God...my clit was starting to tingle. *Seriously?*

Stop, Evie. Just stop.

All thoughts finally came to an abrupt halt when he squeezed so hard that tears formed in my eyes. "Ouch! That hurts!"

He let go. "It's out."

I reached around and rubbed my derrière. "Jesus. Did you cut off a piece of my flesh?"

"It was deeper than I thought. I had to squeeze hard." Merrick pointed to the cabinet next to us, under the sink. "There should be a first aid kit under there. Grab it, and I'll put some Bacitracin on this and cover it up."

When he was done, he gave a little smack to my right cheek. "All done."

I stood and adjusted my shorts. "Thank you."

"No problem. I think I need a drink after this welcome. You want one?"

I nodded. "Yeah. I'm just going to wash up first."

After Merrick left the bathroom, I took a few minutes to compose myself before finding him in the living room. He'd opened a bottle of wine and was sitting on the couch. When I walked over, he slipped a throw pillow from behind his back and tossed it toward the other end. "You might want more than one of these to sit on."

"Thanks." I picked up the much-needed glass of wine and sat down. "It might be the first time I'm glad I have a little extra junk in the trunk. I don't really feel it now."

"I wasn't going to say anything, but since you brought it up... You do have a pretty full ass for a little thing."

"I get it from my mom. I hated it when I was younger. But the Kardashians have made it fashionable, so I've learned to appreciate it."

Merrick brought his wine to his lips. "I'd say I appreciate it too, but I'm afraid I might get whacked in the head again."

"I really am sorry for that. You sure you're okay?"

"I'm fine. Can't do too much damage with a plastic toilet bowl brush. Next time, maybe try for something a little sturdier."

"It was all I could find. And you should be glad about that."

Merrick smiled. "True." He sipped his wine and pointed his eyes to the coffee table. I'd left out a piece of orange sea glass when I took a shower. "Kind of ironic that you got a piece of your lucky charm stuck in your ass, don't you think?"

I took the sea glass from the table and rubbed it between my fingers. "Don't blame the sea glass for trouble you caused."

"What's the story with those anyway? How did they become your good luck charms?"

"About a year before my mom left my dad for good, he had done a number on her and we took off for a week—my mom, my sister, and me. Mom took us to this beach in Virginia that we'd never been to. It was sunny and beautiful, and one day I spent hours on the beach collecting sea glass. I remember my mom telling me she wasn't going to go back to my dad this time." I closed my eyes and could still feel the happiness in my chest from that day, could still smell the salt air. "I remember feeling so free and happy. I guess the sea glass just kind of stuck with me as a reminder that it was possible to feel that way. My mom did end up going back to my dad, but I never forgot the feeling I had on that trip. Still to this day, I go to the beach when I'm feeling down or need to clear my head."

"That must be hard in New York City. Not sure I've ever seen sea glass on the beach. Maybe some broken beer bottles, but not anything to collect."

I smiled. "Then you haven't been to Glass Bottle Beach in Dead Horse Bay, Brooklyn, have you?"

"Dead Horse Bay? No, I haven't. That's not the most enticing name..."

I laughed. "Definitely not. But it's covered in sea glass. The bay got its name because a lot of horse bones have been found there. It's near the Marine Parkway Bridge, and when they built that, they used garbage to build the land up around a small island they were trying to protect. Unfortunately, they didn't cover the trash with enough sand, so it started rising to the surface in the fifties. Every day more and more seventy-year-old trash washes up, and a ton of it is now sea glass. You have to walk with thick-soled shoes, but it's a collector's paradise. I go there often to comb the beach. It helps me clear my head."

Merrick's eyes looked back and forth between mine. "You're definitely a unique person, Evie."

I sipped my wine. "You're hard to read. I can't tell if that's an insult or a compliment."

He smiled. "It's a compliment."

"Should I write down the date? I get the feeling they're given out pretty sparingly."

"Well, as long as I'm feeling generous, I need to thank you for rushing down here to take care of my grandmother."

"Oh, you're welcome. But no thanks needed. I'd do anything for Kitty. She's an amazing woman. Stubborn, but amazing."

"I'm sorry I didn't text you back to let you know I was coming. I fell asleep on the flight from China, and when I woke up, we were getting ready to land. I read your message and had to turn off my phone for a while. Once we were on the ground, I turned it on to text you back, but it only had one-percent battery left. I'd plugged it in to charge on my flight, but apparently the port wasn't working at my seat. Then I was able to get on a connecting flight to come down here, but I had to rush to make it, and there was nowhere to charge my phone on that flight."

I nodded. "I did worry a little when I didn't hear from you, but I figured something like that must've happened."

"What the hell was my grandmother doing roller skating anyway?"

"If you'd like another whack to your head, you should ask her just like that."

He laughed and drank his wine. "True."

"As much as having one ankle broken and the other twisted is bad, it might've been a blessing it happened. Apparently, she's been having bleeding and uterus pain for a while and hadn't gone to a doctor or told anyone. They only found out because she was anemic at the hospital and the doctor asked questions. This afternoon, she let me go online to the hospital's patient portal and read the ER summary and lab results. The attending wrote that the gynecologist consult believes she might need a hysterectomy. So we really need to talk her into going back to the doctor, and I don't think she should be alone until her blood count is in a normal range. It was so low I'm surprised she didn't pass out at some point before the roller-skating incident."

Merrick shook his head and dragged a hand through his hair. "That's Kitty. Takes care of everyone else, but doesn't prioritize herself."

"Yeah. My grandmother was the same way."

"Is she in two casts?"

"One hard cast and a removable boot for the sprain. She's not happy about it. If there's any kind of saw in the garage, we should probably hide it. I wouldn't put it past her to try to take it off herself."

"Good idea."

Over his shoulder, I noticed Merrick's briefcase sitting near the front door, but when I glanced around the room, I didn't see any suitcase.

"Where's your luggage?"

"It didn't make the flight to Atlanta. The connection was too tight. Hopefully it will show up tomorrow."

"Oh, that stinks. Well, my suitcase is in the guest room, but I'll move it out and stay on the couch after I finish this wine. You must be tired from all the traveling."

"You're not sleeping on the couch. I'll be fine right here."

Kitty's two-bedroom house was small, and so was her furniture. I eyed the tiny sofa. "You won't even fit on that thing."

"I can fall sleep anywhere."

I looked around the room and sighed. "It feels so strange to be here and not be able to go next door. It's the first time I've been down here since my grandmother's house sold. I'd rented it for two years after I moved because I wasn't ready to part with it yet."

"I'm sorry. That must be hard."

I smiled sadly. "At least I have a lot of good memories. Your grandmother used to come over and sit on my grandmother's porch every night after dinner. When I was working on my PhD, I practically lived at the library. Sometimes I'd come home at ten or eleven, and the two of them would still be out there, laughing their asses off and often loaded on spiked sweet tea. They used to drink it out of mugs so the neighbors would think they were drinking regular tea. I'd walk Kitty home and make sure she got inside alright, and she'd twist my arm to have a goodnight shot of whiskey with her. Then I'd go back next door, and my grandmother and I would sit outside a little longer on the porch."

Merrick smiled. "I was eight when my grandmother gave me my first taste of whiskey. I remember my mother being pissed."

"The new owner took down the treehouse in the back. I loved that thing."

"I remember the treehouse. I was in it a few times."

"You were?"

"Yeah, when I was a kid and I'd come down to visit my grandmother, sometimes I'd go check it out when they were sitting around on the porch. I remember it had a lot of pink in it—pink plastic refrigerator, pink pillows, pink frilly lampshade, even though there was obviously no electricity."

I smiled. "That was all me. I hadn't honed my decorating skills yet."

"Wasn't there a poster of some boy band, too?"

"Not a boy band. Burt Reynolds."

"Burt Reynolds? The old actor who died a while back?"

"Yep. I had a major crush on him. He was the voice of the German shepherd in *All Dogs Go to Heaven*. I loved that movie and his voice. I watched it over and over again. One day my mom and I were in some store, and I found an anniversary movie poster of Burt Reynolds in *Smokey and the Bandit*. I made her buy it for me. I thought he was so good looking."

"Ah... So this is a pattern for you," Merrick said.

"What do you mean?"

"Finding older men attractive. I do have three years on you, you know." He winked.

I snort-laughed. "It's funny how we both spent so much time here, but never ran into each other." I shrugged. "At least I don't think we did. To be honest, I don't remember too much before the age of ten."

"How come?"

"It's called dissociative amnesia. Our brain sometimes blocks things out, often as a protective mechanism after a traumatic event. I was ten when we left my dad for the last time. Usually his abuse came at night, when he'd come home drunk and start with my mom, so I was already in bed. I had this little pink clock radio with rhinestones on my nightstand. If I heard screaming start, I'd bring it under the covers with me and put the music on next to my ear." I paused a moment. "That last time, he was perfectly sober, and I wasn't in my room. It happened here at my grandmother's. We'd come to stay for a few days, and he wasn't happy about it. So one afternoon, he waited until my grandmother went out and then snuck inside. I don't remember all the details, but apparently my dad made my sister and me sit on the couch and watch while he beat Mom up pretty badly. It was an extra punishment for her because she'd left without ironing his shirts."

"Jesus Christ."

I shook my head. "It was pouring that night. After, my sister locked herself in the bedroom, and I ran to the treehouse. But when I got to the top rung of the ladder and was trying to climb in, the ladder fell away from the tree, and I wound up dangling from the edge of the treehouse floor. I was crying hard and the rain was pelting down, and my fingers were slipping. The boy across the street, Cooper, saved me by putting the ladder back. Do you remember him from your visits?"

Merrick shook his head. "No, I don't think so."

"Well, at least I think it was Cooper who helped me. I didn't stop to look once I got back on the ladder. Years later, I asked him about it, and he said he didn't remember. But I prefer to think it was Cooper who saved me, rather than that I unknowingly accepted help from my father—who could have come out of the house. Anyway, I remember that treehouse and that little rhinestone clock so clearly, but I can't remember a lot of other things about my childhood. That treehouse made me feel so safe. My grandfather built it for me for my fifth birthday. He died the following summer."

Merrick frowned. "I'm sorry you went through all of that."

I shrugged. "It made me stronger in a lot of ways. Not being able to remember got me interested in how the brain works, which eventually led me to study psychology and become a therapist. And that treehouse I loved so much is where I got the idea for my Airbnbs. I know my grandparents would be thrilled at what I did with their property, and all of the profits are donated to an Atlanta DV shelter— the one Kitty founded."

"God, you must think I'm such a dick." Merrick rubbed the back of his neck. "I basically made fun of your rentals when you told me about them during the interview, and all the profits go to my grandmother's charity."

"Nah. I know renting treehouses and a glamping site sounds a little odd. I didn't think you were a dick for that." I grinned. "There were so many *other* reasons to think you were a dick. You know, like you telling me you were hiring me because I was the least-competent candidate." I paused and smiled. "Sorry. We had a deal that I wouldn't bring that up anymore."

Merrick hung his head. "I really am an ass."

"At least you own it."

"You know, I ridiculed your upbeat personality when we first met because we're so different, and I didn't understand it. But maybe I can learn something from you."

I cupped my ear and leaned to Merrick. "What was that? I didn't hear you. I think it might have been *another* compliment. Can you repeat it?"

Merrick lifted his glass of wine. "If you tell Will I just said that, I'll deny every word."

"Your secret is safe with me."

"I don't think I ever actually apologized for the way I treated you at first. So I'm sorry."

I smiled. "Thank you. But you can't appreciate the beauty in someone without seeing the ugly. You just got your ugly out of the way to make it easier to appreciate the good parts."

His eyes swept over me. "I'm not sure that's always true. I haven't seen any ugly side of you."

Oh wow. That made my belly feel all mushy. You know what goes good with mush? *Wine*—lots of it. So I drank half mine down.

A few minutes later, we'd both emptied our glasses, and Merrick yawned.

"What time zone are you on right now?" I asked.

"I have no damn idea."

"Welp, on that note, I think it's time for me to let you get some sleep. Are you sure you don't want the bed? I really don't mind the couch at all."

"I'm good. But thank you."

I went and grabbed a blanket and pillow from the guest room and returned to set them down on the couch. When I got to the doorway, I stopped and looked back over my shoulder. "Thanks again for, you know, saving my ass."

Merrick's eyes dropped to my butt, and his lips formed a dirty grin. "Anytime you need to drop your drawers and bend over a knee bare assed, I'm your man. Let's just say, it wasn't miserable for me."

I winked. "I might've enjoyed it a little myself."

CHAPTER 15

Evie

Holy shit.

The next morning, I froze mid-step as I walked into the living room. Merrick was sound asleep on the couch, one arm slung across his forehead partially covered his eyes, but that was pretty much the only part of his body I couldn't see. Well, that and one foot covered by the blanket I'd given him last night, which was now bunched up in a ball at the bottom of the couch.

And I couldn't stop staring.

He wore only a pair of tight, black boxer briefs. I grew hot taking in his sculpted eight-pack, narrow waist, and the sexy V carved into his beautiful, tanned skin. Not to mention, there was a pretty large bulge in those skin-hugging underwear. Merrick Crawford was a sight in a suit, but this... This was next level. At any second, he could've opened his eyes and found me staring, but I was pretty sure even that wouldn't have stopped my ogling. Some guilty pleasures were worth the consequences.

Damn. I might have to go back to my room for a little while, or maybe even take a cold shower.

But then Merrick shifted on the couch, and I held my breath while he settled in. I waited for him to open his eyes and find me drooling like a teenage girl. When he didn't, I blinked myself back from my fantasy and managed to put one foot in front of the other and make it to the kitchen.

Fifteen minutes later, I sat at the table, drinking a cup of coffee and fantasizing about my boss's body, when the door swung open. Merrick seemed surprised to see me.

"Oh, hey." He raked a hand through his bed hair, which really worked for him. "What time is it?"

I pressed a button on my phone. "Seven thirty."

He now had on his dress pants from last night, but still no shirt, and the top button of his slacks was unbuttoned. A thin line of hair led from his belly button down into the waistband of his underwear. It didn't matter that he was now wide awake and standing only a few feet from me, my eyes had a mind of their own. They took a slow tour up and down his body. It was impossible for Merrick to not see it.

He shrugged. "Sorry. I don't have any clothes until my luggage gets here."

I tore my eyes away and lifted my coffee mug to my lips. "It's only fair that you show a little skin after last night." I pointed over my shoulder. "There's coffee made."

After Merrick poured his caffeine fix, he took the seat across from me.

"How did you sleep?" I asked.

"Pretty good. You?"

"Not bad." It had taken me forever to fall asleep. Visions of me lying over Merrick's knee, *without* a piece of glass in my ass, had played in my head over and over.

"I checked on Kitty just now. She's still sound asleep."

I nodded. "Yeah, I checked on her earlier, too. The doctor prescribed a pretty strong pain medication, and it makes her sleepy."

"Ah... Well, that explains it. She's usually up early."

I sipped my coffee. "I was looking at flights on my phone before I got out of bed. There's a five thirty direct into JFK this afternoon, if you want me to stay today so we can try to talk to her about going to a gynecologist."

Merrick looked alarmed. "You're leaving?"

"Well, yeah. I figure you're here now, so things are under control."

"I pride myself on having control of most of my life, but Kitty's always been the exception. I have no control over that woman."

I laughed. "Do you want me to see if there's a later flight?"

"If later means tomorrow or sometime after that, the answer is yes."

My brows pulled together. "Are you staying?"

"Yeah, but you can't leave me alone with her—not to talk about her woman problems."

"You actually sound a little afraid."

Merrick shook his head. "Not a little. A lot. Can you stay? At least until tomorrow. Maybe we can play it by ear."

"I guess so. I have some patients scheduled, but I suppose I could reschedule them. My boss is kind of a jerk, though. I hope he doesn't mind me taking a day when I'm so new."

"Your boss might give you a raise if you stay."

I smiled. "That's not necessary, but I'll stick around a little longer if it makes you feel better. I'd do anything for Kitty."

"It does." His shoulders dropped. "Thank you."

We finished our coffee while sharing stories about our grandmothers. When I got up to pour a second cup, I heard Kitty calling from the bedroom. "Yoohoo! Everly, darling, are you up?"

I smiled. "I almost forgot she doesn't know you're here yet."

He lifted his chin. "You go first. I don't want to scare her."

I went down the hall to Kitty's room. When I opened the door, Merrick stayed behind me, out of view. "Good morning."

"Good morning, darling. I'm sorry to be a burden. Do you think you can give me a hand getting out of this bed?"

"I'd love to, Kitty, but there's someone else here who might be a little stronger." I stepped aside, and Merrick walked in.

Kitty's face lit up like a Christmas tree. "Merrick! You're here!"

"Of course, Grams. I came as soon as I could." He walked over to the bed, leaned down, and kissed her cheek. "I'm sorry it wasn't sooner."

She waved him off. "You're such a busy man. I hate to bother you."

"Bother me? What bothers me is that you didn't call me yourself. And we're going to talk about that. But I'll let you get up and have your coffee first."

He carefully helped her into the wheelchair I'd left by her bedside.

"I need to make a pit stop in the loo."

Merrick looked at me with panic on his face. I smiled. "Why don't I help you with that?"

He wheeled Kitty to the bathroom, then scooped her out of the chair and set her down on the toilet, fully dressed, before rushing out the door. "I'll leave you to... whatever."

There was something kind of comical about how freaked out he was, but I kept that to myself. After I helped Kitty get settled, I told her I'd wait outside and to yell when she was done so I could get her back into the wheelchair. Of course, she hobbled on one hard-casted foot and one boot to get herself out of the bathroom anyway.

I shook my head as she sat back in the chair. "Kitty, you're not supposed to put weight on either of those legs."

"Oh, doctors are such wimps these days." She put up a hand. "No offense."

I pushed Kitty down the hall. "None taken. I'm not a medical doctor anyway."

A few minutes later, the three of us sat in the kitchen drinking coffee. When it felt like it might be the right time to broach the subject of Kitty's gynecological problems, I motioned with my eyes to Merrick, and he nodded.

"So, Kitty..." I said. "Merrick and I want to talk to you about the gynecologist."

"No need." Kitty put up her hand. "I'm going to go."

Oh, wow. "That's great, Kitty. I'm so glad. The doctor they recommended is affiliated with the hospital you went to, so I can go online and make an appointment for you, unless you have an established doctor you'd rather see."

"That's fine. It's been nearly twenty-five years since I've been to the vajayjay doctor. I'm sure my old guy is retired by now. Or worse."

Merrick shook his head. "Not that I'm complaining, but didn't you refuse to stay at the hospital or discuss your condition after they finished with your feet?"

"Yes." Kitty sipped her coffee.

He squinted. "So why the change of heart?"

Kitty shrugged. "Marvin said he's not having sex with me until I see that doctor and make myself well down there. He thinks he's going to hurt me or something." She leaned toward me and lowered her voice, unfortunately not low enough. "He is rather well endowed, and the little blue pills are a miracle worker, though I'm pretty sure he isn't going to do any damage. But whatever. Boys and their egos."

Merrick cleared his throat and pushed his chair back from the table. The legs skidded loudly across the tile. "I need to go call and check on my luggage."

I burst out into laughter. "Yeah, that's a good idea."

CHAPTER 16

Evie

"There you are." Kitty motioned to the chair across from where she sat on the couch. "Come sit with me, sweetheart."

"I was just going to ask if you'd like me to make you some tea."

"That would be nice. But sit first. I want to talk to you, and we don't have much time."

I sat. "I'm not leaving until tomorrow, Kitty."

"Oh, I know. I meant much time before my grandson gets off the phone. He just went outside on the lanai to call the airline about his luggage again."

"Oh, okay."

"Do you trust me, dear?"

"Of course, Kitty."

"Even though he's my flesh and blood, I would not steer you into something I thought would cause you any harm. I know he can come off as an ass sometimes... Let's face it, a lot of the time, but he's a good man. When he loves, he loves with his heart and soul."

I shook my head. "I've never doubted that he was a good man. Well, maybe he wasn't so friendly during our first meeting. But since I've gotten to know him, I can see he's not as impenetrable as he wants you to think he is."

She pointed to me. "You hit the nail on the head, sweetheart. Of course you did. You're a smarty pants. Merrick is a roaring lion on the outside, but inside he's a kitten. He thinks the way to protect his heart is by acting like he doesn't have one."

I smiled sadly. "He's been through a lot. We have that in common. People respond to trauma in different ways. I've baked and snacked my way through the last six months, and Merrick has thrown himself into his work more than ever."

"Has he told you about the twit?"

"Amelia?"

Kitty nodded.

"I don't know the whole story, but I know Merrick was hurt and she died."

Kitty nodded again. "I knew she was a twit the day I met her. I regret minding my own business and not telling him so. Which is why I'm meddling now. At my age, you can see things that fit, often before a person tries them on. It's a gift you get in exchange for your memory, teeth, and hearing." She leaned over and patted my hand. "Can I be frank, dear?"

"Oh boy. You mean all of these years you were holding back?"

She smiled. "He carries a lot of guilt for things he shouldn't feel guilty about. You both have a lot of baggage, but you were meant to help each other unpack."

"I don't think Merrick sees me in that way, Kitty."

"He's different when he's around you—calmer and more at peace."

"That might be because he finally took a break from the office."

She shook her head. "It's not. And that's not even how I know he's falling for you."

"Okay..."

"He smiles because of you. Whether he's talking about you or to you, I haven't seen him smile this way in forever."

"I think maybe that's because he's laughing *at* me. You did hear me tell the story about last night, right? How I attacked him with a toilet bowl brush and wound up with a piece of glass in my ass?"

She smiled, but ignored my comment. "You know what else I think?"

"What?"

"I think you feel the same way. But both of you are too chicken shit to do anything about it. Often the things that scare us the most are the ones that have the potential to change our lives. But if you open your heart and believe your happiness can happen, it will."

I wasn't so sure about manifesting happiness, but she wasn't wrong that something about Merrick terrified me, and not the way he wanted to keep people at a distance. But I thought she was off base that Merrick had feelings for me—well, the feeling of *lust,* maybe. That's all it was.

Kitty smiled. "You don't believe me, even though a part of you wants to. I've had my share of gentleman friends over the years, but there was only one love of my life. You know how I knew my Redmond felt the same way?"

"How?"

"I kept catching him watching me when he didn't think I was paying attention. My guess is you might have already noticed it once or twice with my grandson, but you haven't been ready to let yourself consider the meaning."

I had caught Merrick watching me once or twice, but he was an attentive man. It was a large part of the reason he was so successful.

When I didn't say anything, Kitty patted my hand. "Humor me. Next time you're in the same room with him, don't pay him any mind. Then look over at him when he doesn't expect it. I'd bet my house that you'll find him already looking at you."

Our conversation was interrupted by the sound of Merrick grumbling from the other room. "Damn airlines."

Kitty lowered her voice and leaned forward once more. "One more thing—I've changed his diaper. You won't be disappointed. Sometimes zigging and zagging not only finds you a new path to take, but it makes getting there a hell of a lot of fun, too."

―――――

Merrick swiped his cell phone off. That was his third call to the airline since this morning, and it was now going on three in the afternoon. "They finally have my luggage in Atlanta."

"Oh good. Are they delivering it?"

He shook his head. "Not if I want it sooner than one to three days. They're backed up, so I'm going to have to go to the airport to pick it up."

"Oh, that stinks. Do you want me to take a ride with you so you don't have to park? I can drop you at the terminal and circle while you pick it up and come back." I looked through the sliding glass doors that led to the lanai. Kitty was sitting with Marvin, both her casted and booted feet up on his lap. They laughed about something. "I think her stud muffin can take care of her while we're gone."

Merrick groaned. "Please don't use the words *stud* and *grandmother* in the same sentence."

"Oh yeah. Of course." I grinned. "Do you prefer I call him her rocket ride or boy toy?"

"You're going to be over my knee again in about two seconds."

Does he think that's a deterrent? Just the opposite.

Marvin slid the glass door open. "I'm going to cook the four of us some dinner tonight—a stick-to-your-ribs, southern meal." He looked back and forth between us. "You're not those types who only eat rabbit food, are you?"

I smiled. "No, neither of us is vegetarian."

"Good."

"Marv, are you planning on staying here this afternoon?" I asked. "Merrick needs to run to the airport to get his luggage, and I was thinking of taking the ride with him, but I don't want to leave Kitty unattended."

"I'll be here taking care of my girl all day. She's got a Zoom call with one of the new relatives she found on Ancestry later, and I like to read the Sunday paper from cover to cover. So take your time. It's a beautiful day out there."

I nodded with a smile. "Okay, thanks, Marvin."

A little while later, Merrick and I borrowed Kitty's car and headed to the airport. He drove while I looked out the window, feeling a lot of emotions. When we came to the Buckhead exit, I pointed. "I would be living somewhere out there if things hadn't derailed between me and Christian."

Merrick's eyes slanted to me before returning to the road. "You were going to live down here?"

I nodded. "Christian is from Atlanta. I think I told you we met when we were both students down here. We moved up to New York so he could work for a few years at his family's corporate headquarters, and I did my internship there. But he wanted to move back after our wedding. His company has a huge research-and-development facility down here that he was being trained to run."

"Is that what you wanted? To live down here, I mean?"

I shook my head. "Not really. I like it down here, but I love New York, and I wanted to be near my sister. I always imagined we'd have kids at the same time and they'd grow up together."

"Yet you were going to move anyway?"

I shrugged. "Christian hated New York. He hated apartment life and not having a big yard, and he absolutely loathed public transportation and busy sidewalks. Both his parents are originally from Atlanta. They divorced when he was five, and he mostly lived with his mother after that. His father relocated to work in the family business in New York, so he went back and forth. I think part of the reason he hates the city so much is because of what it represents to him—his family being torn apart. It's easier to blame something other than your parents."

"How long were you two together?"

"Three-and-a-half years."

Merrick nodded.

"What about you? Did you always live in the city?"

"I spent a week every summer down here with Kitty and my mom. But yeah, born and raised in New York. My mom went to college in the city and never came back. She was one of the few women on the trading floor in her day. She passed away six years ago of breast cancer."

"I'm sorry."

"Thank you."

"What about your dad?"

"He retired to Florida last year. Never remarried after my mom. My sister lives down there and has kids, so he moved not too far from her."

"You were...engaged once, too, right?"

Merrick's eyes flashed to me quickly before returning to the road. His lips pursed. "You like to dig around, don't you?"

"It's an occupational hazard. I ask questions and try to fit the pieces together to see the whole puzzle."

"Oh yeah? What pieces have you managed to put together about me?"

I didn't want to mention the comment Will had made—that his fiancée had annihilated him—so I was vague. "I've heard around that you were engaged to your business partner and it didn't end well."

Merrick stared at the road. I thought maybe that was the end of our discussion, but then he cleared his throat.

"You've shared a lot about your life, stuff that wasn't easy to live through. Yet you seem to have found a way to make peace with it. I have a harder time talking about things."

I nodded. "We all handle things in different ways. That's okay. I didn't mean to pressure you into discussing something you aren't comfortable talking about."

Merrick went quiet for a long time. It surprised me when he started to talk again. "Amelia and I started the business together, though she didn't want to be an equal partner and didn't want her name on the door."

"Why not?"

He drummed his fingertips on the steering wheel. "She said she wasn't a people pleaser. She wanted nothing to do with any personnel or dealing with a board of directors. Used to say she wanted to play Monopoly for a living but didn't want to own Hasbro."

"Why be a partner at all then?"

Merrick frowned. "I pushed her into it. She was smarter than me and understood people more, even though she didn't want to get involved with most. Plus, she out-earned every trader in the industry her first year, so she deserved more."

"Wow. Sounds like she was some sort of a whiz kid."

"She was."

He didn't offer more, so I debated whether to push. But I was curious. I knew she'd died, but I didn't get the feeling it was her death that had annihilated Merrick.

"Can I ask what happened between the two of you?"

The exit for the airport was coming up, so Merrick put on his blinker to get into the right lane. Our eyes caught briefly as he looked over his shoulder before changing lanes.

"My story isn't that different than yours. I found out I never really knew the person I thought I was going to marry."

"I'm sorry."

We exited the highway to the road leading to the airport. Merrick pointed up ahead. "There's a cell phone lot right over here. Customer service said to follow the signs to passenger pick up and go into the office in the baggage claim area. Hopefully it won't take too long, but why don't you drive around and wait in that cell phone lot. I'll text you when I have it."

"Okay."

I wanted to ask more questions, but I thought Merrick might have intentionally changed the subject.

"How's your ass today?" he asked. "That shard was in there pretty deep."

"It's sore. But I looked this morning, and it's not too red or anything."

"If you need a second opinion, just let me know." He winked, and it set off a flutter low in my belly.

Lord, crushing on this man was such a dead-end road. Not only was he my boss, but we'd both had disastrous relationships with people we worked with. And my sister had been right to remind me that Merrick's battle was harder. He had to move on from a ghost. Yet the more time I spent with him, the more I liked him, and even worse, the more frequent my fantasies became. Could there be something to what Kitty had told me?

We pulled up at the terminal. I walked around to the driver's side to take the wheel, and Merrick went in. Before I could even get back to the cell phone lot we'd passed, he'd called to tell me he had his luggage. So I headed back.

"That was fast," I noted when he opened the passenger door.

"Yeah, it was pretty painless. The office was empty, and my bag was sitting to the side with a few others."

"Do you want to switch places and drive?"

"Not unless you want me to."

"No, I'm good."

Merrick clicked his seatbelt on. "I was thinking, since Marvin is at the house, why don't we take a little detour?"

I shrugged. "Sure. Where to?"

"You said your Airbnbs aren't too far from here, right?"

My eyes widened, and I smiled. "They're only about a half-hour drive. Part of it is on the way back to Kitty's, but I get off the highway earlier and head east for a bit."

"Let's check 'em out. I've never stayed in a treehouse or a campsite."

"That's *glamp*site."

Merrick smiled. "I stand corrected."

I shifted the car into drive and started on my way. "I'm so excited. I'm not sure if they're rented or not, but I can check the website when we get there. If they are, I'll just show them to you from the outside."

"Sounds good."

For the entire drive, Merrick let me rattle on about all the different things I'd done to make what I thought was the perfect rental experience. "Both the treehouses have two large skylights, so there's a ton of natural light during the day, but it's absolutely incredible at night. The property is sixty acres, so there isn't too much light pollution, and on a clear night you can lie in the bed and see the stars."

I felt Merrick's eyes on my face, so I looked over. "What?"

"Nothing." He shook his head with a warm smile. "You just light up when you talk about them."

"I do? Well, then I must look like a Lite-Brite because I've been chewing your ear off for the entire drive."

Merrick chuckled. "It's alright. I enjoyed it. It reminds me a lot of when I started my company. I talked about it all the time."

I pointed to a road coming up. "This is it. The entrance is a mile or so down there. Then there are dirt paths that lead to the different rentals." I put my blinker on. "I'm just going to pull over once I turn and check the website to see if they're vacant."

"Sounds good."

I don't think I'd ever been so excited to see two of the places *not* rented today. Both the glamping site and one of the treehouses had guests who'd checked out this morning. I nearly squealed as I put the car into drive again. "There's one treehouse open and the glamping site. Which one do you want to go to first?"

"Whichever you want."

"The treehouse, definitely."

After we arrived at the property entrance, wooden signs with arrows pointed the way to the different rentals. Merrick looked around. "This must be tough to find at night."

"Yeah, definitely. We always tell people it's best to get here during daylight. If not, they have to go slow and use their high beams to see the signs on the trees."

As we approached the first site, I pointed up. "This is the first one."

Merrick ducked his head to get a better look out the windshield. "That's pretty awesome."

We parked, and I showed Merrick around the site. A freshwater stream ran through a few of the acres, and I'd selected the spots for the treehouses so they'd be nearby. Today it was running fast and loud.

"There's no better sound to fall asleep to than this."

"You can hear it from up there?" Merrick asked.

"Yep."

"Nice."

I pointed to a dirt trail that ran away from the stream. "If you follow that, it loops you on a nice hike through the adjoining state land. There's a small lake about two miles off the trail. We have a map on our website, but there's no clear trail to follow."

"Is that who mostly rents these? Hikers and nature enthusiasts?"

"That and city people who need to get away for the weekend." I waved for him to follow. "Come on, let's climb up to the house."

Once we were inside, I held my pointer to my lips in the universal *shhh* sign. The window had been left open, and you could hear the sound of the stream running. Every ten seconds or so, the wind blew, causing the leaves to rustle in perfect harmony with the water.

I smiled proudly. "What do you think? Magical, right?"

He looked around. The treehouse was only about two-hundred-and-fifty square feet, but it had all the essentials: a small fridge, cooktop, sink, bathroom with shower, and a bed with one nightstand. The floors were Pergo, but I'd picked it to match the outside of the tree, and the interior was painted a pale yellow.

"It's pretty incredible," he said. "People pay for soundtracks like that to fall asleep to at night. I'm not sure what I expected. I guess maybe dirt floors and a cot or something. But this looks like an efficiency in Manhattan." His brows pulled together. "Wait... How is there electricity and plumbing in here?"

"Ah, it's hidden. All of it runs down the back of the tree. You don't see it when you climb up the ladder, and it's camouflaged with all-weather paint to make it less conspicuous. The pipes run from the base of the tree under the ground to a small generator next to the storage shed behind the bushes in the back. I actually got all the electric done for free. When I was in school, I bartered home health care for an electrician's sick mom for some electrical work my grandmother needed done. So I called the same electrician when I was building these. I was planning on paying him, but then he asked if I wanted to trade for some counseling sessions for his daughter who has OCD."

"Damn. And you could only get me cat biscuits for my sperm. I think I'm kind of insulted."

I snort-laughed and gave him a shrug.

Merrick scanned the room again. "This is a little fancier than the one in your grandmother's yard. Although I don't see a rhinestone phone or pink plastic fridge anywhere."

"I know. But it does have this..." I walked over to the bed, laid down, and patted the spot next to me. "Come. You need to get the full effect."

Merrick looked amused, but played along. He laid back on the bed, the two of us side by side, and stared up at the skylights. The trees blew in the wind around the edges, but most of what we could see was simply blue sky.

"Close your eyes," I said.

I heard the smile in his voice. "Okay."

"Now, imagine it's nighttime. There's no light coming from anywhere, except the stars twinkling above you." I was quiet for a moment as I pictured it. "Now imagine those twinkling stars and listen to the sounds all around us."

We were quiet for a long time. When I finally opened my eyes, I looked over and was surprised to find him watching me.

"You're supposed to be looking at the Big Dipper," I said.

Merrick's eyes dropped to my lips and lingered before returning to meet mine. My belly did that little flutter it often seemed to do around him.

"You're pretty amazing, you know that?"

"Does that mean you like my treehouse?"

He chuckled softly. "I do. But I'm referring to the whole package. You're smart and funny, didn't think twice about hopping on a plane to help Kitty, and you seem to care deeply for your patients' well-being. But more than that, you're probably the most resilient person I know. You grew up around abuse and anger. Most people would have carried that with them like a shield and used it to keep people at a distance. But instead, you built sanctuaries where people can come and escape life—with all of the profits donated to a domestic violence shelter." He paused and looked away. "Your ex was a goddamned coward who couldn't handle the woman you are, so he acted like a boy."

Merrick's words seeped into me, making my chest feel full. I shook my head. "No one has ever said anything so nice to me. I'm not even sure what to say..."

Merrick smiled almost sadly. "If that's the nicest thing anyone has ever said to you, then your ex was more than just a coward. He was also a fucking idiot."

I rolled onto my side to face him, tucking my hands under my cheek. "Can I ask you sort of a forward question?"

He raised a brow. "I'm intrigued..."

My heart pounded, and I shook my head. "You know what? Let's just forget it."

"You can't pack a question like that back in the box. Spit it out, Vaughn. It's not like you to tiptoe around something."

"Well, Kitty sort of... Well, she thinks you're attracted to me."

Merrick smiled. "My grandmother is a wise woman."

I hadn't expected him to admit that. I thought maybe I'd misunderstood. "Are you saying she's right?"

"I think you already know the answer to that."

I nodded and looked away a moment. "So how come you..."

He lifted a brow. "How come I haven't mauled you?"

I laughed. "Yeah, that."

Merrick slipped a curled knuckle under my chin and tipped my head up so our eyes met. "Because while I think the attraction might be mutual, I get the feeling it might be something you'd regret after. Am I wrong?"

I looked into his eyes. "It's not you. I have some big trust issues, obviously. Not to mention, you're my boss, and I really like my job. And you...you lost someone you loved." I shook my head. "With all of that going against us, of course I'm nervous."

Merrick smiled sadly. "If it's meant to be, you'll come around when it's time."

"How will we figure out if the time is right?"

His eyes darkened. "I guess we'll know when my tongue is down your throat—or better yet, something else."

I laughed and play-smacked his chest. He sat up from the bed and offered his hand. "Come on. We better get out of here before it's too late."

"Oh, there isn't anyone checking in today."

"That's not what I meant."

"Why do we need to rush out of here then?"

"Because five more minutes of lying on this bed with you, and I'm going to have your clothes on the floor."

CHAPTER 17

Merrick

The next morning, I woke up early. Kitty's house was still dark and quiet, so I didn't bother pulling on a shirt before I headed to the bathroom. As I reached for the doorknob, the door suddenly opened.

Evie stood before me, wrapped in only a towel. Her hand flew to her chest. "*Shit*. You scared the crap out of me."

"Sorry. I didn't think anyone was up yet."

"I wanted to shower before Kitty woke up, so I wouldn't be in the way. But I realized I forgot my conditioner in my bag."

"Do you mind if I use the bathroom while you get it?"

She shook her head and tightened the corner of her towel. "No, of course not. Go right ahead."

After I relieved myself, I found Evie waiting in the hall outside. I didn't mean for it to happen, but my eyes surveyed the contours of her body. The towel only hung to the top of her thigh, and the way it was wrapped around her chest, her cleavage really wanted to spill over. I might've gotten stuck in that area for a few heartbeats. When my eyes finally found their way back to hers, she offered a knowing smile.

"Pervert."

My brows shot up. "I'm a pervert? You're half naked, and you've already shown me your ass. Actually, I saw you in your bra in that dressing room, too. You really need to stop coming on to me like this."

She put her hand on my chest and nudged me to one side of the doorway. Then she squeezed into it with me. Our bodies weren't touching, but they were damn close. She pushed up on her toes and looked into my eyes. "I bet if I left the bathroom door open a bit, I could prove who the pervert is."

I swallowed. *Fuck.* I had the strongest urge to show her exactly how perverted I was feeling at the moment. In fact, she was about ten seconds away from finding out, because her attitude was making me hard. She was going to be in for a surprise when it hit her belly. But then Evie slipped past me into the bathroom and wiggled her fingers.

"You might want to step away so I can close the door, pervert." She grinned.

I groaned. "You're evil."

It took every ounce of willpower to walk away as she pulled the door shut. I stood just down the hall for a few minutes, second-guessing myself. Luckily, my ruminations were cut short by my grandmother's voice. It was just the cold shower I needed.

"Merrick!"

I took a relieved breath before walking to her room. "Morning, Grams. How'd you sleep?"

"A little better. I took that damn boot off."

I shook my head. "You're supposed to keep it on so you don't cause further damage."

She waved me off. "That foot feels fine. They just wanted another thing to bill my insurance for."

I looked around the room. Finding the soft cast on the dresser, I walked over and grabbed it. "At least put it on before you get up."

She grumbled but let me help her with it before we went out to the kitchen.

"You still take your coffee with enough sugar to induce a diabetic coma?" I asked.

Grams used her hands to lift the leg with the hard cast up on the chair next to her. "When you're as sweet as me, you have to replenish the supply somehow."

While my grandmother was certainly one of the kindest humans I knew, *sweet* wasn't the way I'd describe her. "If your personality comes from what you ingest, I'm surprised you don't put lemons in your coffee," I teased. I prepped two mugs and took the seat across from her, sliding hers across the table.

"Thank you," she said. "So tell me, what are you going to do about Everly?"

"Evie?"

Grams raised her mug to her lips. "Mmm-hmm."

"I guess she'll go back after your doctor's appointment. I know she wanted to be here for it. I'll see if there's a flight for her tomorrow morning."

"I wasn't asking for her itinerary, dumbass. I was asking when you're finally going to make your move."

"What move?"

"I see the way you look at the girl when you think no one's paying attention. A woman like that won't be single for long. So stop dilly-dallying and throw your hat in the ring."

Oh, Jesus. I shook my head. "We're not having this conversation, Grams."

"Why the hell not? When was the last time you had a girlfriend? I'm not talking about a hookup—I mean a nice girl to date."

The word *hookup* should never come out of anyone's grandmother's mouth. "I've been focused on my business the last few years. Besides, that's not what Evie wants."

Grams frowned. "That twit really did a number on you. I worry about you, Merrick. When you close your heart to opportunity, you miss out on love."

"I'm not doing that."

"Okay. So then humor me for a minute. Do you think Everly is attractive?"

I sighed, knowing Grams would never let it go if I didn't play along. "She's a beautiful woman, yes."

"Got a great ass, too."

I shook my head with a laugh. "Yes, Evie also has a nice figure."

"Do you often find yourself wondering what's going on in her head?"

"Yes, but she's a therapist. So she has a unique way of looking at things."

"See a future with her?"

I didn't want to throw Evie under the bus and say it was her who was stopping anything from happening. But it was becoming inevitable.

"Grams, you're talking to the wrong person. Evie knows I'm attracted to her."

"Of course she does. But she also sees a man who's closed off from his feelings and angry at the world—a man who can quickly answer questions about his attraction to her, but say the word *future*, and you change the subject. You're two good-looking people. Lust isn't the problem; it's being afraid of love."

"I'm fine, Grams. Really. You don't need to worry about me. I'm not afraid to fall in love."

Grams's face turned serious. "Oh, I never thought you were, sweetheart. I think you're afraid you won't be loved back."

"Thank you so much for coming today." I shook my head as I drove. "I would never have gotten her to agree to have surgery without you. What did you say to her when you asked for a few minutes to talk alone?"

Grams, Evie, and I had all gone in to meet with the doctor after she examined Grams. The doctor laid out all of the reasons my grandmother needed a hysterectomy, but Grams was adamant that things would heal on their own. She wanted to give it some time. Then Evie asked if they could have a few minutes alone. Twenty minutes later, my grandmother was signing consent forms and getting scheduled for this coming Wednesday.

Evie smiled. "Do you really want to know?"

I sighed. "Never mind. But thank you."

Grams had asked us to drop her off at Marvin's, so now it was just the two of us pulling into her driveway.

"You're welcome," Evie said.

I put the car in park and killed the ignition, but made no move to get out. "I think I'm going to work from down here until she's out of the hospital and back home safely. I'll probably arrange a nurse to come by and check on her, too, which will piss her off."

Evie smiled. "It definitely will. But I'm glad you're going to stay. I'm going to see if I can get a flight home late tonight or tomorrow morning. I didn't cancel tomorrow's patients yet, and I hate to have people think they aren't my priority when I just started."

"I don't think that's the case, but I understand."

"Would it be okay with you if I came back? Her surgery is on Wednesday, and the doctor said she would only be in the hospital two or three days, so she'll likely be home Friday or Saturday. I could come down for the weekend."

"I'm sure she'd like that. Though I can only have you come back under one condition."

"Oh?"

"I'm paying for your flight. And I'm reimbursing you for the one you already paid for."

"No, it's fine. I'd have done it for Kitty even if you weren't my employer."

"I know you would have. But it will make me feel better."

She nodded, but I had a feeling she had no intention of giving me the bill, so I made a mental note to tell Joan in HR to put a bonus in her next check.

We went inside, and since the market was open today, I had some work to do and a bunch of calls to make. Evie went online and booked a ticket for 6 AM tomorrow morning and then said she was running to the store to pick up some things to make dinner.

It was almost six by the time I joined her in the kitchen. "It smells good in here."

"I'm making chicken piccata, but I think it's the cookies I'm baking that you smell."

"Uh-oh. Should I be nervous about why you're baking?"

She smiled. "No, I'm in a good mood. It was nice to be down here, and I'm relieved Kitty is feeling well and going to have the surgery."

"Yeah, me, too."

Evie turned to face me and leaned against the kitchen island. "Can I say something and you won't get offended?"

"That's never a good start to a conversation..."

She laughed. "It's not terrible. Just an observation."

I folded my arms across my chest and leaned against the counter across from her. "Go ahead. Lay it on me."

"Well, you're a very different person out of the office. You come across as cold and hard, but you're actually warm and soft."

"*Soft* is not a word a man likes to hear himself described as, for many reasons."

Evie smiled. "If you showed even just a glimpse of this side of you in the office, I think it would go a long way."

I looked down, quiet for a moment. "I think I might have forgotten that there was another side of me. Maybe the trip down here was a reminder I needed."

"Your grandmother is a special lady. She brings out the best in people."

I looked up and caught Evie's eye. "She is a special lady. But I'm not sure she's the one who brought about the change."

Evie's lips parted, and I couldn't stop staring at them for the longest time. When I finally forced my eyes up to meet hers, I found her watching me just as intently as I'd been watching her. But then...

"Merrick! We're back!" Grams yelled from the other room. "Just wanted to let you know in case we're walking in at a bad time."

Evie and I looked at each other, breaking into smiles. I wasn't sure if Grams had bad timing or good.

CHAPTER 18

Evie

I'd been looking forward to my Friday-morning patient all week for a few reasons. First, there were far more male traders than women, and I had only met with one other female trader so far. But secondly, Merrick had said Colette Archwood hated him. So I was curious what insight today's session might bring.

My sessions were forty-five minutes, and for the first forty of Colette's, we made small talk and I collected background. I hadn't picked up on any discord with her job or Merrick, at least not until now.

"So how did you come to work at Crawford Investments?" I asked her. "I feel like just about everyone I've spoken to so far had a connection to Merrick or one of the managers."

Colette frowned. "One of my close friends brought me on...Amelia Evans."

"Oh."

Colette sighed. "I take it you've heard about Amelia."

I usually prided myself on not showing a reaction or judgment during sessions, but apparently, I'd let my mask slip. I shook my head. "Only that she was one of the found-ers and that she passed away."

Colette harrumphed. "Passed away. That's a nice way of putting it."

My brows pulled together. "She didn't pass away?"

"Oh, no. She's dead alright. But passed away makes it sound...I don't know, peaceful. Like she was sick and when her time came, a sweet angel walked her to the Pearly Gates."

"Was she not sick?"

Colette shook her head. "Amelia died in an accident."

"I'm sorry."

"Actually, I wish she would have died *in* the accident. Then maybe she would've had some peace. But she lived for months after the crash. It was horrible. And the man you work for, whom we both work for, didn't give her one minute of peace."

"Merrick was in the accident, too?"

"No. He—"

My phone interrupted with a light chime to signify the end of our session. I grabbed it and turned it off. "I'm sorry about that. Go on..."

But the moment had passed. Colette straightened in her seat. "It's fine. I've learned over the years that I need to focus on good memories with Amelia and not her death. She was a very good friend—imperfect like all of us, but a woman I admired and loved." Colette stood. "It was very nice to meet you. I wish you the best of luck here at Craw-ford. Since our chat is confidential, there's no harm in tell-ing you this will probably be our only session. I'm leaving the firm soon. I have a little more than five weeks left."

"Oh, I didn't realize that."

She smiled. "That's because you're the only one who knows. I'm not giving notice. The day my employment contract expires will be my last day here. I've spent four years waiting for this day to come. Well, that's not true. I've only hated it here for three. But I do believe adding your position is a step in the right direction for the employees, many of whom I care about. So I mean it when I wish you good luck." Colette extended her hand before I could say anything else. "Take care, doc."

The first thing I did when we landed was turn on my phone. I'd taken an evening flight down to Atlanta after work, and we'd taken off a few minutes late, so it was eleven now that we were on the ground. It had been a long day, but it was important to me that I'd completed all of my appointments before heading to the airport at five.

By the time I grabbed my luggage and got an Uber, it would probably be midnight when I arrived at Kitty's. But she hadn't been discharged yet, so I wouldn't be interrupting her sleep by arriving so late. Merrick had offered to pick me up, but I'd declined, not wanting to put him out. Yet when my phone finished booting back up, the first thing I saw was a message from him. I swiped to read.

Merrick: I'm at the airport. Text me when you're walking out and I'll pull around.

Okay...well, so much for needing an Uber.

My bag came down the carousel pretty quickly, so I texted Merrick to let him know I'd be out in a minute. He was already waiting at the curb when I arrived. He stood next to the car, leaning against Kitty's hot rod wearing a black T-shirt and jeans—and dammit, if he didn't look sexier than ever.

He squinted at me as I approached. "What's going on in that head of yours? That's one hell of a mischievous smile you're wearing."

"I was just thinking how funny you look standing in front of Kitty's souped-up Charger."

"What? I can't pull off a hot rod?"

I smirked. "Definitely not."

Merrick took my luggage and lifted it into the trunk before opening the passenger door. "Listen, *Prius*, don't judge."

I pulled my seatbelt across my lap as he climbed in. "I told you I'd take an Uber. You didn't have to come out at close to midnight."

Merrick shrugged. "I don't mind. You're doing me a favor by coming. It's the least I can do."

"It's not a favor at all. Kitty is my friend."

He looked over and smiled warmly before returning his eyes to the road. "I know she is. That's one of the things I like about you. You're very loyal."

"One of the things, huh? That must mean there are others?"

Merrick chuckled. "How was the office this week?"

"Well, no fist fights broke out, so you being offsite must have a positive impact on the stress level," I teased.

"It was *one* fist fight."

I smiled. "The office was pretty quiet. I got to see a lot of new people, and I had lunch with Will one day."

"You had lunch with Will?"

"Yeah. He said he ordered the same Chinese food he always orders, but they arrived with your usual, too. So he had an extra meal. I guess they know you guys pretty well."

"How did that go?"

"Lunch with Will? It was fun. He makes me laugh."

Merrick had been smiling since I walked up to the car, but now his face wilted. His lips were pursed, and it seemed like he was jealous. I couldn't resist screwing with him.

"Will's single, right?"

The muscle in Merrick's jaw ticked. "Depends on the day of the week. Why?"

I shrugged. "Just curious."

His eyes narrowed. "I wouldn't go there."

"Go where?"

"It's not a good idea to get a crush on Will."

There was no mistaking the angry set of his jaw. "Oh? Is there a policy against office romances? I read the employee manual cover to cover, and I thought only supervisor-and-subordinate relationships were prohibited—like us, for example."

Merrick's grip on the steering wheel visibly tightened. "Will's not looking for anything serious."

"Maybe I'm not looking for anything serious, either. In fact, it's been a while, and a hookup sounds sort of appealing." At this point, I could barely keep myself from laughing. Merrick's face was red. He was so mad. What had started as a light and happy trip to Kitty's suddenly became heavy and quiet. I felt bad and cracked, laughing as I spoke. "I'm teasing. I'm not interested in Will in that way."

"Why the hell did you say all that?"

"It looked like it was pissing you off. I thought it was funny. Were you...*jealous*, Merrick?"

Merrick cleared his throat. "No."

I smiled. "Uh-huh."

"Why would I be jealous?"

"I don't know. Why *would you* be jealous?"

"I think you're misreading the situation."

"Mmm-hmmm."

Merrick rolled his eyes. But he was also no longer white-knuckling the steering wheel.

"How's Kitty?" I asked.

"The nurse told me that right before she went under the anesthesia, she asked the doctor if he could fix her up to be like a fifteen-year-old virgin again."

I covered my mouth and laughed. "She's such a trip."

"I think it's probably funnier when she isn't your grandmother."

"I'm sure. But she sounded great when I spoke to her. Although she's definitely very anxious to come home."

He nodded. "I wish they would keep her longer. She'll probably be released tomorrow morning."

It was after midnight when we got back to Kitty's house. The house was dark except for the light streaming from the hallway, but it was enough to illuminate the living room.

Merrick tossed the keys in the bowl on the table by the door and put his hands on his hips. "You gonna turn in? I'm going to have a glass of wine first, if you want to join me."

I set down my purse. "I'd love that."

Neither of us turned on any more lights, so when we sat together on the little couch in the dim room with our wine, it felt intimate. I traced my finger around the top of my glass, thinking how long it had been since I'd enjoyed this feeling.

"Thanks again for picking me up," I said.

Merrick smiled. "My pleasure."

I tilted my head. "We've come a long way from our first meeting, if you're saying it's a pleasure to be in my company."

He smiled again. "I guess we have."

I sipped my wine and stared into the glass. "Want to know a secret?"

"Do I have to share one too?"

I laughed. "No."

"Then sure."

"You used to make me nervous." I shrugged. "Not just during my interview when I wasn't sure if you recognized me or not. But even after that."

"How come?"

"I guess because I wanted to prove you wrong—that I wasn't incompetent. And part of me wasn't sure I could."

"You're good at your job. You've already given me things I can do to improve the work environment, and everyone seems to love you."

"Thank you. I feel like I'm good at my job again. I don't think I realized how much the events of the last six months had shaken my confidence. It's logical that finding out your fiancé is cheating would make you doubt relationships and the opposite sex, but it did so much more than that. It made me doubt things I'd been so certain of—like my professional abilities and my ability to make simple decisions. I think I felt like, if I had been so sure of my relationship that I was going to marry someone, what else could I be wrong about? Does that make sense?"

"It does." Merrick was quiet for a minute. "So I don't make you nervous anymore?"

I shook my head. "Not really."

He winked. "I'll have to try harder."

I smiled. "Give it your best shot, bossman."

Merrick chuckled. He leaned down and took off his shoes before kicking his feet onto the coffee table. "So who did you see this week?"

I rattled off my appointments in order as I mentally went through my schedule. I knew I'd met with sixteen people, so I counted on my fingers. At fourteen, I tapped my pointer to my lip, trying to figure out who I was missing. "Oh, I know. I forgot John McGrath. He was my first appointment when I got back. And Colette Archwood. She was my last session before I left today."

Merrick frowned. "How did things go with Colette?"

Confidentiality kept me from telling him that her days with Crawford Investments were numbered, and it also kept me from mentioning what she'd said about him and Amelia. So I answered vaguely.

"She was actually pretty open and forthcoming."

Merrick hung his head. "Oh boy. I guess I should be grateful you came back tonight if she was open with you."

I smiled and sipped my wine. "You've mentioned that you think she hates you."

"Not think, know. Mostly because she's told me as much. If I remember correctly, that was right before she spit in my face."

My eyes widened. "She *spit* in your face? Or do you mean she was so upset when she was yelling at you that she spittled?"

Merrick shook his head. "*Spit*. As in *hock-choo*. Coughed it up and all."

"And she still works for you? Is that because she has a contract?"

"All of my employment contracts have an insubordination clause that allows me to terminate anyone for being unprofessional or disrespectful."

"So why didn't you fire her?"

"It's complicated. At the time, emotions were running high. She was close with my ex and didn't know all the facts about what was going on. Trust me, I wanted to fire her. But what she did had nothing to do with business. It didn't even happen at the office, so I waited to see how she acted when I saw her at work the next time. I wasn't sure she'd show up the next day. But she did. She was frosty, but did her job, and she does her job well. And I was too caught up for months in other things to let it bother me much. By the time I had my head screwed back on, Colette and I had fallen into a speak-when-spoken-to relationship and mostly ignored each other. There's always been a management level between us at work, so we don't need to interact one-on-one much anyway." Merrick paused and looked down for a long time. "My ex, Amelia, had an accident. She was in the hospital for a long time. Colette didn't agree with some of the decisions I made as time progressed."

I nodded. "I'm sorry. I heard she was in an accident. But I didn't know any of the details. That must've been tough."

Merrick nodded and gulped back the rest of the wine in his glass. "Do you want some more?"

"No, thanks. I actually had two on the flight. I'll wind up with a headache in the morning if I have any more."

"Lightweight." He smiled and got up to refill his glass.

When he sat back down, it looked like his mind was elsewhere. He stared off at nothing in particular with wrinkles in his forehead. Eventually he drank down half of his new glass of wine and turned to face me. "You want to know a secret now?"

I rubbed my hands together. "Absolutely. I love secrets. My mom always teases that it's the reason I became a therapist."

Merrick smiled. "Well, don't get too excited. My secret isn't that thrilling."

"I'll take it anyway."

"I may have been biased against bringing on a therapist at the office for more reasons than I originally indicated."

"Oh?"

"Amelia and I were having some problems before her accident. We went to a therapist a few times. It didn't go well, so I might've been prejudiced by that."

"Wow. Okay. Well, that makes sense. If you didn't have success with it, it's no wonder you thought it was a waste of time."

Merrick nodded.

"Thank you for sharing that with me."

He smiled sort of sadly. "Thank Kitty."

"She encouraged you to tell me you'd been to counseling?"

He looked down into his glass. "Something like that."

There were so many questions spinning in my mind. Like why did they go to counseling? What decisions didn't Colette agree with after Amelia's accident? But I wasn't sure how long Merrick's openness might last, so I chose to ask the question I'd been most curious about, just in case it was the only question he answered.

"I hope you don't mind me being nosy, but could I ask how Amelia died? What kind of an accident was it?"

Merrick rubbed the back of his neck. "She died after a plane crash. She was taking lessons to get her small-craft pilot's license."

"Oh my God. That's awful. You weren't with her, were you?"

He finished off his second glass of wine and was quiet for a long moment before setting the glass on the table and shaking his head. "No, I wasn't with her. The other guy she was sleeping with was."

CHAPTER 19

Merrick

"When am I going to see my little Amelia Earhart in action?" I wrapped my hands around Amelia's waist. She was getting dressed to go to the weekly Sunday flying lesson she'd started a few months ago.

"You'll make me too nervous."

I frowned. "I'm going to call bullshit on that. You're missing the nervous gene."

Amelia wiggled out of my arms and grabbed a baseball hat before walking over to the mirror to position it on her head and pull her ponytail through the back. "You'll be a distraction, and I need to focus."

I could have argued, since we both knew she was full of shit. Ever since we'd moved in together last year, it felt like Amelia had taken up a half-dozen hobbies, none of which included me. Before flying lessons, it was sky diving and rock climbing, and before that she was flying all over the place on the weekends to play in poker tournaments. She'd always been a daredevil and an adrenaline junkie, but nothing like this.

"Don't pout." She walked back over and grabbed two fistfuls of my shirt. "Why don't you do what the couple's therapist said and get your own hobby?"

"Why don't you do what the therapist said and spend a little time with me?"

She rolled her eyes. "We spend eighty hours a week together at the office, and we live together."

"That's not spending time together. It's working and having a roommate."

She pushed up on her toes and pressed her lips to mine. "A roommate who let you wake me up this morning by sticking your dick in me."

I was about to remind her that it was the *only* time we'd had sex in two weeks, and interrupting her sleep was the only time I got from her lately, outside of discussing trades at the office. But the therapist had told us to try to avoid unnecessary confrontation, so I bit my tongue and kept things positive. "How about dinner tonight?"

"I probably won't be back until seven."

"It's fine. I have a mountain of work to do at the office. I'll make us a reservation for eight at that little Italian place we ordered from that you liked."

She nodded. "Okay. Why don't I meet you there in case I'm late?"

I kissed her forehead. "Sounds like a plan. Stay safe. Don't go rogue on your instructor like you do your business partner most days."

She finally cracked a smile. "I'll try. No promises."

***

"Would you like another cocktail, sir?"

I shook the ice in my empty glass. "Sure, why not? Apparently I need something to occupy my time."

The waiter smiled and nodded. After he walked away, I checked my phone for the tenth time: eight thirty-five now and no missed calls. Amelia had texted around five thirty, right before she was about to go up for her lesson. She'd said they were getting a late start and confirmed she'd meet me at the restaurant. But even if she didn't take off until six, her forty-five-minute, in-air lesson would have been done in time to get here at eight.

Fifteen minutes later, I'd sucked back my second drink, there was still no sign of her, and my calls kept going to voicemail. So I raised my hand to call the waiter.

"I'm sorry. It looks like the person I've been waiting for is not coming to dinner."

"No problem. Would you like to order for yourself?"

I shook my head. "Just the check, please."

He nodded. "Of course."

After I signed the bill, I took cash from my wallet and tossed enough on the table to cover the hour I'd wasted. As I got up, my phone buzzed.

"About time," I grumbled.

But when I pulled my cell out, it wasn't Amelia's number on the screen. Though it was a local one, so I swiped to answer anyway.

"Hello?"

"Hi, is this Mr. Crawford?"

"It is. Who's this?"

"My name is Lucy Cooper. I'm an ER nurse over at Memorial Hospital."

I froze. "Memorial Hospital? Did something happen to Amelia?"

"I'm sorry to tell you this, but there's been an accident."

"What kind of an accident? Is she okay?"

"Ms. Evans was in a plane crash. She's in very serious condition, Mr. Crawford."

A giant lump formed in my throat and made it hard to speak. "I'm on my way."

"Can you tell me where Amelia Evans is?" I'd paid the Uber driver an extra five-hundred bucks to blow any light he could to get to the hospital faster.

The woman behind the glass frowned. "And who are you to Ms. Evans?"

"I'm her fiancé."

She nodded. "I was here when she came in. I think they took her upstairs. But let me check."

She disappeared and came back a few minutes later. "May I see some identification, please?"

I pulled out my wallet and slid my license through the opening at the bottom of the glass. The woman examined it and slid it back. "Thank you. Ms. Evans is upstairs. They're prepping her for surgery. But the gentleman who came in with her said he was her husband. They both came in via ambulance and went straight to the back, so I didn't question it or see any ID."

My brows pulled together. "Amelia doesn't have a husband."

The woman offered an apologetic smile. "Sometimes people lie about who they are so we won't kick them out since they aren't family. But your name is in our system as Ms. Evans's next of kin. It's on file from a prior admission for surgery."

I nodded. "When her appendix ruptured last year."

"Anyway." She pointed to the left. "You can come on through the door. I'll buzz you back. Then you're going to walk straight down the hall to the elevator bank and go up to the fifth floor. The nurses at the station on the surgery floor should be able to give you an update on her condition."

"Thank you."

I saw a large desk right when I stepped onto the floor, so I walked over and waited for the woman in blue scrubs to get off the phone. When she hung up, I couldn't even wait for her to acknowledge me. "I'm here for Amelia Evans. The nurse in the ER said she was in surgery. Can someone tell me what's going on?"

"And you are..."

"Her fiancé, Merrick Crawford."

The nurse looked over to a waiting area. There was a guy sitting by himself. He had his head in his hand and was tugging at his hair.

"Then who's that?"

I looked over again. This time, the guy looked up. Our eyes met, and a look of recognition seemed to come across his face. That made him the only one who understood anything around here. I turned back to the nurse. "I have no idea who the hell that is."

The guy stood and walked over. He looked hesitant. "I'm Amelia's flight instructor, Aaron." He turned to the nurse. "This is Amelia's fiancé."

The nurse frowned and shook her head. "Can I see some ID from both of you, please?"

I again pulled my license from my pocket, while the guy standing next to me shook his head. "I don't have anything on me. I leave my wallet and phone in a locker when I do lessons."

The nurse ignored him. She typed into her computer, and then her eyes moved back and forth from the screen to my ID. "I'm sorry, Mr. Crawford. There seems to have been some confusion."

"Whatever. I don't care. Can you just tell me how Amelia is?"

She nodded. "Of course." She started to speak but then stopped and looked over at Amelia's instructor. "Can you excuse us, please?"

"Oh... Yeah, of course."

Aaron walked back to the waiting area. The nurse lowered her voice. "How much do you know so far?"

I shook my head. "Not a damn thing."

She nodded. "Okay. Well, Ms. Evans was brought in following a small-plane crash. She suffered serious injuries to the head and spine. The head injury she sustained is sometimes called a hinge fracture, but it's basically a fracture of the skull. We were told by the crew that brought her in that the top of the aircraft collapsed on impact, so that's possibly what caused the injury."

I raked a hand through my hair. "Jesus Christ. Is she going to be okay?"

The nurse's face was solemn. "The impact has caused swelling in her brain, and the doctors are working on relieving some of that. The next few hours are going to be crucial. She also suffered a few broken vertebrae, which the doctors will treat if they're able to stop the swelling."

"If...they're able to stop the swelling? What happens if they can't?"

The nurse shook her head. "It's imperative that they do, Mr. Crawford."

I felt like I was in a dream after that. The nurse kept talking, but her words sort of floated through the air around me, unable to sink in. When she was done, her eyes darted over my face.

"Are you okay?"

I shook my head. "How long will she be in surgery?"

"It's hard to say. But she has an amazing team of doctors working on her. She only went in about fifteen minutes ago. I'll go back in a little while and see if they can give me any update, okay?"

I nodded. "Okay. Thanks."

She motioned to the waiting room. "Why don't you take a seat? Ms. Evans had some jewelry and personal items on her when she came in. We removed them in case of swelling. I'll go in the patient safe and get them for you, and you can sign for them. I also have some paperwork you can fill out for her."

"Okay."

Even though she'd told me to take a seat, I stood at the desk after she disappeared, trying to make sense of everything. After a while, I remembered Amelia's flight instructor was here. Maybe he could tell me something more. So I walked over. But just as I started to ask him, the nurse came with a Ziploc bag and some papers clipped to a clipboard. Looking down, she lifted the top page.

"Okay, so I have here that we collected two necklaces and one engagement ring." She held out the bag to me. "I just need you to double-check what we're turning over to you and sign for them at the bottom of this page."

I nodded. "Okay."

She passed me the clipboard and a pen, along with the baggie. I scribbled my name and handed the papers back to her before looking down at the bag.

"Thank you." She nodded. But as she walked away, I lifted the Ziploc to see what was inside. There were two necklaces I recognized right away. But the engagement ring...was definitely not hers.

The nurse was already halfway to her desk, so I called after her. "Hang on a second."

She turned back. "Is something wrong?"

I shook my head. "This isn't Amelia's engagement ring."

Her forehead wrinkled. "I took the jewelry off of Ms. Evans myself."

"Well, this isn't her engagement ring."

The flight instructor stood. "It's Amelia's ring." He frowned. "Just not the one from you. That's the one from me."

CHAPTER 20

Evie

On Saturday morning, I slept later than I wanted to. Merrick was already showered and dressed, drinking coffee in the kitchen when I walked in. He held up his mug and smiled.

"Morning, sleepyhead."

"I can't believe how late it is—almost seven thirty. Why didn't you wake me? Kitty can be discharged as early as eight."

"She called this morning. She developed a fever last night, so they're doing some bloodwork now to make sure it's not an infection." He shook his head. "If she gets out today, it's definitely not going to be early. So I figured I wouldn't wake you."

"Oh no. That's not good. An infection after surgery can be serious."

He nodded. "Hers is a low-grade fever, right at a hundred. The nurse made the mistake of telling Kitty that some people can go home if the fever is very low. But someone her age they usually keep to monitor."

I covered my laugh with my hand. "Oh shit. And that nurse now has a cast that matches Kitty's."

"I wouldn't be surprised."

I sat down at the table across from Merrick. His eyes fell to my chest and lingered, causing me to look down. *Shit*. I'd forgotten to put on a bra. It was warm in my bedroom, but the kitchen window was wide open, and the temperature change had my nipples peaked against my thin T-shirt.

Merrick cleared his throat and looked away. "Anyway, Kitty asked me to ask you if you would mind bringing her some monkey bread. I don't know what that is, but she said you'd know."

I smiled. "It was my grandmother's specialty. It's sort of like a cinnamon bun, but made into a cake. My grandmother made it with southern-style biscuits and loads of sticky cinnamon-sugar icing. Not exactly healthy, but everyone loved it, especially Kitty."

"Where do we get some?"

"I make it." I stood and walked over to the fridge. "It doesn't take very long. If she has all the ingredients, I can make the buns and then hop in the shower while they cook." I started to pull out things I'd need. "It looks like she only has one stick of butter, and I'll need more than that."

"Make me a list. I'll run to the store."

"You don't mind?"

"Not at all."

"Okay." I finished searching the cabinets and wrote down three things I needed. "I'll get in the shower while you're gone to save time."

He nodded. "Sounds like a plan."

A little while later, we were back in the kitchen together. I tossed the biscuit ingredients into a bowl and started to whisk. "Can I ask you something?"

"No."

I turned to look at Merrick. He grinned. "I've learned that whenever you say, 'Can I ask you something?', it means you want to get inside my head."

"I think you're exaggerating."

He sipped his second cup of coffee. "I'm not. But I was teasing. What do you want to ask?"

"Last night you said you'd had a bad experience with therapy. Why do you feel it didn't work out? I'm not asking to pry into your problems but to understand your experience in a clinical way."

Merrick rubbed along the rim of his coffee cup a moment. "I'm not sure you can fix things the patient doesn't perceive as broken."

"Are you referring to Amelia or yourself?"

He shrugged. "I don't even know anymore. To be really honest, it was my idea to go to couple's therapy, but I didn't feel like *we* needed therapy. I mostly did it because I was hoping someone could fix Amelia. She was the type of person you could only get so close to or get to know so much. She had a wall she kept up. I guess I thought the therapist could help break it down or something."

"Was she receptive to therapy?"

Merrick shook his head. "In hindsight, I think she was doing the same thing as I was—going so the therapist could fix me."

"She thought you were broken?"

"Just like I couldn't understand why I couldn't get closer to her, she couldn't understand why I would want to."

I nodded. "If you go into couple's therapy hoping it will change your partner, that's usually not a good sign. You have to be in the mindset that it will help you."

Merrick tilted his mug at me. "Which is why I had an issue with my employees being required to go to therapy. They need to believe in it and want it for it to work."

"True. But what we're trying to accomplish in the office isn't all that different from couple's therapy. If you look at management as the people on the other side of the relationship with the employee, the goal is to get both parties to take ownership for things that happen and make changes to avoid a repeat in the future. Just like with couple's therapy, if one side thinks it's all the other side's fault and are just waiting for them to change, it won't work."

Merrick nodded. "Okay. I get it. I'll try to be more open. Can I ask you a question now?"

"Uh-oh. Does this mean you're trying to get into my head?"

Merrick smiled. "I guess I learned from the best."

I finished the biscuit mix and began spooning dollops into a muffin pan. "What's your question?"

"You seem to get a solid grasp on people's mental state so quickly. Yet you didn't see what was going on with your fiancé?"

I shook my head. "Didn't you ever hear about the plumber with leaky pipes?"

Merrick laughed. "I guess."

"The bottom line is therapists are human. We're trained to help others and look for certain things, but sometimes we don't examine our own relationships enough."

"How do you learn to trust again after going through what you did?"

"Are you asking for me or for you?"

Merrick shrugged. "I'm not sure anymore, doc."

I smiled. "I think there's always a risk in love. But when the right person comes along, we'll feel like it's worth taking that risk."

Merrick looked into my eyes. My heart raced, and my belly felt all melty at the same time. But then his cell phone rang. He looked down. "It's my grandmother. She probably wants to make sure I asked you about the monkey bread."

He swiped to answer and lifted the phone to his ear, still looking at me. "Hey, Grams, what's up?" He smiled. "Yes, Evie is making it right now."

I turned around to put the tray in the oven and set the timer. The moment had been ruined, but it was just as well. Merrick didn't seem anxious to continue our conversation after he hung up either.

"I'm going to go get ready while that's in the oven," I said.

He nodded. "I need to make some calls before we head to the hospital. I'll do that in here and listen for the timer."

"Thanks."

When I came back, Merrick was on the phone with Will, his nose buried in some chart on his laptop screen. "Alright, that sounds like a plan," he said. "Start slow on Monday, so we don't set off any alarms with people watching us who might jump on without knowing why we're buying." He was quiet. "I'm not sure. If she gets out today, I'll have a better idea. I want to see how she feels once she's home. Yesterday I mentioned having a visiting nurse come in when I left, and she told me not to let the door hit me or the nurse in the ass on my way out. So we'll see..."

I heard Will talking again, and then Merrick's eyes jumped to me. "Don't be a dick. Goodbye, Will."

I chuckled as he swiped his phone off. "That conversation seemed to take a quick turn."

Merrick shook his head. "It's one of the dangers of working with your friend. He doesn't know how to stick to business when he should."

I opened the oven and took out the monkey bread, setting it on the stovetop to cool.

"Holy shit. That smells incredible," Merrick said.

"You want a piece?"

"Hell yeah."

I cut off a chunk for each of us and brought it over to the table. "It's better than an orgasm when it's hot."

Merrick's eyes gave a wicked gleam before he bit in. "That sounds like a challenge, Dr. Vaughn."

"Oh, doc," Kitty said. "This is the lady I was telling you about this morning."

I turned to smile at the physician in the room. Wow. *Just wow.* The doctors didn't look like this when I was in the hospital, that's for sure.

He smiled and flashed perfect teeth as he extended his hand. "Therapist, right?"

I shook. "Yes."

"Ms. Harrington here tells me you went to Emory."

"I did."

Kitty put her hand on the doctor's arm. "I told you to call me Kitty."

He smiled and nodded before turning his attention back to me. "Ms.—I mean, Kitty and I figured out that you would've started the semester after I graduated."

Yeah, I definitely would've remembered if I'd seen this guy on campus.

"Dr. Martin is single, dear," Kitty said. "He almost went into psychiatry. And he likes to hike. I was telling him all about your land and your Airbnbs. You two should grab some coffee when he goes on his break. I bet you have a lot in common."

"Did the doctor spend any time examining you?" a stern voice from behind me asked. "Or was he too busy using his patient as a matchmaker?"

Oh boy. The look on Merrick's face could only be described as murderous. His eyes were narrowed, jaw set hard, and he stood with his hands folded across his chest.

I flashed him a dirty look which he promptly ignored, so I shook my head and spoke to the doctor. "I'm sorry."

Dr. Martin looked back and forth between Merrick and me and gave a curt nod. "Why don't we move on to Ms. Harrington's health, shall we?"

For the next fifteen minutes, Dr. Martin went over Kitty's post-op stats, current vitals, and what they had done so far to rule out less-common causes of her fever. "It's not unusual to have a low-grade fever after a big surgery like Ms. Harrington had. Most likely, it's an inflammatory stimulus reaction to tissue damage and the exposure to foreign materials that occurs during surgery. It almost always resolves on its own within a few days. But because she also broke her ankle and is in a cast, and she's not moving around so much, she's at a higher risk of DVTs. These type of blood clots can also cause a low-grade fever. We did a sonogram to rule that out, but we're going to keep her monitored for another day or two and do a repeat before we discharge her to be sure."

I nodded. "That makes a lot of sense."

The doctor smiled at Kitty. "To be clear, this has nothing to do with age. I'd recommend the same to a thirty-year-old."

I laughed, knowing Kitty had already read him the riot act. "Good to know."

Dr. Martin looked to all three of us. "Any questions?"

I turned to Kitty and Merrick. Merrick still looked cross, but he shook his head. "I'm good. Thank you."

The doctor nodded to Kitty. "I'll stop back later before my shift ends to check on you."

Kitty batted her eyelashes. "Thank you, doc."

After he left, she fanned herself. "If only I was twenty years younger."

Merrick raised a brow. "Twenty?"

She squinted at him. "It's going to hurt a lot more than usual when I kick you in the ass with this cast on."

I chuckled. "I'm sorry you're not going to get to go home today like you'd hoped. But they're being thorough and taking good care of you."

"Oh that one was thorough alright," Merrick grumbled.

Kitty's eyes gleamed. "Something wrong, my darling grandson?"

"It's hot in here," he mumbled. "I'm going downstairs to the cafeteria to get something to drink. Either of you want anything?"

"No, thank you," I said.

Kitty barely waited until Merrick was out the door. Her smile bordered on wicked. "That one has it bad."

CHAPTER 21

Evie

"You two should go," Kitty said. "You've been here all day."

Merrick looked up from the newspaper he'd been reading. "Visiting hours end in fifteen minutes."

Kitty pointed to her iPad on the hospital tray next to her bed. "Oh, that's plenty of time for me to show you the updated family tree..."

Merrick shut the paper and stood. "On second thought, we probably shouldn't wait for them to kick us out."

I chuckled at Kitty's smirk. She certainly knew how to push her grandson's buttons.

I stood. "I'm leaving tomorrow afternoon, but I'll be back in the morning. My flight isn't until four."

"Don't rush back early, sweetheart. Get some sleep. I appreciate you coming at all."

I bent and hugged her, then stepped aside so Merrick could say goodnight.

Outside, it was a beautiful evening. The air was warm and unusually dry for late summer in Atlanta. When we approached Kitty's hot rod, I got an idea. "Can we put the top down on the car? I've never been in a convertible."

"Really?" Merrick said.

"Nope, never."

He shrugged. "Sure."

I was surprised that folding away the ragtop was as easy as pushing a button. Before we were even out of the parking lot, I was in love with the feeling of the wind blowing through my hair. I held my hands in the air. "This is ahhmazing."

Merrick looked over. "You're not very hard to please."

He made a left and a right and then we were on the highway, going pretty fast. I let my head fall back and stared up at the dark sky as my hair whipped all around me.

"You hungry?" Merrick yelled over the wind.

"Starving! Can we get junk food?"

He smiled. "Whatever you want. Did you have something particular in mind?"

"How about Wendy's?"

He narrowed his eyes. "Cute."

I laughed. "Any chance you know a place called Mix'D Up Burgers? It's not exactly on the way back to the house. It's more on the way to my Airbnbs. I stumbled on it one night when I was trying to find gas."

"I don't know it, but I'm sure I can put it in the GPS."

"I'd be your best friend if you did."

He handed me his phone. "Here, type it into Waze and see if it comes up."

It did, and I spent the rest of the drive enjoying the warm breeze while salivating at the thought of what I was going to order. When we arrived, Merrick pulled into the parking lot. "You want to go inside to eat or take it home?"

"Can we order a meal and eat the fries on the way home?"

He smiled. "Good plan. "Do you know what you want?"

"I do. I want The Pile. It's a burger loaded with cheesy fries. But you also get a side order of fries."

He laughed. "You're killing me. Between the monkey bread this morning and now this, I'm going to have to hit the gym a little harder next week."

"Oh God. Don't remind me. I don't even want to think about weight. I've been on a junk food tear since my wedding debacle."

Merrick's eyes raked down my torso, stopping to linger on my breasts. "Trust me, junk food works for you."

"Do you mind waiting out here a second?" Merrick unlocked Kitty's front door and pushed it open halfway.

"Umm, sure?"

He held out the fast-food bag to me. "I'll just be a minute."

"Alright, but I'm going to eat your dinner if you take too long."

"You already ate most of the fries we were supposed to share."

Two minutes later, he came back outside, carrying two familiar mugs. My eyes lit up. "Oh my God! The Waffle House mugs they used to drink their spiked tea from. You know they stole those from the restaurant."

Merrick smiled. "That doesn't surprise me."

I sighed. "Those bring back such great memories." I pointed over to what had been my grandmother's house. "They would sit on that porch for hours every night getting loaded, and all the neighbors saw were two little old ladies drinking hot tea."

He smiled. "I know. Guess what's in here?"

"Don't tell me it's spiked sweet tea?"

"Yep." He nodded toward the house next door. "The neighbors who bought your grandmother's house are away. I met them earlier this week. When they mentioned they were going out of town, I asked if they would mind if the old owner's granddaughter sat on their porch. You said you'd give anything to bring back the sweet-tea days. I know it's not the same, but I figured we can eat on the rocking chairs and drink the spiked stuff."

My heart swelled. "I can't believe you did that for me."

He nodded toward the porch. "Come on. Let's go over."

At first it was strange to sit on my grandmother's porch without her here. But when we were done eating and sat on the rocking chairs, doing nothing but sipping out of our Waffle House mugs, I felt a warmth in my chest.

"How did you know they drank out of these particular mugs? I don't think I mentioned it the other day."

"You didn't. My grandmother did."

"Oh."

"She's pretty much talked about you or your grandmother all week. I think having you down here brought up a lot of memories for her, too." He held up his mug. "She must really love you, because she gave me her spiked sweet tea recipe when I said I wanted to make it for you. You know southern women hold their tea recipes just below the Bible when it comes to sacred things."

I smiled. "Well, the feeling is mutual."

We sat side by side, rocking and sipping quietly for a few minutes. Eventually, I pointed to a house a few doors down and across the street. "Remember the story I told you about when I almost fell from my treehouse in the rain? That I thought a boy named Cooper saved me?"

Merrick nodded. "I remember."

"That was his house. He had a dog with three legs named Woody."

Merrick squinted down the dark street. "I remember the dog. He used to walk on his back two legs like a human, right?"

"That's the one."

"Yeah, I remember the dog. But I don't remember the kid."

"I definitely do. He was also my first kiss."

"Really?"

"Yep. I'm sure he remembers me, too. Because aside from being his first kiss, I also caused his first dental procedure."

"Did he go in for the kiss too fast and your teeth clashed or something?"

"Worse. But let me stop my story and give you a little background. When I was fifteen, we were living in Chicago. All of my friends had kissed boys before, but I wasn't anxious to start down that road because I already had trust issues because of my dad. Anyway, a cute boy in my school asked me out, and we went to a movie. He had the absolute worst breath. I mean, I was sitting in the theatre and could smell it next to me, even when he wasn't facing my way." I shook my head. "I don't know if it was the braces or what, but it was horrendous, and I was dying for the movie to be over. Long story short, he tried to kiss me at the end of the night, and I stopped him. He accused me of being a prude. So to defend myself, I told him the truth—that his breath smelled like ass."

Merrick cracked up. "So you haven't changed much from fifteen, huh?"

"*Anyway*, the next day he lied and told the whole school that he had kissed me, and I was the worst kisser ever." I shook my head. "I obviously knew what really happened, but I developed a paranoia that I was going to be a terrible kisser. Dumb, I know. But whatever. Fast forward to the following summer, and I'm now sixteen and still haven't had my first kiss. We came down to visit my grandmother for a week, and me and Cooper used to ride bikes together. I knew he was attracted to me, and he seemed like a nice kid, so I figured maybe it would finally happen. One night, he'd gotten a flat tire on his bike, and we were in his garage. I was holding the box wrench when he pulled off the tire, and when he stood to take it from me, he told me I was beautiful and leaned in for a kiss. At the last second, I remembered I had eaten fish for dinner and not yet brushed my teeth, so I lifted my hand to my mouth. Except I still had the box wrench in my hand. He chipped his front tooth on it."

"Damn. Poor guy."

"I know. I felt so bad that I came back the next morning and kissed him."

"I bet you cleaned your teeth first."

"I definitely did! I think I scrubbed them for ten full minutes."

We both laughed at that. It felt so good to sit here again. "So let's hear your story," I said.

"What story?"

"Your first kiss."

He smiled. "Ah... Daniella Dixon. Her parents knew what they were doing when they gave her the initials of double D."

I play-shoved his arm. "So the obsession started at an early age, huh? I've seen your eyes linger on my boobs more than once."

Merrick's eyes glinted as they dropped again now, speaking directly to my breasts. "You started it, showing them to me in that dressing room."

I laughed and pointed up. "Eyes up here. Now go on with your story about Daniella."

Merrick shrugged. "Not much to tell. She was a little older, and we made out in her basement."

"How much older?"

"Two years, I think. I was fourteen, and she was sixteen. As far as I remember, her breath was okay, and I didn't injure her."

I smiled. "Boring."

"I'll take boring over bad breath any day."

I pointed to him. "True."

He knocked back the rest of his drink. "You want another?"

"Sure."

When I went to get up, he stopped me. "I got it. Enjoy the porch."

Rather than thinking of the many times I'd spent in this exact spot with my grandmother, I couldn't stop thinking about the man who'd arranged this. It was such a simple gesture—asking the neighbor if we could sit here and making the drinks that brought back good memories for me—yet it meant so much more than that.

Merrick listened to me. He paid attention. We'd certainly started out on the wrong foot, but this week he'd even implemented my suggestion to mandate that employees use the majority of their vacation time. It was funny—normally it felt like your boss stood in front of you, but with Merrick, it felt like he stood beside me. He was also smart, cared deeply for his grandmother, and I was insanely attracted to him. Not to mention, he'd made it clear that he was into me.

So why was I afraid to give us a chance?

While I mulled that over, Merrick came back with our drinks. He passed me mine before sitting back down.

"What time is your flight tomorrow?"

"Four."

He nodded. "As long as she gets out Monday, I'll probably come home by the end of the week. I contacted a skilled nursing company. I just hope she lets them in when I make the arrangements."

"Oh, that reminds me. When I stepped out of Kitty's hospital room to go to the ladies' room, one of the doctors talked to me about some equipment that might help her at home, at least until her cast comes off. I didn't mention it in front of Kitty because I figured you might want to ask for forgiveness, rather than permission. I have a brochure for the company in my purse."

"Which one?" Merrick asked.

"Well, there's a chair that looks like a recliner, but it tips forward to help the person stand. And there's also a motorized base for under her mattress that can help her get up with less struggle."

"No. I didn't mean which equipment. I meant which doctor approached you?"

"Her doctor, Dr. Martin."

Merrick frowned. "Did he write his number on the back of the brochure?"

"Jealous much?"

"My grandmother was trying to goad me by setting the two of you up."

"And...did it work?" I didn't realize I'd bitten down on my bottom lip until Merrick's eyes fell. He groaned and shook his head.

"Of course it did. I'm jealous of your damn teeth right now—and that little shit whose tooth you chipped, too."

I snort-laughed. The alcohol was definitely starting to go to my head, but I loved that Merrick and I could talk this way.

We stayed on the porch for hours after that, rocking and laughing, all while sipping spiked tea from Waffle House mugs. At midnight, I still wasn't ready to call it a night, but it started to drizzle, and the warm breeze blew it into our faces.

I took off my wet glasses and wiped them dry with my shirt.

"You ready to go in?" Merrick said.

The truth was, the longer I spent with him, the more I fell. So while I would've been perfectly happy sitting in the rain a little longer, I nodded. "Yeah, I don't have windshield wipers for my glasses."

He took my empty mug and his, and together we walked next door. The house was dark and quiet, with only the light from the front porch illuminating the room. Since we'd walked across the grass, our shoes were wet, and we both slipped them off at the front door.

"You going to bed?" Merrick asked.

I nodded. "Yeah, I probably should."

Merrick shoved his hands into his pockets. "I'll see you in the morning."

In the guest room, I leaned my head against the door. I heard Merrick walking around for a few minutes and then footsteps grew louder as he entered the small hallway just outside my door. The two bedrooms we were sleeping in were separated only by the bathroom, so I expected to hear a door open and close, but instead there was stillness. Had he gone that quietly, or was he standing in the hallway right outside the door, struggling like I was?

I couldn't remember the last time I'd wanted a man as much as I did Merrick. It made me feel like Christian had done me a favor. He and I had been perfect on paper—compatible and goal oriented. We got along well enough before everything blew up. But I'd never realized what was missing until now: passion. I felt heat in my belly when I was near Merrick—whether that was arguing our views or tracing the broadness of his shoulders when he wasn't paying attention. Deep down, I knew what the problem was. Sure, he was my boss and I'd made that mistake before, so it would be stupid of me to go there, but that wasn't the reason I'd been keeping him at arm's length. The real reason was that the feelings he ignited in me scared me. I'd kept away from anything that caused highs and lows for all of my adult life, preferring to sail smoothly down comfortable lane. With my past, you didn't have to be a therapist to understand why I'd take that route.

I was afraid of passion. My parents had it. They'd swung from crazy in love to him abusing her. It was like a pendulum that never stopped. So I'd sought the metronome of relationships—one steady beat that never got out of sync.

Outside in the hallway, things were still quiet. I started to think I just hadn't heard Merrick go into his room—until I heard movement outside my door. I held my breath as my heart raced, expecting him to knock. But then the footsteps fell away. When the other bedroom door finally clanked open and closed, I let out a disappointed breath.

It's better this way.

At least that's what I told myself as I got ready for bed and slipped under the covers. But when I shut my eyes, my thoughts went in the opposite direction. I wanted Merrick in the worst way. I wanted him to bite my lip and be jealous. I wanted the fire I saw in his eyes to come alive in his touch. Forget the romance—brushing my hair behind my ear, the sweet things he said to me—I wanted the man to lift me over his shoulder and drag me to his bed like a damn caveman.

The vision of that in my head caused a thin sheen of sweat on my forehead. I was never going to fall asleep with every muscle in my body knotted in a tight ball of lust. Frustrated, I stared up at the ceiling for a long time.

I knew what I needed to do to fall asleep. But Merrick's room was only eight feet away down the hall.

What if he heard me?

Though I could be quiet, couldn't I?

Oh my God, what if he was doing the exact same thing right at this moment?

That was it. The thought of his big hand wrapped around his cock was too much to bear. So I closed my eyes, slipped one hand under the covers, and skimmed my fingers over the smooth skin of my belly until I reached the lace of my panties. My clit was already swollen, just thinking about what was to come, so I spread my legs wide and dipped my hand inside. This was going to set a record for how quickly I could get myself off...*or so I thought.*

But for some reason, I couldn't get there. Two fingers massaged my clit in small circles. I felt tension build, but it wasn't enough to push me over. I tried to imagine the fingers were Merrick's and slipped them inside myself. It felt so damn good. My breathing quickened as I found my rhythm, fingers pumping in and out of my wetness.

Thoughts of Merrick flashed in my mind.

Him lying on the couch with his bulging cock and flat stomach.

That sexy line of hair that led from his belly button down into his underwear.

The V—that damn V. I imagined my tongue licking up and down the deep crease of it.

Merrick standing in his office, fully dressed in a suit with his feet spread wide and arms folded over his chest in a power stance. Lord, he was almost as sexy dressed.

Oh.

Yeah. That's it.

So close.

I panted as I raced toward the finish line. When I thought I was about to get there, I reached my thumb up to touch my clit, knowing that almost always detonated the impending explosion.

It felt good, great even, but no matter how gently or firmly I rubbed, how fast or slow I pumped into myself, I couldn't close the deal. I even tried using my other hand to massage my breasts and pinch my nipples, but it was impossible. After a while, definitely longer than I'd ever had to pleasure myself before, I finally gave up.

God, I can't even do that right.

Frustrated and on edge, I blamed Merrick.

The man had stolen my damn orgasm.

Another half hour or so went by, but I still couldn't relax enough to fall asleep. I thought maybe I'd make some chamomile tea—perhaps the warm drink could help me wind down a little. So I got out of bed and creaked open my door. There was no possible way I could face Merrick after what I'd just done to thoughts of him. Luckily, his bedroom door was closed, and I didn't hear any signs of moving around. So I slipped out of my room and tiptoed to the kitchen. But when I pushed the door open, I froze.

Fuck.

Merrick was inside, leaning against the counter, and he wore only a pair of low-hanging gray sweatpants—no shirt or shoes.

"Hey." His voice was gravelly.

I couldn't look at him, so I spoke to his feet. "What are you doing up?"

I didn't raise my eyes, but I could see through my peripheral vision that he lifted a glass. "Couldn't sleep. Came out for some water."

I nodded and went to the kitchen cabinet next to where he stood, still not able to look at him. Though I definitely felt his eyes following me.

"Everything alright?"

"Sure. Just thirsty, too."

Merrick went silent. He didn't say a word while I took down a glass, walked to the sink, and ran the water before filling my cup.

"You feel okay?"

I guzzled almost the entire glass before answering. "Fine, why?"

He reached out and felt my forehead. "Your face is red." He brushed the back of his hand over my cheek. "And you're clammy."

I tried to hide my embarrassment, but I felt my face heating even more. "I was under the covers. That room gets warm."

Again, he was quiet, and I continued to stare down at his feet.

Seriously? Even his stupid feet were sexy.

Tension built in the room with every second that passed. Eventually Merrick set his drink on the counter. He slipped the glass from my hand and set it next to his. My eyes darted up, but I quickly looked away.

"Look at me, Evie."

Fuck.

The moment was already awkward, and all I wanted to do was run back to my room and hide under the covers. But that would make things even worse. So instead, I put on my big-girl panties and took a deep breath before looking up.

Our gazes locked, and I watched as Merrick studied me. Long seconds ticked by as my heart ricocheted against my rib cage. I watched in fascination as his pupils grew darker and larger, and a ghost of a devilish smirk tugged at the corner of his lips. Merrick shifted from next to me to in front of me, putting one hand on either side of the counter.

"You want me as much as I want you, Evie. I can see it."

I felt like a deer caught in the headlights with a car barreling down the road. Yet I couldn't seem to get my feet to move. Maybe they didn't want to.

Merrick's eyes were filled with so much heat, I actually started to sweat.

"Tell me I'm wrong," he said.

"You're..." It felt like he could see right through me, so rather than lie, I told him something that was true. "You're my boss, Merrick."

He looked down for a minute before locking eyes with me again. "Is that the only reason?"

"Isn't that enough?"

A wicked grin spread across his face. He held up one finger and then took a few steps to grab his cell from the kitchen table. Looking at me, he swiped and tapped before holding his cell up to his ear.

"Who are you calling? It's after one in the morning."

He held my eyes as he spoke into the phone. "Hi, Joan."

My eyes flared. He was *not* calling the head of HR in the middle of the night, was he?

Merrick listened for a minute and then nodded. "Yeah, everything is fine. I'm sorry if I woke you. But I've been struggling with something and wanted to run it by you."

I couldn't hear what she said, but I was positive we were both thinking the same thing: Our boss is a damn crazy person.

He continued. "I think it's best that we build a wall between myself and Evie Vaughn. If employees are supposed to be able to confide in her, they should know her boss can't pressure her to reveal anything they might disclose. The best way to do that is to not have her report to me."

My mouth dropped open.

Merrick looked over and covered the phone. He motioned with his hand for me to close my mouth and whispered, "Rest that jaw. I'll need it open later."

Oh

My

God.

He continued on the phone without missing a beat. "I think it's best she reports to you for day-to-day issues. And since the board brought her on, they should have hiring and firing authority."

Merrick's eyes sparkled as he stared at me, still listening on the phone. After a minute, he smiled. "Perfect. Except this can't wait until next week. I'd like it to be effective immediately. Thanks, Joan. Sorry again for waking you."

He swiped his phone off and tossed it on the table, looking pretty damn proud of himself. "Problem solved. Anything else we need to take care of?"

He looked at me with so much determination, I got the feeling I could tell him the house needed to be picked up and moved, and he'd find a way to lift it onto his back.

Something Kitty said to me a while ago suddenly jumped to the forefront. *"If you want to be happy, you need to see it in your future and believe it. Find a new path, you can't be afraid to try new turns. Make a left instead of a right. Zig instead of zag."*

But then again, hadn't I gone down this path—a man I worked with? I knew where that landed me.

My eyes lifted to Merrick's carved stomach. *I definitely never explored a path like that*—one filled with peaks and valleys of taut muscle. I salivated at the thought of running my tongue over them all.

I want this.

No, I *need* this.

I groaned. *"Fuck it."* I flew into his arms. Mr. Confidence apparently hadn't been expecting it, because while I was busy wrapping my arms around his neck and climbing him like a tree, he stumbled back a few steps. Once he regained his footing, he crushed his lips to mine. Our mouths opened in a tangle of desperation with teeth clashing and tongues frantic to find each other. One of his hands slid down to my ass, while the other gripped the back of my neck and pulled me yet closer. I couldn't get enough. He was overwhelming all of my senses at once.

Merrick walked with me in his arms until my back hit a wall. Then he pressed his hips to me, pinning me in place while he reached around to the back of his neck, gathered my hands into one of his, and stretched them up and over my head. I kissed him hard, feeling desperate to dig my nails into his back, but so turned on that I couldn't because he was restraining my hands.

He bent slightly, used one hand to pull my thigh up, and suddenly I could feel his erection grinding into my clit. I whimpered, feeling a little breathless, and that only seemed to egg Merrick on. He growled, rubbing between my legs with his rock-hard cock, and I swear I almost came right there. We were just kissing, and he was going to get the job done faster than I'd been able to.

He shifted his head to my neck and sucked along my pulse line. "You had your fingers inside your pussy earlier, didn't you?" he whispered.

I couldn't form words, but nodded.

"Were you thinking of me?"

I nodded again.

Merrick growled, and I felt it in my belly.

"Did you come?"

I shook my head.

"Good. I want you on edge."

Oh, I was already there. If he kept talking dirty, he wouldn't have to do much more for me to fall over.

"My room or yours?" he mumbled.

"Mine. I couldn't...in Kitty's."

Merrick released my hands and gathered me in his arms again. He walked toward the kitchen door, but I yelled, "Wait!"

He froze. The look on his face was actually kind of comical.

I bit my lip. "Do you think you could...put me over your shoulder?"

He arched a brow.

I shrugged. "It's kind of a fantasy I had going."

Without warning, he plucked me from around his waist, lifted me into the air, and tossed me over his shoulder. "This is just the first one I'm going to make come true, sweetheart."

Merrick carried me to the guest bedroom and sat down on the edge of the bed before setting me on my feet between his legs.

"I want to taste you, but first I need to see all of you." He reached up to the hem of my shirt and slowly lifted it over my head. I had already changed for bed, so I didn't have a bra on.

Merrick shook his head. "You're beautiful."

His head was perfectly aligned with my breasts, and my nipples stood at full attention, begging for his touch. Leaning forward, he sucked one into his mouth and looked up at me. When our gazes locked, he sucked harder before biting down and tugging with his teeth.

My eyes closed. *Fuck. I need him to touch me.* I'd been aching for him for *hours* and felt so damn needy.

When he moved to my other breast, he shimmied my sleeping shorts down my legs, leaving me completely bare.

He leaned back to get a better look at me. "You said you fantasized about me. I don't think I could dream up something this perfect."

My body was already on fire, but his words made my heart melt. He stood and guided me to switch places with him. Once I was on the edge of the bed, he nudged my knees open.

"Wider."

I spread my legs a modest amount, but it wasn't enough apparently.

"More... Wider."

Any self-consciousness I had was quickly forgotten when Merrick licked his lips, staring at my pussy. "So pink and perfect," he said. "I want you to watch me eat you."

Oh God.

He leaned forward and licked at me, his tongue flattening to lap between my parted lips as it traveled from one end to the other. Reaching my clit, he fluttered his tongue over and over before sucking it into his mouth.

My eyes shut, and I dug my fingernails into his scalp. *"Merrick..."*

Without warning, he slipped a finger inside of me, pumping a few times before adding another. I'd been riding the edge of a wave for so long that it didn't take long before it began to crest. My body trembled, and my insides clamped down on his fingers. Merrick sucked once more on my clit, and the free fall hit.

Falling.

Falling.

Falling.

I wasn't sure I could feel anything else in the lower half of my body. It was as if every nerve ending from the waist down had shut down to magnify the intensity of what was happening between my legs. When it was over, I collapsed back on the bed, one arm slung over my face.

Merrick climbed up and hovered over me. "Not good, huh?"

I moved my arm enough to peek at him through one eye and gave him a giddy smile. "Holy shit. You're going to be doing that...*a lot.*"

Merrick flashed a triumphant look. "My pleasure." He peeled my arm away and kissed my lips gently. "I'll be right back."

He returned with a sad face and held up two condoms. "I only have two."

I smiled. "I think that will hold us."

"I'm pretty sure I'm going to fill two the first time."

I laughed and held out my hand. "Come here."

Merrick climbed over me and pressed his lips to mine. The kiss started slow and sweet, but didn't take long to grow heated and desperate. A few minutes ago, I'd been sated and content, and yet already I was growing needy. I grabbed the waistband of Merrick's sweatpants and started to push them down, but he took over and finished.

I'd seen the bulge between his legs that one time on the couch, but that didn't prepare me for what I found when I slid my hand between us and tried to wrap it around his cock. The thing was pretty damn big—not that I'd experienced a vast array, but it definitely put Christian to shame. That gave me a weird sense of satisfaction. Not only had I moved on, I'd traded up, too.

Merrick broke our kiss and sat back on his haunches, grabbing one of the condoms he'd dropped on the bed. His cock bobbed against his belly as he grasped the wrapper between his teeth and tore it open. Pausing as he sheathed himself, he caught my eyes.

I pointed. "That thing is bigger than my vibrator."

He winked. "Don't worry. I'll take my time when I feed it to you later."

Merrick positioned himself over me and took my mouth in a languid kiss as he pushed inside. He eased in and out gently, careful to give my body time to adjust to each thrust. When he was fully seated, I felt his arms shake, yet he stopped to check in with me.

"You good?"

I nodded and smiled. "Very."

Merrick clenched his jaw as he continued, looking into my eyes in a way that made me feel bare—and it had nothing to do with being naked.

"You feel...fuck, so good," he muttered.

My eyes closed as I felt the familiar wave taking form once again.

"Open your eyes, Evie. I want to..." He thrust deeper. "*Fuck.* I want...to watch you come."

When our eyes met again, I felt the intensity of our connection deep in my chest. We were giving each other so much more than our bodies—what I was feeling came from the soul.

Merrick's thrusts quickened. He lifted one of my thighs, causing him to sink even deeper into my body—hitting just the right spot.

"Merrick..."

"That's it, sweetheart. Wrap your legs around my back." He tightened his hold and fucked me hard and fast. His hips ground down, pinning me to the mattress, and it took all my strength to match his thrusts. "I'm so deep inside you... You're so fucking tight..."

I felt desperate, my nails digging into his pumping ass as my climax started to build once again. We were slicked with sweat, our bodies slapping into each other, playing the most erotic tune I'd ever heard.

My orgasm hit faster than ever before, and with so much intensity it felt like it might blow me to smithereens. I cried out Merrick's name while his eyes blazed so hot, the green of his irises turned dark gray.

When I finally started to loosen my grip on his ass, it was his turn. Merrick bucked one, twice, and on the third time he planted himself to the root with a roar. The veins in his neck bulged, and every muscle in his body tightened as he released inside me. Even through the condom, I could feel spurts of hot cum.

Rather than rolling off or collapsing on top like most men do, Merrick kept going. His mouth slid over my shoulders and neck, licking and kissing while we caught our breath.

"Wow," I finally managed. "Now I understand why you thought we needed more than two condoms." I smiled goofily. "You're good at that."

Merrick chuckled. "My ego would like to take all the credit, but that was us, sweetheart. It's been there from the very start."

I knew he was right. There'd been a spark of something since the first time I'd stepped into his office. That day I would've bet that *something* was friction from the clash of our personalities. To be honest, a little of that might still exist, but our connection had gone somewhere I'd never imagined it would.

I cupped his cheek. "You were very unexpected."

He turned his head into my hand and kissed my palm. "Sometimes the best things come along that way."

CHAPTER 22

Evie

"**H**ave you ever used your barter system for sexual favors?" Merrick was propped up on one elbow, tracing the outline of my areola.

I laughed. "Can't say that I have."

"Good answer. I can't wait to be the first."

"How do you know you have something I want?" I teased. "I don't barter with just anyone, you know."

He leaned down and brushed his lips with mine, keeping them there while he spoke. "Change your flight. I'll spend the entire day showing you I have something you want."

I made a pout face. "I wish I could. But I have appointments bright and early tomorrow."

He made the sound a buzzer makes when you give a wrong answer. *Bzzzzt.* Then pinched my nipple.

"Owww!" I laughed. "That's not a toy."

"I disagree. But it wouldn't be an issue if you gave the right answer, now would it?"

I ran my fingers through Merrick's hair. "I wish I could stay. But it's important to me that people learn to trust me, and keeping appointments is the first step toward that."

He frowned.

I cupped his cheek. "You're adorable when you sulk. But I think it's even more important for me to keep my schedule now that we...you know."

"Fucked?"

"I probably would have used a nicer word, but yeah."

He went back to tracing my areola. "There's no nicer word than *fuck*. You can use it when you're pissed off, happy, or to describe my new favorite hobby. Tell me another word in the English language that is so diverse."

"Okay, but...this does complicate things. If, you know, this becomes more than a one-time thing."

Merrick's finger froze. "What do you mean?"

"Well, last night just sort of happened. We didn't talk about it, so..." I shrugged. "I don't know. It doesn't have to be more than it was."

"Are you saying that's what you want?"

I shook my head. "No, I just...didn't want to make you feel like there were any expectations or anything."

His mouth flattened to a grim line. "I expect it wasn't a one-night stand. I'm not the one who's been running from this, Evie."

I looked away. "I guess I'm just trying to say I don't expect anything of you."

Merrick was quiet for a long time. "Evie, look at me."

I did.

"I like you. A lot. Do I see potential pitfalls because you work at my company and we both have enough baggage to fill JFK?" He nodded. "Of course. I don't even know if I'm capable of a normal relationship anymore, it's been so long. But what I am sure of is that last night was not a one-night stand for me."

My heart felt hopeful, which scared me more than a little. But I took a deep breath and nodded. "Okay. But could we talk about the office?"

"I'd rather celebrate our new understanding that last night was not a one-night-only thing with my head between your legs." He shrugged. "But sure, let's talk about the office."

I laughed. "I'm being serious."

"So am I, sweetheart."

"Well, hold that thought then." I turned over on my side to face him. "Having a relationship with the boss is fraught with risks under normal circumstances, but our circumstances make it even messier. For me to do my job, people need to confide in me and trust that nothing they say is going to make it back to the boss."

"Well, you don't work for me anymore."

"While I think having me report to Joan is a good idea—though it should have been implemented at a more reasonable hour of the day, obviously—it doesn't change the fact that you *are* the company. It's already a steep hill for people to accept that the guy who signs all of our paychecks isn't my boss. It becomes a mountain if I'm also sleeping with that boss."

"So what do you propose?"

I shook my head. "No one can know about us. At least not at the office."

Merrick frowned. "How am I supposed to fuck you in my office if people can't know?"

My eyes widened.

Merrick cracked a smile. "I'm kidding."

"Oh, thank God."

He shrugged. "I'll need to get rid of the glass walls before we can do that." When he saw the look on my face, he laughed. "I get it. You don't have to worry. I learned my lesson about people in the office knowing my personal business after Amelia. I don't even bring dates to work functions anymore. My private life doesn't need to be on display."

Hearing him say that made me feel slightly less anxious. I nodded. "Okay, great."

"One exception though."

"What?"

"Will. He was my closest friend long before I started Crawford Investments. Besides, he loves to fuck with me. So if he doesn't know, he's going to continue to flirt with you relentlessly to piss me off."

I smiled. "Okay. Hopefully Will can keep it quiet."

"Thank you." He reached out and rubbed my bottom lip with his thumb. "How come you haven't worn that red lipstick you had on during your first interview again?"

My nose wrinkled. "What lipstick was I wearing?"

"It was a bright red."

I covered my mouth and cracked up. "That wasn't just lipstick. I'd stained my mouth bright red by eating cherries while I was on my way to the appointment. I did the best I could to even it out, but that lipstick was mostly cherry stains."

"I liked it. I might've fantasized about you with just those red-painted lips and nothing but a pair of high heels on more than one occasion."

I laughed. "I knew you were a perv. If you're good, maybe one day I'll make that fantasy come true."

"Promise?"

I pressed my lips to his. "Sure, boss."

He brushed a lock of my hair behind my ear. "Anything else you want to talk about?"

I shook my head. "I don't think so."

"Good." Merrick abruptly rolled us so I was on my back, making me squeal. He leaned down and kissed my lips softly. "Heads or tails?"

"You don't even have a coin in your hand."

"Pretend I do. What would you pick?"

I shrugged. "Heads, I guess."

"Good choice. I couldn't decide."

"Decide between what?"

"Going down on you or taking you from behind while you're up on all fours." He slid down my body. "Head it is."

CHAPTER 23

Evie

A week and a half went by before Merrick returned Thursday morning. I was a mix of anxious and excited. I knew it might be awkward to pretend nothing had changed between us, but I missed seeing him every day.

Kitty had needed to stay in the hospital a few days longer than originally expected. Her slight fever had turned into a pretty elevated white blood count, and they'd started her on IV antibiotics. She'd finally come home on Wednesday morning, so Merrick had the nurse he'd hired start that day. Late that afternoon he ran out to the grocery store, and when he came back the nurse was gone. Kitty had fired her the first opportunity she had alone with the woman. So Merrick had stayed another week, until he felt comfortable Kitty was recovered enough from her surgery to be left alone with only Marvin's help. He'd taken a flight this morning.

I was talking to Joan in the break room when he walked in. The sight of him stopped me in my tracks.

"Hey." A smile spread across my face, but I realized it was a bit overzealous and reined it in. "You're back."

He walked to the coffee pot and gave me a grin that made the butterflies in my stomach flutter awake. My eyes darted to Joan to see if she'd noticed anything, but she didn't seem bothered at all.

"Welcome back," she said. "I don't want to bombard you, but I have a few things to talk to you about when you have time."

He filled a coffee mug and nodded. "Can they hold until tomorrow?"

"No problem."

His eyes twinkled as he raised his mug to his lips. There was something mischievous in their depths. After he drank, he set the mug on the counter. "I almost forgot. I found something I think might be yours, Evie." He reached into his pocket and pulled out a lipstick. "Did you drop this? It was on the floor right near your office."

I shook my head. "No, I don't think so."

He looked at the bottom of the lipstick case. "You sure? It's called Cherry Stained." Merrick's eyes dropped to my lips before he looked down at my shoes with a dirty smirk. "It's still sealed, I think."

Oh my God. I felt my face heating up. He'd been back five minutes and was reminding me of my promise to wear red lipstick and nothing but heels for him while standing with the head of HR. If this was any indication of his discretion, I was in trouble. When Joan turned her back, I shot him a warning glare. But that only heightened the gleam in his eyes. The jerk was still holding out the lipstick, so I took it.

"You know what? Maybe it is. I only wear it with this one *special* outfit, so I forgot I even had it." I looked at my phone, not even catching the time. "Ohhh... Look at that. I have an appointment. I need to run. Welcome back, Merrick." I smiled at my new boss. "I'll talk to you later, Joan."

I had back-to-back appointments the rest of the afternoon, so I didn't have time to check my phone. A little before four, I took a break before writing up my last patient's session notes. I had a few texts waiting... One from my sister, one from the real estate agent who was going to show me a few apartments tonight, and a flurry of activity in a group chat I had with my grad-school friends. But I went to the one that made me smile just seeing the preview.

Merrick: Thinking I need blinds on the glass walls of my office...

I swiped to open, saw that it had been sent almost an hour and a half ago, and texted back.

Evie: Sorry, was in sessions. Blinds? Maybe I want people to watch...

I watched as the dots started to jump around, then stopped, and my phone rang. Merrick's name appeared on the screen.

I was glad my office glass was frosted because otherwise people would see the big smile I had when I answered. "Yes?"

"That scenario is my heaven and hell, sweetheart."

Sweetheart. My heart let out a big sigh. "Oh yeah, why is that?"

"Because the thought of fucking you in front of people, showing them what's mine, is heaven. But anyone else seeing you naked is my personal hell."

"Sounds like a conundrum."

"What are you doing right now?"

"Sitting in my office taking a short break before I have to write notes, and then I have one more patient in forty minutes. You?"

"I have an overseas call in twenty. Meet me upstairs in five."

"Upstairs?"

"In my apartment. I promised you I'd be good in the office. That doesn't mean the entire building. Look in your top drawer. I snuck a key in it while you were talking to Joan before I came into the break room."

I slid open my desk drawer. Sure enough, there was a key ring with a single key. He'd placed it right next to my turquoise sea glass. I took it out and dangled it in my fingers. "That was very presumptuous of you."

"I prefer to call it confidence."

As tempting as it was, I didn't think it was smart to start sneaking away in the middle of the workday. "Not sure that's a good idea, Merrick."

"It's probably not, but..." He was quiet for about ten seconds before speaking softly. "I fucking miss you."

His voice was so tender and vulnerable, it obliterated my willpower on the spot. "Don't leave your office for five minutes. I don't want anyone to see us going together."

I heard the smile in his voice. "Yes, ma'am."

A rush of adrenaline hit before I even swiped the phone off. I folded the key into the palm of my hand and decided not to take my purse or anything with me in order to look as casual as possible. Halfway out of my office, I had a brilliant idea. So I turned back and swiped something from the corner of my desk with a smile.

Might as well make it memorable.

Merrick took a few steps into his apartment and froze. "Holy fuck."

The last two minutes of standing in his living room wearing nothing but Cherry Stained lipstick and my high heels had started to make me question whether I'd lost my mind. But the answer was clear the minute I got a look at Merrick's face. *He* was the one losing his mind at the moment. He licked his lips and stared as he took off his suit jacket and tossed it on the floor.

"Fifteen minutes is not going to be enough." He shook his head and yanked at the knot of his tie while his eyes raked up and down my body. "I might need fifteen *days*."

I tilted my head coyly. "Well, fifteen minutes is all we have, so we're going to have to do it my way."

The slow grin that spread across Merrick's face gave me goosebumps, even from ten feet away. "Any way you want, sweetheart."

I curled a finger at him. "Come here. No touching."

"No fucking way I can promise you no touching…"

"You're wasting time, bossman."

His eyes sparkled as he walked over and stood toe-to-toe with me. Merrick was always an imposing figure, but this stance was a power move. He was fully dressed and looking down, while I was naked and had to tilt my head back to see him. But I had a power move of my own up my nonexistent sleeve.

I dropped to my knees.

Merrick bent his head back and mumbled a string of curses as I unzipped his slacks. The sound of his buckle clanking open and the zipper teeth coming apart had me salivating. By the time I yanked his pants to the floor, I couldn't wait any longer. He was hard and ready.

I licked my red lips and opened, sucking in the wide crown of his smooth cock.

"*Fuck…*" Merrick growled. "Take it. Take it all, Evie."

He dug his hands into my hair and wrapped clumps of it around his fists, giving a hard tug as I ran my tongue along the underside. The soft nip of pain made me wild.

Looking up, I tilted my head back to give him a better view from above. Then I bobbed my head up and down, taking him farther and farther with each thrust forward.

"Jesus Christ, keep doing that," he growled. "Suck harder. Take more."

The desperation in his voice had me so turned on. I could feel him trying to restrain himself, in his touch and the shake of his words. That made me want to break that last bit of self-control he was trying to hold on to. I looked back up, and the image of such a powerful man, still dressed in his custom-made shirt and tie, looking so out of his mind with carnal desire, made me crazy.

He swelled in my mouth, growing impossibly thicker as I worked my tongue over the bulging veins and opened my jaw still wider. I started to jerk him with one hand while I pushed past the spot in my throat that wasn't always easy. When he slipped in deeper, his grip on my head tightened, and I felt his body shake as the switch flipped from *getting* head to *taking* it. Merrick began fucking my mouth.

He held my head in place while he took over, pumping in and out, grumbling curses with every thrust in.

"I'm going to come... *Evie*."

His grip in my hair loosened, giving me a chance to pull away if I wanted to, but I wanted it as much as he did. So I answered by taking him as deep as I could.

"Fuck. Fuck. Fuck." He groaned.

My eyes started to water as he emptied into me for a very long time. I wasn't even sure how I managed to not choke on the never-ending stream he unleashed down my throat.

He was still panting like he'd run a marathon when I stood. I wiped my mouth and grinned. "Thank you for the lipstick."

Merrick chuckled and shook his head. "I'll buy you the entire cosmetics store if just a lipstick makes you that happy."

I smiled. "It's not the lipstick. It's... Well, where did you get it?"

"I stopped at the store the other day when I was running errands for my grandmother."

"How did you know what color to ask for?"

"I didn't. I went to the counter and told the lady I was looking for a color that looks like the stain cherries would make. I had no idea there was one called Cherry Stained."

I smiled. "I didn't either. But that's my point. It's not the lipstick. It's that you were thinking of me and went to the store to do that."

Merrick pulled up his pants. "Well, I'm glad my perverted thoughts make you happy because I've got plenty of them."

I pushed up on my toes and kissed his lips chastely. "I have to get dressed."

"What? No. You can't do that and not let me take care of you."

"That's sweet. But..." I looked at my watch. "You have an appointment in five minutes, and I have a session in a little while, and I still need to do some things before that."

Merrick's bottom lip jutted out. "I don't like this."

I grabbed my panties and bra and started to get dressed. "Oh? You don't like coming into your apartment to a naked woman and getting a quickie blowjob? I'll have to remember that."

"Wiseass." He wrapped a hand around my waist and tugged me to him. "Can I see you tonight?"

"Can I get back to you? I might have plans."

He frowned.

I smiled. "Relax. It's with your friend the real estate agent. I'm looking at apartments."

"Oh. What time?"

I buttoned my blouse. "What time will I be done?"

"No, what time are you going? I'll try to get out of the office early."

I stopped buttoning. "You want to go with me to see apartments?"

He shrugged. "Can I convince you to skip that appointment and come up here and let me fuck you all night instead?"

I shook my head. "I need to get out of my sister's place."

Merrick shrugged again. "Then what choice do I have?"

"We could see each other tomorrow night after work?"

"That's not an option."

I smiled and finished getting dressed in a hurry. "I'll text you when I know my plans. You should take the elevator down first since you have a call."

"They won't start without me. You go. I need a minute after what just went down here."

I kissed his cheek. "Hope the rest of your afternoon is as pleasant as this has been."

⟿

"Do you have anything available on an upper floor?" Merrick asked Nick, the real estate agent he'd introduced me to.

"Not in this neighborhood."

We'd just looked at our third apartment. This one was a brownstone that wasn't too far from my sister. It was already empty and ready to move in, and had so much sunlight. I loved it. "I love that it's on the ground floor, especially since it's a walk-up."

Merrick frowned and pointed to the big windows. "You can see right in from the street. Not to mention, it's easy to break right in, too."

I shrugged. "I can get blinds, and I want to get a dog anyway." I turned to the real estate agent. "They allow pets, right?"

He nodded. "Under thirty pounds with an extra security deposit for damages."

I smiled at Merrick. "Problem solved."

"How does that solve your problem? What's a dog under thirty pounds going to do if someone tries to break in?"

I put my hands on my hips. "Are you insinuating size makes a difference in toughness?"

"No, but it makes a difference in the sound of a bark. And a tiny dog yapping isn't going to scare off an intruder. Plus, how are you going to have a dog when you work all day?"

My face scrunched up. "What's that got to do with anything?"

"What's it going to do, sit around all day?"

"What do your *fish* do all day?"

"The same thing they do when I'm there, swim. Because that's all fish can do. Dogs are a lot of work."

"So are relationships..."

Nick watched our bickering like a tennis match. When my last comment stumped Merrick, he looked at me. "So... you're taking it? This place has my vote. I love it, too."

"Thanks for being on my side, buddy," Merrick grumbled.

I bit my bottom lip. "How soon can I move in?"

After I signed all the paperwork, we stood outside. Merrick looked up at the window, shaking his head again. "How about an alarm?"

"I don't think that's necessary."

"It'll make me feel better."

I bumped my shoulder to his. "I thought I'd already made you feel better today. Greedy boy."

He smiled. "I'll take being greedy if it makes you safe at night."

"Alright. I'll think about an alarm."

"Good. I'll have my security company come over once you get the keys."

I shook my head. "You're bossy."

"I'll tell you what, you can pick where we eat to show you how amicable I can be."

I raised a brow. "*Anywhere* I want to eat?"

He shrugged. "Sure."

Twenty minutes later, we were sitting in Gray's Papaya. Merrick had let me order for him, so we both had hot dogs with the works.

He picked his up. "I can't tell you the last time I had one of these."

"You're too busy at fancy restaurants because you're all..." I waved my hand around. "Fancy..."

He smiled and sipped his soda. "So what kind of dog do you want to get?"

"Any kind. As long as he likes to snuggle. As soon as I move in, I'm going to go to the shelter to pick the ugliest one that no one wants."

"I figured you had a certain type of breed in mind."

I bit into my delicious hot dog and spoke with my mouth full. "Nope. Just one who needs a home."

"Did you ever have a dog?"

I nodded. "Once. For a week. Arnold was the best dog ever."

"Why'd you only have him for a week?"

"He bit my dad when he...you know." I grinned. "That's why he was the best dog ever."

Merrick frowned. "I guess that's why he only lasted a week?"

"Yeah." I wiped the corner of my mouth. "What about you? Ever have a dog?"

"Once. Growing up we had a black lab. It got sick when it was maybe five or six and died young."

"I'm sorry. Is that why you have fish now?"

He shook his head. "I inherited them. They were Amelia's."

"Oh."

"She always had pet fish. She had a lot of trouble sleeping, so she would keep them on her nightstand and watch them swim when she went to bed at night. The funny thing is, they never lasted more than a year until they became my problem. It's been years now."

I was quiet for a minute. Then Merrick caught my eyes. "What? Does it bother you that I still have them?"

"No, of course not. It would bother me if you flushed them."

"Then why does it look like something's bothering you?"

"I don't know. I guess..." I shook my head. "I noticed they're still on the nightstand. So you haven't moved them or anything in the last three years?"

Merrick looked back and forth between my eyes. "Where am I supposed to put them?"

I waved him off. "Sorry. You're right. I'm being silly and reading into something. It's an occupational hazard."

Merrick nodded but was quiet after that. At least I thought he was, but maybe he was just chewing and I was doing it again. When we were almost done, my phone rang. "It's my sister. Excuse me for a second. I'm going to answer it just in case she wants me to pick up something on my way home."

"Of course."

I swiped and brought my phone up to my ear, though I could have left it on the table and heard her the way she screamed. "Why aren't you answering my texts?"

"I was looking at apartments and then eating. Is everything okay?"

"No!"

"What's the matter?"

"I'm pregnant!"

"What? Oh my God. Are you serious? That was so fast! The implantation was only a little over a week ago."

"I know! Apparently, soccer loving, tech guru number 09376230 has super swimmers!"

I laughed and held my hand over my heart. "I'm so excited! I'm going to be an aunt!"

"Now you need to hurry up and get pregnant, too. How's hot boss's sperm count?"

I looked at Merrick to see if he'd overheard. His arched brows told me he had. I shook my head. "I'll be home in a little while. I guess I'll have to drink both our wine to celebrate!"

"Ugh. Don't remind me. No wine for *soooo* long."

I heard someone knock on a door through the phone. "Greer? Are you in there?"

"Yes, I'll be right out! I'm on the phone." She came back on the line and whispered. "Shit. I didn't think he'd be home for another hour. Don't tell him I told you first or he'll be upset."

My eyes widened. "You didn't tell Ben yet?"

"He worked late and wasn't supposed to be home until ten. I wanted to tell him in person. But I had to tell someone!"

"Oh my God. Go tell the poor man!"

"Alright. But hurry home. I want to start a list of potential names!"

I laughed. "I'll see you in a little while. And congratulations, Greer."

As soon as I hung up, Merrick smiled. "I guess your sister didn't need me after all?"

"I can't believe the artificial insemination worked the first time."

"That's great. Congratulations."

"Yeah. They've been trying for five years. I'm so happy for them. She's going to make such a great mom. Greer was like a second mother to me in a lot of ways because she's ten years older. She's a natural caretaker. Which reminds me, I told her about us when I got back from Kitty's, and she's already bugging me to invite you to dinner one night."

"Should I bring a lab report with my sperm count when I come?"

"You heard that, huh?"

"It was kind of impossible not to."

I sipped my soda. "Do you want to have kids someday?"

Merrick looked away. "If you'd asked me a few months ago, I would've said no."

"And now?"

He reached across the table and took my hand. "I don't know. Things can change, I guess. I'm only now realizing how much I've let my past control my future. I don't want to do that anymore."

"You mean things with Amelia?"

He nodded.

A worker walked over and pointed to the trays in front of us. Our plates were both empty. "Can I take those?"

"Oh, that would be great. Thank you."

Merrick took out his phone. "I was planning on kid-napping you and bringing you home with me. But it sounds like you need to go home to your sister's."

I nodded. "Yeah, I do."

"Tomorrow night? Bring what you need with you to the office so you can stay. I'll make you dinner."

"You're going to cook?"

"You don't seem so hard to please, considering we had hot dogs tonight. I can top that."

"Okay." I smiled. "Sounds like a plan."

He lifted his cell as we stood. "I'll call you an Uber."

"That's okay. I'll just jump on the train. There's a station at the corner."

Merrick ignored me and typed into his phone before looking up. "It'll be here in three minutes."

"Do you have something against the subway?"

"I have something against you not staying safe—same reason I think you should have an alarm in a first-floor apartment."

As soon as we walked outside, the Uber pulled up. I kissed Merrick goodnight. "Thank you for coming to look at apartments with me. Oh my God—I didn't even tell Greer I found a place."

He leaned down to open the Uber door. "You had a lot of excitement tonight. I'll have to work to make tomorrow evening as good."

I wiggled my brows as I got into the back of the car. "I can't wait."

CHAPTER 24

Evie

"**C**ome in!"

The door to my office opened, and Merrick poked his head inside. Finding just me, he let himself in.

"Hey." I closed the notebook I'd been writing in. "Good timing. I'm done for the day."

"Wish I could say the same thing. I'm running behind. The market went a little crazy today because of some unexpected news. The analysts just finished working on what it means so we can talk about it and decide on our holdings. Sorry, but I'm gonna be another hour or two."

"Oh..." I shrugged. "That's okay. I can find something to do."

Merrick looked at his watch. "It's already six thirty. Why don't you go up and get comfortable? Order some dinner since it's going to be too late to start cooking by the time I'm done."

"I'll just work some more."

Merrick frowned and held out a key. "I noticed you left this behind yesterday when you left my place."

"I figured you were just loaning it to me to let myself in. I didn't think you wanted me to keep it."

"Will it freak you out if I tell you to hold on to it? This is a copy."

"Do you want me to answer that honestly?"

He smiled. "How about you take it and go up now, and we talk about it later?"

I nodded. "Okay."

Merrick handed me the key. "Go get changed and settle in. I don't want you to stay just because I'm stuck for a while."

I tilted my head. "You're just hoping I greet you like I did before, aren't you?"

He chuckled. "Go. You can snoop around some more."

"I don't think you realize the danger of making that statement to someone like me."

He closed my palm with the key inside. "Have at it. I've got nothing to hide."

It wasn't lost on me that my ex wouldn't even let me look at a picture on his phone without hovering to take it back. But then again, there was no comparison between Christian and Merrick. "What do you want me to order?"

He shrugged and pulled his wallet out of his pocket. "Whatever you want. I'm not picky. But use my card to order it."

"I can pay for dinner myself. Though, technically, I think you wind up paying for dinner either way, since you pay me the money I use to eat."

His lip twitched. "Use my card, please. I gotta run. I have six people waiting in my office."

"I'll see you soon."

A little while later, I headed to the elevator. I'd just entered and pushed the button for the top floor when Joan opened the double glass doors to the office and walked toward the waiting car.

Shit.

Merrick's floor was illuminated. But I couldn't very well close the elevator doors now that we'd made eye contact. So I panicked and did the only thing that came to mind. I hit every button on the panel.

Joan noticed as soon as she stepped inside. "Oh my."

"Yeah, someone must've thought they were being funny."

"We might be better off waiting for the other car. Looks like we're going up before we even start heading down."

"Good idea."

We stepped back out into the hallway. Once that car left, we pushed the button to call the other one.

"Everything okay between you and Merrick?" Joan asked.

I was already nervous, so that question freaked me out completely. I tried to school my features. "Why wouldn't it be?"

"No reason. I just saw him coming from your office earlier and wanted to make sure he wasn't pushing you for information on any of your patients. Not that you can't talk to him, of course, but I figured I'd check in. He can be very persuasive when he wants to."

Don't I know it. I forced a smile past the nerves in my face. "No, he wasn't doing that." I'm not sure whether I felt guilty for hiding the truth, or Joan was actually waiting for more, but I felt the need to elaborate. Once again, I went with what popped into my head first. "He was talking to me about coming in for therapy."

Joan's eyes widened. "Really?"

I nodded. "Yep. It was a surprise to me, too." *Oh boy. I'm making this worse.*

By the time we arrived at the lobby level, I felt like I might suffocate in the damn elevator. I was relieved when the doors slid open. Joan and I walked to the exit together. My train was to the left, so I pointed as if I were going home. "I'm this way."

She smiled and pointed in the other direction. "My bus is that way."

I couldn't get out of here fast enough. "See you Monday," I called, already moving down the sidewalk.

When I got to the subway station, I waited a few minutes in case Joan had forgotten something. You'd think I'd just stolen the Hope Diamond the way my heart hammered inside my chest. When I returned to the building, I held my breath until I arrived safely at Merrick's floor.

Inside the apartment, I still felt tense. But then I stepped into the living room and saw something on the coffee table.

Was that...?

I walked over for a closer look. Sure enough, two orange goldfish were swimming around in a bowl. And it was not the same bowl that had been on the nightstand in his bedroom.

He got more fish? Or...

I dropped my purse on the couch and headed to the bedroom to investigate. As I opened the door, the jitters I'd had since Joan were finally pushed out by the warm feeling in my chest.

The fishbowl on the nightstand was gone. Merrick had moved it to a new home, in a new room. It was so minor and silly, but he'd taken the time to think about the comment I'd made last night, and he'd done something to alleviate my unvoiced concern.

Maybe I didn't have to worry about fighting the shadow of another woman after all. It seemed Merrick wanted to let the sun in himself.

"Oh my gosh. That sounds like a huge undertaking."

"Nah," Kitty said. "It'll give me something to do while I'm stuck here in the house. It's only been two weeks. Eight more with this cast is going to make me go cuckoo if I don't have something to occupy my time."

"When would this reunion be happening?" I asked.

"I was thinking spring next year or the year after that, depending on the availability of the dude ranch."

The front door opened, and Merrick walked in. I pointed to the phone and held up a finger. "Did you say dude ranch?"

"What better place than that? A lot of open land, night fires, horseback riding, and cowboys. Who doesn't love a cowboy?"

"Well, I can't argue with you there. What's not to like about a cowboy?"

Merrick's face scrunched up.

"But do you feel up to that already, Kitty?"

Merrick slapped his hand to his forehead and shook his head as he walked toward me.

"I'm fine—was fine last week when my jackass grandson thought I needed a nurse, too."

I was pretty sure Merrick heard that last part. When I looked up, he held his palm out for the phone, but I shook my head. He took it from my hand and brought it to his ear anyway.

"Hey, Grams." Merrick looked at me as he spoke. "No, I'm not working. And neither is Evie. We're about to have dinner...alone in my apartment."

I heard Kitty saying something else.

Merrick nodded. "Yep. You were right. So do you mind if she gives you a call tomorrow? Because while Evie is too polite to rush you off the phone, I'm not." His eyes swept over me, lingering on my lips. "Thank you, I will. Goodnight, Grams."

Looking pretty proud of himself, he tossed the phone to the couch and hooked an arm around my waist. "Now kiss me."

"What if I don't want to? That was kind of rud—" My words were swallowed in a kiss. And not just any kiss, but one where I had to cling to his shirt to make sure I stayed upright because the man could seriously make my knees weak with his mouth. For lack of a better description, he kissed the shit out of me. I was breathless when we broke.

Merrick pulled back to gaze into my eyes. His were hooded and filled with enough heat to make between my legs start to throb. "Sorry I made you wait."

I smiled. "I like your apologies."

His eyes sparkled. "Yeah? I'll have to piss you off more."

"Did you just out us to your grandmother?"

He nodded. "Should I apologize again?"

I laughed. "I think you should."

Merrick resumed kissing me, this time slow and sweet. He pulled back and rubbed his nose with mine.

"You just angel kissed me!"

"I don't think that's what you call it."

"It's what my grandmother used to call it. Whenever we would leave my dad and go stay with her, I had trouble sleeping when we first arrived. So when she put me to bed, she would give me an angel kiss, which meant the angels would watch over me while I slept. No one else has ever done that to me."

Merrick kissed my forehead. "Maybe it means I'm supposed to take the job from the angels now."

I blinked. "That's so incredibly sweet."

He looked around the room. "Did you eat yet?"

"No, I waited for you. I ordered Chinese. It's in the kitchen."

"Come on, let's eat so I can get you naked. We're saving some sweet and sour sauce so I can lick it off your tits later."

"Aaaaannnnd we go from sweet to dirty in three sentences."

He winked. "It's a talent."

We sat at the island eating Kung Pao chicken and Szechwan shrimp while Merrick filled me in about the problem that had kept him and his team late tonight.

I shook my head. "You basically gamble for a living. Does that mean you like casinos, too?"

"Depends on the game. I only like to gamble when there's more to it than playing the odds. If you sit at a table playing blackjack, the dealer is just putting cards on the table and turning them over, and you're guessing based on statistics. If you're playing poker against others, it involves reading people and studying their habits. That's basically what I do at work, except with companies."

I held out a shrimp with my chopsticks, and he took it in his mouth. "I never actually thought about it, but our jobs are similar in some ways," I said. "We both study people to learn more about them. We look for the things they don't tell us to put the pieces of a puzzle together."

Merrick held out a piece of chicken. "Tell me what you've learned about me that I didn't tell you."

I thought a moment. "I've learned that you're a caretaker from the way you treat your grandmother, but also by the small things you do. For example, if we're walking down the street, you always walk on the outside. You never want me to take the subway at night, and the first thing you noticed about my new apartment was that it needed an alarm."

He nodded. "Anything else, doc?"

I looked over at the fishbowl on the coffee table and pointed my chopstick. "You also reflect on things people say, long after they've been said."

Merrick followed my line of sight and then turned back to me. "I didn't think I was capable of moving on, but it turned out, I'd never really tried."

I set my chopsticks down. "So what have you learned by studying me?"

He reached over, plucked a piece of broccoli from my plate, and popped it into his mouth. "You like your hair pulled and when I talk dirty to you."

I smacked his arm. "It figures you'd take this conversation there."

He finished chewing and swallowed. "You're gun shy about men because the ones you loved hurt you really badly."

I sighed and nodded. "I don't think that one was too hard to figure out."

"Maybe not. But you're also the most resilient person I know. Most people who went through the shit you've gone through, whether it's with your dad or your fuckwad ex, would feel like the victim. But not you. You don't know how to be the victim in your story. You only know how to be the heroine, and the heroine always dusts herself off and goes on."

"Thank you for saying that. But there have definitely been days where I've let myself wallow and feel like the victim."

"Well, you'd never know it."

"You probably won't be saying that next week. I have my first court date with Christian next Friday."

Merrick frowned. "Still can't believe that guy is suing you. Why don't I come to keep you company?"

"It's sweet of you to offer. But I think it's something I need to handle on my own."

He nodded. "The offer wasn't coming from an entirely sweet place. I'm a little territorial when it comes to you. But I understand."

After we finished eating, I packed up the leftover food while Merrick got changed. Then we sat in the living room and watched TV for a while. Merrick had his feet propped up on the coffee table, and I lay down with my head on his lap.

"Oh, I forgot to tell you." I turned on my side to look up at him. "I almost got caught coming up here. When I got in the elevator, I pushed your floor, but then Joan walked out of the office and joined me in the car."

"Did she notice?"

"No. Because I panicked and hit all the buttons on the panel before she entered, so she couldn't see what I'd pressed."

Merrick chuckled. "That's one way to handle it."

"It was the best I could think of in the moment. But I think it worked. Oh, and she saw you coming out of my office earlier, so I told her you'd stopped in to let me know you wanted to start therapy yourself."

"*I'm* starting therapy?"

"I felt like she was looking for a reason you were in my office, now that you're not my boss anymore. I pulled that out of my ass. Then I had to walk to my train and wait until the coast was clear before coming back up. Let me tell you, I was a nervous wreck until I made it safely up here."

Merrick stroked my hair. "You know I don't want to hide you forever."

Those damn butterflies in my belly went crazy once again. Merrick was not a man who spoke first and thought about his words later. So the fact that he'd used the word *forever* hit me hard. The signs were all there that I meant something to him, but I hadn't let myself believe it yet.

"Maybe we could tell Joan soon," I said. "That way I'm not lying to my boss. But I do think we should keep our relationship quiet when it comes to the employees, at least while I'm working to establish trust and let them get to know me."

Merrick leaned over and brushed his lips with mine. "That sounds like a good compromise."

I rested my head back in his lap and stared at the goldfish on the table, watching them swim before rolling on my back to look up at Merrick again. "Thank you for moving the goldfish."

He smiled. "My apartment might be big, but I thought it was important to show you there was room for you."

***

The next morning, I dragged Merrick out on a Saturday shopping trip to get things for my new apartment. I was going to get the keys on Monday, and I needed to get a bed before I could move in, so that was first on my list.

"What do you think of this one?" I lay back on a plush-top mattress and made Merrick do the same.

"I'm not sure. How about you get up on all fours so I can see if I'm gonna like it."

I pulled the pillow out from behind my head and whacked him in the face with it, laughing. "I'm serious. A good night's sleep is as important to your health as eating right and exercising. What bed do you have? Yours is really comfy."

Merrick shrugged. "No idea."

My nose scrunched up. "Oh."

Merrick looked over and his forehead creased before a look of understanding crossed his face. "It's not because another woman picked it out, if that's what you're thinking. Well, one did. But she was an interior designer. I hired someone to pick out everything I needed when I moved in."

"She chose your mattress too? What if you didn't like it?"

He shrugged. "I'd get a different one, I guess. She picked out everything. I basically just showed up one day and moved in."

"Did you give her direction, like colors and stuff?"

Merrick shook his head. "Nope." He looked around the mattress showroom. There were two salespeople, both currently helping other customers. Then he rolled on top of me and started jumping around, making the bed move up and down.

"Oh my God," I laughed. "Stop it."

He jumped a few more times before planting a chaste kiss on my lips. "This one will work. Let's get it."

After the mattress store, I dragged him to HomeGoods. For a man who didn't even want to pick things for his own apartment, he was incredibly patient. My cart was soon full of bedding, candles, housewares, and even a stuffed pig, which I couldn't resist buying for my soon-to-be niece or nephew. The checkout line was twenty deep when we joined the end of it. A little girl sat in the seat part of the cart in front of us. She had braces on her legs, and she pointed to the pig in my cart.

I smiled. "Aren't you adorable?"

Merrick had been scanning messages on his cell, but he looked up at the little girl. He seemed to squint like she looked familiar, but I didn't think anything of it, and he resumed scrolling on his phone.

"*Puh! Puh! Puh!*" she yelled, pointing to the pig again.

Her father turned around to see what his daughter was getting excited about. He smiled at the little girl and spoke as he simultaneously began to sign. "That's right. Puh for Pinky, your pig." The man looked at me. "She's deaf and just started working with a facial-prompt therapist to learn sounds. She has a pet guinea pig named Pinky, and all stuffed animals are him lately." Reaching into his cart, he pulled out a small stuffed frog. The little girl reached for it, making a *Puh* sound again. "I already got suckered into buying one today."

The line moved up, so the guy pushed his cart forward. I followed, but Merrick didn't. When I looked up, I found him staring at the little girl.

My brows furrowed. "Merrick?"

It was like he didn't even hear me. He just kept staring. I finally rested my hand on his arm.

"Merrick? Are you okay?"

Through my peripheral vision, I saw the guy in front of me turn back around. Merrick's eyes shifted to him and narrowed to daggers. My head volleyed back and forth. The man was also now staring back at Merrick.

Feeling a bit freaked out, I stepped in front of Merrick and nudged him a bit. "Merrick. What's going on? Talk to me."

He shook his head. "Nothing. I'll meet you outside, okay?"

"Yeah, sure. If you're okay?"

His eyes shifted from the man to the little girl one more time and held for a moment. Then he stormed toward the front door.

I blinked after him, unsure what the hell had just transpired, before turning back to the man with the little girl.

"Do you two know each other or something?"

He lifted his daughter from the cart and held her tight. "I'm Aaron Jensen."

The name meant nothing to me. I shook my head. "I'm confused. Should that be familiar to me?"

The man looked at his daughter. "Eloise's mother was Amelia Evans."

"Amelia, Merrick's ex?"

He nodded.

I stared at the little girl. "How old is she?"

"She'll be three in two months."

CHAPTER 25

Merrick

THREE YEARS AGO

"**W**hat the fuck did you just say?" I had to have misheard this guy.

The flight instructor looked at the nurse. He had cuts and dirt on his face and burn marks on his arms. "It's her ring—Amelia's."

The poor nurse looked panicked. "Ummm... Okay." She looked between us and spoke softly. "I'll let you know when I have an update, Mr. Crawford."

"What the fuck are you talking about? The ring from Amelia's hand is *your* ring?"

He shook his head and looked down. "She was never going to marry me. She made that clear from the start."

"The start of what?" I raised my voice. "What. The. Fuck. Are. You. Talking. About?"

"Amelia and I have been seeing each other. It began right after she started flight lessons. I've always known about you. She never kept you a secret."

Well, she obviously kept some secrets from me. "And you're...engaged?"

He frowned. "I bought her a ring a month ago. I thought maybe if she knew I was committed, she might take things between us more seriously. It was just a fling for her. I was the only one who wanted more. But she turned me down... Said she was going to marry you. I wanted her to keep the ring, but she wore it on her right hand. She never planned for us to be more than we were."

"Which was what exactly?" My head was spinning. It hadn't even sunk in that Amelia was in surgery, and now this? I raked a hand through my hair. "You were fucking her?"

Aaron frowned. "I should go..."

"Go? You shouldn't fucking *be here* in the first place."

He kept staring down. "I'm sorry you had to find out this way. And I'm sorry this happened."

"Were you in the plane with her?"

Aaron nodded. "The landing gear only came down on one side, apparently. I didn't know until after they pulled us from the wreckage. If I'd known, I never would have let her land the plane. She didn't have enough experience."

I was quiet for a long time, letting things sink in. "Why aren't you hurt more?"

"We landed on the pilot's side, and the top caved in. The passenger side held."

My heart wanted me to punch this guy in the face. But my head wouldn't let my arms or legs move. I just stood there, shell shocked.

Eventually, Aaron took his jacket from the chair behind him. "I'm going to go. I hope she's okay. And I'm very sorry, Merrick. She loves you."

Maybe I would've left by now if she'd had anyone else. But Amelia was on her own for the most part, except for me.

She had been since high school. Well, apparently, she had fucking Aaron, too. I'd spent the last eight hours while she was in surgery trying to piece it together. Actually, if I were being honest, I'd been trying to understand Amelia Evans since the night we met years ago in college. I'd sort of come to terms with the idea that there were parts of her she was never going to let me see. I always felt like she hid them as some sort of self-protection mechanism, since she'd been in and out of foster care her entire life and never fully trusted anyone. But I wasn't sure I could accept that some of those missing pieces of her were with another man.

The nurse had come over and given me updates every few hours. The last time she'd said it would probably only be another hour. Since that had been almost two hours ago now, I was getting antsy. Just then a doctor wearing blue scrubs, with a matching blue surgical cap and mask, walked over to the nurses' station. When the nurse pointed at me, I stood.

Taking down his mask, the doctor extended his hand. "Mr. Crawford?"

"Yes."

"I'm Dr. Rosen. I'm the neurosurgeon who operated on Ms. Evans."

"How is she?"

The doctor put his hands on his hips and sighed. "I wish I could answer that question. As you know, Ms. Evans suffered a severe head injury. She was brought in with a fractured skull, several cracked vertebrae, and some pretty significant cranial swelling and bleeding. All things considered, the surgery went as well as could be expected. We were able to perform a craniectomy to stop the bleeding and make room for the swelling to avoid even more compression damage. She's alive, and her vitals are amazingly stable after such an immense trauma and difficult surgery.

But when we tried to bring her out of the anesthesia, she didn't wake up. That's not to say she will not regain consciousness at some point, but it's obviously not a great sign. So at this point, all we can say is that she seems to be holding her own. It's going to take some time to know how extensive the damage is."

He paused and looked me in the eyes. "But I think you need to brace yourself for the possibility that she might not make it through the next few days. Or if she does, that she could wind up with some pretty significant deficits."

I sat down in the chair behind me. "Can I see her?"

Dr. Rosen nodded. "They're finishing cleaning her up now, and then she'll be moved to the ICU. Her face is very swollen, which is common after a head trauma, and we're going to leave the top of her skull off for a while—her brain needs the room. But yes, you can see her when we're all done. Just be very careful moving or touching her."

"How long will her head be open?"

"It's hard to say. We're going to freeze the bone flap we removed so it can be reattached in the future."

It was difficult to breathe, so I swallowed. "Okay."

"Ms. Evans filled out a health care proxy when she was here for another procedure."

I nodded. "She had her appendix out last year."

"That form names you as her agent—the person who makes health care decisions for her when she's unable to make them herself."

I rubbed the back of my neck. "She doesn't have contact with any of her family."

He nodded. "I'm sure once everything sinks in, you're going to have a lot of questions. I'll stop back in the ICU once she's settled in and examine her, and we can talk again."

"Thank you."

He started to walk away, but then turned back. "I'm sorry. I got so wrapped up in her neurology, I didn't even mention that the baby seems to be doing well. We have an order in for an OB to come examine her while she's in the ICU, but the pregnancy appears intact at this point. It's pretty incredible."

"Pregnancy?"

The doctor's eyes narrowed. "Amelia is at least a few months pregnant."

⌒

"Would you like to hear the heartbeat?" The obstetrician smiled at me. "It's very strong. I can't imagine what you're going through right now, but I find a baby's heartbeat often instills a sense of hope in parents."

I looked at the screen, at the life growing inside Amelia. "Sure."

The doctor fiddled with a dial, and a sound echoed in the small glass ICU room. *Lub-dub, lub-dub, lub-dub.* "It's fast. Clocking in at a hundred-forty-seven beats per minute. Right where it should be." She clicked a bunch of keys on the keyboard and moved the wand around Amelia's belly some more.

How had I not noticed the small bump? I felt guilty, at least until the questions the right side of my brain asked were answered by the left.

Because she rarely let you see her naked anymore.

Because she was fucking some other guy.

Holy.

Fucking.

Shit.

Was it even mine? How had I not even given that any thought over the last hour since the first doctor had told me Amelia was pregnant?

Is that why she didn't tell me?

Just when I thought I might be able to start to digest it all...

The doctor interrupted my thoughts. "The baby is measuring about seventeen weeks, so we're in our second trimester. We usually do a sonogram at about eighteen to twenty weeks and can see the sex at that time. But your baby's anatomy is pretty clear. Would you like to know if it's a boy or a girl?"

What I wanted to know was if it was *mine*. But she was waiting for an answer, and all I had were questions. I shrugged. "Sure."

The doctor smiled. "You're having a girl. Congratulations, Daddy."

CHAPTER 26

Evie

"**D**o you want to talk about what happened inside?" I'd finished putting my purchases in the trunk and clicked my seatbelt into place in the passenger seat.

Merrick's eyes closed a moment and he sighed. "Not really."

I thought he probably just needed a little time and space, so I nodded. "The landlord is having my new apartment painted today. He said I could drop things off while it's being done. Would you mind stopping there so I can deliver all this stuff I bought?"

"Sure."

He was quiet during the ride. When we pulled up, Merrick double parked out front and helped me get everything inside.

"You're not staying here until the bed gets delivered, right?" he asked.

"No. I still need to finish packing all my stuff at my sister's anyway."

He nodded and shook the keys in his hand. "You want me to drop you off at your sister's?"

"Oh...yeah, sure. That would be great." It wasn't like I expected him to spend the entire weekend with me, yet the ending to our time together felt sort of abrupt. I hadn't even taken my overnight bag when we'd gone out to the stores. "My bag is at your apartment, but I don't need anything from it. I can just grab it before I leave the office Monday."

He nodded.

The drive to my sister's apartment was short, and I was glad since the silence was getting pretty loud in the car. I tried not to take it personally. Clearly seeing Amelia's daughter had upset him. Unless I was doing the math wrong, which I didn't think I had, she'd had a baby with another man while they were together. I could've sworn Merrick had said Amelia passed a little less than three years ago, and it seemed like they'd been together up until the end. But maybe I'd gotten that wrong. Now was not the time to ask.

When we arrived at my sister's building, Merrick pulled to the curb. He left the car running and came around to open my door.

I forced a smile. "Thank you for coming shopping with me."

"No problem."

"I guess I'll see you Monday?"

He nodded, then leaned down and kissed my forehead. "Take care."

Merrick waited until I got into the building to get back in the car. I wanted to think whatever had happened would blow over, yet I couldn't help the sinking feeling in the pit of my stomach as I watched his car pull away. Call it women's intuition or whatever, but something told me my heart was about to be broken...again.

"Hey. What are you up to?" My sister tossed her keys on the kitchen counter and walked into the living room, where I'd been sitting for a long time. It must've been after eight already since she was closing the store tonight.

"Not much. Just watching TV."

Greer looked at the television and back to me. "Ummm... It's not on."

I blinked a few times. "Oh... I meant I was about to watch television."

She eyed me suspiciously. "Okay, well, mind if I join you?"

I shook my head. "Of course not."

"I'm just going to go get changed. I ordered some alcohol-free wine. I'm going to put it in a wine glass and pretend it's real."

"Alcohol-free wine? So grape juice?"

"Basically. It's a cabernet."

She came back a few minutes later wearing sweats and an Emory sweatshirt I'd bought her at least seven or eight years ago. She held two glasses and passed me the one in her right hand.

"Yours is real. You looked deep in thought, so I thought you might need it."

"Thanks." I sighed. "I do."

She sat down at the other end of the couch and tucked her legs underneath her. "So what's going on that you're staring at the TV and don't even know it's not on?"

I smiled. My sister knew me so well. "It's nothing, really. I'm just overthinking things."

She sipped her faux wine and wrinkled her nose.

"Not good?" I asked.

"You know when you leave an open bottle of wine around for a few months, and then you want to have a glass of wine and that's the only shit you have left?"

I chuckled. "Sadly, I do."

"It tastes like that."

"It's going to be a long nine months," I said.

"You ain't kidding." She sipped anyway. "But talk to me. What are you overthinking?"

I sighed. "Well, today Merrick and I went shopping for my new apartment. When we were in line at HomeGoods, there was a little girl in the cart ahead of us. Merrick kept staring at her. It seemed like he recognized her or something, and then he abruptly said he was going to wait in the car."

"Okay…"

"The little girl was with her dad, and he looked a little freaked out too, so after Merrick left, I asked him if they knew each other. Turns out, the little girl is his ex's daughter. Merrick told me Amelia had cheated on him, and he found out when she had her accident. But the little girl wasn't even three, and I could've sworn Merrick said Amelia died around three years ago."

"Hmmmm… Could you have gotten the timeline wrong?"

"Maybe. But what's bugging me is how Merrick acted afterward."

"How did he act?"

"He barely spoke and then just dropped me off here. I didn't even have my bag with me."

"So seeing the little girl upset him?"

"That's what it seems like. Maybe I'm overreacting, but it felt like the thirty-second exchange they had rewound the clock on our relationship."

"I do think you're reading into it. It was probably just an emotional reminder of a hard time. Things like that can pack a punch if they're thrown at you when you least expect it."

"Yeah, I guess..."

"Do you know Amelia's last name?"

I nodded. "Evans. Why?"

Greer picked up her phone. "You said she died in a plane crash, right?"

"Yeah."

"There must've been some press coverage." She shrugged. "Let's Google."

Before I could reconcile why googling a dead ex felt wrong, my sister turned the phone to show me a headline.

"Woman survives crash during flight training. She didn't die on impact?"

"I don't know all the details, but no."

My sister scanned the article. "This was written in July a few years back, so it would've been thirty-one months ago. How old was the little girl you saw today?"

"Her dad said she was going to be three in two months. So thirty-four months?"

"Welp, then that little girl was in her mom's belly when the plane crashed, and Amelia survived for at least a few months after."

Oh, God. There was a lot more to the story than I knew. I sighed. "Well, I guess there's a reason for a lot of emotions to bubble up then."

"That's probably all it was."

I nodded. "Yeah."

Yet deep down, I wasn't so sure.

Monday morning, I walked into the office with an anxious feeling in the pit of my stomach. I hadn't heard from Merrick since he'd dropped me off on Saturday afternoon.

Whatever uneasiness I had was magnified tenfold when I unlocked the door to my office and opened it.

The overnight bag I'd left in his apartment was on the couch.

I froze, feeling the wind knocked out of me. It took a solid thirty seconds before I walked over. When I did, I unzipped it and peeked inside, not certain what I was looking for. But whatever it was, it wasn't in there, because I found only my clothes and toiletries packed neatly. I looked around the room—to my desk, the coffee table, the small end table next to where I usually sat. What was I trying to find? A note, perhaps? But there was nothing.

Again, I did my best to convince myself I was overthinking. Merrick had returned my bag before I got here so I didn't have to sneak upstairs to get it later. He probably thought he was being helpful. He knew I was paranoid about people here at the office knowing.

I walked over to my desk and forced myself to start the day.

Yeah, he was being thoughtful.

I was being silly for reading into it.

I could picture it now. He probably went out for his morning run and brought it here on his way down when no one was in the office yet.

Maybe he thought I might need something from it early this morning.

It was actually a sweet gesture...

Wasn't it?

I looked over at the bag on the couch again, and my heart sank.

If it was such a sweet gesture, why did it feel like my bags had been packed and I'd just been kicked to the curb?

Luckily, I had an eight o'clock appointment, so I didn't have too much time to dwell. Since the market was open from nine thirty to four, I'd quickly found my schedule filled with a lot of 8 AM and 4 PM appointments. Which I was grateful for right about now. I needed something to distract me.

My first patient was a woman I'd met only briefly when HR walked me around on my first day. Her name was Hannah, and she was a junior-level trader, but probably about thirty. We did a typical first meeting, getting to know each other a bit and letting the conversation flow where it may. When the conversation came to a lull, I nudged our chat around to the office.

"So you work for Will, right?"

She nodded.

"How is that, if you don't mind me asking?"

"I like him. He's very open and honest, even when I'm not going to like his feedback. He has a way of softening a blow by making you laugh, but I always know where I stand with him."

"That's really great to hear."

"Yeah, it's why I'm happy in my position and don't have a desire to move up too much farther. I don't think I could work directly for someone like Merrick."

"Oh? What makes you say that?"

She shrugged. "He seems nice enough when you talk to him one-on-one, which I've had occasion to do when Will was out. But you never really know what's going on in his head. My friend Marissa was a manager here. When her boss left, she wound up reporting to Merrick for a while. After a few months, he called her in to talk about her position. She thought she was getting a promotion, that he was giving her the open position her boss had held."

"That didn't happen?"

"Merrick fired her instead. Can you imagine? She went in thinking she was getting a promotion, and instead," she got canned." She shook her head. "I'll stay where I am with a layer between us. Besides, my income isn't limited by my position. It's only limited by my abilities and what I put into it."

I did my best to smile, but her comment hit home.

By midday, the tossing and turning I'd done last night had started to catch up to me, and I needed a cup of coffee. There was none made in the break room on my floor, so it was the perfect excuse to take a trip upstairs. I had to walk past Merrick's office on my way. Unfortunately, his lights were on, but no one was inside, and his assistant was on the phone. My shoulders slumped as I made my way down the hall. When I walked in, Will was standing at the coffeemaker.

I walked up next to him. "Oohh... You just made a fresh pot?"

He offered his usual grin and pointed to the coffee dripping down. "This is the good shit. From my personal stash."

I smiled. "Are you going to share *the good shit* with me or hog it all for yourself?"

"I'll share. Although, I should warn you, my stuff is not cheap, but it is addictive." He winked. "Kind of like me."

I chuckled. Hannah was right. Will was pretty great.

The pot finished brewing, and Will filled my mug before pouring himself a cup. He leaned a hip against the counter. "So how long is the boss gone for?"

My forehead wrinkled. "Gone?"

"Yeah, he sent me an email yesterday saying he was flying out to California, but he didn't say when he'd be back. I figured you knew."

I couldn't hide my frown. "No, I didn't even know he wasn't in today."

One of the reasons Will was successful was because he was very perceptive. His eyes swept over my face, and he quickly changed the subject. He lifted his chin, motioning to my mug. "So what do you think?"

I sipped. The coffee was good, but at the moment everything had a bit of a sour taste to it. I forced a smile. "Delicious."

By six o'clock that night, I still hadn't heard anything from Merrick, so I bit the bullet and sent him a text.

Evie: Hey. Just checking in. Heard you were in California. You hadn't mentioned the trip, so I wanted to make sure all was okay.

Even though I wasn't an emoji person, I included a smiley face at the end, trying to make the text feel casual. I sat at my desk, turning a piece of sea glass over and over between my fingers as I waited for a response. After a minute, the text went from delivered to read, so I held my phone in my hand, expecting a message to come in any minute.

But a few minutes passed.

Then ten minutes.

A half hour ticked by.

And suddenly it was almost seven thirty and still no response. Of course, I tried to give myself a pep talk again.

He was probably in a meeting.

It would be rude to text.

He'd message me back soon...

Unfortunately, soon didn't happen until after ten o'clock that night. And the response did little to alleviate my bad feeling.

Merrick: Just a business trip. If you need anything, Will should be able to help you.

I frowned. I definitely needed something, but it wasn't Will who could give it to me.

CHAPTER 27

Evie

At least the week had gone by quickly. I had taken today off because I had to be in court at nine for the ridiculous lawsuit my ex had filed against me. My lawyer had said it would only take an hour or two of my Friday, that the judge would hear any motions and the trial calendar would likely be set. It was the absolute last thing I felt like doing after Merrick's disappearing act this week, but I tried to make the best of a day off and scheduled my bed for delivery this afternoon. I could finally move into my apartment this weekend.

I arrived at the courthouse early and waited outside at the top of the steps for my lawyer, but while I scanned the crowd coming in, I saw Christian instead. The jerk had the balls to wave. I greeted him with a less friendly flick of my hand—flipping him the middle finger.

This week had been such an emotional one, and seeing his face brought so much animosity to the surface. I hadn't heard from Merrick again after his short text response on Monday, and seeing Christian was a flashing-neon-sign reminder that I had misplaced my heart and my trust before.

It all bubbled to a boil once we got to the courtroom.

"Your Honor," my lawyer said. "I have a motion to dismiss for failure to state a claim. Even if everything in the plaintiff's petition were true, Mr. Halpern has no damages."

Christian's lawyer shook his head. "His reputation has been ruined by the defendant, Your Honor."

I leaned forward and scowled at my ex. "I think your reputation was ruined by you sleeping with my best friend the night before our wedding."

The judge narrowed his eyes at our table. "Please keep your client from speaking out of turn. She'll get to say her piece when the time comes."

Yeah, like any of this would bring me *peace*. I rolled my eyes but shut up.

My lawyer responded. "Yes, Your Honor. But back to the matter at hand. There is nothing in the petition that remotely indicates how Mr. Halpern was harmed that he should be made whole by my client. What is the basis of any damage claim? How was it calculated?"

"The damages are non-economic," Christian's lawyer said. "He was humiliated, suffered emotional anguish, had a loss of enjoyment of activities—"

I couldn't help myself. I leaned forward again. "*He* was humiliated? *He* suffered a loss of enjoyment?"

The judge wagged his finger. "Not another peep, Ms. Vaughn. I'm warning you."

My attorney held up his hand. "Could I have a word with my client, Your Honor?"

"By all means." The judge threw up his hands. "We have nothing better to do with our time this morning."

"Just one moment, Your Honor."

My lawyer leaned over to me. "You're going to wind up locked up for contempt if you don't listen. This is the judge who's going to rule over a trial, if it comes to that. You do not want to start off like this."

I took a deep breath and nodded. "Sorry."

My lawyer held my eyes. "Tread lightly."

I managed to refrain from speaking for the next forty-five minutes. In the end, the judge set a trial date, but stressed that he believed it was in both our best interests to settle the matter out of court.

After it was over, my attorney and I spoke for a while in the hall. Then he had to go upstairs to a different hearing, so I headed out on my own. As I made my way down the marble stairs, Christian was suddenly by my side.

"Can we talk for a minute?" he said.

"Why?"

"Because I want to put this behind us as much as you do."

I kept walking. "So drop the lawsuit."

"I will...if you just have dinner with me."

That stopped me in my tracks. My entire face wrinkled. "What?"

"Have dinner with me. And I'll drop the lawsuit."

"What are you talking about?"

Christian looked down. "I fucked up, Evie."

I snort-laughed. "You think?"

"Please have dinner with me."

"For what? What would be the purpose of that?"

"So we could talk?"

"We're talking right now. Say what you have to say and drop the lawsuit. I just want to move on with my life."

Christian looked up. "I can't move on with my life without you, Evie."

Oh my God. Is he serious? I shook my head and held up my hands. "I don't even know what to do with that. I'm not having dinner with you."

"Come on, Evie..."

I had no words. So I started to walk again. "Just sue me, Christian. I'd prefer that than having to look at your face for an hour over a meal."

I went into the office on Saturday morning to take care of a few things since I'd been out yesterday. There were a few people milling around, but Merrick's door was still closed. I'd taken out my notepad and started reviewing my scribbles so I could type up a session summary when I noticed my hairclip on my desk.

I picked it up and stared at it. I hadn't left it there, had I? I didn't think I'd ever brought one of these to the office. The only time I ever used one was when I washed my face and got ready for bed. Then it hit me—I might've left the one I'd used at Merrick's on his bathroom sink. I thought back to a week ago Friday night...

I'd gone into the bathroom off Merrick's bedroom to wash my face and brush my teeth. I was just finishing when Merrick walked up behind me. He looked in the mirror with a dirty smile, unclipping my hair as he reached up underneath the T-shirt I'd been wearing. I couldn't remember putting my clip back in my bag after that. I suppose Merrick could have left it on my desk the other day when he placed my bag on the couch. But I can't imagine I wouldn't have noticed. And why would he have placed it there and not in the bag with the other stuff he'd collected?

The only logical explanation was that he was back, and he'd left it on my desk either yesterday when I was out, or this morning. If that was the case, he might be upstairs right now. I thought about texting him again or picking up the phone and calling, but something was clearly going on, and I needed to see his face to know he was okay. Merrick was not the type of man to shy away from things, so maybe he was hurting more than I understood. I took a deep breath and went to the elevator.

Halfway up, I started to second-guess my decision, and I pushed the button to go back down to the office. But it wasn't like the elevator had a cancel button, so I had to ride up to the top floor before I could take it back down. Which is exactly what I'd planned to do, until the door slid open and Merrick stood in front of me.

"Oh...hey," I said.

Merrick looked up and frowned. My heart nearly broke right then and there.

"Hey." He shoved his hands into his pockets and looked anywhere but at me.

"I was just coming up to see if you were back. I, uh, found my hairclip on my desk today so I thought you might be."

He nodded. "I found it in the bathroom last night."

Merrick didn't look well. His skin was sallow, and dark circles rimmed his normally bright green eyes—which were pretty damn bloodshot. He was also a wrinkled mess, which was very unlike him.

I stepped forward and reached out. "Are you okay?"

Merrick stepped back. It would have been less painful if he'd slapped me across the face.

"Are you sick?"

He shook his head.

"Are you hurting because of seeing Amelia's daughter?"

His eyes jumped to meet mine. I'd never mentioned that the man had filled me in on who he was.

"He told me after you left the store," I whispered.

The elevator doors slid closed behind me. It made the hall feel so much smaller.

"Will you talk to me? Maybe I can help."

Merrick shook his head. "I don't want this."

For some reason, I assumed he meant me giving him therapy. "I won't try to psychoanalyze you or treat you like a patient. Whatever is going on, I can just listen as your girlfriend."

"I'm sorry, Evie. I made a mistake. We should never have happened."

I instantly went from sad to angry. It was one thing to dump someone, but another to say it was a mistake. "A mistake? You're calling what happened between us *a mistake*?"

"It's my fault."

My hands flew to my hips. "You're damn right it is. You know why? Because you wore me down. I wasn't ready to go down this road—*you* chased *me*. Not to mention, I thought it was a bad idea to get involved with someone at work, the boss, no less." I looked up and laughed maniacally. "Oh my freaking God. I did it again. Fell for a guy who is full of shit. Tell me, Merrick, is there a woman in your apartment, too? Because I left my phone downstairs, so you don't have to worry about any video going viral, at least." I shook my head. "Is that what this is? You were growing bored so you went back to fucking models? I mean, your neighbor would be convenient and seemed pretty interested."

Merrick hung his head. "No one is inside. I'm sorry. It's just... I can't be in a relationship and be responsible for someone else."

My neck pulled back. "Responsible for me? When did I ever ask you to be responsible for me? I'm an adult and perfectly capable of taking care of myself. Now you're just pulling excuses out of your ass. You know what, you were right to begin with. This was *a mistake*. But the mistake was completely on my part. I should have never fallen for your shit. That's what the mistake was."

Merrick met my eyes, and I waited a few heartbeats. A small part of me held out hope that he'd apologize and say he was wrong. But realizing I was clinging to that hope only made me more upset. I needed to get the hell out of here.

So I spun around and pushed the button—ten times. Merrick didn't seem to have moved from where he stood, though I couldn't be sure since I didn't turn back to check. Luckily, the elevator was super quick. I slipped inside before the doors had even finished opening. Pushing the button, I looked up at Merrick one last time. "You're just like the rest of them."

CHAPTER 28

Merrick

THREE YEARS AGO

It had been three days with no change.

I stood back, watching the group of doctors who came by each day for their morning rounds. Dr. Rosen lifted one of Amelia's eyes open and moved a pen light back and forth. First one, then the other. The frown gave me the answer before he even spoke.

"No change," he said. "I'm sorry."

I nodded.

He looked me up and down. "Have you left the hospital yet?"

"No."

"It looks like this is going to be a long haul. You might want to consider getting some rest. If you don't take care of yourself at the beginning of the marathon, you won't make it the full distance."

I nodded. "I don't want to leave her alone in case she wakes up. Her friend is coming today, so maybe I'll leave for a while then."

Dr. Rosen lifted the iPad he always carried around and started to type into it. "I'd like to consider starting her on a course of methylphenidate. It's a central nervous system stimulant. In some cases, it can help bring the person out of a coma. We're not there yet, but it's something for you to consider, maybe in a few more days if there are no new developments."

"Okay... And that's safe with the baby?"

"There's a recent study that showed it to be relatively safe during pregnancy."

"Relatively?"

"There are possible side effects with just about any medication. It's rare, but medications in this class can cause heart defects in an unborn child, though what's been studied is mostly the effects in the first trimester, which Amelia is past."

I blew out a deep breath. "What if we don't give it to her?"

"Well, there are a lot of very real risks for long-term coma patients. Blood clots, infection, loss of higher brain function..." He paused and looked over at Amelia. "We're not there yet. But these decisions are hard, and it often takes a family time to make them. As Amelia's health care proxy, that falls to you. So it's something to start considering."

I sighed. "Okay."

Dr. Rosen took a small pad out of his pocket and jotted something before ripping the sheet off and holding it out to me. "This is the name of the drug and a website where you can read up about it."

"Thanks."

After he left, I walked back over to the bed and stared down at Amelia's belly. The bump was barely visible, especially with the blankets over it. It was bad enough I had to make life and death decisions for her, someone whom I suddenly felt like I'd never known at all. But now I had to make decisions for a child who might not even be mine.

Colette stopped at the door, staring at Amelia a moment before walking into the small, glass ICU room.

"Hey." She forced a smile. "How are you holding up?"

I was a fucking wreck, yet I nodded. "I'm hanging in there."

She set her purse down on a visitor's chair, walked over to the bed, and took Amelia's hand. Tears fell from her cheeks. "I'm sorry I couldn't get back sooner."

Colette had been off work this week to take care of her mom, who'd had major neck and spine surgery yesterday. But we'd spoken every day since the accident. She was one of Amelia's few friends, and they were pretty close.

"How's your mom doing?"

"She's okay. They moved her out of the ICU last night into a surgical unit. So that's good."

I nodded. "Glad to hear it."

She stared down at Amelia. "I just can't believe this happened, Merrick. It's like a bad dream. Any news today?"

I shook my head. "No change. If nothing improves in a few days, they want me to consider approving a treatment that might stimulate her nervous system and bring her out of the coma."

"Oh great. Are there any risks to her? Like could it make her worse?"

I hadn't yet told Colette about the baby, or about the man I'd met when I walked in. She'd had her mother to deal with, and the news about the accident had been bad enough to tell her on the phone. But I was curious whether she knew about Aaron. If there was one person Amelia would tell, it would be her.

I took a deep breath. "The risks to her are minimal. But there are some risks to consider...for the baby."

Colette's head whipped up. "Baby?"

I nodded. "Apparently, she's more than four months along."

Colette's forehead wrinkled. "Apparently? So you didn't know?"

I shook my head.

Colette looked perplexed, but then understanding came across her face. She looked away, and I knew in that moment that she knew about Amelia's affair.

"You know about Aaron?"

Colette's eyes widened. "Did she know you knew?"

"No."

"How long have you known?"

"Since they brought her in wearing another man's engagement ring, and I found him in the waiting room."

She put her hand over her heart. "Oh, Jesus. I'm so sorry you found out that way, Merrick. I really am."

"Me, too."

I wanted to ask her so many questions, but I was fucking exhausted. Sleeping on the chair next to Amelia and all the noise of an ICU didn't lend itself to more than a half hour of rest at a time. "Are you going to stay for a while?" I asked.

"If you don't mind. I don't have anything else I need to do. Will has me covered this week since I was supposed to be down with my mom."

"Would you mind if I went home for a few hours?"

She looked me over. "Have you not gone home since everything happened?"

I shook my head.

"Oh, God. Definitely go home. I can stay all day, overnight even. If anything changes, I'll call you."

"I'll come back after I get a few hours of sleep."

She nodded. "Whatever you want. But I'll be here, so take as long as you need."

"Thanks, Colette."

I walked over and held Amelia's hand for a moment before squeezing. "I'll be back in a little while."

Colette nodded. "You look like shit, boss. Get some sleep."

I took the elevator down to the lobby and was halfway to the door when I noticed someone sitting alone in the large waiting area. Aaron met my eyes. He swallowed and stood. For a few seconds, I debated going over and punching his lights out, but I didn't have the fucking energy. Plus, there was something I needed to know. So I walked toward the seating area. The guy was still dressed in the clothes he'd been wearing the day they brought Amelia in. And his face still had dirt and bruises. Guess I wasn't the only one who'd been here three days.

"How is she?"

"I'll answer that if you answer one question for me first."

He nodded his head. "Anything."

"Did you use protection?"

"What?"

I raised my voice. "When you were *fucking my fiancée*, did you use a condom?"

"Yes, always. Why?"

I felt as relieved as I could. "She's still in a coma. There are brainwaves, and *my daughter* is holding on."

The guy blinked. He hadn't known either. "Amelia's... pregnant?"

My lip curled. "I answered your question. You might as well go home because you're never getting in that room to see her. I'll kill you before that happens."

Later that night, I was back at the hospital alone. I sat in the chair beside Amelia as the night nurse came to examine her. After a quick check of her vitals, she put the stethoscope on her belly and held it there listening. "Oh wow..." She removed the listening part from her ears. "I just felt the baby move."

I sat up. "You did?"

She nodded. "Come here. Put your hand right where the stethoscope is now."

I hesitated, but eventually set my hand on Amelia's belly. Her skin was so warm and soft. At first, there was nothing, but after a minute, I felt a roll in her stomach. My eyes widened. It was the first time I'd smiled in almost four days. "I felt it."

She nodded. "That's an active little bugger."

"Figures. She's probably just like her mother."

The woman smiled. "It's a girl?"

I nodded. I felt the movement again, this time it was more like a poke than a roll. "I think she just kicked me."

She laughed. "Well, her heartbeat sounds good, and it's a good sign that she's kicking at this age. Some people can't feel the baby for a few more weeks."

I kept my hand on Amelia's belly and looked up at her. I'd been afraid to even consider that the baby could be mine before now, before the other possibility confirmed they'd been careful. Amelia and I weren't, though she'd been on the pill since we met. But something happened in that moment—feeling the baby move for the first time.

She went from being Amelia's baby to *our* baby. I was so fucking mad at Amelia, but it wasn't fair to take it out on this little one.

I'd been so lost in thought that I almost forgot the nurse was there until she spoke. "I'll come back and check on her in a few hours."

"Okay."

After she left, I laid my cheek on Amelia's stomach, right over where I'd felt the movement, and shut my eyes.

I'm having a baby.

A little girl.

For the first time, I let the gravity of that sink in. Something bloomed in my heart, but the weight of everything else felt like it was crushing my chest.

What if Amelia doesn't wake up?

What if my little girl has to grow up without a mother?

What if I lose them both?

My throat constricted. I tried to swallow the taste of salt, but I was no match for the wave that was coming. For four days, I hadn't shed a single tear. Anger and sadness had blocked them. But suddenly, my body wanted to make up for lost time. Tears began to flow, streaming down my face and falling from my cheeks onto Amelia's belly. My shoulders shook, sobs wracking over me as I let out a harrowing sound.

I have no idea how long I cried, but it felt like hours. At one point, the nurse even came back to check on me. When my tears finally dried, I turned my head and kissed Amelia's belly.

"I'm sorry. I've been so mad at your mother that I haven't even acknowledged you. Forgive me. It won't happen again. From now on, I promise to be there and take care of you every step of the way, my precious little girl."

CHAPTER 29

Evie

"That's the last of it." I collapsed onto my new couch on Sunday afternoon after crushing the last box we'd unpacked. It had taken two days for Greer and me to find a home for everything that had been delivered from my storage unit to my new apartment, which was a fraction of the size of the place I'd moved from.

"You know, there's a great singles' bar down the block. I went a few times before I met Ben," my sister said.

I guzzled the last of a bottle of water. "I have zero interest in dating for a very long time."

Greer frowned. I'd told her what had gone down between Merrick and me last week. "I know, but that's usually when you meet someone. I met Ben less than a week after Michael and I broke up, remember?"

Christian and I had been together for years and been engaged, yet I didn't think it would be nearly as easy to get over Merrick as it had been with him. It made me realize that time together didn't matter. Some people just work their way deeper into your heart.

I shook my head. "It would be easier to move on if I understood what happened."

"It sounds to me like he saw that little girl, and it reminded him of what he didn't want—commitment and a relationship."

Of course, that was entirely possible, but I didn't think so. "I don't know. But I think I'm going to start looking for another job."

"What? You love your new job."

"I do. But I reopen a wound every time I see him down the hall or pass by his office. And half of my sessions involve talking about him." I sighed. "I'm in love with him, Greer."

She smiled sadly. "I know you are."

My doorbell rang. "Is that Ben? I thought he was going to pick you up later this evening?"

My sister shrugged. "He is. He went to the office for a few hours."

It wasn't my brother-in-law at the door when I opened it. Instead, it was a guy in a uniform holding a clipboard. "I'm here to install the alarm."

"I think you have the wrong apartment." I shook my head. "I didn't order an alarm."

"Oh, sorry." He lifted a page on his paperwork. "It's for an Evie Vaughn. Do you happen to know what floor she lives on? I pushed the only button that wasn't labeled."

My face wrinkled. "I'm Evie Vaughn. But I didn't order an alarm system."

The guy looked as confused as me. He shuffled through more of his papers. "Well, it says here someone prepaid for installation and a three-year contract."

Then it hit me. Merrick had been adamant that I have an alarm. He could have ordered it before we broke up. "Can you tell me who ordered it?"

"If it was paid with a credit card. Most orders are placed over the phone, so the office gives me the receipt to give the homeowner when I do the job."

"Could you tell me the name on the card?"

He scanned more papers before pulling one from his clipboard and holding it out to me. "Looks like it was paid for by a Merrick Crawford."

I looked down. The amount was shocking. "Forty-three-hundred dollars?"

He shrugged. "He bought all the bells and whistles—window security, doors, even two panic buttons that silently call the police in an emergency."

I shook my head. "I'm sorry. I can't afford this. The person who paid for it... Well, we broke up."

"Did you break up with him?"

"No."

He smiled. "Then why not take it as a parting gift?"

"I can't do that."

"It's not refundable. The guy signed an electronic contract, and it's only cancelable for three days. New York requires a three-day right of recission. That was up yesterday. Trust me, the company I work for doesn't let anyone out after that, so you might as well use it."

My forehead creased. "The contract was signed three days ago?"

He looked down at the paperwork once more. "Order was placed four days ago. It was a rush request. This is the first day we would do an install since customers have the right to cancel the full contract within three days."

That made no sense. Merrick and I had broken up more than a week ago. "Could this date be wrong?"

"I don't think so. Everything gets printed the date the contract is signed."

Greer came to the door. "What's going on?"

"It's an alarm company coming to do an install. Merrick prepaid it for three years."

"Nice. At least he did something right before he broke your heart."

"Actually, that's the strange part. It seems he placed the order after we split up." I thought back to the other day at the office, to the conversation I'd had with Andrea in the break room. "Now that I think about it, his assistant asked me if I was working today. I thought she was just making conversation, but I told her I'd be home unpacking all weekend."

"Awesome." My sister smiled. "You should have an alarm on the first floor anyway. I didn't even think of that."

"But I can't let Merrick pay for an alarm. I wouldn't have let him even if we were still together." I shook my head at the installer. "I'm sorry you wasted a trip."

The next morning, I went to the office early so I could speak to Merrick about the alarm, but he wasn't around. For the rest of the day, he was in a meeting whenever I was free. Then he was out of the office Tuesday and Wednesday. When he returned on Thursday, I was determined to get in to see him at some point, because the alarm company had called me twice to follow up after I didn't allow their installer in. At six, I'd just finished up with my last patient and readied myself to go by his office when my phone rang. It was my lawyer, so I swiped to answer even though anything to do with Christian's lawsuit gave me an instant headache.

"Hello?"

"Hey, Evie. It's Barnett Lyman."

"Hi, Barnett. How's it going?"

"Good. Listen, I just wanted to check in to see if you've given any more thought to Christian's offer."

"You mean his ridiculous bribery attempt? That if I have dinner with him, he'll drop the lawsuit?"

"I know it's ridiculous. And I'd never advise a client to meet with someone who is actively suing them. But his lawyer says they'll put it in writing so he can't back out."

I leaned back in my chair and sighed. "Can't we just tell the judge what he's trying to pull to prove Christian's acting in bad faith?"

"We can. But we'd have to file motions and take more time in court, and there's a good chance the judge won't kick the case even if he doesn't like it. But the bottom line is, I'm five-fifty an hour, and I don't like to waste a client's money. Filing a motion is an hour prep, then going to court... That easily racks up to a few thousand dollars. I'll do whatever you want, but if you can save all that and get rid of it, why not try? Let me ask you, are you afraid to meet with him?"

"You mean like in a physical sense?"

"Whatever."

Christian was the world's biggest jerk, but I wasn't afraid of him physically, and he couldn't hurt me emotionally anymore. I shook my head. "No, I'm not afraid of him at all."

"I could try to negotiate it from dinner to a lunch, if that would help."

It was the last thing I wanted to do, but Barnett was right. I didn't have thousands of dollars to waste, and all I really wanted was to put the last of it behind me. I hated it—but it was the right move. I sighed. "Okay. If you can get him to agree to a lunch, that would be great."

"I'll get back to you soon."

After I hung up, I sat at my desk for a while, staring out the window. A knock on my office door interrupted my thoughts. Merrick stood in the doorway.

"My assistant said you came by and asked if I was in?"

He looked only minimally better than he had the day he dumped me. His naturally tanned skin was still sallow, and dark circles remained below his green eyes. But I couldn't let that affect me. Especially not after the call I'd just finished. So I took a deep breath and exhaled. Just as I was about to speak, a trader walked down the hall behind Merrick, so I motioned to the door. "Could you come in and close that? I'd prefer we discuss this in private."

"Of course."

He shut the door, but stayed on the other side of the room. Which was just fine with me.

"An alarm company showed up at my house the other day. They said you pre-paid for service and the installation."

"I did."

"But you did that after you dumped me. Why?"

Merrick's face fell. "I told you I would, and I didn't think you would do it on your own."

I stood and put my hands on my desk, leaning forward. "You told me you would? Well, why keep that commitment when you didn't keep the one that convinced me to trust you? You know, the one where you *promised you'd never hurt me?*"

He had the audacity to look like my comment upset him. Merrick rubbed the back of his neck. "I'm sorry."

"Oh, you're sorry?" I nodded and rolled my eyes before sitting back down. "Thanks for that. It helps a lot."

Merrick took a step toward my desk, but I put my hand up, stopping him in his tracks. "Don't," I said. "I don't need another apology, and I certainly don't need you to pay for an alarm system out of some sense of pity or whatever it is. So unless you have something else to say, like maybe explaining the truth of what happened between us, there's nothing more we need to discuss."

Merrick finally looked in my eyes. He looked sad, but I didn't care.

"You know what?" I said. "You once told me my ex was a coward. And you were right, he is. But so are you." I shook my head. "Just please go before I get upset."

CHAPTER 30

Merrick

"I am a fucking coward," I grumbled, staring down into the bottom of my empty glass. Well, not empty, considering the ice I'd tossed in when I'd filled it three quarters of the way up with whiskey fifteen minutes ago hadn't had a chance to melt yet. Now the bottle—that shit was almost empty.

I stared over at the coffee table, at the upside-down box and its contents that I'd spilled all over the place two nights ago, after Evie had asked me to leave her office. Leaning forward, I swiped a picture from the pile, one I'd stared at for hours on end over the last two days, trying to find my nose and my chin—the ones I'd so clearly known were mine the day my little girl was born. Yet now all I saw was Amelia's face—her nose, her chin, her dark blue, distant eyes. I wanted to rip up the damn photo and never see it again. But I'd cherished the day it was taken even more than I hated the ones that came after.

The alcohol started to hit—either that or my apartment was spinning faster than a ride at Disney. So I laid back on the couch with the photo still in my hands, and I shut my eyes with one foot on the floor to keep me grounded. It didn't take long until I drifted off to sleep. Sometime later, a loud banging on my door woke me up.

At least I *thought* someone had been banging. But as I sat up and glanced around, my apartment was silent. *Ugh. But my head.* Apparently, the pounding I'd thought was coming from the door was coming from my brain.

Tha-thump, tha-thump.

Fuck. It felt like a little drummer boy was inside my skull practicing for a solo. I dropped my head into my hands and massaged my temples. But then the loud banging in my head turned into surround sound, and a voice joined in with the band.

"Crawford, open the damn door before I break it down. I know you're in there."

Fuck.

I needed Will riding my ass right now like I needed a hole in the head.

"Go away! I'm fine," I yelled back.

"Not good enough. Get your ass up and open the door."

I closed my eyes and shook my head, knowing the pain in the ass was not going anywhere. Basically, the faster I dragged my ass to the door, the faster I could get rid of him.

When I stood from the couch, I barely stuck the landing.

Damn, I suck at drinking.

I tried to move my head as little as possible as I treaded to the front door and unlocked it.

Will opened the door and looked me up and down. "Jesus Christ, those are the clothes you were in two days ago. I knew you weren't out of town." He leaned forward and sniffed. "And you stink like stale liquor." He shook his head. "How many times do I have to tell you to leave the drinking to me? You never could develop a tolerance worth shit."

I started back to the couch without saying a word. Unfortunately, seeing I was alive wasn't good enough. Will shut the door behind him and followed me in.

"What the hell is going on with you?"

I sat down on the couch with my head hanging. It was too heavy to hold up.

Will looked at the shit strewn all over the coffee table. "Oh fuck. What happened?" He bent and picked up the tiny baby cap Eloise wore the day she was born.

"Don't touch that," I managed to grumble.

He sighed loudly and walked away. I hoped maybe he'd realized I was going through something and decided to respect my privacy. But he came back two minutes later.

"Take these." He held out a few pills and a tall glass of water. "Three Motrin and hydrate to start." Then he started typing on his phone. "I'm ordering Gatorade, bananas, and a pastrami on rye from the deli down the block that delivers."

I squinted up at him. "There's no way I could eat pastrami."

"That's not for you, jackass. It's for me. I'm starving. You'll have the Gatorade and bananas. You need electrolytes and potassium." He finished typing and tossed his phone on the couch, taking the seat across from me. "Talk to me. What happened?"

I was in no mood to converse. I shook my head.

"How long have we been friends?" he said.

"Too long," I grumbled.

"Then you should know by now that I'm not going anywhere until we talk it out."

"I can barely keep down the Motrin you just gave me. I'm not up for conversation."

"It's alright." He shrugged. "I'm in no rush."

Great. He's here for the long haul.

"Why don't you lie down for a bit and wait for the headache to subside? I have some emails to answer anyway."

I would've preferred he just disappear, but I'd take silence if that was all I could get. So I did what he said and laid back down on the couch, propping my feet up on the armrest and shutting my eyes. I was in and out of consciousness for a while after that, until the sound of a bag crumpling opened one eye.

"Any better?" Will asked.

I swung my legs down to the floor and sat up. It felt like a Mack truck had run me over, then backed up and run me over a second time in reverse, but the Motrin seemed to have taken the edge off the pounding in my head, at least.

I rubbed the back of my neck. "You got that Gatorade?"

Will held it out, along with a banana.

Twenty minutes later, I still didn't feel like talking, but at least I was capable of it. Will had finished his sandwich, kicked off his shoes, and had his feet propped up on a corner of the coffee table with his arms spread wide across the top of the couch.

"What's going on, my friend?"

I sighed. "I ran into Aaron Jensen."

"Okay..."

"He had Eloise with him." I'd been looking down at the ground but raised my eyes to meet Will's. "She's deaf."

Will frowned. "But she's okay, otherwise?"

I shrugged. "She has braces on her legs, and her..." I couldn't bring myself to call him her father, even after three years. "Aaron was signing to her."

Will digested the information. "Okay, well, you knew there was a possibility she might have hearing deficits and some developmental issues. That's tough, but doesn't mean she won't be able to live a perfectly happy life."

I closed my eyes and pictured her in the shopping cart. The face had haunted my thoughts so much that not even drowning in alcohol could stop it. "She looks just like Amelia."

Will was quiet a long time. "You need to nip this shit in the bud before you blow things with Evie."

I looked up at him.

Will shut his eyes. "Shit. You already did."

"I fucking did this to Eloise." I shook my head. "I don't even know if that's her name anymore."

"Did what to Eloise?"

"Everything. It was the choices I made that killed her mother and caused her to be born prematurely. If I'd just let nature take its course..."

Will's face wrinkled. "What are you talking about?"

"You know I made all of the medical decisions for Amelia and the baby."

"Yeah, and?"

"She went into labor from a drug I approved giving her."

"Yeah, because the *team of doctors* treating her recommended it. I know you're a smart dude, but you didn't go to four years of medical school and do eight years of residency like the neurologists did. Not to mention, there's no proof that the medicine caused her to go into labor early. Her body was giving out long before that." He shook his head. "Things happen. Women who aren't in plane crashes go into early labor and have babies with far more issues. There's shit in life we can't control."

I heard Will talking, but I was too distracted by the memories flashing through my mind to really listen to him. One, in particular, was the hardest to tune out. It was the day I'd found out my daughter wasn't my daughter. I'd left the hospital to wallow in self-pity marinated in vodka and come back to an empty bed.

"I didn't say goodbye to her," I choked out.

Will stared at me as tears rolled down my cheeks. "What do you mean, you didn't say goodbye? I was outside the room when you held her—" He stopped abruptly. "Shit. You don't mean Eloise, do you? You're talking about Amelia. This isn't just about the baby."

A few minutes passed without either of us talking. Eventually Will sat up. He took his feet from the coffee table and leaned his elbows on his knees. "Do you love Evie?"

I wiped my tears and nodded. "I do."

"Then you need to figure out a way to move on."

I thought I *had* moved on...until I saw Eloise's sweet face. "How do I fucking do anything now?"

"You stop letting things from your past destroy your future. I'm no shrink, but I think the first step is letting it out. It's been three years, and this is the first time you've let the emotions in. After Amelia died, you came back to work a few days later like nothing happened. You can't erase people from your heart to move on." He tapped his fingertips to his chest. "You have to accept that they're always going to have a piece and let it heal as best it can. A person who loves you will take your heart, scars and all."

CHAPTER 31

Merrick

THREE YEARS AGO

"**M**r. Crawford?"

I looked up from the rocking chair. I'd been sitting and staring down at my little girl for the last hour. She was five days old today, and it was the first time she'd been stable enough to come out of the incubator.

The NICU nurse who'd handed her to me was standing at the door with another woman I didn't recognize. She wore a suit, rather than scrubs like everyone else. The nurse walked over. "We need to put Eloise back in now. It's important she gets sufficient time under the lights for her jaundice."

I nodded and leaned down to kiss my daughter's forehead. She was tiny, so freaking tiny.

When I was ready, the nurse scooped the baby from my arms and set her back in the incubator. She smiled warmly at me as she pointed to the woman standing in the doorway. "Mrs. Walters would like to speak to you. She's the hospital's in-house attorney."

My eyes jumped to the woman. I guessed they'd sent in the big guns since I'd refused to sign the DNR for Amelia so far. I nodded and stood. "Can I hold the baby again later?"

"Of course. We'll just do it in short sessions." She looked at her watch. "It's three o'clock now. Maybe around seven?"

"Thank you."

The attorney stepped outside the nursery and waited for me to join her. "Hi, Mr. Crawford. I'm Nina Walters from the hospital's legal department. Would it be okay if we went somewhere to talk for a few minutes?"

I looked back at the incubator, at my daughter safely sleeping inside again. "Sure."

We walked to the waiting room, which was empty, and sat down.

"Your fiancée's medical team has filled me in on everything that's transpired over the last few months. I'm very happy Eloise is doing so well."

I nodded. "She failed her hearing test, but they said that was common and may work itself out."

My little girl was tough. She had some fluid stuck in her middle ear, and they couldn't guarantee there wouldn't be developmental issues as time went on, but she was one hell of a fighter, born at only twenty-nine weeks.

Nina took a deep breath and exhaled. "You've been through so much already. I hate to even talk to you about this, but the hospital received a court order today."

"Because I didn't sign the DNR? From who? Amelia hasn't spoken to her mother in years."

The woman shook her head and held out some official-looking documents with a blue back. "This isn't related to your medical decisions for Amelia. The court has ordered the hospital to collect DNA from Eloise for a paternity test. The petitioner is someone named Aaron Jensen."

The following afternoon, I was sitting in Amelia's room when the monitors suddenly started going off. I stood and watched the normally steady lines start to jump all over erratically. But Amelia hadn't moved a muscle. A nurse ran into the room, took one look at the screen, and yelled back to the nurses' station.

"Code blue! Grab the crash cart!"

A half-dozen people piled into the room in the next thirty seconds. The doctor listened to Amelia's heart, while another nurse grabbed an arm and counted the heartbeats from the pulse on her wrist.

"Mr. Crawford, can you please step outside?"

I backed up to make room for them to work. "I'll keep out of the way, but I'm staying right here."

They were too busy to argue with me. The shit that happened after that played out like a scene from a TV show.

Her heart rate display on the monitor fell to a flat line.

The doctor fired up the defibrillator paddles and told everyone around the bed to clear their hands from the patient. Then he pressed them to her chest and shocked her.

Amelia's body jumped, but it went right back to the limp state it had been in since the day she arrived here.

Everyone stared at the monitor.

Nothing.

They shocked her a second time.

Still nothing.

A nurse injected something into her IV and measured her pulse manually again. She looked up at the doctor and shook her head with a frown.

"All clear!"

The doctor adjusted the knobs on the machine before setting the paddles once again.

Amelia's body jumped even higher.

The monitor made a blip sound and the flat line started to jump up and down again.

The doctor's shoulders visibly relaxed.

"Why did that happen?" I asked.

He returned the paddles to the portable machine they'd wheeled in. "Could be a number of reasons." He shook his head. "A blood clot, electrolyte abnormalities, or even just her system shutting down because it's exhausted. The last few months have been tough on her body, including her C-section."

"A blood clot? Because of the medicine she was given? They told me that was a risk when they asked for permission to try it."

The doctor held up his hands. "Let's not get ahead of ourselves. We don't know that there was a blood clot yet. And even if there was, patients who spend months in a coma are at a high risk for such a thing."

I rubbed my forehead. "Is she going to be okay?"

He looked over at the monitor. "She's stabilized now. But like it's been since the beginning, we have to take this one step at a time. Let's start with running some tests to see what we're up against now."

I nodded and blew out a loud puff of air. "Okay."

The following morning, I'd just finished holding Eloise in the NICU again and returned to Amelia's room to check on her. The monitor showed her heartbeat was normal, so I sat down by her bedside and shut my eyes for a minute. I'd been here all night, afraid to go home and have something else happen. Then a woman knocked at the open door.

She smiled. "Hi, Mr. Crawford. I'm Kate Egert. I'm from the hospital's social services department. We met a while back when Ms. Evans was first brought in."

I nodded, though she barely looked familiar, and stood. "Sure. Good to see you."

She seemed hesitant. "Do you think we could talk outside for a minute?"

It was never good news when they didn't want to talk in front of Amelia. But how much worse could shit get than the last two days? "Sure."

Outside in the hall, she pointed. "Why don't we go sit in the family room?"

I glanced back at Amelia and shook my head. "Could we just talk here? She's had a rough twenty-four hours."

"Oh, sure. Yes, of course." She took a deep breath before holding out a folded paper. "I'm sorry to pile on with everything you're going through. But the paternity test came back."

I froze.

She unfolded the paper in her hand and looked into my eyes. "According to the DNA test, you are not Eloise's father."

CHAPTER 32

Merrick

I stood across the street for a third day in a row.

It felt like I was starting to establish something of a routine: Get up hungover at the ass crack of dawn. Take two Motrin with a gallon of Gatorade and let the water sluice over me in the shower. Put on a baseball cap, sunglasses, and dark zip-up sweatshirt, walk down more than forty flights of stairs and slip out the service entrance to minimize the chances of running into anyone from the office. Then hike it over to 19th Street to stand in a doorway that reeked like piss and watch a man I loathed from a distance.

I wasn't even sure what the hell I was looking for. But just like the prior two days, Aaron had left with Eloise about twenty minutes ago. His day seemed pretty scheduled, so I expected him back soon. Ten minutes later, he strolled up to his building. Only this time, he stopped at the front door, turned...and stared right across the street at me.

Shit.

After a few seconds, he walked to the curb, looked both ways, and jogged across the street. I usually ran five miles a day, so I could have pulled the bill of my hat down and taken off. He never would have caught me, especially not with the adrenaline flowing through my veins at the moment. But I couldn't move. Not even when he walked right up to me.

"Do you want to come up and talk?" he said calmly.

I held his eyes. He had to see the hatred in mine. "How do you know I didn't come here to kill you?"

He shrugged. "I don't. Do you want to come up anyway?"

I didn't know what the hell I was doing here, yet I found myself nodding. My body was rigid the entire ride up in the elevator, and when he opened the door to his apartment, I paused but ultimately followed him in.

Aaron went straight to the kitchen. He stood with his back to me at the counter. "Coffee or whiskey?"

"Whiskey."

He nodded, and while he pulled a bottle and glasses from the cabinet, I walked over to the refrigerator. Hand-drawn pictures hung from various magnets all over. One, in particular caught my attention. It was mostly a bunch of scribbled circles, but I could make out that they were supposed to be people. One was in pink and small, and the one next to her was three times the size and blue. A third pink circle-person was at the top of the page, next to a bunch of dark blue scribbled lines.

Aaron walked up and offered me a glass. He pointed at the drawing as he sipped his drink. "She knows her mother is in heaven, and heaven is above, so she puts her next to the clouds."

I nodded.

To the right was a picture of Amelia. She was sitting in the pilot's seat of a small plane, smiling at the person taking the photo from outside. I gulped down the entire glass of whiskey while staring at it and held the glass out to Aaron. No conversation was necessary for him to refill it.

"Why don't we sit at the table?" he said, holding out a full glass again.

We took seats across from each other.

"Did you come here to punch me or to talk?" Aaron asked.

I shook my head. "I'm not sure."

"Well, I deserve the punch. So have at it, if it'll make you feel better."

We stared each other down for a moment. "How long was it going on?"

Aaron set down his glass. "About six months, I guess."

"Why didn't she break things off with me?"

"Because she loved you. I gave her an ultimatum once—told her it was me or you. She said if she had to choose, it would be you. That it would always be you."

I was quiet for a long time. "Why then? Why'd she do it?"

He shook his head. "That's a question I've asked myself many times—in addition to why *I* did it, knowing full well she wasn't available. I was just a selfish asshole. But I don't think that was the reason for Amelia. I actually don't believe it had anything to do with me. I think she wanted you to find out."

My forehead wrinkled. "Why?"

"So you'd break it off, so she could hurt you before you hurt her."

That wouldn't make much sense for a lot of people, but he'd clearly gotten to know Amelia pretty well. His theory wasn't that far-fetched. Though his answer just made me angry, and I wasn't sure why I'd asked those questions to begin with.

"Is Eloise...okay?"

Aaron's face lit up. "She's very okay. At the rate she's going, she'll be smarter than me in a few years."

I smiled for the first time in a week. "And her hearing?"

He nodded. "She's completely deaf. It's common in premature babies."

"Her legs?"

"Just a little bowlegged. Doc says she should be done with the braces in a few months. Other than that, she's perfectly healthy. Small for her age, but that's also another common preemie issue. She caught up a bit in her first year. But I think she's just going to be on the low end of the height chart, like her mother."

I blew out a deep breath. Since I hadn't planned on talking to Aaron, there wasn't much else I needed to say. I nodded. "Thank you."

"I know I must have caused you a world of pain during those difficult times, and I'm very sorry for that. Not that it helps, but on the rare occasion I get out and meet a woman, I run the other way if she's involved in any way."

Aaron walked behind me to the door. He opened it, and I stepped into the hall and lifted my hand in a wave before heading to the elevator.

"Merrick?" he called after me.

I turned back.

"Would you like to see her? To get to know Eloise a bit?"

I wasn't sure I could handle that, but I appreciated the offer. "Can I get back to you?"

He smiled. "Sure. You obviously know where to find me."

CHAPTER 33

Evie

"I wasn't sure you'd come today." I sat down in my usual chair, across from the patient couch. "Today is your last day, right?"

Colette nodded. "It is. But I have a lot of mixed feelings about it. I thought it might help to talk to someone. I don't have a lot of friends anymore, and the ones I do have I'm more likely to discuss my day's buy orders than feelings with."

"Well, then I'm glad you came." I pointed to a giant tray of cookies on the table. "Please have some. I've been on a baking spree, and if I take them home, I'll eat them."

Colette smiled and grabbed a cookie. Biting into it, she looked around the room. "This place was my first job out of college. For the last three years, I couldn't wait for this day to come, but now that it's here, I don't feel relieved and excited like I thought I would."

"What are you feeling?"

She shook her head. "Sad, mostly. Maybe a little regret."

"Regret for leaving?"

"No. It's time. The regret is more to do with Merrick."

I wished I could have said, "*I feel your pain, Colette.*" Then maybe cracked open a bottle of wine and shared stories. But I was a professional, and my own feelings needed to be kept out of it. So instead, I said, "Tell me about that. Can you pinpoint what it is you regret?"

She shook her head. "It's so many things... Some of them don't even make sense."

"Like what?"

Colette looked down. "Well, for some reason, lately I've been thinking a lot about the times I went out to dinner with my then boyfriend and Merrick and Amelia. I knew she was having an affair, yet we all went to dinner and acted like everything was normal. I'm not sure why those memories keep popping into my brain after so long."

"Oftentimes the secret we keep is irrelevant. It's the fact we kept it that bothers us most."

She nodded. "Maybe."

"You said *lately* you've been thinking about the secret you kept during dinners. Does that mean these are new thoughts, or that they've just popped into your mind more in recent times?"

"I never gave the fact that I kept my friend's affair a secret any thought until the last month or so. That might not say a lot about me, but it's the truth."

"Did something happen recently that made you think of the affair?"

"Not really. But I did notice a change in Merrick. I'm not sure if that's relevant or not."

"What kind of a change?"

"Well, he hasn't been around much the last couple of weeks, but before that I noticed that he smiled more in meetings. And he laughed more. It wasn't until I saw him seeming happy the last few months that I realized how long he must have been unhappy. It made me realize how much he suffered after Amelia's death."

My forehead creased. "Did you think he didn't suffer?"

She shrugged. "I don't know. I blamed him for her death. But maybe I just needed someone to blame."

"Why would you blame him for her death?"

"Because he was her health care proxy and made all the medical decisions. He found out she was having an affair when she was brought into the hospital, and then got to decide what drugs she would take and what procedures she would undergo."

Oh, God.

Colette noticed my face and nodded. "Yeah. It was screwed up."

It was difficult not to take what she'd just told me and focus on Merrick, but he wasn't my patient. He wasn't even my boyfriend anymore. So I forced myself back to what I should've been doing—helping Colette untangle her feelings.

"Let's back up a moment. It sounds like you're starting to question whether the things you've been holding Merrick accountable for are really his fault. And at the same time, you're reminded of things you kept from him when you were once friends. You're bringing a lot of guilt to the surface. Why do you think that's coming up now? Because you're leaving?"

Colette smiled sheepishly. "Well, I'm taking some clients with me. That's against my noncompete. Merrick won't be happy about it, though it won't make a blip in the firm's profit. But I also know he won't do anything about it because I'm not the only one who's held him accountable for what happened."

"What do you mean?"

"The only person who was tougher on Merrick than me was Merrick."

⌒‿‿⌒

That evening, even though it was Friday night, I didn't feel like going home. I hadn't been able to stop thinking about Merrick since my session with Colette earlier in the day. I'd even broken my week-long streak of staying on my own floor and not going upstairs in an attempt to catch a glimpse of him, but he was nowhere to be found. It was just as well since I was feeling vulnerable, and the last thing I needed was a reason to justify the way he'd acted and give myself hope that things could work out.

It was a beautiful night, so I decided to take the bus to Glass Bottle Beach in Brooklyn instead of going home. I walked the shoreline for an hour, picking up sea glass and sidestepping sharp pieces the ocean hadn't taken for a long-enough tumble yet. But even my happy place wasn't cutting it tonight. I sat down on a big rock at the ocean's edge to watch the sunset. The sky lit with a mix of purples and pinks, and I closed my eyes to listen to the soft jingle the beach played as it hit all the glass. It seemed louder with each breath—so much so that I opened my eyes to look around and see if the waves had changed. But it wasn't the ocean jingling; it was a set of keys.

I blinked, assuming the person holding them in his hand was an apparition.

But he wasn't.

I lifted my hand to shield my eyes from the sun as my heart started to race. "Merrick? What are you doing here?"

"I came to find some lucky sea glass."

"Did you know I was here?"

He shook his head. "I've been coming every night around this time for the last few days."

"But...why?"

He smiled sadly. "Is there room on that rock for two?"

I was afraid, but I couldn't stop the hope from blooming in my chest. I scooted over to make room for him. "Sure."

Merrick sat down beside me and looked over at the sunset. Since I had to face his direction to watch, I used it as an opportunity to take a closer look at him. It looked like he'd aged a few years in just a few weeks. I was angry as shit at the man, but I was human, and it looked like he needed a friend. So I pulled out my lucky orange sea glass and held it out to him.

"Give it a rub. It looks like you could use it."

His eyes washed over my face before he shook his head. "I've treated you like shit the last two weeks, and you offer me something you treasure."

I shrugged. "It hasn't been doing its job anyway, lately. Maybe you'll have better luck."

Merrick reached over and closed my open palm, leaving the glass tucked inside my hand. He stared down at my fist for the longest time before lifting his eyes to meet mine. "The day of Amelia's accident, I found out she was having an affair and was also more than four months pregnant. I knew it was possible it could be someone else's child, but I somehow convinced myself it wasn't." He shook his head. "I was certain the baby was mine. I was so damn angry at Amelia for what she'd done. But I eventually found a way to let some of that go by falling in love with my daughter." Merrick swallowed. "It was like I had all this hatred and animosity in my heart, and the more I fell in love with a child I'd never met, the more those feelings pushed out the bad ones. I read to her for hours every night, played her all of my favorite songs, and even told her stories about her mother and me when we met in college. The nurses gave me my own stethoscope because I would borrow theirs to listen to her heartbeat all the time."

It didn't matter that Merrick had broken my heart, I opened my hand and entwined my fingers with his, keeping my sea glass inside our meshed palms.

"Over the next few months, I had to make a lot of difficult medical decisions. The more time that passed, the more Amelia's life was at risk. But Eloise needed her mother because she wouldn't have survived if she was born too early."

"You had to make all those decisions for them by yourself?"

He nodded. "Her parents weren't in the picture, and she wasn't close to many people. But at the time, I wasn't even sure *I* knew what she'd want, considering I'd had no idea she was having a long-term affair with another man. After a few months, Amelia's health took a turn for the worse. It turned out she had some blood clots that were breaking off. It was still pretty early for the baby to be born—only twenty-nine weeks. But I agreed to try a new drug because they were both at risk. It caused Amelia to go into early labor. Eloise was born and went right to the NICU, but Amelia just kept declining. None of the medications were working."

Merrick paused for a breath, and when he spoke again his voice was hoarse. "In the meantime, the hospital had been served with a court-ordered paternity test by the guy she'd been sleeping with. A few days after they swabbed Eloise, Amelia flatlined, and they were able to bring her back. The next morning the social worker came in and told me..."

Tears streamed down Merrick's face, and mine followed.

He shook his head. "It's been three years, and I still can't bring myself to say I'm not Eloise's..."

The look of pain on his face sliced right through me. I reached up and wiped his tears. "It's okay. You don't have to say it."

He took a minute to pull himself together before continuing. "When they told me about Eloise, I left the hospital, went to the closest bar, and got piss drunk. I came back and found Amelia's bed empty."

My eyes widened. "Oh, God. She..."

Merrick nodded. "Alone. Amelia died alone. I lost them both that day."

I could barely wrap my head around what he'd gone through. After months of agonizing struggle, everything had come crashing down around him.

He took a deep breath. "I went to see Aaron the other day—the other man."

"You did?"

He nodded. "He actually seems like a pretty nice guy. He offered to let me get to know Eloise."

"Wow. Did you say yes?"

"I told him I needed to think about it. But I think I'm going to. There's a big part of me that feels like I lost a daughter. I know I can never get that back. But maybe having Eloise in my life in some capacity is important."

"I don't even know what to say, Merrick."

He shook his head. "There's nothing you need to say. It's me who owes you all the words. There's no excuse for what I did to you, running away when you'd just opened your heart to me. Before you walked into my office that first time, I thought I'd moved on and was back to living. But I hadn't healed. I'd just shut off that part of my heart.

Falling in love with you opened me again. And when we ran into Eloise, everything just came rushing back, so my gut reaction was to shut down again, because that was the way I moved on last time."

I blinked a few times, stuck on his words. "You love me?"

Merrick cupped my cheeks and looked into my eyes. "I was a goner the day you called me out for being an ass-hole and walked out of my office. I stupidly tried to fight it because I was a coward, but it was useless." He pulled my face closer, so our noses were almost touching. "I am so in love with you that it scares the living shit out of me. What I feel is more than a want. I *need you*, Evie."

Tears rained down my face again. This time, happy ones. "I love you, too."

"I'm so sorry I hurt you, Evie. But if you'll give me the chance, I promise to spend the next, I don't know—ten years making it up to you."

I laughed as I wiped my tears. "Only ten?"

He smiled. "We'll just take it one decade at a time."

The next morning, I didn't wake up until a quarter to eleven. Merrick and I had spent half the night reconnecting, and I would have preferred to stay in bed all day today, too. But I had an appointment I was dreading in a few hours— one I hadn't mentioned to the man with his arms currently wrapped around me from behind. Merrick was still sleeping, so I tried to gently extract myself from his grip without waking him. But as I put my first foot on the floor, a long arm tightened around my waist and hoisted me back to the center of the mattress.

I yelped in surprise. "I was trying not to wake you."

Merrick took my wrist and dragged my hand down between his legs. "I'm wide awake, sweetheart."

That he is. I gave him a little squeeze. "You know, I think this thing might be broken. It was wide awake like four times last night."

"I'm about to show you how broken it is..." He leaned in to kiss me, but I stopped him.

"Okay, but we have to be fast. I have an appointment at noon, and I need to shower still."

He pouted. "Cancel it."

"You have no idea how much I would love to do that. But I need to get it over with." I paused and looked into Merrick's eyes. "I'm having lunch with Christian."

He froze. "Come again?"

"It's not what it sounds like. Christian agreed to drop the lawsuit if I have dinner with him and hear him out. My lawyer negotiated it down to a lunch. It's the last thing I want to do, but I also don't want to be buried under legal costs just to defend myself in a ridiculous lawsuit."

"Fuck that. I'll pay your legal fees."

"That's very sweet of you. But I can't let you do that."

"Then I'm going with you to lunch."

I shook my head. "I don't want any reason for him to back out of this deal. So I'd rather not antagonize him."

Merrick frowned. "I don't like it."

"I understand. And I'm sure I'd feel the same way if the shoe was on the other foot." I cupped his cheek. "I promise to make it up to you when I get back."

"What time do you have to go?"

"I'm meeting him at a diner in Midtown at twelve. So I need to get out of here by eleven thirty."

Merrick reached over to the nightstand next to him and grabbed his phone. "I'm messaging my driver. He'll take you and wait for you to get done."

"That's not necessary."

He ignored me and continued typing. When he was finished, he placed it back on the nightstand. "I told him to come at eleven forty-five. It's Saturday, so traffic will be light. Plus, I need the full hour to help you get ready."

I arched an eyebrow. "You're going to help me get ready? Like blow dry my hair and do my makeup?"

"Nope. I'm going to make sure you smell like sex, and my cum is inside you while you're sitting with that asshole."

I chuckled. "Possessive much?"

"You have no damn idea." Merrick crushed his lips to mine, and it didn't take long before I was lost in the moment. He broke the kiss but kept my bottom lip between his teeth and tugged. "I want to come inside you. Not use protection. Can I do that, Evie?"

I swallowed and nodded. "I'm on the pill."

Merrick trailed his knuckles down my cheek. "I love you."

"I love you, too."

He buried his head in my hair and nuzzled my neck, sucking along my pulse line as he made his way to my ear.

"I'm going to apologize before we even start," he said. "Whether I have any right to or not, I feel territorial right now knowing when we're done, you're going to meet another man. So I need to fuck you hard."

I liked the sound of that. Spreading my legs wide beneath him, I grinned. "Well, get to it, bossman."

Merrick didn't need to be told twice. He licked his hand and slipped it between us, making sure I was lubricated. But I'd been ready since he'd said the words *I want to come inside you*. His pupils dilated as he realized how wet I was. He aligned his swollen head with my opening and pushed inside with one deep thrust. His eyes closed as he stayed in place, looking like he'd found nirvana. When they opened, he began to move—like he'd never done before. Merrick pulled almost fully out and slammed back in hard, over and over again.

"Fuck, Evie. I'm going to fill this pussy so it's still dripping out of you when you go." He pulled back to look at me and groaned as he sank in. "*Mine.*"

My nails bit into his back as I climbed toward climax. "I'm going to..." I didn't even make it through the sentence before my body started pulsating on its own. "*Oh, God.*"

Merrick sped up. It was hard and raw, each thrust going deeper until he finally let out a roar, "*Fuuuuck.*" Then his hips bucked one last time before he planted himself deep inside me.

We kissed languidly for a long time after that. Merrick smiled as he brushed a lock of hair from my face. "Since you won't let me join you for lunch, at least you'll have a bit of me inside you now."

"We don't need to have sex for that to happen." I placed my hand over my heart. "You're already in here. So you're with me wherever I go."

EPILOGUE

Merrick

ONE YEAR LATER

"I didn't take you for someone who would get freaked out by a little turbulence."

"Hmmm?" I looked over my shoulder before merging from the airport onto the highway. "What are you talking about?"

"On the flight here," Evie said. "You were so tense. Every time I looked over at you, you were white-knuckling the armrest."

"Ohh..." The thought that a few bumps on a plane would bother me after all these years of travel was pretty comical. I'd once slept through an emergency landing. But I nodded anyway. "Yeah, I thought I hid it well."

Evie chuckled. "There was sweat beading on your forehead at one point."

We'd just landed in Atlanta for Kitty's long-planned family reunion picnic, which was two days from now, though Evie thought the party was tomorrow. She also thought we were going straight to my grandmother's.

I cleared my throat. "It's only seven. My grandmother has her weekly card game until nine. I told her to have it since half the time flights are late anyway. Do you want to take a ride to your Airbnbs, to check in on things, since we have some time?"

I had no backup plan, so I was banking on her saying yes.

"Oh yeah, that would be great. Let me look on the app and see if they're booked."

Shit.

Of course it was booked. I'd booked it a month ago under a fake name thinking I was slick, but I hadn't stopped to consider she'd want to check before we went and would find it was rented.

Evie typed into her phone. "They're both booked."

"You want to do a drive-by anyway, just check on the property? What about the glamping site?"

"No, it's okay. Maybe if we have time on the way home. It looks like they're open on Sunday, so that might be better."

I felt like kicking her ass. *Think. Think.* I was nervous as shit, so my brain couldn't come up with anything. "You sure?"

She looked over at me and squinted. "You don't want to get to Kitty's while all her card friends are there because last time they made a comment about your cute bum. Is that it?"

"Yep. Yep...you got me. They might look like sheep, but those ladies are wolves."

Evie snickered. "Fine. You know, for a man with such a dirty mouth, you really can be a prude sometimes."

I drove the rest of the way to the Airbnbs barely saying a word. I traded billions in high-risk stocks every year, and never once had I felt like this. Evie had been on my ass about softening my tone a bit when I spoke to the new traders, because I apparently made them nervous. If this was the shit they went through, I really was a dick, and they should all quit.

"Oh, I forgot to tell you," Evie said. "I got tickets to Sesame Street Live for Abbey and Eloise for their birthdays. The show isn't for a few months, but Abbey is obsessed with everything Sesame already. I thought Eloise might like it too. I got three tickets for two different shows. I wasn't sure if you'd want us to take Eloise, or if you just wanted to gift them all to her for her birthday, and Aaron could take her and a friend."

A few weeks after the day Aaron and I had talked, I took him up on his offer to get to know his daughter. It was awkward at first. I just wanted to stare at her and look for the baby I'd once thought was mine. But it didn't take long before that wore off. Since then, I'd visited often. Aaron and I had even formed some sort of friendship. I never thought I'd be grateful to have that guy in my life, but I was. Because I couldn't unlove a child I'd fallen for months before she was even born. I'd introduced Evie to them, and the last few times we'd gotten together, she'd brought along her niece, Abbey. Eloise loved her and treated her like a doll.

"Do you want to go?" I asked her.

"Sort of. My mom never had the money to take us to shows when we were kids. I guess I'm kind of curious what it is."

"Okay," I said. "So we'll take her."

"Really?" Evie's eyes widened. "I never thought you'd agree to go to Sesame Street Live."

I shrugged. "I'm going to spend a few hours with my little friend and then go home and get a blowjob because I did something you wanted to do, right?"

She chuckled. "Probably."

"Sounds like a pretty damn good day to me. Don't care where we are if it makes both of you happy."

Evie's eyes went soft. "You say the sweetest things without even realizing it."

"It was the part about the blowjob, wasn't it?"

She smacked me.

Ten minutes later, whatever calm I'd channeled talking to Evie went out the window again as we turned off the main road and onto the one that led to the treehouses. I parked when we arrived, just as the sun was starting to set.

Evie looked around. "Look at that sky. We couldn't have timed this better if we'd planned it."

I almost laughed. *Someone did plan it.*

"It doesn't look like the guests have arrived yet," she said.

"So let's go up and take a look."

"What if they come?"

"We'll tell them we're the cleaning crew."

She looked me up and down and smiled. "Even without the three-thousand-dollar suit, no one would ever believe you were the cleaning crew."

"Why not?"

"Because you just look like the boss. I don't want to get caught poking around after check-in time."

I got out of the car and opened Evie's door, extending a hand to help her out. "Come on, it'll be fun. You like almost getting caught. Remember how hard you came when I ate you out on your desk last week without the door locked?" I rubbed the hair at the back of my head. "I'm missing a chunk of hair from how hard you pulled."

She took my hand. "I'll go, but I'm warning you... You're going to be missing the rest of it if we climb up there and you try something like that again."

At the ladder, I smiled when she looked around again to be sure the coast was clear.

"After you," I said.

Evie was wearing a sundress, so the view from below went a long way toward making me forget what I was about to do.

"Stop looking at my ass," she yelled without looking back.

I chuckled. "You appreciate your views, and I'll appreciate mine."

Inside, she took a few steps in and stopped short as I climbed in behind her. "Oh my God. There's champagne chilling. The people must've already checked in. I bet they went for a walk. They'll be back any second since it's almost dark. We better go."

Evie turned toward the door, but I grabbed her wrist. "Hang on one minute. I want to talk to you."

"We can talk in the car."

I did the only thing I could think of to make her relax. I cupped her cheeks and pulled her mouth to meet mine. She tried to pull away, but after ten seconds her shoulders loosened and she gave in. It was supposed to calm her down, but it started to have the opposite effect on me, so I forced myself to cut it off. Though I kept her cheeks in my hands and her face close.

"Just give me one minute, okay?" I whispered.

She blinked a few times, looking a little out of it, but nodded. I loved that even after all this time, I could still make that happen. Bringing her hand to my lips, I kissed the top before taking a deep breath and stepping back. Then, I dropped to one knee.

"Evie, I wanted to do this here because I know the significance of these treehouses. They're a place you came to feel safe at times in your life when you wanted to escape the world. I might not have climbed into a treehouse, but I've definitely spent my share of years wanting to escape life—until you walked through my door."

Evie covered her mouth, and tears welled in her eyes.

"Since the day I met you, my life has been changed. You've made me want to live again, to be a better person, and you've made me want so much more out of life than money and power." I reached into my pocket and pulled out the ring box I'd been carrying around since we left New York this morning. "I worried you might think I was playing pocket pool with the way I've been reaching into my pocket so much to make sure I didn't lose this."

Evie laughed.

I opened the ring box. Inside was a four-carat princess-cut diamond, with two smaller stones set into the filigree on either side. The smaller stones were from her grandmother's ring and Kitty's. It had taken a few people to get this made. Next to the ring in the black velvet box was the orange piece of sea glass she kept in her purse and never went anywhere without. I took out the glass and held it up to her. "I hope you don't mind that I stole this from your bag this morning. I needed every bit of luck I could get today."

She took the sea glass and held it next to her heart. "I think the feeling in my heart right now might be better than the one I had on the beach twenty years ago when I found it."

I smiled. "Evie, I want to wake up with you every morning and fall asleep next to you every night. I want you to be my wife, and I want to have a family with you. But more than anything, the reason I wanted to do this here is because I want to replace your treehouses, sweetheart. I want to be the person who will always be there for you, the place you run to when you need to feel safe." I paused and took a deep breath. "Will you marry me, Evie?"

Tears spilled down her face. She wrapped her arms around my neck and kissed me. "Yes! Yes!"

My heart raced out of control as I took her mouth in a kiss. When it broke, we were both panting. I pushed the ring onto her finger, and she stared at it.

"The stones on either side are from our grandmothers' engagement rings, given by their one true loves. Greer helped me find your grandmother's ring, and Kitty couldn't wait to give you hers."

"Oh, Merrick, that means the world to me." She held out her hand. "It's absolutely stunning."

"Well, then I guess I got the right one. Because it matches the woman wearing it."

THE END

(But sometimes life is a circle
and leads back to the beginning...)

BACK TO THE BEGINNING

Merrick

NINETEEN YEARS AGO

"**H**ey." My sister walked into the garage where I was practicing shots on my grandfather's old pool table. She picked up the five ball I had bent over to shoot. "Grams needs you to take a ride to the market to pick up some sugar."

"Can you put the ball down?" I said. "I'm playing a damn game."

She tossed the solid orange ball into the air and caught it. "Don't you sit in your room playing with your balls enough?"

I snagged the ball the next time she tossed it up. "You're funny. But looks aren't everything."

She rolled her eyes. "Original, kid."

Kid. My sister Lydia was fifteen, barely two years older than me, but she acted like our age difference was at least a decade. I glanced out the garage window. It had just started drizzling. "Why don't you go to the store?"

"I just blow dried my hair."

I shrugged. "So? Wear a hood."

"If you don't shut up and go, I'm going to have to call Dave..."

I set the five ball back on the table. "Good. Ask him to bring me a Big Mac. You know that threat stopped working when I was like six, right?"

"Big Macs are McDonald's, doofus. Not Wendy's."

I shrugged and leaned over to take my shot, whacking the ball into the corner pocket. "Grams would've come in here to ask me herself if she wanted me to go. I know she asked you, and you're just trying to pawn it off on me."

Lydia shrugged. "It doesn't matter. You have to listen to me because I'm older."

"I hate to tell you, but that's not a thing. You don't get to order me around just because you're a little older. But while you're at the store, pick me up some peanut butter. We're out."

She scrunched up her nose. "How do you eat that stuff three times a day?"

"Don't knock it until you try it." I walked over to my sister and stood close, looking down at her. I was at least six inches taller already. "Maybe if you ate some, you could grow to be a normal size."

"I'm five foot one. That *is* a normal size for a girl."

I smirked. "If you say so..."

She folded her arms across her chest. "If I go, I'm not getting peanut butter for you. I'm only getting Grams' sugar."

I rolled my eyes. *Of course.* "Fine," I grumbled. "I'll go when I clear the table. But only because I want a sandwich."

A little while later, I rode my bike to the market, all of three blocks away, and picked up sugar and peanut butter. But while I was in the store, the drizzle turned to a full-on downpour. I lifted my bike from under the awning. "*Great.*"

By the time I made it back to my grandmother's, I was drenched from head to toe. I pressed the button to open the garage door, but as I did, a flash of long, blond hair streaked across Grams's friend's yard next door. I watched through the downpour as a girl slid across the wet grass and raced up the ladder to the treehouse in the back. On the fourth rung, she slipped and lost her grip, and landed flat on her ass on the ground. But she got right back up, looked over her shoulder toward the house, and began climbing again. The second time she made it almost to the top before her foot slipped. Somehow she kicked the ladder out from under her while trying to grab it with her legs. I thought she was going down with it, but she grabbed the treehouse and now dangled from it.

"*Shit.*"

I raced over to Milly's yard. Rain pelted me in the face as I hurdled the little white picket fence and lifted the ladder from the grass, hoisting it back up next to the girl. She hooked her legs around it and managed to get herself back on. As soon as she was steady enough to climb again, she bolted up the last few rungs and into the treehouse, slamming the door behind her.

I waited a minute, but she didn't come out again. And since the rain was definitely not letting up, I ran back to my grandmother's. When I reached the garage, I heard a man yelling from inside Milly's house. I figured the girl had probably done something wrong and gotten in trouble, so I put my bike back in the garage and minded my own business.

Inside, Grams took one look at me and shook her head. "Boy, you look like a drowned rat. What the heck are you doing playing out in that rain?"

I unzipped my sweatshirt and took out the bag I'd tucked inside to keep dry. "I went to get you the sugar you asked for."

"You mean your sister's sugar. She's the one who wanted it to make rock candy."

I freaking knew it. I shook my head. "She told me you wanted it."

Grams chuckled. "Sounds about right. I'm one of eight, and shit flows downhill. I probably would've done the same thing to my little brother when we were your age." Her phone started to ring, so she walked toward where it hung on the wall, motioning to my clothes. "Go get changed, and I'll make you a snack."

I was so soaked, I even had to change my damn underwear.

When I came back out, Grams was hanging up the phone. She pulled her raincoat from the coat closet and grabbed her car keys from the key holder that hung near the front door. "I have to run out. You and your sister be good."

"It's pouring. Where are you going?"

Grams shook her head. "To help a friend. I'll explain when I get home."

"Okay."

After she left, I made myself a peanut butter and jelly sandwich. When I put the dirty butter knife in the sink, I looked out the window and noticed my grandmother's hot rod in the neighbor's driveway. A woman was getting in the passenger side. Grams's friend Milly walked around the side of the house with her arm wrapped around the girl who'd almost fallen from the treehouse a little while ago. I watched as they all piled in, and then Grams took off, flying down the road.

It was hours later when she came back, and I was half asleep on the couch, watching a poker tournament on TV. She walked over and grabbed the remote, flicking it off.

I sat up. "Is everything alright?"

She sighed. "It is now—for the time being anyway."

"Did something happen to Milly next door? I saw her getting in your car with some other people."

"No, Milly's fine."

"Oh. When I came back from the store earlier, a girl ran out from Milly's. She almost cracked her head open climbing into the treehouse in the back when the ladder slipped out from under her."

"That must've been Milly's youngest granddaughter, Everly."

"I heard a man yelling, too."

Grams frowned. "That was her father. He's a bad man, honey. But he won't be coming around anymore, at least for a while."

"Is the girl okay?"

Grams nodded and patted my hand. "She will be."

I nodded.

"Come on. You've been watching that boob tube long enough. I want to show you something I've been working on."

I followed Grams to the kitchen where she unrolled a piece of oak tag paper. Inside were probably a hundred rectangles, all connected with various lines.

"What is that?"

"It's our family tree. I thought it would be nice to map out our ancestors."

I shrugged. "For what?"

"To know where we came from, silly. What do you mean, *for what*?"

She pointed to the top of the chart. "This here would be your great, great, great, great grandfather, Merchant Harrington. He was a tailor." She lowered her finger down the chart. "He made his daughter's wedding dress, which was worn by two more generations. I have a picture of it on my computer. Maybe you'll wind up being a tailor, too."

I snort-laughed. "Definitely not."

"Why not?"

"Because I'm going to be rich."

"Oh yeah? And how exactly are you going to get rich?"

"Easy. I'm going to play the stock market."

Grams smiled and returned her attention to her chart. She spent the next hour telling me about every person on it. When she got to the bottom, there were squares under my parents' names, as well as my and Lydia's names, and then empty squares next to us.

I pointed to the one next to my name. "What if I don't get married? Your tree branch will wilt?"

"You'll get married." She wagged her finger at me. "I see it in your future."

I shrugged. "Whatever."

She mussed my hair. "Why don't you get some sleep?"

"Alright. Goodnight, Grams."

The next morning, the wind woke me up. The rain had stopped, but the spare bedroom window had been left open a crack, causing a loud whistle to squeak through. I got up to shut it and couldn't fall back asleep. So I went to the kitchen to get some juice. After chugging a full glass, I looked out the window over the sink at the treehouse in Milly's yard. The ladder I'd put back last night had fallen again. So I went to the garage, got a hammer and some long nails, and walked across to take care of it once and for all.

When I came back in the house, Grams was awake and sitting at the table with her family tree open again.

She smiled at me. "What made you go over and fix that ladder?"

I shrugged. "I don't know. It was on the ground again. I don't want the girl to get hurt next time when I'm not around."

"That was very nice of you."

I looked down at the paper. "You adding more names to your tree?"

"Just one."

"What ancestor could you have found since last night?"

Grams rolled up the chart. "I added a *descendant*, not an ancestor."

"What's that?"

"It's a person in the family who comes after me, not before me."

My brows pulled together. "Like Mom and me and Lydia?"

"Exactly."

"But you already have us on there."

Grams looked toward the window over the sink and smiled. "I'm manifesting."

"Manifesting?"

"It's putting something out there into the universe to believe in, so you can make it happen someday."

I snorted. "How about manifesting me a peanut butter and jelly sandwich?"

Grams stood, tucking her chart under her arm, and walked over to kiss my cheek. "I think I can do better than that. You just wait and see."

OTHER BOOKS BY VI KEELAND

The Summer Proposal

The Invitation

Inappropriate

We Shouldn't

The Spark

The Rivals

The Naked Truth

All Grown Up

Sex, Not Love

Beautiful Mistake

Egomaniac

Bossman

The Baller

Left Behind (A Young Adult Novel)

Beat

Throb

Worth the Fight

Worth the Chance

Worth Forgiving

Belong to You

Made for You

First Thing I See

Well Played (Co-written with Penelope Ward)

Cocky Bastard (Co-written with Penelope Ward)

Playboy Pilot (Co-written with Penelope Ward)

Mister Moneybags (Co-written with Penelope Ward)

British Bedmate (Co-written with Penelope Ward)

Park Avenue Player (Co-written with Penelope Ward)

Stuck-Up Suit (Co-written with Penelope Ward)

Rebel Heir (Co-written with Penelope Ward)

ACKNOWLEDGEMENTS

To you—the *readers*. Thank you for allowing Merrick and Evie into your minds and hearts. I'm honored my story provided you an escape for a short while, and I hope you'll come back soon to see who you might meet next!

To Penelope – Could you just write yourself a sappy acknowledgement detailing what a good friend you are and read it into this section? Neither one of us will remember who wrote it anyway. ;-)

To Cheri – Thank you for your friendship and support.

To Julie – The craziness of 2022 has been a reminder of what friendship means. I can't wait to watch you dig your toes into the sand next summer on Fire Island.

To Luna –Thank you for always being there, day or night. Your friendship brightens my day.

To my amazing Facebook reader group, Vi's Violets – more than 23,000 smart women (and a few awesome men) who love to talk books together in one place? I'm one lucky girl! Each and every one of you is a gift. Thank you for all of your support.

To Sommer –Thank you for figuring out what I want, often before I do.

To my agent and friend, Kimberly Brower – Thank you for being there always. Every year brings a unique opportunity from you. I can't wait to see what you dream up next!

To Jessica, Elaine and Julia – Thank you for smoothing out the all the rough edges and make me shine!

To Kylie and Jo at Give Me Books – I don't even remember how I managed before you, and I hope I never have to figure it out! Thank you for everything you do.

To all of the bloggers – Thank you for inspiring readers to take a chance on me and for always showing up.

Much love
Vi

ABOUT THE AUTHOR

Vi Keeland is a #1 New York Times, #1 Wall Street Journal, and USA Today Bestselling author. With millions of books sold, her titles are currently translated in twenty-six languages and have appeared on bestseller lists in the US, Germany, Brazil, Bulgaria and Hungary. Three of her short stories have been turned into films by Passionflix, and two of her books are currently optioned for movies. She resides in New York with her husband and their three children where she is living out her own happily ever after with the boy she met at age six.